The WINDOWS of HEAVEN

The WINDOWS of HEAVEN

A NOVEL OF GALVESTON'S GREAT STORM OF 1900

Ron Rozelle

Texas Review Press
Huntsville, Texas

FIRST EDITION, 2000

Requests for permission to reproduce material from this work should be sent to:

Permissions
Texas Review Press
English Department
Sam Houston State University
Huntsville, TX 77341-2146

Cover design by Kellye Sanford
Photographs courtesy of the Rosenberg Library, Galveston

Library of Congress Cataloging-in-Publication Data

Rozelle, Ron, 1952-
    The windows of heaven: a novel of Galveston's great storm of 1900 / Ron Rozelle.--
1st ed.
        p.   cm.
    ISBN 1-881515-27-3 (paper)
    1. Galveston (Tex.)--History--Fiction. 2. Hurricanes--Ficton. I Title
PS3568.0994 W56 2000
813'.54--dc21

                                                    00-025125

For Karen
and Kara and Haley and Megan

. . . the same day were all the fountains
of the great deep broken up, and
the windows of heaven were opened.
—Genesis 7:11

PROLOGUE

It started raining after midnight.

At first a few heavy drops, as large as pebbles, splattered against windows, and spotted the dry pavement of the streets. They plinked into half-full troughs of dirty water outside the saloons on Postoffice Street; horses tied there winced against the stings. People inside the saloons—sailors and dock workers and whores—paid no attention to the steadily quickening tattoo being pelted out on the tin sheets or slates of the roofs, but kept to the business at hand: the drinking, and gambling, and the sweaty, brief stabbing away at the very oldest of human exertions.

Some of Galveston's people, in other parts of the city, listened to the rain from their beds. A few, who had looked up that day at the Levy Building on Market Street and noticed the pair of warning flags that flew from the fourth floor offices of the Weather Bureau, knew that this was the first, slow calling card of a tropical storm. Isaac Cline, the chief of the bureau, had hoisted the flags on Friday morning, and they had danced and popped in the brisk north wind all day. The red one, with the black box in its middle, meant that a particularly malevolent storm was a possibility. The white one, above it, meant that if it came, it would come from the northwest.

But not too many people had seen the flags. And now the first big drops of rain plopped into the sand dunes and salt grass of the island, and slid through the muted light of the gas street lights in town, and nobody paid much attention to them. Those in bed closed their eyes, and let the tapping of the rain sing them to sleep.

It had come a long way, this storm.

Almost two weeks before, somewhere on the immense, swaying surface of the eternal Atlantic, a small portion of the sea had rebelled against the unremitting late summer heat, and heaved itself up in protest. Africa lay a thousand miles to the east, over the vast, bowl-like curve of the world, and many more thousands of miles of ocean and sky stretched endlessly to the west. The air above the place had become suddenly full of new, burdensome moisture. Feeble clouds

1

had emerged, fattened with warm seawater, and fled upward, thousands of feet above the turbulent, rolling place.

Once it had pulled up enough wind and water, it took its first steps, in a slow, counter-clockwise rotation, and found its voice. Hollow, booming thunder rumbled and cracked throughout it, as it answered the ancient beckoning. To the west.

For the next three days it grew, and swept slowly across the empty breadth of the Atlantic, feeding on the deep ocean water that it sucked in, marching over the edge of the world.

It moved over Santo Domingo on the first day of September, and bent the tall palm trees over, and blew the roofs off some houses, as if only testing its strength. Then it launched back into the sea, and gained new energy from the two hundred miles of open water between Haiti and Cuba. On the fifth, it raged through Havana, and headed for Key West. Arrogant now, and old—unusually old for a hurricane—full of warm water, it was nearly four hundred miles wide, containing 150,000 square miles of boiling, seething rage.

It moved resolutely north for a day, and the Weather Bureau, having received reports from stations it had passed, issued warnings for the upper coast of the Gulf of Mexico, and even along the eastern seaboard. Then, on the night of Thursday, September 6th, it made a last grasp at living even longer and headed due west, consuming acres of gulf water with every second, and gaining speed.

By Friday, the outer curved finger of the monster encountered a ship, not a very big one. The crew had just dropped two offerings, wrapped in burlap, into the choppy water. A boy, not a very big one, his cap pulled down over his handsome eyes, watched the offering, and then turned to see the blue-black thing that filled up the eastern horizon of the already cloudy sky.

It hadn't taken the captain long to steer hard to port, in an attempt to fight through the thing's leading bands and race for New Orleans. Soon, the ship had plowed, bow first, into the wind and rain of the monster, already older than any hurricane in recent memory, and still feeding on the warm water that fueled it, and drove it stubbornly on, directly toward the city that the ship had sailed from, on the narrow island that stretched calmly along the edge of the sea.

Now it was Saturday morning, and the rain was coming down in torrents, driving straight down from the low, gray clouds that blanketed the city as if something up there couldn't get rid of it fast enough. It pounded into the foamy water that already stood in the low places in streets, and boiled and gurgled in deep puddles. When enough of the water had congregated in one place, it swirled around, looking for a place to go, and then it traveled along the edges of the streets, lapping at the tall sidewalks.

People ate their breakfasts beside solid sheets of gray rain that shrouded their windows like curtains, or watched it push down off the awnings over sidewalks and hammer into the little rivers forming in the streets. In Church Street, and Market, and Ship's Mechanic, and Strand. All of them sent the dirty water along, until a network of shallow waterways covered the city that would soon be entirely navigable by toy boats, if any toy boats could withstand the pounding. Even Broadway, the highest part of the city, at eight and a half feet above sea level at several places, held standing water on either side of the elegant esplanade that ran down its wide middle. The oleander bushes in the esplanade gyrated through little dances in the straight, hard rain, and the massive trees in the yards of the mansions on Broadway slowed it down only enough to diffuse it into a gray splattering of steamy murk. Postoffice Street sent its own little river along, beside the windows of sleeping whores.

The wharves, beside Avenue A on the bay side of the island, stood under more water than the streets did. Sailors from all over the world, most of them still snoring in the dry, snug confines of ships in their berths, would not have needed more than a glance to determine that most of the water on the docks hadn't fallen from the sky.

By midmorning, the word had gotten around that the waves were enormous, and Galveston's people came out.

Entire families took the trolleys out to the beach, or, if they wanted to save the nickel fares, waded through the ankle deep water in the streets. What they found there was, indeed, a spectacle. The water wasn't deep enough on the beach road to keep them from standing on it, though they did hang on tight to their small children. The mountainous waves, bigger than any they had ever seen, exploded into the pilings of the big piers built out over the Gulf of Mexico. Even the biggest of the piers—Murdock's, and the Pagoda Bath House— swayed and groaned in the onslaught. The pelting rain stung people's faces and drenched their clothes, but they all figured it was worth it to see such a thing.

When the massive waves crashed against the pilings and the sides of the sprawling wooden structures on them, they shot high enough in the morning air to splatter, with the falling rain, onto the people standing on the road, and everybody agreed it was great fun.

And when the waves began to tear the buildings on the piers apart, like cardboard, and sent the broken planks spiraling into the wind like so many missiles, the people on the road decided it wasn't as much fun as they had first thought. And they began herding their families back to their homes, to wait for whatever the day would bring.

CHAPTER ONE

The little man in the buggy shook the reins with determination, and encouraged the horse on in the same high-pitched voice he had used to call out to everyone he passed. Though they could hardly see the man through the driving rain, many of the people wading through water on the beach road recognized him, since not too many men in Galveston wore a white suit every day of the year, in every climate, with the top button of a stiff collar pinched tight at the neck, and a wide brimmed Panama hat. Many men wore mustaches, but they were usually coarse, unkempt affairs; not too many wore close-cropped whiskers, the color of salt and pepper and trimmed to perfection each morning with a tiny pair of scissors, ordered all the way from a shop in New York City. The people who recognized him were no more surprised to see him driving a buggy through a storm than they would have been to see a rooster crowing, or a seagull darting down to snatch a fish out of the gulf. For this little man was Isaac Cline, and the weather was as much a part of his being as were his hands and his head and his heart.

The people in the road who didn't know him waved back as he passed, and leaned forward in the stinging rain to listen to his admonitions. Some of those who did know him called out to him that it was raining too hard, and they pointed to the heavens, as if, because Isaac knew the weather like a preacher knew the Bible and studied it as closely as a mother listened to the heartbeat of a sick child, he might possibly have some control over it.

"I've never seen the waves so high," one man told him, as he grasped the side of Isaac's still rocking buggy, and shook rainwater from his face and hat. His wife and two small children stood beside him, as soaked as he was. "How much higher you figure they'll get?"

Isaac shook his own head now.

"High enough to make you people go on home, I hope," he said. Drops of rain nestled and shone in his mustache like small, perfect eggs in a bird's nest. He tilted a thumb toward the huge waves that thundered on to the beach. "They ought to be that high already." He leaned toward the family now, and let his gaze rest on the children, shivering close to their mother. "A child has already been swept out, over by Murdock's pier. A piece of lumber hit her in the head and knocked her down, and a wave just came and got her. And that's a fact." The horse shook his head, as if to confirm it.

The mother held the children closer to her, and looked first at the big waves, and then at her husband, who had more than likely suggested the outing, Isaac thought.

The man looked at the waves, too.

"We just wanted to see it," he said, as much to himself as to Isaac. "I ain't never seen it like this, and . . . ." He didn't add that he had lived here all of his life, since almost everyone on Galveston had lived here all their lives. The man was still thinking about the child that had been swept away and didn't speak again.

Isaac lifted the reins. "Go on home," he said, loud enough to be heard over the rain and the waves. "And tell everybody else you see to do the same thing. If your house is close to the beach, then get yourselves to higher ground, at the center of the island, and don't take any long time about doing it."

The man watched the rain pouring off the brim of Isaac's hat. His wife had taken a step closer to him, away from the heaving, gray gulf, and clutched the two small children hard enough to hurt them. Thunder cracked in the low, thick clouds and rolled along mournfully for a long moment, spending itself completely before dying away.

"It will get considerably worse before it gets any better," Isaac told them. "And that child won't be the last to die today, would be my guess."

He didn't wait for them to say anything, but clicked at the horse and went on to tell everybody else he saw the same thing. Many of Galveston's people were still out, milling around in the hard rain and rising water, not wanting to miss a bit of something that didn't happen every day. And waves big enough to knock down big buildings built out on piers fell pretty easily into that category.

Isaac chided those that paid any attention to him and pointed his small hand toward the center of the island and called out to the horse when he wasn't calling out to people. The buggy pushed on through water that was deep enough to cause a wake, and Isaac's white suit and hat shone out through the pelting downpour like a particularly bright rock at the bottom of a murky pond.

When he had covered several times the part of the beach road that he could get to, he jerked the horse's reins toward town, and drove him on. The buggy's tall wheels threw water up into the yards of the small houses it passed, and sometimes even on the housewives sitting on the covered porches, watching their barefooted children splashing in the deep pools standing at the edge of the streets. Several children had fashioned miniature boats out of whatever material had been at hand. They pushed them along in front of them, and were glad of the little waves sent up by the buggy.

At every third or fourth house Isaac slowed the horse to a trot, or stopped him all together, and told whoever was on the porch to gather up their children and start walking up toward town, and to find a brick building to get in. He tried to call out in a voice loud enough for several households to hear him, but his high-pitched efforts didn't carry too well in the current conditions.

"You can't stay here," he yelled, while the buggy bounced under him. "You're too close to the beach. You've got to find a good building to get into, before this water gets any higher."

One of the women on the porch leaned forward in her chair, and stopped fanning herself with the folded paper she was holding. She almost smiled.

"It ain't even up in the yard good, yet," she sang out at him, and pointed with the paper, to show him. "Then it's got right smart of a high porch to come up afore it gets in any house."

Isaac watched her children as they giggled and splashed by the road, and thought again of the little girl who had been swept away so quickly a little while ago. Her father, who should have been holding on to her, had still been watching the wind peel away a large section of the Pagoda Bath House when the child disappeared in the brown water. The man and several others had darted out toward the surf, but it was useless. Isaac stayed only long enough to see that everything was being done that could be, and then resumed his Paul Revere imitation.

"It'll come up it," Isaac told the woman. "And then it will fill up the house, I imagine, that is if there's any house left after the wind we're likely to get here in a little while." He pointed toward the center of the island, and looked from one porch to another. "Believe me now," he begged them, "and don't take the chance of this not being as bad as I figure it might get. Go on toward higher ground while you can still get there." He knew that the husbands of the houses were already in town, or at the wharves or the warehouses, at work.

He moved on, stopping several more times to deliver the same warning and advice. The rain still barreled as straight down as if it had been plumbed to do it and exploded into the slowly rising water. Isaac knew that soon, when the water lapped up high enough to make everyone realize what was happening, people out too close to the beach would start moving toward a better place to be. But by then

6

the going would be harder, especially for those families with small children, who by that time would have used up all the fun of the experience, and would have started crying, and wanting to be held. And almost all of the families had children that small, Isaac knew, and older ones too, since most of the families produced children with the industry and regularity that farmers grew crops.

Isaac didn't even bother to shake water off now. He was soaked through, and was sitting in an inch or two of rain that had accumulated in the depression of the buggy seat. His own children, three daughters, were at home now, with his wife, in a house no further away from the beach than these were that he was passing. Cora Mae was pregnant again—maybe a son this time, he thought, for the thousandth time—and there had been complications with this one. So he had chosen not to try to move her that morning, but to put his faith and hope in the large, two-story frame house that was sturdier than most, since Isaac had designed it himself, and supervised its construction, making sure it was not only sound, but raised up high enough to allow average overflows to move beneath it.

He clicked at the horse, and balanced the soggy leather reins in his hands. He just pointed now at the people he still passed who were heading out to the beach to see the waves, indicating that they would do better to turn around and go back in the direction they had come from.

On Market Street, he brought the little rig to a stop outside the Levy Building, then took the steep steps up to the fourth floor two at a time.

"How often are you telegraphing reports to Washington?" he asked, as his brother Joseph handed him a copy of the latest one.

"Every two hours. But with the wind already rising, who knows how long it'll be before the lines blow down?" He looked at his brother. "Why don't you change into something dry?" He knew that Isaac kept a change of clothes in his office. A white suit, of course. A fresh collar as stiff as planking.

Isaac wiped the moisture from his glasses, and read the report.

Unusually heavy swells from the southeast, intervals one to five minutes, overflowing low places south portion of city three to four blocks from beach. Such high water with opposing winds never observed previously.

He laid the paper on the desk. "When we lose that north wind—" His voice trailed away as he considered that certainty. As he looked at the chart laid out on the table before him, the water on his clothes dripped on it. "The thing's not even here yet, and it's pushing the gulf up all over us. I hate to think how high it's finally going to get."

The day before, after Isaac had sent the two warning flags up the short pole into a perfect Friday morning, the telephone started ringing. He let Joseph man it. Joseph was his chief assistant, and the best assistance he could give him then was to answer the same question with the same answer every time the bell jingled.

Joseph told every caller that, yes, that was indeed the storm flag, and he was aware that it was a pretty morning, but that the latest advisory from Washington had said that it wasn't likely to stay pretty for long. He nodded his head and tapped a pencil on the desk and said to just use caution, and to get to high ground if they were down by the beach if the weather turned ugly. Don't be fooled by the sunshine, he told the callers, since that could change quick enough.

Most of the callers had posed one last question, and it always stopped Joseph. "It's not a bad idea," he finally said to each one, "but we're not ready to say it's a necessity."

After one of the calls, he dropped the heavy receiver into its cradle, ran his thumb around the rim of the mouthpiece, and told his brother he wished he could give a better answer.

"I wish you could, too," Isaac said as he looked again at the map where he had attempted to plot the progression of the storm, with the scant information he had been given.

"I wish I knew where the damned thing *is*, too. And where it will come ashore. And I wish the city aldermen had risen above their bickering and politics for once and built a seawall." Then he looked up from the map, to his brother.

"And I wish Cora Mae would have steak and champagne on the table every day for our dinner."

Then he looked out one of the tall, wide windows of the Weather Bureau office, at the bright September morning. Wagons and buggies clattered through the intersection of Market and Twenty-Third Streets, the horses pulling them clopping along the uneven wooden blocks of the pavement. The deep bellow of a steamship announced its imminent departure from what was, in this first year of the new century, one of the busiest ports in the world. Scraps of conversations filtered up to him, and a few shouts from children, a couple of seagulls sang out, and the two warning flags popped in the breeze not very far above him. Most of Galveston's people, on the streets below him, were wearing hats, the brims wide, as protection from the relentless sun. The hats floated along on the mass of people, like small, bobbing

8

boats on the sea. Some of the ladies sported parasols and twirled them beside the hats. An automobile, one of three on the island, sputtered across an intersection a couple of blocks away.

"How can we tell people to leave the island?" he said, knowing that it was the question that Joseph had been asked. "When we just don't know." He took off his small spectacles, and rubbed his eyes.

"We just don't know."

Now it was twenty-four hours later. And they did know.

The one long bridge that connected Galveston to the mainland was a narrow one, running along beside the single railroad trestle. It was reputed to be the longest wooden bridge in the world, and the islanders were proud of that. But neither the bridge nor the trestle, Isaac knew, were built high enough over the bay to be of much use for very long in a storm like this one. And the boats that ferried people across the Bolivar roads would have already shut down their operations.

The western end of the long island was underwater by now, he knew, and he hoped that the few people who bothered to live out there at all, on the low, scruffy ridges among the swamps and salt grass, had already come in to town.

Isaac had wondered many times what Galveston must look like from high overhead, to a bird, sailing in wide, slow circles so high up that he was barely a speck to someone on the ground. On a pretty day, and cloudless, a bird gliding that high up would see a long, narrow island hugging herself close enough to the mainland to be able to claim rights to it, but far enough removed to maintain her independence. From her southwestern tip, at San Louis Pass, to her northeastern, where ships from all over the world sailed into and out of the Bolivar roads, was a distance of just over twenty miles. From the air she would resemble an awkward creature trying to take flight, her head, wider and heavier than the rest of her, making an effort to lift all of her up and away, the long, slender body lagging behind. The side of her short wings, straining to pull her up, was the pointed jut of land above Offats Bayou, and most of the rest of her was sand and salt grass, the curving beach separated from the flats and marshes by sand dunes, odd shaped structures born of wind and tide. Only toward the head of the creature had much civilization taken hold, as if the town had grown out of the thing's brain, and been blown back over its body by the wind accompanying its ascent.

If a bird dipped lower, over the town, it would see—on a clear day—the precise, parallel streets, laid out in a north/south grid. The buildings of the business district, ornate and sturdy, would look, from up high, as much a natural part of the place as the dunes and the beach. The busy harbor, beside Avenue A, would be full of ships, big and small, some giving off clouds of steam, some relying on the most ancient of engines, standing tall and naked above them. At the center of the island there would be trees, palms and oaks and pecans, and oleander everywhere. Churches and houses would point up out of the trees, and some of the houses, gigantic and splendid, would be bigger than some of the churches.

Standing at the window, Isaac watched the rain falling hard and steady outside, and looked up at the low, slate colored mass of clouds that had settled over the city.

"One day," he said, almost to himself, "we'll surely have a way to get up above everything, and look down into such a storm as this one, and see what it's doing." He looked at his chart again, and at the row of colored pins in it. "And where it's going."

He thought of Galveston's people, out on the beach road, and in the lowest streets of the city, that he had spent most of the morning calling out warnings to, and that he would go back out now to yell at again.

He looked at Joseph. And listened to yet another deep, slow peal of thunder move slowly through the clouds. The thin panes of the tall windows shuddered in their frames.

"But not today," he said.

CHAPTER TWO

Almost three miles away, out the gently curving beach road, toward that end of the island Isaac Cline knew would go under water first, the rain rolled off the steep roofs of the two buildings of the St. Mary's Catholic Orphanage.

Sister Zilphia, one of the ten Sisters of Charity of the Incarnate Word who saw to the day-to-day operations of the place, just wanted for this particular day to be over and done with.

She had lived and worked in one of the two long two-story wood frame buildings since Spring, fascinated every day and night by the close proximity of the imposing Gulf of Mexico, separated from the two buildings by a thin strip of sand and some grass-topped dunes. She studied the clockwork comings and goings of the tides and listened closely to the other nuns, who had been there much longer, when they talked of storms.

And they had often talked of storms.

This morning, the tides seemed to have tossed aside their timetables, and the foamy gray water of the gulf sloshed against what was left of the sand dunes and filled up the yard that surrounded the buildings. And the nuns weren't doing any more talking about storms, except for Sister Mendulla, who Zilphia suspected would probably enjoy a good storm, since it would match her disposition.

Zilphia had gone out to one of the porches hours ago, long before daylight, to find the yard full of water, already slapping against the steps. She went back in to wake Reverend Mother Camillus, but met her on the stairs, already headed out to see about things first-hand.

The two women went back out on to the porch and a quick gust of the steadily increasing wind caught the heavy folds of their black habits, popping them with the force of a rug being shaken out. Camillus, old enough to be Sister Zilphia's grandmother, steadied herself against the younger nun's arm and told her to wake the other sisters and tell them to get the children up and dressed. And to pray, she had said, which surprised Zilphia not in the least, since the old lady's advice about everything was to pray.

Zilphia told her, as they went back inside, that she would ask Sister Catherine to cook breakfast right away—even though the sun wouldn't be up for an hour or more, if it bothered to come up at all on such a dismal day—since it was no telling when they would eat again.

Camillus nodded in agreement as she lifted up the hems of her long habit before taking the first steps. Then a final word came out, as naturally as the rain fell: Pray.

Then some busy hours passed. Camillus did considerable praying in the narrow room that served as her study, and Mendulla frowned even more than usual through the unfortunate birthmark that covered much of her face, and Catherine sang bits of songs as she cooked and served up the breakfast, and Sister Elizabeth led some of the children in their prayers, and Sister Zilphia didn't pray at all.

It had been daylight now for some time, and everyone had their breakfast and sat or stood at the windows of the two long buildings, watching the water rise around them.

Sal Casey, who was not an orphan, read a story to a group of the youngest children. The smallest of all of them sat huddled in Sal's tiny lap. Her name was Mary, and everyone called her Wee Mary, since there were currently seven Marys at the orphanage. At one time there had been ten.

Wee Mary had taken a liking to Sal, who came the three miles out from town nearly every day all summer to read stories and to play with the children. She leaned back against Sal, and watched her lips as she read the words from the book.

Sister Zilphia watched her, also, and wished, again, that she had gotten Sal home safe to her family yesterday afternoon. She had intended to take her back in the wagon, but she didn't learn until late that one of the wagon's wheels was broken, and by that time the massive waves were washing over the edges of the beach road, so walking to town was out of the question.

The orphanage didn't have a telephone, since the lines didn't run out that far, and Zilphia couldn't have called Sal's mother anyway, since Sal told her they didn't have one in their house either. If the orphanage had a telephone, Zilphia could have rung up the big Kempner mansion on Broadway, where Sal's mother was the cook, but surely she hadn't gone in to work on a day like this. So there wasn't a way to get in touch with her, to let her know that Sal was safe, so Zilphia resolved to worry about things that she could do something about.

She turned her attention from Sal's reading back to the storm, which was blowing with greater force than it had been. This storm was another thing Sister Zilphia couldn't do anything about. Her thinking concerning fate had changed considerably of late, and she was almost glad of it, since she wouldn't have to worry now about why she had ended up in this place, on this precarious stretch of beach, in this storm. Once, she would have spent much of her time wondering about fate, and questioning it, and making futile attempts to see the good in actions and situations where it was just possible that no good resided. Once she would have been certain that fate had brought her to Galveston.

Now she knew that it had been infinitely simpler than that. And that what had brought her was nothing more philosophical or meaningful than a train.

She watched little spurts of spray shoot up between the boards of the porch floor. Only the tops of the dunes in front of the two long buildings were visible now, after all the battering of the wind and water. Gray waves swirled around and between them, and Zilphia knew that the beach just beyond them must by now lie under a couple of feet of the gulf. She squinted her eyes and tried to see out there, but saw only the foamy crests of large, agitated waves which were the same color as the air around them.

"It's not looking any better," Sister Elizabeth said, behind her.

As if to concur with her assessment, the sea sent an odd-shaped piece of driftwood through the dunes. It tumbled over a section of picket fence that had been pushed down and swept quickly to the porch, clattering against the steps.

Zilphia watched it, and didn't speak for a moment. When she did, she didn't look back at Elizabeth, but kept her gaze locked on the worsening conditions outside.

"Has the water ever gotten this high before?" She pinched the narrow strip of molding that separated two panes of the window. "I mean, up to the steps like this, and sloshing through the porch?"

Elizabeth, hardly ever at a loss for words, was quiet a while before she answered.

"Not that I've seen," she nearly whispered, so nobody else could hear. "But some of the others might have seen it, before I came. Sister Mendulla's been here the longest."

Zilphia had just been thinking of Mendulla, of how the dark sky and waves were the exact color of her wide birthmark. She wondered if Elizabeth had called her "Sister Blister"—as the children did, out of her hearing—just now. Surely not.

Zilphia nodded slowly. "Since the original flood, I imagine."

On Thursday, just two days before, Zilphia and Elizabeth had gone with several of the children through the dunes and out to the beach at the end of the day. It was a cloudless afternoon, and the two nuns watched as the children got in their last romping play of the afternoon, their laughter and shouts blending with the squawking of seagulls that swooped down and rose again, as if jerked along on the nimble strings of a talented puppeteer.

They watched, too, for the occasional rattler that might make its way out of the dunes. Elizabeth yelled at the children, as they barreled through the dunes toward the beach, that not a single one of them had once looked where they were going, and how many times was she going to have to tell them to be careful there? Then she told Zilphia—not for the first time—about the little girl who had been bitten two summers ago, and how they had barely gotten her to the infirmary, miles away in town, over on the bay side of the island, to save her. Bless her heart, she told Zilphia—she was so sick, for ever so long. Elizabeth had thought of it for a long moment and then shook it out of her head and inspected the last of the day. The sky was cloudless, and the gulf had mirrored its fading light on its churning, frothy breakers and, beyond them, on the still, flat plane of the sea which stretched to the horizon.

Zilphia tried to find the horizon now, beyond the pounding rain and the gray spume that boiled up from where the beach used to be, but she couldn't. It had been perfectly visible then, in the last light of that nice afternoon, when she and Elizabeth had herded the children back to the buildings, and darkness descended on everything like a curtain. The breeze had played through the long grass at the tops of the dunes, the first stars had sputtered to life in the vast heavens, and even then, Zilphia thought, as she looked again at the surging upheaval all around her, even then, on that most perfect of afternoons, this monster must have already been crawling toward them from the east, way out past the still, straight edge of the world.

A particularly insistent wave collided with the front of the porch, and sent enough splattering spray up on the window to make the two nuns lean backwards. They blinked their eyes and looked again at the surging water and driving wind, hoping to find that it had lessened some.

It hadn't.

The weather, if anything, had grown even more foul. The weather in Galveston was something that Zilphia had spent the summer coming to terms with. Most of the time it was hot and awfully humid, and the mosquitoes were large and hungry. But the gulf still offered its spectacular visage every time she looked at it—at least until today - and the breeze that came off of it whisked into the windows of the orphanage day and night, and danced in the thin curtains by her bed.

She was still coming to terms, too, with Reverend Mother Camillus, who seemed to lurk always in the background, waiting for Zilphia to make the decision she had been sent here to make, and with Sister Mendula, whose splotched face seemed to be a barometer of her foul mood, and who treated her like one of the mosquitoes. But the other sisters, especially Elizabeth, standing behind her now, had been wonderful to her.

And the island had, too. The gulls called her to consciousness every morning, and the slow pulse of the surf sang her to sleep at night. The sight of the countless dunes, spread out along the edge of the beach like bubbles on a pie's crust, was beautiful to her. And the night sky over the gulf exploding, for a few seconds, with thin fingers of lightening and sharp cracks of thunder, was magic, beyond any that she had ever known. She loved to stand on the porch of one of the buildings and search the beauty of a perfect red sunset, not for anything in particular, not for evidence of anything philosophical, or theological, not for justification, or guidance.

She had determined to no longer attach symbolic baggage to such things as sunsets, or thunderstorms over the dark sea. But to see them through the eyes of one merely content that they somehow occur.

For she was coming to terms with Someone else, too. She was far from sure of the relationship there, and all communication between them had long since ceased, but she was sure of one thing: His handiwork was magnificent, and nowhere more so than on this island.

Out of the corner of her eye, Zilphia saw someone moving quickly through the body of water that was where the yard had been until this morning. Samuel, the black man who did odd jobs around the place and lived in a room behind the shed, finally reached the porch and pulled himself up out of the murky water. He slung water from the brim of his hat, and put it back on. Zilphia and Elizabeth met him at the door.

"I ain't got no other wheel for the wagon," he said, having to talk louder than he usually did over the whistling wind and the roar of the big waves crashing into the dunes. "And that other one is busted up too bad to fix."

Zilphia leaned out the door and looked down the beach toward town. The road had completely disappeared under the tide.

"It doesn't matter," she said, leaning close so he could hear her. "We couldn't get anywhere in the wagon now anyway." She read the

15

fear in his eyes. "Come on in and get dry."

He starred at her.

"Come on," she said, and managed a smile. "We'll all be all right."

When he and Elizabeth went in, Zilphia walked to the edge of the porch and looked again at the churning, gray surface that heaved and fell in front of her, almost as if it were breathing. A wave struck the steps with enough force to send water over her shoes.

The least of her worries, she knew, was that she had wet shoes. Or that she had just told Samuel a lie.

Inside, she told two of the boys to quit their rough-housing, and to settle down.

"It's going to be a long day," she said, "and I can't do a thing about it, but I guess I can still send the two of you upstairs to copy down enough scripture to keep you occupied for a while."

The pair found another place to be, and Zilphia joined the group of children that had been listening to Sal's story.

Sal closed the book, and Wee Mary said that it was a good one. Margaret, who was not much older than Wee Mary, but considerably taller, sucked loudly on the piece of hard candy that Sister Elizabeth had given to her.

"It wasn't as good as the one about the dog that jumped over the moon," she said, and shifted the candy to the other side of her mouth.

"It was a cat," Sal said.

Margaret thought about it.

"I ain't never liked cats," she said.

Another wave hit the front of the porch, and some of it slammed against the door. Then the first water crept in under it, spreading out over the wood floor like the daily tides on the beach.

The children watched it, then looked at Sister Zilphia, then at Sal.

"Maybe you don't like them because Chester is a dog," Sal said, "not a cat." Chester was the large yellow dog that lived at the orphanage.

Margaret thought again, and sucked at her candy.

"Naw," she finally said. "I didn't like cats even before I met Chester."

CHAPTER THREE

Galveston's people—even the ones who had come into contact
with Isaac Cline, and hadn't paid any attention to him—had finally
come to realize that this wasn't any day to be out wandering around
and looking for interesting things to see.

The pounding rain and increasing wind had proven to be too
bothersome to contend with, and a dry change of clothes and a good
chair to sit in offered more promise. Husbands had waded home from
their jobs by mid morning. Those offices that opened at all had closed
soon, and the big warehouses ceased their operations. Stores in town
shut down, and the merchants went on home, too, hoping that the
water rushing through the streets would stay there, and not come up
over the tops of the high sidewalks, and inside.

Even the wharves, which usually churned with as much activity as
an anthill, stood empty now, except for the two or three feet of bay
water that covered them. The ships in port had put out all their
available mooring, and the captains and crews settled in and hoped for
the best. The *Norna* and the *Red Cross* and the *Comino* hugged tight
to their berths, and the *Guyller*, from Norway, and the *Benedict* and
Roma, from England. The old *Alamo* was at Pier 24, sitting low and
heavy in the water, full of cotton bales. The slip assigned to the
Maydelle stood empty, the gray waves sloshing up against the pilings
and docks. The handsome English schooner had sailed on Thursday
night, its curious cargo of odd-shaped wooden crates and two tightly
wrapped burlap bundles stowed carefully beneath cotton bales in the
deepest recesses of the hold.

The first mate of the *Kendal Castle*, a British steamship at Pier
31, found the captain on the bridge.

"All we got is down," he told him, flinging off the heavy parka he
had worn to make his inspection. "I don't think we got another
goddamned inch of line."

The captain listened to the rain beating against the hull, and felt the
big, empty ship already starting to rock slightly in the wind. He looked
again at the barometer that he had studied countless times this

morning, and wasn't surprised to see that it was still falling.

"It may not be enough," he said.

Many blocks away, toward the beach, a tall black man had just waded out of the water that he had been walking in for the last hour. It had been almost up to his knees for most of his journey, and he was glad to be out of it. Now if he could just get out of the rain, and the wind, and maybe find a little something to eat, he figured his immediate situation would improve considerably.

Tucker didn't own a watch. And it was too dark and rainy for him to even guess what time it was. But he didn't have to guess that it was past time for breakfast. His growling stomach told him that.

If he was at work this morning, like he ought to be, Mrs. Ivy would have already brought out a cup of coffee with sugar stirred in it, and one of Minnie Casey's biscuits, lathered up with butter and mayhaw jelly. Tucker ate the breakfast that Mae, his wife, put on the table every morning, but he was always thankful for the second one, and ate the biscuit and drank the coffee while he leaned up against the big post oak in the side yard of the huge Kempner house on Broadway, where he was the yardman and, sometimes, when Mr. Ike Kempner or his mother needed to be taken somewhere in the buggy, the groomsman.

Tucker was moving in the same direction that the other people out on such a morning were going: towards town, and the middle of the island. He figured that the small wooden houses he had been wading past for so long had not offered enough hope to the people who lived in them, so they were headed for the brick buildings along the main streets of Galveston. He was headed there, too, since his home was in one of those buildings.

He had already seen one dead man this morning, or at least he suspected that he was dead, laid out on a porch like he was, with his people around him. Some of the people had been crying, and one woman was holding the man's hand. The storm wasn't bad enough to kill folks, Tucker thought, at least not yet. So maybe the man had just died on a stormy day, or maybe he had fallen down in some of the high water and couldn't get back up, and he drowned. He had looked pretty old. Tucker hadn't gone close enough to see about any of it. He had had to haul two dead people around on Thursday night, and clean up the blood that had spilled out when they died, and he didn't fancy dealing with any more corpses if he could help it.

One little boy, wading beside his family, had started crying this morning, and Tucker volunteered to carry him. But the boy's father took a long look at Tucker and picked the boy up and carried him himself, which was certainly all right with Tucker, since he was too tired to be toting a child anyway.

His stomach growled again, loud enough for him to hear it over the splashing rain and the wind, and he thought again of that biscuit that he would be eating if he *was* at work. He guessed he wouldn't be leaning up against that tree this morning, even if he was at work, where he ought to be, since even the Kempner's yard, on the highest part of the island, must have a lot of water in it by now. But he could have sat in the carriage house, and talked to the horse, and eaten the biscuit and drunk the coffee.

Tucker always felt a little bad about eating two breakfasts every day, when Mae and his babies only had one. But, so far, the bad feeling hadn't kept him from eating whatever Mrs. Ivy handed out the back door to him.

He was tired, and had walked a long way, in all that water. And the rain hadn't let up any. He had spent the night on a raised loading dock, as far up under its tin awning as he could get, and he tried to not do any thinking about his current dilemma, since he had thought about it so much and for so long, and worried about it, and had tried to figure out how in the world he had ended up in such a predicament. So he had tried to put it all out of his mind last night, under the awning of the loading dock, and let the rain tapping on the tin roof sing him to sleep, like Mae sang his babies to sleep every night.

Now, he knew, as he made his slow way home, he might never eat another biscuit under the big tree at the Kempner's, since he surely wouldn't have a job there anymore. Not that it would matter much, since he was most likely going to end up in Mr. Ketchum's jail. Mr. Ketchum was the chief of the Galveston police, and his jail was always full of people that he and the other policemen caught, Tucker heard. And if Mae hadn't taken the babies and left him already, she would surely do it then, since Mae was a Christian woman, and wouldn't abide living in the house with anyone who had been thrown into a jail.

Some people sat on the porches of the little houses he passed, and some children still played in the water in the yard. The people on the porches were all white folks, so they didn't even bother to wave at him. Some of the youngest of the children, who hadn't learned better yet, smiled at him, or waved. He nodded in their direction and kept on his way. The rain pelted down steadily, and Tucker was soaked through. And hungry.

After all the bad business on Thursday night, he had gone out to the beach and slept in the dunes. On Friday morning, he was awakened by a loud, rumbling sound that he couldn't immediately identify. He thought, as he blinked frantically to try to figure out where he was, that some kind of animal might be after him. The muffled growling had *sounded* like an animal.

He got quickly to his feet and looked all around for the animal, but didn't see one. He saw, instead, the big dark waves rolling over each other and crashing on the sand.

Later that day, after another nap, he moved back further from the dunes, since the waves had reached them by then, and he sat on the edge of the beach road.

He watched the waves and determined that they didn't show any interest in going back to where they were supposed to be. Then he got up, walked across the road, and looked at the salt grass that stretched out toward the other side of the island. It looked awfully low out there to Tucker, and he decided that the only thing to do was to start walking back toward town, and just be careful to keep his eye out for Mr. Ketchum. Which would be a hard thing to do, he had thought, since he didn't know what Mr. Ketchum looked like.

Now, it was Saturday morning, and Tucker was no closer to making up his mind about what to do than he had been on Thursday night, after everything went so wrong. All he was doing now was walking, toward the rooms off the dingy little alley that was his home. Finally, he came to some more water that he would have to walk through. This water, he knew, must be coming from the bay, rather than from the gulf. He was too tired to try to figure out what that meant, so he just waded on in.

Eventually, he reached the alley. There was no water standing in it, but he knew that it wouldn't be long before it would be, since he had been wading in water for blocks. The alley was off the sidewalk, which was a few feet up off the street. And when the water got in the alley, he knew, it would get in the rooms where his family lived, since their only door opened into it.

Mae and the children were gone. Tucker sat down at his place at the table, and thought some more. They might have gone to their church, he knew, to try to pray the storm away—Mae was much given to praying—or to watch the little preacher jump and holler while it blew in.

But the church house was an old wooden building not even three blocks from the beach. Surely nobody would go out there. Tucker knew that the little preacher, and Mae, and lots of other folks who went to that church put their trust in Jesus. But surely, with a bad storm coming in off the gulf, and with not all that sturdy a church to pray in, they would be better off doing their trusting somewhere in the middle of town.

Tucker thought he might need to walk out to the church house, just to make sure, but he knew that the water must be higher out there now than it had been a little while ago, when he had waded within a block of the place.

He wondered why he hadn't thought about looking in the church while he was out there. That would have been the thing to do. But he was getting tired of wondering why he had done, or not done, things in the past week. What he needed to do, right now, was eat.

He built a fire, and made coffee. He opened a tin and found some of Mae's cornbread wrapped up in a towel. He lifted the can of cane syrup down from the shelf and, when the coffee began to boil, had his breakfast.

While he ate, he tried to think of places where Mae might have taken his babies. Maybe she thought she ought to find a better place to be than here for a storm. But this old building was made out of bricks, and had come through many a storm and overflow. The water might come in on the floor, but there were beds and a table and chairs for them to get up on till it went back out.

Tucker chewed on a piece of cornbread and drank his coffee. He couldn't think of anyplace that Mae might go, and he had been here long enough for her to come home, if she had walked down the street to a store.

A low peal of thunder rolled over the building, and shook it a little. Tucker watched the coffee send out tiny waves to the edge of his cup. He had saved the worst fear for last.

What if Mae had left him? Maybe Mr. Ketchum had come here, and told her that she was married to a thief, and maybe even a killer. Tucker knew that he should have told Mae about everything that had happened on Thursday night himself, so he could have explained it to her. But, as usual, he had done the wrong thing. And what if she had figured out how he had come by the money he had given her? What if she prayed about it, and Jesus told her not to stay married to a killer and a thief? What if she had used some of the money and bought train tickets and gone to her sister's in Angleton?

The emptiness in the room told him that she had.

He was still hungry, but he pushed the cornbread away. He wished that Mae and the children were here, and that this storm wasn't, and that he was at his job at the Kempner's, sitting under the post oak, drinking his coffee there, or working in the yard, or tending to the horse in the carriage house.

He hoped that horse was safe, and not having to stand in water. He hoped that somebody had remembered to feed him, and brush him —he liked to be brushed—since he hadn't been there to do it since

Thursday afternoon.

Another crack of thunder shook the window and the door of the room. Tucker went outside and walked in the stinging rain to the front of the alley. The water was nearly level to the sidewalk now, so it would be in the room soon. He looked down the street and saw that the water was higher toward the wharves, being pushed in from the bay by the stiff north wind.

Tucker went back to the room and sat down at his place at the table. He looked at the empty chair where Mae always sat, and at the others, where his babies usually were. He knew he ought to be hungry, but he wasn't. He knew he shouldn't be tired, since he had slept more than usual the last couple of days. But he was.

He watched the bottom of the single door, until he saw the first tenuous finger of brown water slip under it.

Debris of all sorts was traveling around the new system of waterways in the streets, moving beside, and in the way of, and sometimes colliding with Galveston's people, who were still clamoring for a good place to ride out the worst of a storm that was already bad enough to suit them.

Pieces of fencing and wooden porches moved along in the water in the streets like rafts. Bulkier objects, like chairs and harness riggings, tumbled end over end if the water was deep enough, or got caught up at the edge of a sidewalk or a store if it wasn't.

On his way out his own side gate, Ike Kempner was almost hit by a big section of a pecan tree as it scraped its way down the street. There wasn't enough water standing in this section of the city yet to float the limbs, but the wind was moving it anyway, in spurts, and one of the brisk spurts nearly caused it to broadside the scion of one of the wealthiest families in Galveston.

Minnie Casey, the Kempner's cook, stood at one of the kitchen windows, and watched Ike step back and let the tumbling contraption roll on by before he started off toward his office.

It was just like him, she thought, to go down there today to make even more money than he already had, when a bad storm was blowing in, and when he had almost been knocked down by a piece of a tree before he even left his own yard. Jews. She thought, and clicked her tongue, and turned her attention back to the kitchen.

It was a big kitchen, at the corner of the house, with slender windows along two of the walls that reached all the way up to the high ceiling. A mammoth black stove dominated one end of the room, its oven still emitting the heat that had cooked the breakfast biscuits. Several of the biscuits lay on a plate on the table where Mrs. Ivy, the housekeeper, and Pearl, the maid, and Minnie ate their meals. A jar of Minnie's mayhaw jelly still stood open beside the plate. The tall windows were all open a few inches, just enough to let in a little fresh air, but not any of the rain, and they had screens on their outsides to keep out mosquitoes. A fly had found one of the several holes in the screens and then found the jelly. In the winter, the Kempner's elderly cat would be curled up beside the stove, in spite of the fact that Minnie did not hold with animals in the house, much less in the kitchen. But today, it was sleeping, safe and sound and dry, beneath one of the potted palms on the covered front porch, while the rain poured off the roof and down the steep steps and along the red brick walk, through the ornate iron gate, and out into Broadway, the widest boulevard of the city.

Minnie had waded through water for all of the sixteen blocks between her home, on Ship's Mechanic Street, and here, and complained about it all morning, which Mrs. Ivy and Pearl had expected her to do. She complained about everything.

"Why did you even bother to come in at all," Mrs. Ivy had asked her, early, as she poured her a cup of coffee. Mrs. Ivy and Pearl both lived in the house, up in the servants' rooms at the very top.

Minnie dabbed at her uniform with a towel and tied on her apron.

"I've never missed a day of work in my life," she told them. "I don't guess a little bit of a storm will make me do it." She had been in America for sixteen years, but her brogue was as rich as the day she had left Ireland. She had taken the cup from Mrs. Ivy, tried a sip, and said she'd better make another pot, first thing, since this was no more than colored water.

"We've all been up since before daylight," Mrs. Ivy told her, "and you're the first to complain about it."

Minnie poured the contents of the cup into the sink. "That may be," she said, "but when I drink a cup of coffee, I like a little coffee in it."

Then she looked at the wood box, and the few pieces at its bottom. "I guess the nig . . ."—Mrs. Ivy's expression had stopped her—"I guess Tucker still ain't showed up." One of Tucker's jobs was to keep the woodbox filled. She clicked her tongue, as if encouraging a horse to move on, and said she'd have to have more wood than that to cook any breakfast.

Mrs. Ivy tilted her big head. "I've got a good fire going, though I know it probably isn't to your liking. But it's enough to cook breakfast. There's no need for you to get drenched again, now that you're dry." She pulled a chair out from the table. "Why don't you sit down and rest a minute, after wading clear across town. Mr. Kempner isn't going down to his office until ten. He's got an appointment, or he wouldn't go then."

"I don't need any rest," Minnie snapped. She studied the fire and determined that it might do.

"I didn't get any rest last night," she said, as she pulled out the heavy skillet, "nor a minute's sleep, either. So why should I rest now?"

Mrs. Ivy certainly hadn't seen the logic of it, but long association with Minnie had taught her that it would be a waste of time to say so.

"Thurmon was the only one of my family to come home at all," Minnie went on, slamming the skillet around on the surface of the stove till she got it where she wanted it. Thurmon was Minnie's husband, about whom she never had anything good to say. Not that she ever had good things to say about anyone, but even Mrs. Ivy, who looked for and found the good in most people, thought that Minnie might be justified in her opinion of her husband, since, by all accounts, he was a drunkard, and couldn't hold a job.

Then Minnie began cracking eggs on the side of a porcelain bowl and pouring their contents into it.

"Sal never came home at all, and is out at that orphanage, I imagine, reading stories to orphans who could as easily be reading them to themselves—if they can read at all—and doing the work of a bunch of lazy nuns. She lifted a wooden spoon and whipped the eggs with such vigor that Mrs. Ivy was afraid she would sling them out of the bowl and across the kitchen. "And Joe . . ." Minnie gave enough of a snort to indicate that there was just no telling where Joe was. Sal and Joe were her children.

"All I can do is pray about Joe," she said. "Since I can't do anymore about what he does than I could with a stray dog that wanders up to eat every once in a while."

Mrs. Ivy had looked at the solid sheet of rain that was blowing against the windows.

"Well," she said, "let's hope that Sal and Joe are safe. And dry." Minnie threw two more pieces of wood into the fire, and clanged the metal door shut.

"Let's hope this storm starts rainin' dollar bills, too," she said. "While we're hopin'."

Now it was nearly ten, and no brighter outside, and Minnie was

24

preparing the mid-day meal. Pearl was seated at the table, polishing silver.

"And another thing," Minnie said, since there always seemed to be another thing, "you've got to bear down to it when you shine the things, and not sit all dainty like you're waitin' for Queen Victoria to call. It's work we're doin' here, girl, and not play. And the sooner you've learned it, the more good you'll be to me." She turned her pinched and pained expression back to the chopping of vegetables for the soup, but not without adding the last word. Minnie was awfully good at adding the last word.

"It's a cozy position you've got here, and at a better wage by far than when I started, I can tell you. You'd best see to keepin' it, since any girl pulled in off the street could do it as well."

Pearl considered saying "Yes, m'am," to Minnie, as she would have to Mrs. Ivy, but decided to keep her mouth shut. She had lived in the Kempner house for almost three months now, in one of the small attic rooms down a narrow hall from Mrs. Ivy's, and she had never once called Minnie "m'am." The less said to the sour bitch, the better, she figured. She resumed polishing a teaspoon, and had nearly finished it before she noticed Mrs. Ivy in the doorway. In fact, there wasn't much of the doorway left when the large woman stood there.

"Pearl," the housekeeper said, "go upstairs and see if any of this rain is coming in around any of the windows. It did some in the last blow, and we'll need to stuff towels along the places where it leaks."

Pearl started for the door. Mrs. Ivy stopped her and arranged the wide collar of her uniform, before giving her a smile and patting her on her way. She waited until she was down the long hallway before she turned her attention back to Minnie.

"That girl," she said, still standing by the door, "doesn't work for you." Minnie stopped her chopping and turned toward the house-keeper, who continued. "She works for *me*! And I'll do any fussing that needs doing." She stepped over to the counter and lifted a few bits of carrot that Minnie had been cutting. "Correct her when she makes a mistake, but there's no need to be pestering her all the time. Mrs. Kempner sees everything, believe you me, and she won't abide any such behavior."

Minnie started to protest, but Mrs. Ivy shushed her. "Just you pay attention to what I'm saying. That girl came from hard times, and this job is a blessing to her." She nodded her big head as if she had just remembered something else. "And she has much on her mind right now."

Minnie knew what the girl had on her mind. The rich boy that had been sniffing around her all summer, like she was a bitch in heat, had lost interest. Had gotten all the milk he needed, Minnie figured, and forgotten the cow. She nearly smiled.

Mrs. Ivy picked up another piece of carrot and turned it in her big hand. "Make these smaller," she said. Minnie stared at her.

"And you'd do well to start wearing a bit more of a smile every now and then yourself," Mrs. Ivy went on. "Mr. Kempner has great responsibilities, what with having to take over such a big and important business when his father, God rest his sweet soul,"—she crossed herself—"died so sudden, and he doesn't need to be seeing a bitter expression like yours of a morning before he goes to his office."

She made one of her quick exits. Minnie had always marveled at how someone so big could move about so quickly without knocking things over. When it finally did happen, Minnie knew, the thing would be broken, or, if it was a person, would have to be helped up and tended to.

She resumed her slicing with vigor, the vegetables becoming, for a moment, parts of the big woman whose aura of violet scented toilet water lingered in the kitchen.

Minnie wanted Pearl's job for her girl, Sal, who was only eleven, but would be old enough to have it in a year or two. After all, Pearl had grown up in the St. Mary's orphanage out on the beach road, where Sal went to read to the children and slave away for the sorry nuns, and Minnie knew that a girl with that background wouldn't hold a good job like this one for any year or two. The Kempners were Jews, and as rich as Midas, and Minnie suspected they laid their heads on their ironed pillowslips every night feeling good about giving work to orphans and Negroes, when honest, decent people needed the work. Her own husband, Thurmon, could do the work that Tucker did, she knew, if he wasn't a drunkard. Or her boy, Joe, could have, though he never seemed to be without money, not that he ever gave her any of it to buy groceries for the house, or even spent much of his time there, except to eat the food that she paid for with her wages. Minnie hacked away at the vegetables, thanked the Blessed Virgin that she was a Catholic and of good Irish stock, and hoped that all of her misery was storing up riches in heaven.

There was a knock at the back door.

The woman Minnie saw there, when she opened it, was as drenched as the two small children beside her. Water poured off all three of them in streams.

"What do you want?" Minnie asked.

"I'm lookin' for Tucker," the woman said, pushing the children closer to the door, under the porch roof. "He my husband. I was thinkin' he might be here."

Minnie made no effort to open the screen door that separated her from the waterlogged family.

"He ain't been here in days," she said. "So you'll have to look somewhere else." She started to close the door, and saw the two children in front of the woman. They were shivering, in spite of the heat.

She pushed the screen door open an inch. "You'd best come in and get dry for just a minute," she said. "But don't track up my floor." She pointed to the floor, to show them that this was the one she was talking about.

The woman herded the children inside. "I don't know where else to look," she said. "I'm scared he's caught outside in this storm."

"That ain't no reason for you to be haulin' these children around in it," Minnie snapped.

The woman looked at the children, then at Minnie.

"I ought to of stayed put, I reckon . . . ." Minnie thought she was going to start crying. "I just felt like I needed to find Tucker."

Mrs. Ivy swept into the room. Minnie told her who they were. The housekeeper took matters in hand, and soon had Pearl downstairs and seeing to the children. She went up to the youngest of the Kempner children's closets, got enough clothes to provide a dry change, and even found a frock that would fit the woman.

"You're Mae," Mrs. Ivy said, as she handed her a folded towel. "I know that because Tucker talks about you and his babies all the time." She smiled. "They're handsome children."

Mae smiled back at her and said that Tucker had told her about her, too. She looked at Minnie, and didn't say anything.

"I sure wish Tucker was here," she said. "I been prayin' he was."

"He's all right," Mrs. Ivy said, "wherever he is. Let's just get you and these little ones in some dry things." She sent them off with Pearl.

"Minnie," she said, when they had gone, "I think you'd better make a big pot of your good soup, so we can get something warm into them."

Minnie was already mopping the floor where they had been standing. "If this was a hotel, I guess I'd do just that," she said. "But it ain't no hotel, and . . ."

Mrs. Ivy raised a hand to shush her. "It's going to be a long day, and more people than that poor little family are likely to show up on our doorstep before it's over."

Minnie started to say something else, but Mrs. Ivy went on. "And if they do, we'll feed them, and give them a safe place to be. Because that's the kind of people we are. It's the kind of people the Kempners are."

Minnie looked at her for a moment, then turned back to her mopping.

"I was goin' to do soup, anyway," she said, and clicked her tongue, and cinched her apron even tighter to her thin body than it had been. "So I guess there'll be enough for them to have a little."

While Isaac Cline continued to warn people along the submerged beach road and in the low-lying sections of the city, shouting at everyone he saw to move to higher ground, his brother Joseph monitored the instruments in the Levy Building.

Soon he had collected all the data he needed to prepare his next report, which he would telegraph at eleven. The wind was still coming from the north, at close to thirty miles per hour. The temperature was 82.6 degrees, the barometer read 29.417 and was still falling. Nimbus clouds covered the sky as far as he could see, and a heavy rain continued to fall.

He leaned back in his chair when he was done. The wind, he knew, would increase steadily now, and would soon shift around from the northwest, then it would come from the east, the southeast, and, finally, in great force, from the south.

He knew, too, that when that happened, the hurricane would fling gulf waters up over the island, and that nothing—not the flimsy structures built along the beach, not the north wind that had opposed it all morning, and would no longer be there, and certainly not the seawall that the city should have built long ago, but never had—would stop it.

CHAPTER FOUR

THE CLINE BROTHERS

The small farm where he had been born, in 1861, took up the better part of a gently sloping hillside and a bit of the valley beneath it. It was a remote parcel of the state of Tennessee, which, at the time of his birth, was embroiled in a terrible war which his family and that part of the state had cared not much about. In fact, that little section of Eastern Tennessee had held elections and voted to keep their representatives in the United States Congress. Lincoln himself, in his declaration of war, exempted the place.

By the time he was ten, the boy had known that something bigger and more important than the farm, and the state, and even the war—which was over by then, and had filled up considerable cemeteries—would eventually pull him away and into it for the rest of his life. He didn't know what it was, at first, but he knew that he was fascinated with the changing seasons, and with the clouds that drifted over the fields as he worked with his father, and with the thunderstorms that exploded over the place on summer evenings. His life would be such a business as this, Isaac Cline knew, even as a boy.

He was the oldest of eight children, and was already ranging out over the hills, called knobs there, exploring and hunting and fishing, when he came to the age to begin his formal education. Then he did his exploring and hunting and fishing when he wasn't in the Bulging Grove schoolhouse, or helping his father plant crops, or tend them, or harvest them. The closest his father had ever come to giving him a real thrashing—and it turned out to be not much of one—was for breaking a good pottery jug into pieces because he couldn't get the stopper out of it, and he couldn't stand not knowing what was inside. For he had to know things. And he had spent much of his boyhood wondering just how many things he didn't know.

At sixteen, he said good-bye to the family and the farm and went away to Hiwassee College, where he had learned enough fast enough to get his degree a few months shy of his twentieth birthday. He had assumed his acceptance into the Weather Bureau, then part of the Signal Corps, even if the people who interviewed him had not, so he, at least, hadn't been at all surprised to be hired on, and sent to his first posting, in Little Rock, Arkansas, where he had performed his duties with distinction, and even managed to earn a doctorate in medicine at the university, in what he called his "personal time." From there he had been sent to Abiline, Texas, where he met and wooed and married Cora Mae Ballew, and then had moved to Galveston, as station chief, in 1889.

Though he would never have said it, or maybe even believed it, Isaac knew more about the weather than just about anybody. It was air and food and drink for him, and even when he stood on the beach, on most nice mornings, and watched his three small daughters chase the waves back and forth before he went downtown to work, he followed whatever clouds or breeze that happened to be wandering-across the sky, still in awe, after all those years of study and predictions, of how it all seemed to work so perfectly, and how it sometimes gathered up its considerable fury and hurled it down at unsuspecting creatures below.

Isaac's daughters—Allie, Rosemary, and Esther—were twelve and eleven and six. And they were beautiful, of course, and not just to their father, but to other people, too, and he loved to watch them, on nice mornings, as they waded barefoot along the edge of the gulf.

Joseph Cline was the fifth in that family of eight, and he hadn't stayed on the farm much longer than his brother. He came to Galveston because he overheard some family member mention that Isaac had reported good hunting and fishing there, and he took a job as a teacher in a school whose headmaster had been more interested in how big a fellow was, so he could keep the children in line, than in any college degrees he might have. Joseph had none.

It hadn't taken him long to decide that a new profession was called for—practically any would do. So he became a drummer, which seemed like a good prospect at the time, but had turned out not to be, since he wasn't particularly gifted at selling things to people.

He rented a room in his brother's house and ate the meals that Cora Mae prepared and watched his nieces get taller and prettier, and he did considerable hunting on the mainland and fishing in the bay.

Eventually, Isaac had given him a job at the Weather Bureau office, as an assistant weather observer. Joseph took to it, no doubt influenced by his brother, who usually looked at the sky even when they were sitting in a boat, when he ought to be looking at fishing lines.

Sometimes Joseph missed Tennessee, and the small farm there, on its sloping hillside. Isaac didn't miss it as much, or think about it as often, since he had been away from it longer, and because he wasn't a bachelor, like Joseph, and because he hadn't seen as much of that farm as his brother had anyway, since his attention had usually been focused on the clouds that drifted over it.

There wasn't a smudge of a cloud for Isaac to watch on Thursday, September Sixth. The tall windows of the corner room on the fourth floor of the Levy Building were all open, to catch any breeze that might find them. Isaac adjusted his small spectacles, and read the telegram he was holding for the second time. Then he laid it on his desk.

He had already taken the readings of the instruments on the roof, read the daily report from Washington, prepared the temperature forecasts for growers, and sent it out over the telegraph to the agricultural districts of Texas, marked out on the map behind his desk in geometric patterns.

Before the message arrived, by special messenger from the telegraph office, he had been bored. The courses he taught in medical climatology at the medical college wouldn't start until the fall semester began in another week or so. The temperature forecasts that he prepared daily could have been done by a child at this time of year, and not a particularly bright one at that. It was hot every day. The late fall and winter presented constant challenges, when the variance of a few degrees was crucial to the sugar cane and vegetable growers of the coastal plains. But summer and early autumn usually consisted of just one blistering day followed by another, strung out like pale beads, full of sunshine and humidity and the lazy efforts of people tired of the oppression of the tropical heat, and longing for cooler weather.

Isaac looked out the window. The sky out over the gulf was still and clear, with nothing more in it than a few seagulls floating along. Then he handed the telegram to Joseph, who read it through once and leaned back in his chair.

"Northwest of Key West," he said, and looked at the map where they had been plotting the storm. "It's taking its time."

Isaac stabbed a pin in the newest location and studied the map. "Two hundred miles south of Puerto Rico on the last day of August" —this had been more to himself than to Joseph—"then two hundred south of Santo Domingo City on the First." He removed his glasses, folded them, and placed them carefully in the pocket of the vest of his white suit. "Fifteen miles an hour, pulling up warm water all the way." Then he ran his thin finger along the path of the storm on the map. "South of Haiti at eight in the morning on Sunday, the Second. Between Nicaragua and the Yucatan on the Third, then north to Cuba. Almost thirteen inches of rain in one day in Santiago. Nine hundred miles southeast of Galveston and headed for Florida on the Fifth."

Joseph, still holding the latest advisory, joined him at the map. They worked in the same office every day, six days of every week. They lived in the same house. But they weren't particularly close, these brothers. Entire days of close proximity would often go by without any words passing between them.

"Looks like we dodged this one," he said, and looked at his brother, for confirmation.

Isaac had followed the meandering line again with the tip of his finger, then slowly shook his head.

"It's old now," he said, "and mean. We're not out of its way just yet." He pulled slightly at the small button of his stiff collar. "I called Ed Ketchum last night, just to let him know that a big one is out there, and to encourage him to keep his policemen from wandering too far off over the week-end."

Then he dabbed at the sweat on his neck with a handkerchief. "We'll probably know tomorrow who it's going to bother." He rocked a moment in his straight-backed chair and let the barest trace of a smile touch the edge of his neatly trimmed whiskers. "And if it's somewhere else, I intend to take the buggy out to the west end tomorrow evening and see if the flounder are running in the shallows of the bay." He stopped rocking and gazed, again, at the map and its several pins. "A plate of Cora Mae's flounder would be a fine celebration for missing a storm like that one."

Cora Mae had a way with flounder.

That had been on Thursday. And Isaac Cline hadn't gone fishing on Friday, but still waited to find out where the storm in the gulf was aiming its wrath. By that afternoon, everyone in the Weather Bureau office had seemed convinced that it was bent on Florida, or maybe the coasts of Alabama or Mississippi. Everyone, Joseph knew, except Isaac.

Ed Ketchum, the chief of police, came by the office later that afternoon, exchanged a few fishing stories with Joseph, and asked Isaac about the whereabouts of the storm.

Isaac told him it was somewhere in the gulf, and there was no way to tell where it was going till it got there.

Ketchum said that he guessed he already knew that. What he wanted to know was if it was coming *here*.

Isaac looked at the map and its colored pins making their northward trek. He waited a moment before answering.

"It shouldn't," he said. "Everything says it should go into the upper Gulf Coast." Then he was quiet again.

Ketchum was quiet, too.

"But something on that map of yours doesn't look just right," the police chief finally said. "Is that it? Or something in that wise head of yours."

Isaac looked at the bright blue of the sky outside his tall windows, and at the clock he had just wound. The four clerks and Joseph and Ketchum stood quietly and waited for Isaac's response. The ticking of the clock echoed in its wooden case.

"It's a big one, Ed, and old now, and pretty wise itself." Then he removed his small spectacles, and put them carefully on his desk before he finished.

"And it's not reading any map that's telling it where it ought to go."

Later that afternoon, Isaac drove the buggy out the beach road almost as far as the St. Mary's Orphanage and looked at the huge waves and the unusually high tide. He had checked the instruments on the Levy Building before he left and was glad to see the seventeen mile-per-hour wind was still coming from the north, which should have helped to push back the tide. The barometer had been falling steadily, which he expected. Still, the tide was coming in faster than it should, especially with that much opposing wind. Then he looked at the horizon out over the gulf, searching for the distinctive brick dust coloring that precedes tropical storms, but he saw no evidence of it yet.

He pulled at the reins, stopped the buggy, searched the cloudless horizon again, and didn't find what he was looking for. He thought of the readings on the instruments, and didn't find it there, either. But he did find it in the rolling, thundering surf that filled up considerably more beach than it ought to.

Later, the brothers watched the first wispy clouds, tattered at their edges, creep over the thin line where the Gulf of Mexico met the sky. They followed the shadows of the clouds as they had inched closer, over the unusually turbulent gulf, and then along the streets and the sides of buildings. A big tree, across the street from the windows where they were standing, received the shadow a leaf at a time, drinking it up the way a sponge absorbs moisture. By dusk, low, thick clouds covered Galveston like a blanket that she had pulled up over herself at the end of the day, so she could sleep.

Joseph stayed late at the office that night to complete a weather map that he would send to Texas cities inland. When he finished it, he carried it over to the Post Office, to make sure it would get on the early morning train. Then he walked down Tremont Street, toward the gulf, to Isaac's house.

A few minutes after midnight, as he finished his sixteen-block walk, it started raining. Just a drizzle at first, and then a steady patter.

Four hours later, Joseph sat on the side of his bed, stretched, and listened to the rain that had begun falling hard enough to awaken him. He stepped over to the window and, even in the darkness, saw that the entire yard lay under several inches of water.

Isaac blinked into consciousness when his brother shook him gently and reached for his glasses on the side table.

Cora Mae moved a little, beside him.

"It's begun," was all that Joseph said.

Then they started dressing.

CHAPTER FIVE

At the orphanage, enough water had seeped in under the doors to make the wooden floors damp, so the sisters herded the almost one hundred children into the large upstairs rooms of the two buildings. It wouldn't be too long, the sisters knew, before the water caused more of a problem than slippery walking.

In the long room where some of the girls slept, Sal Casey pulled a brush through Wee Mary's hair. Seven other little girls—two of them being Marys, also—waited for their turn. Margaret sat on the bed beside Sal, but wasn't in line, since she had already brushed her own hair. The room was crammed full of restless children.

"I don't know why we've got to sit up here, all cooped up," Margaret said, "and why we had to get up and get dressed and eat breakfast even before the sun came up if all we was going to do was sit around all day and not even go anywheres."

"Somebody might come out from the cathedral," Sal said, as she pulled harder at a knot in Wee Mary's hair. "Maybe Father Kirwin will come, to take us into town."

"Naw," Margaret said, after thinking about it for a moment.

The rain lashed against the many windows in the room, and they could hear the surf crashing into what was left of the dunes outside.

"How do all of you get to Mass every Sunday?" Sal asked.

Margaret kicked at one of the boys sitting on the floor, since he had gotten close enough to brush his foot against hers. Margaret didn't like to be touched, especially by boys.

"Samuel drives our wagon, and two more comes out to get us from town." She thought for another moment. "But even if they was to send ten wagons today, they couldn't get through all that water."

Sal knew that this was true. She had watched the waves on her way to the orphanage from town yesterday morning. She used one of the nickels that Zilphia had given her and rode the trolley, as far as it went, and then walked along the beach road for the rest of the way. It had been a pretty morning, which had started out scorching, then the wind suddenly changed its mind, and swung around completely, and blew a fresh breeze from the north.

In spite of the sunshine, the waves that Sal watched had been bigger than usual, and louder, booming like thunder when they rolled up on the beach. The surf was choppier than usual for the last week, but now its character had changed all together. It looked, to Sal, like it was upset, though she thought that wasn't the right word.

Angry, she realized, was a better one.

She had kept her eyes on the gray, foamy waves as she walked and felt a little silly when she shivered slightly once or twice, in the brightest of sunlight, on a nice Friday morning, way up on the beach road, above the dunes.

She finished Wee Mary's hair, and another girl backed up to her, on her knees, to have hers brushed.

Sal hadn't worried too much about the big waves yesterday, but she was more than a little concerned about them this morning. If for no other reason than that all of the nuns had spent most of their time standing nervously at the many windows, looking out at them.

Sal was a worrier by nature. She worried about her father all the time, and she was especially worried about him now, in this storm.

She always made sure that she mentioned all of her worries in her prayers, so that maybe God would do something about them. Last night, as Wee Mary lay sleeping in the bed beside her, her soft breathing in tune with the falling rain, Sal had even said her prayers for a second time, since she hadn't been able to go to sleep, and she figured that it wouldn't bother God to hear them again.

She prayed that her mother wasn't worried about her, and that she wouldn't be too very angry about her having to stay out at the orphanage, even though she supposed that it was a wasted prayer, since Minnie was bound to be mad about it. And she prayed that her father was safe and dry, and her brother Joe, too. She prayed for Wee Mary, and for all the other children in the orphanage—though she didn't know all their names, so she lumped them together—and for the sisters, even Sister Mendulla, who she knew didn't like her, and especially for Sister Zilphia, who she knew loved her.

When she had finally gotten sleepy and lost her place a couple of times, she crossed herself and closed her eyes and listened to the rain. Then she imagined her prayer lifting up, rising, like smoke from a fire, through the roof of the orphanage, and through the rain, and the clouds that the rain was coming from, and up through the dark night, until it got all the way to God.

Her last thoughts, before sleep came, were of Pearl, the maid who worked in the Kempner house with her mother, and who had once lived here at the orphanage, and slept in this very room. Pearl was

36

her best friend, was, in fact, her *only* friend, unless she counted Sister Zilphia, who was a grown-up, and the children at the orphanage, who she read to, and were more like her students.

Sal knew that Sister Zilphia had gone to the Kempner's just yesterday to talk to Pearl, because Sal had asked her to. Sal was worried about her friend, but knew that there wasn't anything that she could do to help her. Love and courtship and their attending problems were as far removed from Sal's life as the speaking of Japanese. They were just as foreign to Sister Zilphia, she suspected, but at least she was old enough, and wise enough, to come up with something to say that might help Pearl through her current unhappy situation.

This morning, Sal had been awakened and told to get dressed and then given breakfast, and everything happened so fast that she had little time to worry about Pearl. Then they were all told to go upstairs, and for several hours now they had sat on the edges of the narrow beds, or on the floor, and watched the nuns watch the storm through the many windows. And Sal worried, of course, about the storm, and Pearl, and her father.

Wee Mary went to one of the windows not occupied by a nervous nun and looked at where the yard had been, yesterday.

"How high's that water gonna get?" she asked, barely loud enough to be heard.

Sal began brushing the head in front of her. "Sister Elizabeth said she's never seen it this high before, so she thinks it'll probably start going down soon."

"Sister Blister don't think so," a boy piped up, and turned quickly to make sure none of the nuns had heard him. "I heard her tell one of the others that this here was just the start of it, and it might cover up both of these houses, all the way up to the top, before it's done."

Everybody was quiet for long enough for that to sink in. Two or three of the smallest children began to sniff, as the boy had hoped they would, and Sal told them to come and sit by her.

"Water doesn't get as high as the tops of big houses like these," she said, and looked at the boy. "Sister Mendulla probably didn't say that anyway. You must have heard her wrong." She started brushing, again. "Water doesn't get that high."

The boy started to say something, but another boy pushed him over and they started giggling.

Margaret, at the window now herself, looked outside. "It never got this high, neither," she said.

In the shed, behind the orphanage buildings, Samuel had given up on fixing the wagon's wheel. It would take more tools and supplies and skill than were available to him to get it done.

Every few minutes he looked at the water in the yard just outside the open door. It was rising more swiftly now, and soon it would be in the shed. So he went quickly about the job that Mother Superior Camillus had told him to do, even though it seemed an odd order at such a time.

He measured out sections of clothesline and cut ten of them, each about twice the length of the useless wagon.

By ten thirty, the downpours continued to hammer the island and its city, and the wind had picked up enough speed to dislodge loose shutters and ceiling tiles that people had been meaning to see to, but hadn't yet. Most of Galveston's people had found dry places to be by now, but those who hadn't studied the tops of buildings as they walked, and watched for falling pieces of the roof.

Ike Kempner, in his downtown office, studied a contract. The two men sitting across the desk from him looked nervously at the window, and at the rain slamming against it.

Appropriately enough, they were there to discuss water, specifically the awarding of a contract for damming a creek near Wichita Falls to irrigate several thousand acres of north Texas cotton land. But the water the two high plains businessmen were worried about at the moment wasn't in any creek.

"Ike," one of them said, and the young man, young enough to be either of the businessmens' son, looked up. "I hate to bring this up again, but Henry and I aren't used to these . . . things." He pointed to the window. "Don't you think this might be that storm coming in?" He looked at the man sitting in the chair next to his, who certainly appeared to think that it was.

Ike laid the contract down and looked at the window.

"Well," he said, after a moment, as if he hadn't been aware that the sun wasn't shining out there, "I suspect it is." He smiled. "We don't get a rain like this every day, or we could catch enough of it to haul it up to your country and not have to spend any money on a dam."

The two men laughed nervously.

Their train had rolled into the Galveston station late yesterday afternoon, and they walked the not too many blocks to the Tremont Hotel under clouds no more threatening than the ones that gathered over their town every so often. At tables around them at dinner, there had been talk of a storm in the gulf. Someone said that the flags had been flying all day on the Levy Building.

The two North Texas men didn't listen closely to the snips of conversations, since they hadn't been directed at them, and ate the fresh flounder and redfish that they had looked forward to on the train. This morning, they ate breakfast in the same place, but it was raining hard by then, and the people at the tables around them had paid as much attention to the windows as they had to their food.

Ike Kempner had eaten his breakfast in the large dining room of the house his father had built on Broadway. While his mother talked of politics, he finished a plate of Minnie's biscuits and eggs.

His mother picked at her food with a heavy silver fork, and went on and on about how William Jennings Bryan didn't have any more of a chance of defeating McKinley in the upcoming election than he had in Ninety-Six, and how it was amazing that Bryan still trotted out the abolition of the gold standard as his prize pony, when there had been enough gold discovered in South America to back up American dollars till the sun burned out. Then she caught her breath, and actually ate a bite or two and said that what rankled her more than anything was this "Great Commoner" business. From what she could gather, Bryan was no more common than Mr. Rockerfeller, and had never done a day of manual labor in his life. No more than Lincoln had ever split a rail.

Ike nodded as she held forth, knowing that this daily harangue was important to her, and her only way of taking part in the political process, since she couldn't actually vote. Ike was in a freshly pressed three-piece suit, his collar so starched and tall that he had to stretch his neck away from it every few moments. His father, whose collar had been just as starched and just as tall, had died suddenly six years ago, and the reins of the family business were tossed, all too soon, in Ike's lap. Only twenty-one, he had returned to Galveston from his year abroad and risen to the occasion, as his mother had never doubted that he would, and handled meetings with board members and bankers and lawyers old enough to be his father, or grandfather, with skill and authority.

Soon, Mrs. Kempner's two youngest sons—she had five— appeared to present her with morning kisses, and moved on to the breakfast laid out on the sideboard.

One of the boys dug a large serving spoon into a platter of Minnie's scrambled eggs and mentioned having something better to do than attending Temple that week. Ike, not even looking up from the watch he was winding, had settled that quickly by decreeing that the boys would attend Temple regularly until they were twenty-one, at which time they could find other things to do if they were so inclined.

His mother smiled, and drank her coffee.

In his office now, with the two North Texas men seated across the wide desk from him, he looked at that watch, which had been his father's, and returned it to his vest pocket.

Yet another peal of thunder cracked through the dark morning. The building trembled slightly in its wake. The three men looked at the window.

"We get these blows from time to time," Ike said, and picked the contract back up. "Most of our homes are built up high enough that no water comes into them. Anyway, I was just reading the other day that this famous oceanographer, Commodore Maury, had found that storms that originated where this one did don't put Galveston in their natural path."

One of the men nodded and watched the blowing rain some more.

"It looks like he might be wrong, this time."

Ike smiled and pointed out at the dismal morning. "This isn't the main thrust of the storm you've heard about, gentlemen. The wind isn't blowing hard enough for that. It will come on to the coast somewhere else, or maybe already has, and will keep dumping rain on us here, and you'll have plenty of time to get to the station, and soon be on your train heading north." He looked back at the sheets of paper. "Now, I still need to know a little more about this Clause Six, on the fourth page . . . ."

The two North Texas men looked at each other, both of them hoping that Commodore Maury, whoever the hell he was, was as smart as his young disciple seemed to think he was.

On Ship's Mechanic Street, Thurmon Casey heard someone calling him. It was not his father, though his father, buried for years in the big cemetery between Broadway and Avenue L, did sometimes call to him. And it was not Minnie, his wife, who sometimes called, too, at least in his head. In reality, Minnie was about as likely to call for him as his father was. This was a sweet voice, perhaps real, perhaps not. He hadn't climbed far enough out of his grogginess to know yet. The voice came again.

Sal.

He lay still for a moment, to get his bearings, then he opened his eyes and looked for her. On most mornings, she was there, smiling at him, and leaning down to hug his neck.

Today, he just saw the rusting iron bed frame and the cracked plaster of the tall, shabby room. And he heard the hard rain against the windows.

Thurmon pulled himself slowly to a sitting position, but even that proved to be too fast an effort. The insides of his head began to throb, and felt like water being sloshed around in a bucket.

He had been in several of the saloons on Postoffice street until way past midnight, and then stumbled through the rain until he got home. Minnie started her usual caterwauling, and went on particularly long about something or other. He blinked his heavy eyelids and let his mind reach for it, but he couldn't remember what had set her off. It was too far back in the fog.

He rubbed his head, and wished that Sal was there, to smile at him.

On most mornings, when he woke, his head usually in the dismal state that it was in this morning, Sal would be there, sitting on the edge of the bed and touching the side of his face. And telling him that there was hot water for his shave, and that she had made his breakfast.

But Sal must still be asleep, he thought, in the closet sized area that served as her bedroom. And he'd have to see to his own breakfast, after he tried to wash the putrid taste out of his mouth that had accumulated there in the saloons.

Thurmon spent much of his time in saloons, and stumbling along Galveston's streets between saloons. He usually got drunk fairly early every afternoon and nurtured the condition along, taking in just the right amount of cheap bourbon at precisely the right intervals to sustain that perfect, floating balance between the initial pangs of sobriety and the early, faltering stumbling along the edge of the abyss. On the days that he actually found the odd job to go to—usually at the warehouse of the Cotton Exchange, when they were short-handed— he started drinking a little later than he liked to, for he longed, every day, to drift up, away from his disappointing showing in life, from the dead war hero that was his father, who the city still spoke of, and from Minnie, who only stayed in their poor excuse of a home because of the devotion to Roman Catholicism that she clung to the way a drowning man clings to a rope. The drinking he did in the saloons let him do the floating up that he needed to do to leave it all behind him.

And when he floated he sang, in a rich, full tenor voice, and he didn't slur the words of whatever song he was singing. Neither did he forget them, owing to the fact that he housed only three songs in his repertoire, and he knew those three by heart, either drunk or sober.

It was his singing that got him free drinks in the saloons, that and the Irish banter that he offered. Most of the saloon owners were too cheap to pay anybody to sing, so, when Thurmon wandered in, as he frequently did, they would give him a couple of shots, and suggest a song. It never took a very strong suggestion, and, soon, "My Wild Irish Rose" or something like it would lift through the cigar smoke and the chatter of the place.

With every drink, Thurmon's face took on a deeper shade of red, and his eyelids hung heavier and sadder. The bartenders who watched him sometimes wondered if his eyes would close all the way together if he ever drank enough. With every song, the words took on more sorrowful and tragic significance, so that, toward the end of a performance in a bar, he practically cried the songs. Sometimes tears worked their way out of the narrow slits. And sometimes the people at the tables and the bar would cry too, for their mothers, for their long-lost sweethearts, or for their wasted lives. At the end of it, Thurmon would have another drink or two, this time paid for by the customers, not the owner. Then an internal clock would tell him the time was right, and he would stumble on to another saloon, where a short, thick glass, with its splash of amber at the center, would be placed on the bar in front of him.

The nightly fog he wandered through removed him from everything that was wrong in his life, and morning's light usually shined on the one thing that was right.

Sal.

He stood up, and got his balance, but still he had to run his hand along the wall on his way to the bathroom. After he emptied his bladder, washed his teeth, and threw cold water—the only variety of water in the building—on his face, he studied the sad devil looking back at him from the mirror over the sink. He wasn't actually fat, he supposed. But the stocky, muscular man of his youth was no longer there. His neck was flabby, though only slightly so, and his hairline had receded to the point where more of his forehead was visible than he could ever remember seeing. His eyes, a dimmer blue than they had once been, lay deep in two dark pools, his dry, fair skin running in countless shallow crevices away from them.

He touched one unsteady finger to the image in the mirror, wondering what had become of the young fellow who once caused his father to hold out some hope, though slight, and who took pretty girls to the Pagoda beach pavilion to dance and to look at the colored lights reflected in the foamy surf.

He felt of the stubble on his chin, and knew he should shave, but decided against it. He hadn't shaved since the day before yesterday, and Sal ended up doing it for him then, since his hand shook so that the razor had tapped against the porcelain bowl of hot water.

He looked around the empty room and listened, again, to the heavy rain and wind outside. He reached into his shirt pocket, fumbled for his father's watch, lifted it out and opened it. He looked at the time, then squinted his eyes closely together to try to read the pale in-

scription inside the cover. "To Capt. Casy, from his company. 1883."
The misspelling of the name was owing, he knew, to the literacy level
of that particular unit of the Army of the Confederacy. He turned it
in his hands, letting it catch the dim light, and considered the two
ironies of the watch: that it should have been presented to his father
as the old man lay dying (Thurmon always wondered if the veterans
had suspected that their captain would have need of it where he was
going) and that it should have come finally into *his* unworthy hands.
His father had been a hero in the great business, which he had called,
until his dying day, clutching his new watch in one frail fist, "the War
of Northern Aggression."

Thurmon knew that he had not been cut from the same cloth as
his father, who had taken every opportunity to remind him of it while
he had been alive, and even afterwards. He had sneered at him from
his casket, the several decorations that had been pinned on by Lee and
Davis themselves on the old uniform, the unsheathed saber laid across
his narrow chest, as if he intended to hack his way into eternity. He
sneered at him now from the watch.

Thurmon gently closed it and put it back in his pocket. Then he
felt a crumpled piece of paper there that he hadn't felt before. He
pulled out the single sheet, unfolded it, and read it.

Then he tried to remember where he had gotten it. But he
couldn't.

He read the few, short sentences again, and looked, once more,
at the name printed at the bottom. He got up and went to the bed
where his son Joe slept, when he slept there.

Thurmon wished the boy were in the bed now. He wished, too,
that he could remember where he had gotten the letter, and who had
given it to him, since Minnie would surely have much to say about him
not being able to.

Then the storm that was blowing outside made enough of a racket
to call him to the window.

The first thing he saw was the swirling water cascading along the
river that was usually Ship's Mechanic Street. Something tumbled
through the water, bouncing off the edges of the raised sidewalks. At
first Thurmon thought it was a small buggy that had been separated
from its horse and driver, then he blinked and squinted enough to see
that it was one of the two-wheeled bathhouses that people rented out
at the beach. He watched as it turned over again, then it collided into
the building across the street. In pieces now, it floated away.

Thurmon's mind hadn't crawled up far enough out of his stupor
yet to be of much use. But it was sufficiently clear to remember that
the beach was over twenty blocks away.

He shook his head, listened to the fierce wind and rain bombarding the side of the building, and the one thought capable of jolting him into sobriety hit like an electric current.

He hurried through the tiny rooms, throwing back doors and curtains, until he was sure of it. Sal was not there.

CHAPTER SIX

On Friday afternoon, a ceremony had been conducted in the vestibule of the St. Mary's Infirmary, on Market, between Seventh and Eighth Streets.

"James Bing Tuttle, the Third, and Zachery Scott are hereby graduated," a smiling nun had proclaimed, in as solemn a voice as she could maintain while holding two bedpans wrapped in ribbons, "with the degree of Experienced Orderly, and are presented with their diplomas." The room full of nuns, and a couple of doctors, laughed and applauded, and the two young men were handed their mementos.

"Seriously," the nun said, when the fuss had died down, "we'll all miss you two. You certainly livened the place up, and that's a sure fact." There was more laughter. "And we wish you well in your studies at the Medical College. We expect you to come and visit us every now and then, and maybe mop a floor, or change a bed, to keep your skill levels up." Then she looked at her watch. "It's five o'clock, so you're both officially out of work, but, out of Christian charity, we'll not even charge you rent for staying overnight, before you go home tomorrow."

"We appreciate that," James said, "but don't come waking us up to clean up any spills or empty any of these." He held up the bedpan. "Since we're graduates now, and would have to charge you professional wages."

A cake was brought out, and everybody had a piece before the party broke up, and James and Scott went to the room that they had shared all summer.

Scott's trunk was packed and sitting in the corner. James' things were all over the place, his own trunk open on the floor.

"What time is your train tomorrow?" James asked.

Scott sat on his bed. "Early afternoon. I'll go over to the station about noon. What about you?"

James looked at the bedpan he was still holding. "About the same. We'll go over together, that way you can pay for the rig, and my trunk can get hauled for free."

Scott smiled. "I should make you pay half of it, but I'm happy enough to be through with this job that I might just let you get the better of me." He leaned back against the wall. "For the millionth time this summer."

He waited for a reply, but none came.

"So, back to the ranch for a few days. And back to Beaumont for you."

James tossed the bedpan in the open trunk. "Back to Beaumont." Then he fell back on his bed.

"And . . . ."

James was quiet for a moment. "And . . . I don't know."

"Don't you think it's time to figure it out? It's not all that far to Beaumont, and you ought to have at least a few things figured out when the train gets to the depot."

James nodded. He thought about it and nodded again.

Scott undid the button on his collar and pulled it away from his throat. "I guess I'll miss your snoring. I probably won't even be able to sleep for the first few nights."

"Well," James said, "I don't intend to give up snoring before we get to the college. So you can catch up on your rest then."

"You haven't done as much of it lately," Scott said. "Sleeping, I mean."

James stood up and stretched. "It's Friday, so I guess our fish is on the table. Are you ready to eat?" They both had eaten their meals at the infirmary all summer, since they weren't charged for them. Neither of them was Catholic, and neither was fond of fish, but they had discovered early on that if you ate at a Catholic institution on a Friday, you either ate fish or made do with the ladle full of vegetables that was plopped beside it.

Scott hadn't moved. "Why don't you go see Pearl before you go?"

James looked at him for a moment, then began packing things into the trunk. Later, he lay awake and listened to the first rain as it peppered on the window beside his bed.

As he watched the shadows of the raindrops on the wall, he thought of a pretty girl who would be at the depot on Saturday. And she would be holding a welcome-home gift, wrapped in white paper and tied with a bow. Her parents would be standing beside her, with his own parents. They would be waiting there, as the train pulled to a stop, waiting for him to step down into the place where everybody thought he should be.

An easy thing, he thought as he lay there in the middle of the night, to step off a train and take a wrapped present out of a girl's hands and nod at the smile on her face.

But when he had finally closed his eyes, it wasn't that girl's face that he saw.

Then it was Saturday morning, and he and Scott decided to leave sooner than they had first planned for the railroad station, because of the high water in the streets. They had sent their trunks down earlier, and knew they would have to walk the twenty or so blocks, now that the trolleys had stopped running, and there were fewer buggies or wagons braving the flood. The sidewalks were high enough, they figured, for them to make it without much trouble, and awnings would protect them from the downpour, except when they had to cross streets.

And now here they were, in the middle of the first crossing.

The water was a bit deeper than they had thought it would be, and considerably faster. James kicked at it and said he hadn't intended to swim to Beaumont.

Scott leaned forward, to keep his balance, and climbed the several concrete steps to the sidewalk. They hurried further along under the awning, and stayed close to the building.

"I doubt if you're *going* to Beaumont," Scott said. "The tracks to Boliver aren't far from the beach. Besides, there won't be any boats crossing over to the point in this mess."

They walked to the end of the block and stepped down into the water again. They were quiet until they were half way down the next block.

"My train will be going inland," Scott said, "and has a sturdy bridge to cross to get off the island. Maybe you ought to go on up to Waco with me, then you can catch another train that will get you there."

James kept walking. He knew that whenever he got to Beaumont, and from whatever direction, he would have to take that step down from the train that he was dreading, and into the rest of his life.

"Let's just get to the station," he said, "and see what the railroad has to offer." They stopped and surveyed the next crossing. The water there was lapping up over the tops of the steps.

"Maybe we should just dive in," James said, "and work on our backstrokes."

They finally reached the Union Passenger Depot and found over a hundred of the islanders congregated there, waiting for a train to the mainland. The lines were long in front of the two ticket agents, so they joined what appeared to be the shorter of the two.

The man in front of them turned and shook his head.

"From what I hear," he said, "they'll gladly sell us tickets, but a ticket won't take us to Houston. It'll take a train to do that."

James asked him what made him think there weren't any trains.

"Oh, there's plenty of trains." The man pointed toward several doors that led to the tracks. "A whole yard full of 'em. But the one that just backed in out there looks an awful lot like the one that just left. And I don't figure it came back because somebody forgot their bags."

The doors the man had just pointed to flew open, and the room was suddenly full of more people than it had been, all anxious to share their news. That the bay was up over the bridge now, and there was no way to get off the island.

Everybody was talking at once. Somebody screamed, and some children started crying, without even knowing what they were crying about.

Scott pulled James over to a wall. "We'd best get back to the infirmary, before the water gets any higher."

James watched the mass exodus heading for the front doors of the building. "Let's catch our breath first," he suggested. "Before we have to swim back upstream."

Father James Kirwin, the rector of St. Mary's Cathedral, had spent most the the morning helping people up the steps of the big church. For many of Galveston's people saw as much possibility of salvation in the thick walls of the building as they did in any spiritual solace offered there. Much of the churchyard was covered by water, and all of the streets around it, but, so far, the interior was dry. One man, who Father Kirwin knew something of, grasped the priest's outstretched hand, and pulled himself forward.

"I seen her up there, Padre, through the rain," the man said, through a toothless grin, "and knowed that she was a callin' me to come in out of the storm."

Father Kirwin nodded. He knew that the man was speaking of the statue of Mary on the top of the cathedral's central tower. He knew, too, that the man hadn't been to Mass or confession in years. But his wife had, so Father Kirwin also knew that he slapped the wife on occasion, and the children, too, when he was liquored up enough. The priest continued to hold the man's dirty hand.

"She calls us all," he said, not taking his eyes away from the man's. "She calls us constantly, in every kind of weather, to do our best, and to behave decently."

The man continued to smile, his eyes already darting this way and that, looking for the safest, driest place to be.

Father Kirwin looked, then, at the wife and children standing beside the man. Then the little family moved on, and more people came in out of the morning that was growing darker rather than lighter.

One of the children at the St. Mary's orphanage stood at an upstairs window and watched the brown, frothy water swirling around beneath him. The heavy deluge pelted into it, and pieces of the picket fence, that was already coming apart, spun in the current, bobbing under the hammering rain.

Sister Zilphia put her hands on his shoulders, and watched it too. "It's higher than Chester already," the boy said. "I hope he can swim."

"I happen to know that Chester is in Sister Catherine's kitchen right now," Zilphia said, "eating his food out of a bowl and wagging his tail. I just saw him. He's better off than he usually is."

Margaret was beside them now. "It's a good thing Sister Bli— Sister Mendulla is in the other house," she said. "She don't like Chester."

Zilphia could hear Sal from the other end of the room, reading to some of the children. Two of the other sisters stood at windows, gazing out at the bleak morning. Reverend Mother Camillus, Zilphia knew, was still down in her study, where she would stay, she supposed, until the water got high enough to float her out of her chair. The water hadn't risen high enough yet to come in the buildings, other than to make shallow puddles on the floors, but Zilphia knew that it was just a matter of time.

Every time she had passed the little room where Camillus spent most of her life, she looked in to see the old woman there, at the desk that faced one of the walls, reading one of her collections of meditations, or the Bible. The door was almost always left open to let the breeze from the single window wander through. A crucifix hung over the desk, and Camillus' chair didn't have any cushions, the addition of which Zilphia always thought would surely offer a comfort. But she knew enough about the chair's occupant to guess what her opinion would be regarding cushions: that sitting all day on a hard chair would be as nothing, compared to the misery Christ had felt on the cross.

The window was closed in the study this morning, but the old nun still sat on the hard chair, and read her Bible. And prayed.

The only time that Zilphia had ever been invited into the room, she sat in the only other chair, which had been equally as hard as the one

Camillus sat in, and was told only God knew the answers that she was seeking, and that constant prayer and meditation were needed, and that she must pray to Him, and to the Blessed Mother, and the saints.

Zilphia received the old lady's blessing and nodded her head but said nothing, since she knew that this was a promise she couldn't make. For she hadn't prayed in so long that if she attempted it now, she would have to actually think about the words that no longer held any magic for her, that she had once rattled off continuously by rote.

Sal was beside her now, at the window. Zilphia put her arm around her and drew her closer. Margaret and the boy had gone to find something else to occupy them.

"The water will be in the house soon, I think," Zilphia said. "And that's when the children will need us the most."

Sal nodded that she understood. "I don't know how many more stories they'll listen to."

Zilphia smiled and hugged the girl to her. "I'm so sorry I got you into this. I'm sure your mother will kill me when we see her."

"She'll probably kill us both," Sal said.

They were quiet for a moment and listened to the wind and rain pelting the side of the building and the children making their usual racket.

"What will happen," Sal asked, "when the water comes in?"

Zilphia shrugged her shoulders. "It just . . . comes in, I suppose, and goes out the other side. We'll have to keep the back doors open, to let it go."

Sal looked at her shoes. "What if the wind blows harder?"

Zilphia ran her hand through the girl's hair. "I just don't know, dear. We have to be ready for . . . anything." She looked at her. "I have to keep reminding myself that you're a child yourself, not even as old as many of the children here. They just . . . look up to you so, especially the little ones. It's a bigger job than I should be asking you to do, and I know that, but I'll need your help with Mary, and some of the others, if . . . if the wind does blow harder."

Sal nodded. "Reverend Mother says that we should all pray," she said.

Zilphia touched the side of her face. "That's good advice."

Sal raised her eyes, and looked at her. "Have you prayed?"

One of the nuns shouted that Samuel was coming over from the other building.

Zilphia went quickly down the stairs and out on the porch, shielding her face from the slanting rain. Samuel was halfway between the two buildings, wading through waist-deep water. When he got to the porch, she helped him up on to it and into the house.

Reverend Mother Camillus met them in the entryway.

"Is everyone all right over there?" she asked.

"Sister Mendulla," Samuel spat out, dripping water into the puddles on the floor, "she want to know if you want us to bring all them children over here, so's everbody will be in one place."

Camillus shook her head. "No. I already told her that. It's too many people for one house, especially if we have to all stay upstairs."

"She got them all gathered up over there," he said, "and ready to come over here."

Camillus shook her head again. "Tell her to get all those children upstairs. Now! And to stay put!"

Samuel was shaking his head, too, convinced that nothing he told the nun would make any difference.

Zilphia took his hand in hers. "Samuel," she said, "tell it to Sister Elizabeth. She'll see to it."

"Sister Lizabeth ain't there no more." he said.

Everyone was quiet.

"Where is she?" Camillus asked.

"Sister Mendulla, she sent her up to the that little store."

Camillus' eyes grew wide, and Zilphia shouted her response.

"To the *store*?"

Samuel nodded.

"When?"

"Near a hour ago, I reckon."

Camillus was out the door and almost to the edge of the porch before Zilphia caught up to her. Rain stung at their faces even while they were still under the porch roof.

"I'll go, Reverend Mother," she said. "You stay here."

The old nun didn't stop, or even slow down. In a moment, they were both wading toward the other house. The rushing water pulled at the bottoms of their habits, and Camillus nearly fell once. Zilphia hung on to her. They finally climbed the steps to the house, and Zilphia followed as Camillus threw the door open and stepped into the hall. The large room at their right was filled with children, all standing quietly and waiting for instructions. Zilphia knew that Mendulla had no doubt threatened to deal personally with any misbehavior.

Mendulla stood ramrod straight beside the stairwell, her marred face locked into a frown.

Camillus stood still long enough to catch her breath, and to collect her thoughts.

"You children go upstairs," she said, and turned to face Mendulla. "You come with me. You come, too, Sister Zilphia."

They went to one of the nun's rooms on the first floor, the sound of the children hurrying up the stairway filling up the hallway behind them. Camillus closed the door, and swung around to face Mendualla.

"You sent Elizabeth out into this," she said, and pointed to the window. "Is that correct?"

Mendulla relaxed. "My goodness, is that what this is about? Of course I sent her. We had to have some things. And that store is not even half a mile up the road. And with the water rising like it is, I thought we'd better go ahead . . ."

"You *didn't* think!" Camillus said.

Mendulla resumed her stern stance, but said nothing. The wide blemish on her face seemed darker, Zilphia thought. "What even made you think that the store would be open on a day like this?" she asked. "And how did you suppose that she could carry enough groceries for fifty people?"

Mendulla's scowl said that she was not inclined to answer any questions from Zilphia, but one look at Camillus told her that it would not be the best of ideas to refuse.

"I sent her for candles," she said. "We'll be needing candles. And for hard candy for the children, to keep them quiet during the long hours we'll have to be inside."

Both of the nuns looked at her.

"Surely the girl can carry a sack no bigger than that," Mendulla said, "even if she has to wade a little water."

"Candles and candy," Camillus whispered. "You sent her in this for candles and candy?"

"I thought it was for the best," Mendulla said.

"To risk a woman's life for a few candles . . . ," Zilphia said.

Mendulla swung around to face her. "You have no right to question *me*. And if . . ."

"*I* have that right, Sister!" Camillus shouted. The other two nuns stood transfixed—they had never heard her shout before. "And I *do* question you. But that won't bring Sister Elizabeth back safely." She thought a moment. "Someone has to go far her, to see if she needs help."

Zilphia stepped toward the door, but Camillus touched her arm, to stop her.

"It shouldn't be you, Sister," she said. "Children may be injured in what we're about to face, and we'll need you to tend to them. You're the only one here with nurse's training."

"Elizabeth may need me just as badly," Zilphia said.

Camillus thought a moment, then nodded.

"I'll go, too," Mendulla said.

"You'll be needed here," Camillus said quickly. "We all will."

She followed Zilphia out the door and down the hall, leaving Mendulla, still standing as if at attention, in the center of the room.

On the porch, Camillus gave Zilphia her blessing, and told her to be careful. The wind blew through the folds of their soaked habits, whipping the skirts like flags.

Samuel had waded back over from the other building, and stood beside them. "I'm goin' with you," he announced, as Zilphia stepped down into the water.

"You stay here," she shouted back at him, over the clamor of the wind and rain. "They need you here."

He stepped down beside her. "I ain't lettin' you go by yourself. I shouldn't of let Sister Lizabeth go by herself neither. And I ain't lettin' you."

She turned and started wading toward where the beach road used to be, and he followed her. She was glad that he was going, and felt a new sense of security that she needed, at the moment, to feel.

Camillus had just told her to go with God. But Zilphia was content, under the circumstances, to go with Samuel.

CHAPTER SEVEN

At City Hall, Ed Ketchum, the chief of police, watched the same rain through his window that everyone in Galveston was watching.

He had managed to get a little sleep last night, but not much. He wanted to go to bed early, and catch up on his rest, but several of the smaller of his eight children had no such intentions for themselves, and, even in a large house like Ketchum's, it would have been impossible to find a corner of it far enough removed from small, loud children to offer a quiet enough place to be able to go to sleep. So he had settled in his favorite chair to read the newspapers that had accumulated on the side table.

He read a little about the Boxer rebellion that was still going on over in Peking, China, and a piece about the presidential campaigns. The election was just a couple of months away, and two photographs on the front page of one of the newspapers showed the candidates hard at work garnering votes. President McKinley was waving to a crowd of flag-wielding admirers in one photograph, and William Jennings Bryan's bald head and almost impossibly wide smile filled up much of the other one.

Ketchum had had to follow Bryan around Galveston, when he came in the spring, and five times had listened to the same speech, about the cross of gold that America was having to shoulder. One thing he had to say for the man, he always told anyone who wanted to know about it, was that he never put any more or less energy into that speech wherever he gave it, in front of a big audience like the one at Harmony Hall, or to a bunch of workers on the wharves who had never voted in their lives.

Ketchum had even gone over to the mainland, to Lake Surprise, with Colonel Moody, the cotton magnate, and Bryan to do a little hunting and fishing, and the man hadn't stopped talking even there. After the Great Commoner had left on the train that would take him to Dallas, Ketchum told his friends that no animals or fish had been in any real danger on that outing, since Bryan hadn't shut up for long enough to let them sneak up on any.

The children playing upstairs ran and jumped around enough to make the ceiling shake. The house the Ketchums lived in had been built in 1838 by Michel Menard, who founded the city of Galveston. It was a big house, and had seen its share of storms, and even a taste of war. But Ketchum wondered, as he flipped through the newspaper, and listened to the bouncing going on upstairs, if it might not have met its match in his clamorous offspring.

He read about the recent census, and how there were eight thousand automobiles on the nation's roads now, and ten million bicycles and eighteen million horses and mules, then skipped over a piece about a new book for children that was all the rage, about a little girl from Kansas being transported to some magical place or other. Then he spent a few minutes reading yet another article about Casey Jones, the train engineer who had somehow been elevated to a national hero by running his train into another one in Mississippi last April, killing himself in the process.

Then Ketchum went upstairs and told the children to be quiet and went to bed. The telephone call from Isaac Cline came shortly after four, and he got dressed and came, in the rain, to start what he knew would be a hell of a long day.

When he got to his office, the muted, first light filtered through the blinds on his office window, and he leaned over and pulled the blinds up to get a first view of what the day held. Lead-colored clouds hung low over the city, sending down a steady rain. Water cascaded down the edges of the streets, as if it carried too much energy to stay still while it waited its turn at the several overworked drains. People were about the business of beginning their workday. There were no places at the edge of the street high enough to let them step over the water, so those who had to cross a street just waded through. Those with no business in the street stayed up on the raised sidewalks. Bakery and milk wagons clattered by. The horses were a bit more skittish than usual about all the water, but seemed more concerned with the ominous thunder that rumbled slowly through the low, dark clouds.

Ketchum looked at the murky puddle at the bottom of the cup he was holding.

"Langston," he yelled, and a large sergeant appeared at the office door.

"It's daylight now," the chief said. "Don't you think you might make a decent pot of coffee?" He set the cup on his desk. "I don't know how you night people drink that sludge. We can't even hardly scrape it out of the urn when we get here."

Now it was almost noon, and the storm had grown stronger, and the coffee hadn't improved. People were still scrambling to get to the middle of town and into sturdy, brick buildings, he knew—that is, if they had any sense—and soon those who weren't sucessful would start dying. Because this weather was likely to get considerably worse before it got any better.

The same sergeant stood in the doorway.

"Rowan just got back," the sergeant said. "You want to see him?"

Ketchum sat down and looked at the stack of reports that he should be dealing with today. "Well, I just don't know," he said, "since I don't know where he's been."

A flash of lightning exploded outside. "I guess I forgot to tell you," the sergeant said.

The chief leaned back in his chair, nodded, and watched the sergeant turn and go out the door.

"Langston," he called, and the sergeant stopped and turned back to face him. He waited for the chief to say something.

"Well," Ketchum finally said, but got no response. "I guess you forgot again."

The sergeant lowered his eyebrows to think.

"To tell me where Rowan's been."

The sergeant nodded. "At a cotton warehouse," he said, as he walked out.

Ketchum watched him, and leaned up in his chair. "What happened at a . . . ," he began, then stopped, knowing it would be easier to get it from somebody more willing to give it. "Send Rowan in here," he yelled at the sergeant's back, "and don't go putting any dents or scratches in that urn when you clean it, *if* you clean it, which I guess you don't, from the looks of the mess that comes out of it."

Ketchum was especially protective of his coffee urn, which he believed to be the fanciest and largest on the island. It didn't belong to the police department, but to him personally, and more than a few policemen who had been so foolish as to clang something against it or bump into it had incurred the wrath of its owner and now treated the massive thing like it was made out of egg shells. The chief loaned the urn out on occasion, even to the Confederate Veterans every year, who felt funny borrowing it from a man who had been a bugle boy in the Union army, but they liked Ketchum. Besides, it was a damned fine urn.

The chief sorted through the papers on his desk until J.T. Rowan came in, his clothes soaked from the rain.

"What had you out at a cotton warehouse?" Ketchum asked.

Rowan shook his head slowly. "I ain't sure. I've been over there the last hour, listening to the night watchman and some of the workers, and to the warehouse foreman, and I still ain't sure."

Ketchum looked at the man, and hoped that the rest of his people would be more helpful, and responsive to his questions, than the first two that had been in here this morning. Or he might as well go on home and back to bed.

"The foreman called in a little before midnight, and said there'd been a theft," Rowan said. "He said they was working a crew all night to get everything secure in case there's an overflow, so I didn't get in any hurry to get over there since I had a couple of other things to do first."

Ketchum motioned for him to sit down, so he did.

"When I got there, I asked the foreman what had been stole, and he said he didn't rightly know. Then he showed me a little cement room at the back of the warehouse that was empty. He said that it had been stole out of there. So I asked him, again, what it was that had *been* stole, and he said again that he didn't rightly know."

Ketchum listened to the rain splash harder against his window, looked at the stack of papers on his desk, and then back at Rowan.

"Is this going to be a long story?" he asked.

Rowan smiled. "That's about the end of it. I didn't even fill out no report, which didn't sit too well with the foreman. But, like I told him, I can't hardly write down that something got stole, but nobody knows what."

"So he thought something was stolen out of that room?"

Rowan nodded.

"Was it locked?"

Another nod.

"Was the lock cut?"

"It wasn't the right lock, so they had to cut it themselves, to get in."

Ketchum waved his hand in front of him. "Now, wait a minute. This foreman had a key to the room, and he says he didn't even know what was in it?"

"He knew boxes was in it. Wood boxes, crates. But he didn't know what was in them. And they was all gone when he went in there to check on 'em."

"Fill out a report," Ketchum said, "and just put down that some crates, contents unknown, are missing. In case somebody raises a stink about it. Then forget about it, till after this weather is done, and we'll see what we can make of it."

Rowan got up from the chair that was as soaked, now, as his clothes. "There's one more thing," he said. "That foreman said that two men might have took the . . . whatever it was. One is named

Davenport—he works at the warehouse and didn't show up yesterday. The other one is a nigger, name of Tucker, that sweeps out the place."

Ketchum sat back in his chair.

"Well, that's fine," he said. "We got us two suspects already. But we don't have any notion yet just what it is that they were supposed to have done wrong."

Rowan looked at him, not knowing if he was expected to come up with a response, or any suggestion.

"Go on and file that report," Ketchum said, "and be sure Langston's making some fresh coffee, and not denting my urn in the process."

Soon, another policeman knocked on Ketchum's door and dripped a wide puddle of water on his floor.

"I've been out to the beach," he said, "what's left of it. The Pagoda Bath House got washed away, and Murdock's pier didn't have much left to it. It's probably gone by now. The gulf has come all the way up to Avenue K and don't appear to be slowing down any."

Ketchum studied the map of the city on his wall.

"It'll slow down in just a little while," he said, "because it'll meet up with the water coming in from the bay."

The policeman looked at the map, too.

"There's still people out toward the beach that need to get to higher ground. I told 'um we'd send a patrol wagon out to fetch 'um."

"That would be fine," Ketchum said, "if we had any more patrol wagons. But the ones that we do have are out trying to fetch folks right now."

He looked, again, at the map.

"So, I guess we've run out of patrol wagons," he sighed. "Which won't matter much. Because we're fixing to run out of high ground, too."

The two men from North Texas, who wished that they were there now, had hurried to the Union Passenger Station as soon as their meeting with Ike Kempner was concluded. They stood, now, in the big lobby of the Tremont Hotel, having learned that no trains would be leaving today.

They had waded in more water than either of them had ever seen before, more, even, than they would have believed it possible to have collected in one place, especially in the center of a city.

"At least we still have our rooms," one of the men said. For, in their haste to flee Galveston, they hadn't bothered to check out. "And my mattress wasn't too lumpy last night." He attempted a smile.

A loud clap of thunder rattled the ornate rotunda of skylights high above the lobby.

The other man nodded, but didn't plan on lying down on any mattress tonight, lumpy or otherwise.

James and Scott had returned to the St. Mary's Infirmary to find that they were desperately needed there. Already exhausted from wading the almost twenty blocks to the train station, and then back again, they were met at the door by a frantic nun bursting with the news that the small county hospital, in the next block, was starting to flood.

The two young orderlies found the place in chaos, with nobody quite sure what to do about it. The two looked at each other, and knew not only what had to be done, but who would have to do it. Several of the windows of the hospital had already blown out, and the area where the patients' beds stood was under nearly two feet of water.

They carried one patient after another, first through the turbulent water, then up the steep steps to the second floor of the infirmary. Some of the patients could make it under their own power, but even they had to be guided, and supported. The doctors couldn't help them, since they were treating the increasing number of injured people who had made their way there, and the nuns were either helping the doctors or tending to the patients being brought in.

They didn't stop between trips, and used the return treks to catch their breath. Neither did they waste any of that breath on talking, except once, when James had said that he would surely go ahead and make himself into a doctor now, so that if anything like this ever happened again, he could provide some service other than one which could have been done as well by a jackass.

Three miles away, Sister Zilphia and Samuel were making a slow progress through water that was deeper and faster than any James and Scott were encountering in town.

The slanting rain stung at the sides of their faces and their arms, and the foamy, churning water, already up to their waists, pushed from the right. They constantly shoved back against it, trying to stay on what they hoped was the beach road.

Before she had waded many yards, Zilphia determined that the long, heavy habit, full of water and tugging like an anchor, would be too much of an impediment. So she managed to group the fabric together into a bundle, and hold it tight against her side with one hand and arm, leaving the other one free to keep her balance.

They stayed close to each other as they fought for each yard. Zilphia felt the muscles in her thighs and calves straining, and her lower back was already aching from continuously pushing against the rushing water.

The day was growing darker. Zilphia looked over to see Samuel, only a few feet away, almost totally obscured in the gray salvo of hissing rain.

"That store's not far off, now," he shouted, and pointed in its general direction.

In not too many minutes, they saw its roof. They waded closer, and Samuel, who was in front now, strained his eyes to find someone on its small porch.

"There she is," he shouted.

Now Zilphia could see her, too, the black and white nun's habit unmistakable against the shabby storefront. Elizabeth waved frantically at them.

"I think you're right," Zilphia yelled. "Unless this storm blew a penguin in from somewhere."

Samuel didn't know what a penguin was, and didn't care. All he cared about right then was getting up on that porch for long enough to get a little rest.

CHAPTER EIGHT

SISTER ZILPHIA

She had come to Galveston on a train. The wheels clacked along the rails and sent out a lonesome song. It had been in the early spring.

Three peddlers, a few seats in front of her, had been telling ribald stories so low that she could only pick up enough of the words to discern the nature of the tales. The men, their ties loosened and their coats draped over the backs of the empty seats around them, were laughing in great guffaws, and much knee slapping was going on. One of the peddlers, a tall, thin man wearing a banana colored gabardine suit, had produced a slender silver flask, and it was making the rounds. Two of the men smoked one cigarette after another, and the third, a great heap of a man, as wide as he was tall, churned out dingy gray cigar smoke the consistency of the cloud coming from the loco-motive. The fat man's vest was undone, and his massive stomach lurched and wobbled, barely contained by the thin shirt that strained at its buttons.

Zilphia read the last part of the letter again, though she had long since memorized it. The old woman's handwriting left much to be desired, and one corner of the thick stationary had fallen victim to a spilled cup of tea, making the words run together. Still, she knew the words by heart.

> *You shall report, at Galveston, to Saint Mary's Cathedral, and make your way there to the office of the rector, Father James Kirwin, who will outline your new duties and deliver you to the orphanage. Father Kirwin said, in his letter, that you would be met at the station, but, in the case that you are not, it should not prove too difficult to locate a cathedral. Galveston, after all, appears to be a not very large place. And since you have lived in St. Louis, I should think finding your way around there should present no problem.*

61

Zilphia watched the bleak landscape as it slid by outside her window. She had been anxious to see the Gulf of Mexico, but so far it had not presented itself. She was sitting on the left-hand side of the car because she knew, from the map in her satchel, that the long finger of a peninsula leading down to Galveston would offer its view of the gulf on that side. But the fog was heavy this Sunday morning, and only once had she seen anything that might have been a beach on the other side of the thick bunches of grass beside the tracks. It might just as easily have been a field of dirt, bleached white by the sun.

To make matters worse, the heavy white smoke belched out by the engine seemed to hug itself to the side of the car, before giving up and drifting off. That, along with the fog, made it nearly impossible to see anything. Not that there had been anything very pretty to look at, she thought. The only interesting views had played out soon after the first train pulled out of St. Louis. Much of the trip was in darkness, and there might have been something nice to see then, but the land today, since they had taken on new passengers in Beaumont, was flat and tired looking. The view had gotten worse every few minutes, and more obscured in fog. Zilphia suspected that the terrain would eventually dwindle down to nothing and the train would finally rattle into a simple nothingness that would be Galveston.

The peddlers, who had been quiet for a few minutes while one of them whispered something to the other two, suddenly erupted into laughter. The fat one laughed so hard that he gasped for breath. Two of the buttons on his shirt lost their battle for propriety, and a section of dirty undershirt became apparent. His great stomach jiggled with the steady rocking of the train; his half smoked cigar was wedged between fingers thick as sausages.

Zilphia looked around the car for any thing or person that would offer distraction. Several travelers read their newspapers, and a little girl slept, curled next to her mother. A young man who had boarded in Beaumont sat at the back of the car. He wore a neat, expensive suit and held a small white box, wrapped in ribbon and tied with a bow. She wondered if the box had been presented to him at the station as a *bon voyage* gift, or if he had it to give to someone at the Galveston depot. He was not more than twenty, Zilphia guessed. Just a few years younger than herself. She looked at the box in his lap and hoped that it was for a girl. On such a gray, bleak morning it cheered her to think that it might be, that a handsome young man would give a present to a pretty girl at a railroad station, in celebration of their reunion. She realized that she was staring, not at the box but at the young man, and she gave one of those looks that people give when they are discovered doing such a thing. He smiled at her. It wasn't a smile that indicated that he had caught her out, nor was it one of over-familiarity. It was a greeting, as polite and proper as the nod of a head, or the tip of a hat.

She leaned close to the window as the first spitting drops of rain splattered across it. There was still nothing in the way of an ocean beyond the window, only smoke and fog. Zilphia had never seen an ocean, but she was pretty sure she would know one when she saw it. She lifted the letter again, crumpled now, and showing the evidence of its travels.

> . . . *some time spent working in that corner of the Lord's vineyard where unfortunate innocents have ended up will cause you to forget your troubles and your temptations.*

The rain was coming heavier now, against the window. Zilphia studied her reflection in the glass. "Troubles and temptations," she thought, forming the words with her lips. As if a ride on a train could be a cure for troubles and temptations. She looked at the last of the henscratching.

> *You'll surely be counting your blessings there, among so many who have had so few of them.*

Maybe, thought Zilphia, looking into her own defiant, eyes mirrored in the rain streaked window. And, then again, maybe she would be counting her options.

By the time the train reached the end of the Bolivar peninsula she had been rocked to sleep by the clatter of the wheels and the swaying of the car. The bustle of fellow travelers getting their things together in anticipation of arrival woke her up and she began to look around her for her satchel and the book that she had been reading. The peddlers were still smoking, and the fat one was attempting to button his vest; his face a deeper shade of red from the effort.

Zilphia, having closed the book and packed it away, looked out the window and saw only water. She looked out the other side of the car and saw the same thing there. Leaning up, she looked down in search of rocks and gravel beside the train tracks, but didn't find them there. Only water. She wondered if the train had actually run out into the ocean, or gulf, or bay, or whatever it was. Then she wondered if it was the common procedure to do it, or if it had been by accident. Maybe they were sinking slowly, even now, to the bottom of the sea.

If they were, she thought, they were doing it slow enough for everyone to get out of the train. And, since nobody seemed concerned or hurried, she assumed that something perfectly natural and safe was going on.

She looked out the window again. She had never, until this moment, seen any bodies of water wider than a particularly big lake or river, and the broad expanse all around her, churning and rolling in the light rain, made her clutch the seat beneath her. Soon, she lifted her satchel and followed the others out of the car.

When she reached the door and looked out, the whole ocean seemed to be in front of her. Patches of fog moved across its rolling surface, and the conductor was standing on a narrow wooden walkway, reminding the passengers to watch their step. When he reached up to help her down, she hesitated, not sure that she wanted to leave the safety of the train. It, and others like it, had been a constant burden and misery for the last two days, but they had gotten her here, dry and in one piece. The person behind her pushed a little, and Zilphia took the conductor's hand and stepped down to the deck.

She could see now that the tracks here were on a narrow trestle that ran a long way out over the water, so close to it that the waves slapped up on the train's wheels. A lighthouse stood on the mainland, close to where the trestle met the tracks. She held tight to the conductor's hand until she felt that she had her footing, then she followed the others down the cramped walkway. The fat peddler, three or four people in front of her, took up all of the passageway. He was still smoking his cigar, and its smoke curled into the fog and the smoke from the train's engine and all of it floated out over the choppy water.

When she got to the end of the walkway, and stood on a much wider pier, she trusted her balance enough to look around at the scenery, at least what she could see of it through the fog. It had stopped raining, but the low gray clouds and damp air promised that it could start again at any second. The deep, hollow groan of a fog horn sounded, causing her to jump and grab the arm of the person beside her. A gigantic ship materialized out of the fog in front of them like some ancient creature, churning up the already turbulent water. Zilphia watched it go by. The person who was attached to the arm that she still held tightly patted her hand.

She looked at the well dressed young man who had been sitting in the back of the train. He smiled at her.

"I'm sorry," she said, taking her hand away.

"You can hold on if you need to. Just maybe a little looser. I might need that arm someday, and I was afraid you were going to cut off the circulation."

"I'm not used to seeing ships, especially all of a sudden like that."

He nodded, and pulled his collar up. It had started to mist again. "One thing we have plenty of down here is ships."

The sound of an engine, steadily chugging away, came from the fog, and soon a launch emerged from the cloud and fought the current and the waves long enough to dock at the pier. As the conductor walked toward it, Zilphia stopped him.

"Excuse me," she said, "I was supposed to be met in Galveston by someone from the diocese." For all she could tell, she might be in the middle of the Atlantic.

The conductor stopped. "That may be, Sister. But you ain't in Galveston just yet." He pointed across the bay to the island, just visible in the gray, slow rain. She had to squint her eyes to see it.

"That's Galveston yonder."

In not too many minutes, the passengers and their baggage were on board the launch, everyone holding tight to the side rails, as it made its way through the pitching waves. Zilphia was clutching the rail with such force that she was sure her fingers were white. She hadn't been the best Bible scholar in her class at school, but she did seem to remember that several people in the Bible had been devoured by the sea. And she imagined that it would have been a sea such as this one: gray and choppy and swirling around. This definitely looked like an Old Testament sea to Zilphia. When the voice behind her said hello, she jumped again. When she caught her breath, she wondered how much more of this last stage of her journey her heart could take.

"Sorry," he said, unfolding an umbrella. "I dug this out of my bag, and was wondering if you would share it with me." It was her young man, again. She accepted the offer, and was grateful for the little refuge in the miserable morning.

They stood in silence for a moment, watching the big ships at anchor off in the fog.

"I'll be a student at the medical college in the fall," he said. Zilphia nodded, and continued to look at the ships. "I've been home to Beaumont, to see the folks and . . . and everybody."

Zilphia remembered the wrapped present that he had been holding on the train. She looked for it. He must have put it in his bag to keep it dry.

"I've got a job as an orderly at the St. Mary's Infirmary for the summer," he said.

Seagulls looped through the fog and rain, skirting the surface of the waves. The island grew bigger in the distance.

"Is everything in Galveston named after St. Mary?" Zilphia asked.

"I'm on my way to her cathedral, then I'm off to her orphanage."

The young man smiled. "The papists—pardon me, Sister— *Catholics* have a pretty strong hold on things." He held the umbrella so that Zilphia was under most of it; and leaned in, since his neck was getting soaked. "Have you never been to Galveston before?"

She shook her head slightly. She didn't want to make any more movements than were essential, knowing that much more of the bobbing around of this boat would make her ill.

The rain stopped as suddenly as it had begun, and he closed the umbrella. "Well," he said, as he secured it with a button, "don't let this little trip color your opinion. It's a beautiful city, with big wide streets and fancy houses and nice places to eat. The opera house is one of the best, they say, and lots of good things come here to go and see. The cathedral you're headed to is mighty impressive. And guess whose statue is perched right on top of it?"

"Mary, I'd imagine."

He laughed, and extended his hand. "I'm James Tuttle, Sister. Welcome to Galveston."

"Thank you," she said, shaking his hand. "My name is Zilphia."

"And you're to work at the orphanage?"

She nodded again.

James leaned on the rail and watched a gull skirting along the edge of a wave, dipping and rising to mimic its path. "This is the Bolivar roads," he said, presenting it all to her with a wide sweep of his hand.

"Why are there so many ships at anchor? Is it too shallow at the docks for them?"

"Oh, no," he said. "It's a deep-water port, and always full of ships." He pointed to a building on the shore. "That's the Quarantine Station over there. Some of these ships haven't been cleared to enter port." He leaned further over the rail and breathed in the damp, salty air. "Others are just waiting for an empty berth at the docks. The whole world comes here," he said, looking at the ships, some with tall masts reaching into the gray morning, others with smoke stacks, "and they bring their fevers and miseries with them."

Soon they were at the wharves and she could see, beyond the ships and the cargo stacked on the docks, some of the buildings of the city. James showed her Harmony Hall, its four peaked cornices rising above it like carved headboards of beds fashioned for giants. He told her that Bryan had spoken there last night. Then he pointed to the statue of Mary, on top of the central tower of her cathedral. "The star of the sea," he said. Zilphia could barely see it through the fog. She didn't cross herself when she found it.

Zilphia hoped that the recipient of the wrapped present would be at the dock, but she wasn't. James asked if she needed any assistance, and didn't leave until someone from the cathedral was there to meet her. Then he said good-bye and headed off down the street.

The black man who had been sent for her loaded her trunk into a buggy and helped her into it. "One of the priests would of come for you," he said. "But they all busy at the church, since it be Sunday mornin' and all." Zilphia wondered if he was Catholic, and suspected that he wasn't. She had noticed that Holy Mother Church wasn't particular when it came to getting cheap labor to sweep the floors and clean out the gutters. The man clicked his tongue, and the horse pulled into the street.

They moved at a slow walk, and none of the few people along the sidewalks seemed to be moving any faster. Church bells tolled in the distance, and the horse's hooves clip-clopped along the pavement. Zilphia asked the man his name, and he gave it. Ben. He smiled nervously whenever she looked at him, and she guessed that even if he had to deal with nuns at the cathedral, he probably wasn't comfortable enough with them to sit happily beside one in a buggy. She turned her attention to her surroundings.

The buildings along the streets were handsome and most of them ornate, of the type that architects were already calling Victorian, though their namesake was not yet quite through with her long life. Lush plants, broad-leafed and full, grew close to some of the buildings, and the air itself smelled as rich as the soil. Some of the plants had worked their way up the bricks, and through the iron latticework, so that the buildings themselves seemed to have grown there. It looked to Zilphia as if she could leave her handprint in the soft bricks by simply touching them.

Ben brought the buggy to a stop at the gate of the cathedral, and hurried back to unload the trunk. Zilphia grabbed her satchel and followed him through the front door. He dragged the trunk into a small room off the narthex, and Zilphia looked into the impressive nave. Mass was in progress, and it was full of people looking at the priest's back as he addressed his holy, mysterious words to the altar. The bishop, in his miter, sat on his throne, his crosier leaning against his knee. His eyes were closed, perhaps in prayer. Zilphia suspected he was asleep. Many of the worshipers were whispering the rosary, counting the beads with their fingers. None of them, she knew, could understand the words being recited, unless there happened to be a doctor or a pharmacist or a Latin teacher in attendance.

Someone whispered her name. She turned to see a priest, rather short, not too many years her senior.

"I'm Father Kirwin, Sister," he said. "Let's go where we can talk. Ben will look after your things until we go out to the orphanage."

"You'll be taking me there yourself?" she asked as she followed him along the red carpet of a hallway.

"Oh, I look for any reason to go out there," he said, as they stepped into his study. He motioned for her to take a seat in one of the chairs facing his desk. "I love to go. They're fine children, and so full of life." To her surprise, he sat down in the other chair, rather than behind the desk. He smiled. "You'll see."

She nodded and smiled back. She looked around. On the desk covered with books and papers a huge account ledger was open, a cup and saucer resting on its pages. One wall was taken up with bookcases, overstuffed with volumes. Two windows looked out on a narrow side yard, and an iron fence stood between it and the street.

"Well," Father Kirwin said, "let me be the first to welcome you to Galveston."

"Actually, you're the second. A medical student on the train was the first." He nodded, and said something about the medical school. She was trying hard to listen to him, but her fatigue must have been apparent.

"Are you hungry?" he asked. "Dinner should be almost ready; Bishop Gallagher likes his dinner on the table right after Mass. I'll wager they've got something over there that we can get for you." He started to get up, but she motioned for him not to.

"I bought a boxed lunch in the depot at Beaumont," she said, "and ate it on the way." She smiled again. "To tell you the truth, the combination of the train and boat rides have left me a little queasy."

He laughed. "I've made that trip myself." He stood up, patted his jacket pocket to see if his glasses were there, discovered they were not, and fumbled his hand to his face to collect them. "What we'll do is get you out there as quickly as possible, so that you can rest up. I imagine the sisters and the children won't demand too much of you until tomorrow at least." He took out his pocket watch and glanced at it. "We'll find an occasion to have a good visit at another time."

Zilphia wondered when he would get around to the reason that she had come, or, more precisely, the reason that she had left St. Louis. She thought she'd nudge it along a bit, to get it out and over with.

"Father Kirwin, my Povencial, who you've corresponded with, thought that I should come here to . . ."

"To do God's work," he finished for her, lifting the china tea cup from its saucer to inspect the cold dregs at its bottom. "And, in her opinion, and mine, after studying your credentials, we're fortunate to have you." He clattered the cup back into its place.

68

She looked at him, and lowered her eyes.

"Now, as to your being fortunate to have *us*, is all up to you, and how you look at things." He leaned forward a bit, and he smiled. "And I must say, I can't help but envy you, Sister." She gave him a surprised look. "Working with the children every day, I mean." He looked around the office and at the clutter on his desk. "Sometimes it seems that all I do is sign papers and tell good people that they can't do the things that they want to do." He pointed at the accounts book. Scribbled notes to himself on small slips of paper curled out of the edges of the pages, like leaves waiting to fall. He gazed at the book for a moment before turning his attention back to her. "What you'll be doing is very important." He smiled at her again. She caught herself liking it, and him.

"Are you ready, then," he asked, "for one more journey before you're home?" She nodded.

Soon they were riding in the same buggy, with Father Kirwin driving this time. They crossed a wide street, with an esplanade filled with palms and oleanders running down its middle. Several stately mansions sat in splendor behind massive trees. Down the street, a statue of a woman in a gown stood on top of a huge ornate column in the esplanade. Father Kirwin pointed to it.

"They just put that up a few weeks ago. Wanting to keep up with Rome and Paris, I guess." Zilphia turned her head back to look up at the massive thing, as they crossed the street. "It honors the heroes of the Texas Revolution," he said. "A fellow named Rosenberg left money for it in his will. This is Broadway, where all the rich folks live. It's the highest ground on the island, a full eight and a half feet above sea level."

They rode in silence for twelve or so blocks, until the trees thinned out and the land seemed to fall off into the gray sky. Suddenly, the buggy turned onto the beach road, and there, in front of Zilphia, filling up all of her vision, was the Gulf of Mexico.

They had ridden beside it for several minutes before she spoke. "It's . . . spectacular, I suppose is the only word for it."

"It is that," Father Kirwin agreed.

She continued to stare at the immensity of it. "Do you ever get used to it?"

He looked at the horizon and at the waves where they met the shore. "You'll be a good person to ask, in a few months. The orphanage is right on the beach."

Zilphia leaned forward and studied her surroundings. "The road isn't much higher than the water, is it?" she asked.

Father Kirwin nodded in agreement. "The ongoing argument is

that we need a defensive breakwater of some sort, in the event of overflows."

She looked again at the rolling surf and remembered what he just said about the orphanage being close to the water. "And who's winning the argument?" she asked.

He laughed. "Everybody knows we need it. The biggest proponent is Isaac Cline, our government weatherman." He clicked at the horse, to encourage him along. "His head's full of angles and statistics, and he makes a great case. But it would be awfully expensive to build something like that, and you've just moved to a city, Sister, that's so feebly run that nobody at the city hall even knows who's paid their taxes and who hasn't."

The breakers crashed onto the sand beside them. Zilphia followed the shadows of the low clouds as they drifted across the churning water. It seemed to go on forever, filling up the widest view she had ever seen. She couldn't imagine living next to such a thing. Squawking gulls gyrated and dipped at its surface, and the salty odor from it seemed thick enough to wipe from her hands. She was still looking at it when she realized the buggy had stopped.

She turned her head and saw the orphanage: two long, tall wooden buildings not far off the beach, on the other side of some sand dunes. Covered porches ran the length of them, and several children stood on the porches, watching them.

"And so," Zilphia said, looking at the children and accepting Father Kirwin's hand as she stepped down from the buggy, "I come to my sentence."

He studied her for a moment and smiled. "Better to see it as an opportunity, Sister," he said. He waved at the children on the porch.

"I try to see everything as an opportunity."

One month followed another, and she became part of the place. She was a permanent fixture at one of the long tables during meals, counting to herself sometimes, to make sure one or another of the children chewed their food enough times before swallowing. With the other sisters, she herded everyone off to school every weekday morning, and rode in the wagons with them, every Sunday, to the cathedral for the earliest mass. Since she was a trained nurse, she tended to the various cuts and scrapes that were common there, and to stomach aches and colds and occasional bouts of diarrhea. On one occasion, she tended to an affair of the heart.

After seven months of living on the island, Zilphia drove herself into town in the buggy one Friday morning, barely glancing at Isaac

Cline's two storm flags as she passed the Levy Building, and parked the rig in front of an imposing iron gate. A few moments later, she was sitting with a girl who had lived at the orphanage until recently, when she moved her meager possessions into the maid's room in the very top of one of Galveston's biggest houses. They sat on a handsome garden bench, the sweet presence of honeysuckle and oleander all around them, and thin ribbons of sunlight filtering down through the massive trees of the Kempner's yard. Pearl was in her starched maid's uniform, and watched two squirrels chase each other around the base of a pecan tree. Beyond the dark frame of the low branches, and the hedges that Tucker kept trimmed straight as a table-top, bright sunshine fell on Broadway and its esplanade. Wagons and buggies clattered slowly by, and people walked along the sidewalk. Horses' hooves clopped on the pavement.

"Sal sent you," Pearl said, watching the squirrels bounce down on to the grass, and run to another tree. "I guess."

Zilphia watched an ornate hat, all gauze and lace, progress along the top of the hedge, the lady beneath it completely hidden by the thick leaves.

"You like Sal. Don't you?"

The hat disappeared at the edge of the yard.

Pearl thought of the little girl who had started coming out to the orphanage from town while she still lived out there, to read to the children. Then she thought of some of the orphans, and of Sister Elizabeth, who she missed, and of Sister Blister, who she didn't.

"I'm glad you two are friends," Zilphia said.

Pearl looked for the squirrels. They were gone now.

"And I'm glad Sal comes out every day," Zilphia said. "I like for her to come. We talk."

Pearl moved her attention to the busy street down beyond the brick walk and the iron gate.

"You talk about me, I guess."

Zilphia smiled. "Some days, you're our major topic of conversation."

"What do you talk about? I'm not all that interesting."

Zilphia reached out for a late summer rose, delicate and small on a nearby bush. She leaned it close enough for her to take a sniff, then released it.

"Oh, let me see," she said, resting against the back of the bench. "We talk about your job here, and the pretty dress you bought. And about you going to the German pavilion with Mrs. Ivy." She stopped for a moment. "And James."

Pearl looked down at her lap and straightened the pleat of her uniform before she spoke.

"You two will have to find something else to talk about now."

Zilphia touched her hand.

"I don't know all that went on, Pearl. But if the boy isn't engaged, like Sal told me, then there's nothing to keep the two of you from finding each other again if you want to."

"I *don't* want to!" Pearl said. "I don't want any part of that fancy life, with all those girls looking down their noses at me."

"Maybe James isn't as much a part of all that as you think he is." Pearl gave a little snort, like one of Minnie's. Zilphia leaned toward her.

"Sal told me what you said. About people being better off staying in their place. Do you really believe that?"

Pearl nodded that she did.

"Then, if that's true, we all have to stay in the little pens that have been built around us, or that we've built ourselves."

Pearl shook her head.

"All I'm saying is that somebody like James couldn't ever be happy with somebody like me. He grew up in a house like this one." She let one small hand drift up to wave toward the massive edifice that loomed over them. "And I . . . well, you know where I grew up."

Zilphia looked for a short moment up at the gables and the steep slant of the roof through the trees, then back at Pearl.

"But shouldn't the important thing be that you both grew up *somewhere*? And that, here you are, in the same town, and dancing with each other."

Pearl searched for another argument, but was tired of it.

"I can't say it any better. But I believe it. You don't believe it, and that's your business."

Zilphia nodded slowly, then stood up.

"You think that, because I'm a nun, I don't have enough evidence to think otherwise, don't you?"

Pearl didn't look up at her, but kept her gaze leveled on Broadway.

"You think I've got all this worked out wrong," Zilphia went on, "like a priest would talk about in a homily, that would never really work in life."

She took a couple of steps on the brick walkway and turned back to face her. "As a matter of fact, I used to have it all figured out like you do. That it was safer to stay in one place, like cows in pastures. And best to never go into another place, to meet the people there, since they all will be different, and some of them mean."

"Why did you change?" Pearl asked, still not looking at her.

"Someone pulled me out of my pasture, and into his. His name was James, too."

"Was he a priest?"

Zilphia laughed, and sat back down on the bench.

"No, he wasn't a priest. Do you think that I've only known nuns and priests my whole life? He was a doctor, just like your James is going to be." She looked at Pearl, and read the question there.

"And yes, I loved him."

Only then did Pearl look at her.

"I imagine I felt very much the same way about my James as you do about yours."

A breeze worked its way through the tops of the big trees. Squirrels chattered at each other. The huge bells at St. Mary's cathedral commenced their slow, deep announcement, that it was noon.

"What happened?" Pearl asked.

Zilphia adjusted the folds of her habit, and watched a junebug making its slow journey across the bricks of the walk.

"We paid more attention to other people than to ourselves. And we let the people in our two places pull us back to them. Just like you're doing now, by believing that you could never fit into James' world because of the people there who wouldn't welcome you."

She watched Pearl think about it.

"So, if you could do it all over . . ."

"But *I can't!*" Zilphia snapped. "That's the point, Pearl. I *can't*." She touched the side of the girl's face with the edge of her hand.

"But *you* can," she whispered.

CHAPTER NINE

By mid-day, most of Galveston's people had settled in to where they intended to make the best of what promised to be a bad situation. The winds thundered through the city now, tearing shutters away from windows, working loose the heavy slate tiles that were on the roofs of most of the buildings. Some of the shutters and tiles were stubborn, and let the wind slap them against whatever they were attached to. So the whole city was a cacophony of things being slammed against other things, played out against the overriding din of the wind and pounding rain.

There were not many places that the wind didn't get to. It whipped into corners of alleys, and under tin awnings over the sidewalks, and swirled around and then went on. It wanted in the buildings, Galveston's people knew, like the water did. The wind had already blown out those window panes that were loose in their frames, that people had intended to fix. And it pushed against the ones that were more solidly secured. Later, as the afternoon became even darker, and the wind faster, and the water deeper, those windows would give way, too. And the wind and the water would go where they wanted to go.

Tucker had sat perched on the bed and watched as the water crept under his door and spread out to cover every inch of the floor, as slow as sweat soaked up into his shirt when he swept out the hot warehouse every afternoon. Now, it was a couple of inches deep. The sidewalk, at the opening of the alley, was at least three feet above the street, so Tucker knew that the street was gone now, and the sidewalk, too, covered up with water out of gulf, or the bay, or the dark, low clouds that kept on sending out thunder loud enough to rattle the windows. He wasn't sure where all the water had come from, and he knew it didn't matter anyway since it was here. He leaned over and tried to judge how tall the bed was. Maybe two feet, he figured.

He ate some more of Mae's cornbread. Part of him wanted Mae and his babies to be safe up in Angleton, at her sister's house. But another part wanted them to be right here, sitting up on this bed, and huddled up beside him.

He thought of Mr. Ketchum, who might be looking for him right now, even in all this bad weather. And even if he wasn't, Tucker knew, it wouldn't take long to find him after the storm was over. The little stove-up Englishman had told him that Mr. Ketchum would be after him. And he knew he would be.

Tucker wondered again why he hadn't had enough sense to figure that Mr. Ketchum wouldn't have any problem tying him into the theft. When the little Englishman had told him so, it had been a complete surprise to him. He had been too tired to think about it till then. But it was sure on his mind now.

He looked at the water on the floor. He measured, again, in his mind, the distance from the floor to where he sat. He didn't think the water would rise up another two feet.

But, he thought, as he turned the tin of Mae's cornbread in his hands, he had never figured it would cover up any street and a three foot high sidewalk either.

Isaac Cline pinched the thin wire that held his small spectacles together, and lifted them from his face. He squinted his eyes, and rubbed them with his forefinger and thumb. Then he made his calculations.

He didn't need to rub his eyes or squint them to calculate—he spent much of every day calculating, and almost always with his glasses on. But today his eyes hurt, since they had taken more wind and rain than they ever had. And they needed rubbing.

Isaac figured that the water in the city must be rising at a rate of fifteen inches an hour, give or take an inch or two. The rain gages on the roof of the Levy Building were still in place, though he assumed they would be blown away later in the afternoon, and the driving force of the wind and rain lessened the accuracy of the reading. The water being pushed in from the gulf and the bay was even harder to estimate. But Isaac knew two things with certainty: the level of the water was rising quickly, and it was showing no signs of cresting.

The streets he could see from the Weather Bureau windows were flooded, but none of them were so deep that people couldn't still wade through them, as some were doing at the moment. The high sidewalks were still dry here, but the water in the streets lapped at the edges and would soon be over them, too, and into the first floors of the buildings. Isaac thought of the many stores in Galveston, all of them so crammed full of their cluttered inventory that the prospect of putting it up out of harm's way would have been ludicrous. So, when the brown water came in, it would work its way through sacks of flour and cornmeal and sugar, and into bins of fruits and vegetables and glass jars of hard candy and taffy. The water would inch up into thick, tight rolls of fabric, like syrup being soaked slowly into bread.

He watched one man wading, pushing himself forward against the current, adapting his lanky frame to the present circumstances by taking slow, wide steps, his long arms outstretched like a tightrope walker's, each solid, plodding footfall an anchorage before taking the next one. The precarious, oddly put together human edifice taking nature on headlong.

Isaac recognized the man. He had watched him from this window many times as he crossed Market Street. He wondered if he was going to his family, or maybe looking for a better building to be in. The man finally reached the tall sidewalk and stepped up out of the water. At the edge of the building, the wind caught him, and he had to plant his feet wide again, as he had in the water, to regain his balance.

Joseph was standing beside Isaac now, at the window. Three of the clerks had gone on home, to be with their families. A fourth, who had no family, volunteered to stay here and take the readings on the roof for as long as he could and then to enter current conditions into the log throughout the rest of the day and night. After all, he told the Cline brothers, this building was probably as sound as any other.

Isaac and Joseph would leave soon, to wade the seventeen blocks out to the beach, to the large house where Cora Mae and the girls were waiting for them. The water would be higher out there, they knew, but still navigable for a while yet. They wanted to get just one more report off to Washington, and then they would go.

Joseph pointed to the corner of Market Street and Twenty Third, where the lanky man had just disappeared around the edge of a building.

"He'll be mighty tired when he gets to wherever he's going," he said.

Isaac looked at the empty corner, too. The thick clouds, slate gray and low over the tops of the buildings, moved faster now, but not as fast as the wind. And they continued to send down steady torrents of hard rain that blew so forcefully horizontal that the awnings over the sidewalks that hadn't already been ripped off were of no use anyway.

Now Isaac was watching one family as it pushed through the middle of the street, the smallest child holding tight to her father's hand, the water to her narrow chest. One end of a sheet of tin awning over the sidewalk held tight to its frame, while the other end slapped furiously at the soaked lumber, beating out a loud, steady cadence that accompanied the family's slow progress.

"Lots of folks will be tired before this day is done," Isaac said, almost whispering. He didn't add, since his brother knew it as well as he did, that the worst fury of the storm was still hours away, now howling and ripping out empty expanses of the Gulf of Mexico, waiting its turn to roar onto the already battered island.

Neither did he add that only the very lucky ones would be tired. The rest, he knew, would be dead. How many, he wondered. On this narrow, low, completely unprotected place, with not too many sturdy structures to get in.

How many?

He watched the little family pull itself up on the sidewalk at the same place that the tall man had. The little girl leaned, exhausted, against her father's side. He picked her up, grabbed his wife's hand, and they went on. Isaac closed his eyes, determined not to do any more calculating at the moment.

The wind whistled along outside the window. It echoed off the brick buildings it buffeted, taking on a low, hollow sound. Like moaning.

As if it regretted the horror it was bringing.

On Broadway, Ike Kempner came home to considerably more people than he had left there a few hours before. After sending the North Texas men off to the train station, he read over one more time the contract they had been discussing and locked it in his desk drawer. Then he waded through more water than he had expected to find. On other days, Tucker would have driven him home in the buggy. But Tucker was gone, and nobody seemed to know where he had gone to. Ike's mother didn't know, nor Mrs. Ivy. He hadn't bothered to ask Pearl, the maid, if she had any ideas about it, and he was sure that Minnie didn't know, or care.

Now Ike was home, in the big house that his father had paid a fortune to put up on the widest street, on one of the prettiest corners in the city. And here was Tucker's wife, and his children, and they didn't know where he was, either. Almost twenty other people were in the big parlor, all of them confident that this sizable place offered a sturdier refuge than wherever they had come from.

Ike's mother helped Mrs. Ivy and Pearl get soup and sandwiches for everyone, and Ike went upstairs to change into dry clothes. In the big kitchen, Minnie had used up the last of the bread and meat, and she was glad, since maybe now she could sit down for a few minutes and stop keeping the free food coming for people who, in her opinion, could just as easily be eating their own food in their own houses.

Pearl came in with an empty platter.

"Put that in the sink," Minnie said. "There ain't no more."

"Some more people just got here," Pearl said. "What are we going to feed them?"

Minnie looked in the corner, at the bags and baskets that she and Mrs. Ivy and Pearl had brought in from the shed, in case there was an overflow.

"Give them some of the horse's oats," she snapped. "They're all suckin' it down so fast, they won't taste it anyway."

Then there was a pounding at the back door.

"Now they're comin' straight to the kitchen," Minnie said, as she went over to open it. "So they can get down a sandwich or two before they even say hello."

The big man came in out of the rain and looked around the room. He stood dripping on the floor and finally let his gaze fall on his wife, who didn't complain about the mess he was making on the floor, since the floor was more of a mess at the moment than she could worry about. She stared back at him and, for once, had to fumble for words. She had never seen him in this house, and had never expected to. She looked at him as she might at one of the squirrels from the yard, if it had come in the back door and sat on her kitchen counter.

"Don't tell me they closed the saloons because of a little rain," Minnie finally said. "I never would have . . ."

"Where's Sal?" Thurmon blurted out, stopping the sentence that Minnie had searched so hard to find. She had to take a few seconds to produce another one.

"At that orphanage, I guess." she said. "Moppin' up rainwater for the lazy nuns. If you had bothered to wake up this mornin', I could have told you that."

He looked through the window; at the fury that he had just waded through across town.

"The orphanage is way out on the west side," he said, as much to himself as to his wife. "Right on the beach." He turned to look at her. "It's right on the beach, Minnie."

She saw the terror in his eyes, and felt some of it herself. He made for the door, and she grabbed his arm.

"Wait," she said, and opened a cupboard. She dug around in it until she found what she wanted.

She handed him a small, flat bottle, full of amber liquid. "That's brandy," she said. "For cookin'. You might . . . ." She kept her eyes on the bottle and tapped it lightly with the tip of one thin finger. "You might be needin' it."

He looked at the bottle, too, and put it in his pocket. Then he look-ed at her. One delicate strand of hair had come loose from her tightly clamped bun. He touched it with his fingertip and moved it over to the side.

"Go on," she said, and pushed him toward the door.

He went quickly out, almost running into one of the neighbors, who Minnie knew had come in looking for more sandwiches. The man watched him rush toward the edge of the yard, and the gate, then pushed the door shut behind him.

"Where's that fool going?" the man asked.

Minnie turned toward him, her small eyes ablaze. She held him in her steely glare for a long moment, before shouting that it was her husband.

The man took a long enough look at Minnie to determine that there wouldn't be any more sandwiches offered, at the moment. He backed up a step.

Minnie watched through the window, as the big figure moved quickly through the driving rain.

"He's goin' to get our girl," she said, so softly that Pearl had to look around to make sure that Minnie had actually said it, since she had never heard her say anything softly.

Then they both watched him until he was lost in the dark, gray afternoon.

Chapter Ten

Over by the docks, halfway down a narrow squalid street, that was as flooded now as all of the other streets, a small, stooped Englishman stood in the foamy water that had come into his home. It was a large room, and dark. The windows had long ago been painted over with several thick coats of the darkest color that he had been able to find, and the only light came from a single kerosene lamp. None of the windows had blown out, since the street was as narrow as some alleys, and crooked, like the little man who lived here, and not enough of the wind had found it to do any damage. The big room was something like a cave, or a stable, provided it was a particularly unkempt stable in the last stages of disrepair. The concrete floor was almost three feet above the street, but the water had found it now.

Quin watched the water as it meandered through the cluttered stack of his possessions. He had put some of the most valuable of the things as high up on the stack as he could reach and figured there was nothing he could do about the rest of it. He had already taken all of his folding money from its secret place, and shoved it into the big pockets of his coat.

He felt of the bills now with his misshapen fingers and wondered, again, if he should just stay put for a while longer, or go ahead and try to find higher ground towards the middle of the island. He made his slow, crippled way over to the heavy door, unbolted it, and cracked it just enough to see the water racing by, already up over the tall sidewalk. One of the carts used to haul bales of cotton crashed into the side of the building across the street, then rolled over several times before it continued its journey.

Quin leaned his head out further, into the wind, and looked toward the wharves, but it was raining so hard, and was so dark, that he couldn't see anything except the corner of the biggest of the cotton warehouses.

He knew that a discovery would soon be made there, if it hadn't been already, but he knew that it probably wouldn't be made until after this storm was through. Ketchum and his cops would have better things to do in all of this than worry about a few crates that had gone missing. Besides, all that would be found would be an empty concrete room, and maybe a little stain on the floor. He knew that the other bits of evidence, both of them, would be at the bottom of the Gulf of Mexico by now. And maybe the ship that they had been tossed from, too, since it had no doubt sailed straight into the teeth of this blow.

That was of no concern to Quin. Nothing about the job could be traced to him—he was sure of it. The only other person left behind was that nigger, and Quin had made sure to give him a little warning when he gave him his money: that Ketchum wouldn't take long to figure out that he was the sweeper at that warehouse. Ketchum would put two and two together, he told him, and then would come after him. That nigger's eyes, as tired as they were, got wider then, and Quin wouldn't be surprised if he was north of Houston by now.

He looked again at the small mountain of his hoard, and knew that there was nothing for it but that some of it would get wet. The only chair in the room was a wide, deep one made of thick, rough wood, not too carefully put together, as if a ship's carpenter had fashioned it mid-voyage from the only lumber at hand, with more attention given to bulk than detail.

Quin waded over to it and sat down.

Yesterday morning, he had sat here and addressed his boys. Now that Joe Casey, his best boy, was gone, Quin knew that he needed to let the other boys know that nothing had changed. But his boys— wharf hooligans, the police sometimes called them—had looked up to Joe. So he had put out the word: to show up in inconspicuous groups of no more than two or three at his doorway on Friday morning. Quin, unshaven and unwashed as always, had sat in his big chair and talked them as a coach would a team.

"I've had my ear to the ground, I have," he had said, touching his ear with a dirty finger to illustrate his lesson, "and what I been hearin' there tells me a sad tale." He had leaned forward in the big chair and pointed the finger around the room, at no one in particular. "I hear that certain things have come up missin' around town that I don't know nothin' about. And that tells me," he said, curling his hand into a small fist, "that some thankless little bastard is holdin' out on me."

He reached into one of his pockets and lifted out the jackknife that he was never without and opened it and began to dig delicately at the nail of his little finger. Just the tip of the wide, heavy blade was needed for the task, and Quin had performed the procedure as carefully as a surgeon would an operation.

The boys watched him, waiting for him to lead them deeper into dangerous waters. They knew they were going there, and all they could do was sit and hope they didn't get too wet. All of them kept a piece or two of their take occasionally—not enough so that Quin would notice, but sufficient to make the enterprise and the risk a little more worth their while than the scant pennies he paid them for their crimes—and every boy in the room hoped that the current lecture wasn't directed at him.

Quin examined a small wedge of filth that he had just excavated from under his nail. His voice, when it came, was that of the Wessex countryside of his birth.

"Now," he said, his teeth so soiled and black that they were barely visible when he spoke, "whoever this little bugger is has a choice to make, and he has to make it quick." Every boy sat rigid then, sure that the words were aimed at just him, anxious to hear any option that offered hope.

Quin leaned on one wide armrest of the great chair. "He can give back what's rightly mine, and pray that there's enough charity and forgiveness in old Quin's heart to keep him on as an associate . . . ." He had made a lightning quick slash through the air with the blade, not a wide slash, just enough of one to obliterate a small something or other. "Or he can have his jewels sliced off complete, and leave room in his pants for more of my money."

Each boy had felt a clinching tightness in a certain place. Then Quin closed the knife and returned it to his pocket, its business done, and stretched his short, bent legs out in front of him.

"Now I ain't no monster," he said, lacing his fingers together on his chest, "and I know what goes through your simple brains when you're on a job. You see a shiny, handsome thing, like a pistol or a knife, that you wouldn't mind havin' for yourself. Or maybe you figger you could turn a fine deal on it with some ship's mate, or a buyer." He smiled, to show that he understood their temptations. "But, lads," he said, still smiling, "you'd best remember, when your brain starts takin' you where you'd better not go, that all the buyers work with *me*, and tell me everthing. And anything you keep to yourself you'd have to bury it so deep that I'd never see it nor hear about it. And you can't bury it that deep, unless you was to dig all the way to China." His sudden laugh so startled some of the boys that they jumped. "You'd be safe to stash it in China, since I don't never intend to go back there."

More things had been discussed, like particular places to be avoided for a while, a certain warehouse in particular, or businesses that had been hit too often. He had told them that Joe Casey had left the island for good, and his buddy Danny with him.

One of the bigger boys, standing at the back, asked if it wasn't risky having everybody come over here in the broad daylight.

Quin laughed, and leaned forward in his chair.

"Go over to that grand palace of a city hall some day," he had said, pointing in the general direction of the outside world. "And walk into any room. In that one room you'll see four times more crooks than is in here right now. And them is just the ones sittin' on benches, waitin' to go in the offices to see the thieves and criminals that run Galveston." He leaned back again, satisfied with his appraisal. "I got worried once, 'cause I never paid no tax on this place." He waved his hand around. "So I talked to a fellow that has some pull over there, and he told me that there's so many hands in so many pots, they don't even know who owes what." He laughed again. "That's why the city is as broke as a dropped plate, and can't build that damned cement dike out at the beach that everbody keeps hollerin' about. The big money boys, who live in the castles on Broadway and wear fancy clothes and have niggers to drive them around in buggies, don't pay no more taxes than I do, and I don't pay none."

He rubbed his unshaven chin. "We're little fishes to that crowd. The police is a bunch of stupid billygoats, who can't even handle the big crimes that goes on, and they're not too likely to worry when a piece of silver goes missin', or if some sod from Houston has to go back on the train without his billfold."

The same boy said that Chief Ketchum didn't appear to be no stupid billygoat.

"He's the only one you got to look out for," Quin had said. "And they had to import him from the north—he was a Yankee drummer boy in the war. But he can't be everwhere."

Then the meeting ended and the boys filtered out, in small groups.

Now it was more than a day later, and the big room was empty, and the floor was covered with water.

Quin, still on his throne, looked around him, and listened to the wind scrape across the front of the building. The water had risen an inch or so, and swirled around the base of the chair.

His ramshackle inventory lay in cluttered heaps all around him, all of it on the floor, some of it already drenched. He strained to find in the dark recesses of the room anyplace to put his possessions away from rising water. He couldn't see very well, but he knew that even the brightest of light wouldn't find sanctuary for any of it. There was no ship to haul it up into, or any better place for it to go. He and his various stores would have to sit tight and ride out whatever came.

After all, he figured, this building was made out of bricks, and, even though it was closer to the docks and the bay than he might have wished on a day like this, at least it was as far away from the beach as you could get on this island. And the beach would take the worst of it.

Another explosion of thunder erupted, loud enough to cause the big chair to tremble under Quin. When the noise finally abated, there was still a pounding. At first he thought it was the echoes of the thunder, left behind to bounce off the brick walls, or maybe inside his head.

Then it came again. And he knew where it came from.

He looked at the door, and brought a crooked finger to his lips. The pounding came again, more frantic now.

His mind searched for possibilities as to who it could be. The only people who ever came to his door were his boys, who stood there only long enough to hand him whatever it was they had lifted, and to receive the few coins that he dropped into their dirty hands. Not even the stupidest of his boys would have been out thieving on a day like this one.

Cops, maybe. But why would cops come now, with a storm roaring in, when they had never bothered to come before.

The knocking grew louder.

Maybe, he thought, the *Maydelle* had turned away from this blow, and Captain Barkley had decided to hightail it back to Galveston. Quin disliked that scenario enough to shake his head at it. It wouldn't do for the cargo in the holds of that ship to come back here, ever. And certainly not so soon after it had been taken away. He was thinking about the cargo in the wooden crates; those things wrapped in burlap had surely been disposed of by now.

He waded slowly to the door, hoping that whoever it was had gone on. But the pounding came again. He slid the huge bolt out of its sleeve and cracked the heavy door open just enough to peek through.

Two of the boys who often brought him the things they had stolen stood close together on the sidewalk, their feet covered by the water. They weren't very big boys, and Quin didn't know their names. They were soaked.

Quin gave a low grunt of recognition but didn't open the door any wider.

The taller of the two boys tilted his head.

"We got nowhere to go," he said.

The other one, probably the taller one's brother, nodded quickly, either in agreement or as a spasm against the rain.

Quin opened the door just wide enough to get a better view through the rain, which had grown heavier since the last time he had looked at it, of the portion of the bay that was cascading down his street.

He edged his door back a tiny crack.

"That's right," he said, to the two shivering boys huddled on the sidewalk. "You got nowhere to go."

Then he shut and bolted the heavy door.

Three miles away large waves crashed, one after another, against the porches of the two long buildings of the St. Mary's orphanage. Part of one of the porches was gone, broken up and then washed away. Everybody was upstairs in the two houses now, since the gulf swept through the first floors with enough force to collide with the steep stairwells, and send water lapping up on anyone standing on the landing.

Sal Casey had just received such a sloshing.

Wee Mary and Margaret, who had been standing far enough back in the hallway to avoid getting drenched, looked at her.

"I guess I better stand a little further back," Sal said, wringing water from her hair.

"Naw," Margaret said. "I guess you hadn't ought to go out there at all. You ain't seen nobody else goin' out there. Probly cause they figger they'll get wet."

Wee Mary nodded in agreement.

Sal pulled her wet dress away from her skin. "I just wanted to see if Sister Zilphia and Samuel and Sister Elizabeth were coming back yet."

Wee Mary nodded that she understood, and Margaret started to say something. But she saw sufficient warning in Sal's eyes to know that if she had any doubts about anybody coming back out of a storm such as this one she had better keep them to herself.

Some of the almost fifty children in the room behind them had grown tired of being frightened and had started being noisy. Several of the nuns tried to keep them quiet by getting games started. Sister Catherine sang a little. Sister Felicitas and Sister Genevieve tended to some of the youngest of the children, who were crying.

Sal continued to try to shake her clothes and hair dry, and was glad that Sister Mendulla was in the other building, with the rest of the children and the remaining nuns. No doubt she had her charges quiet and still, and more fearful of the great blotch of a face being aimed in their direction than of any threat from the weather.

Reverend Mother Camillus had gone from one group to another all day, trying her best to give encouragement. The other nuns had difficulty convincing her of the folly of any attempt to get over to the other building to check on the people there. Finally Camillus resigned herself to making her rounds in this building, telling everybody to pray. Pray.

Sal knew that the little old lady would much rather be down in her study, doing her praying in her hard chair, clutching the rosary that she clutched now in her small hands. But the study was chest-deep in the Gulf of Mexico now, and not even the pious determination of the Reverend Mother would keep her from being swept out, chair and all.

"I wish them boys would hush," Margaret said, and a look came over her face which said that she was about ready to go and deal with them herself if the nuns couldn't.

"They're just nervous," Sal said. She stood far enough away from the landing now so that she wouldn't get pelted again.

Margaret continued to look down the long room at the group of rambunctious boys.

"I'm nervous , too," she said, "but I don't see how hoppin' around and yellin' like a red Indian will do anything about it."

Sal wished that Sister Zilphia was back. Not just because it would mean that she hadn't been washed away during her journey, but because she would have already gone down there and jerked a knot in those boys' behinds—as Sal's mother would have put it—and they would be quiet now. Sal had considered going down there and sharing her father's advice about sitting still, and waiting for something good-to happen, but she hadn't.

She was worried about her father and had prayed all day that he was safe somewhere, and dry. She prayed for her mother and her brother Joe, too, and prayed frantically for Zilphia and Elizabeth and Samuel for the last hour or so. But she prayed constantly for her father.

Much of Sal's life had been spent praying for her father.

She liked nothing so much as sitting beside his bed and waiting for him to wake up in the morning. She would have already cooked his breakfast and set the table to look like the tables she could see through the windows at Ritter's. She would have the hot water in the porcelain bowl for his shave and his razor resting on a folded towel.

He would always blink at her when he woke up, then lift an unsteady hand and touch the side of her face. Then he would lift himself up a little and pull her close to him for a hug. She could always smell the whiskey on him from his nights in the saloons.

Sometimes he would get up and get his shave and eat his breakfast and give her a kiss and go on down to the cotton warehouse and the job that he sometimes had and sometimes didn't.

Then Sal would clean up the breakfast things and go to school, and the rooms on Ship's Mechanic Street would be empty, since her mother would have been at her job at the Kempner's for hours and Joe would have already been wherever it was that Joe went. Joe was fourteen, just three years older than Sal, but he had given up on school when he was her age.

On some mornings, her father would linger over the shaving and the eating. He'd splash on some of his bay rum and look a little sad, and Sal might say that she had heard him fighting with her mother last night. Then he would rub some of the bay rum into the back of his wide neck and say that he hadn't been fighting, but just listening, and trying to go to bed. Sal would say that she wished sometimes that he *would* fight her, and he would look at the bottle of bay rum for a long time, and then at her. Then he'd say that it wouldn't do any good to fight with Minnie. Besides, he might add, everything Minnie said about him was right. And Sal would always say that wasn't so, and that her Mama always looked for everything that's bad, and she ought to start looking for the good things, too.

Then her father would pull her over close to him and say that she'd have to look long and hard to find any of those, and he would put his finger to Sal's lips when she started to say something else, and he would say that as long as he had her to take up for him—and he would call her Sweet Potato, as he often did, and smother his words in her hair—then he wouldn't have to fight at all, and he could just sit back and look at her pretty face and be happy and proud.

And she would lean into his hug, and rest her face against his neck, and take in the sweet aroma of the bay rum, like cinnamon and nutmeg, and close her eyes. She'd tell him that she wasn't pretty, and that he knew it. Then he would hold her away from him, and study her face, and get a serious look on his face, and ask her if the sisters down at the school had never told her that the angels in heaven are the prettiest things ever? And he would hug her back to him and say well then, Sal Casey, you're bound to be pretty, aren't you. Her being the only angel of God that he had ever seen.

And on some mornings, he could barely keep his hand from shaking, and she would have to hold his coffee cup to his lips. And he would lie in the bed for a while, and she would let her hand move slowly up and down the side of his face. In a minute or two, he would always smile at her and wink. Then he would whisper his philosophy, as if sharing it for the first time, that if a body would just sit still for long enough, something good would happen.

Margaret and Wee Mary were looking at her now. She didn't know when she had started crying, but the tears were on her face, mingled in with the water that had sloshed up on her. She wiped them away with her damp sleeve. She sniffed, and told the two girls that she wished that Sister Zilphia and Sister Elizabeth and Samuel would get back.

"I wish this storm would stop," Wee Mary said.

Margaret continued to look at Sal.

"I wish you'd get that hair tied back up out of your face," she said, determined to not pay any more attention to the loud boys at the other end of the room.

"It's startin' to bother me."

Chapter Eleven

Tucker

On Thursday, before the storm, when Tucker had still been the
yard man and the groomsman at the Kempner's big house on Broadway, he had spent most of the morning chopping back bushes and
limbs that had gotten too big. Mrs. Ivy showed him which ones to trim,
and some of the first ones that he tended to had been close to the
kitchen window, which was open, of course, in the late summer heat,
so Tucker didn't have any trouble hearing Mrs. Ivy tell Minnie Casey
that Mrs. Kempner wanted a cobbler for dinner. He had even less
difficulty hearing Minnie slam whatever she had been holding down on
the counter and give her reply.

"Well, does she now?" Minnie said. "It's the first I've heard of
a cobbler. She first said she wanted teacakes, so I guess she'll still
be wantin' those, too. And did she expect me to wander around the
island in all my spare time and find a patch of dewberries to make this
cobbler out of?"

"There's apples in one of the sacks in the shed, Minnie," Mrs. Ivy
said. "An apple cobbler would be fine."

Minnie said that she didn't have time to be picking through sacks
of apples and washing them and cutting them up when she still had
dinner to fix and a batch of teacakes to make that wouldn't be needed
anyway if there was to be a cobbler.

Tucker was finished with the bushes by the window and went to
trim the big oleander bushes at the edge of the yard. He knew that
Mrs. Ivy had probably left the room in the middle of the tirade, just as
he knew what would happen next.

In a little while Minnie was at the back door, yelling out to him to
get her some apples, and in another little while he laid them on the
counter in the kitchen.

She wasn't happy with the time it had taken him to do it.

"I guess you had to sit down under that tree and take a little nap to figure out how to fetch a few apples out of a shed," she said.

"No'm," he said as he caught one of the apples before it rolled off the counter. "But I had to tote the limbs I'd throwed in the road up on the yard, so they wouldn't get hit by no wagon." He turned to go.

Minnie frowned at the apples he had chosen. "If you'd thought to put them on the yard in the first place, you'd have saved yourself some work, and me some time."

He went out the back door, but still heard Mrs. Ivy, who had come into the kitchen real quick like she often did, tell Minnie that she ought to speak to both Pearl and him in a more cordial manner. Then he heard Minnie ask her what it could possibly matter how she spoke to a nigger man and an orphan girl.

Late that afternoon he put away the tools with which he had been working, rubbed down and fed the horse which pulled the Kempner's buggy, and made ready to leave for his second job at a warehouse on the wharves. He ran his hand along the flank and neck of the horse once more, looked around to make sure everything was in its place, and left the carriage house.

Outside, Mrs. Ivy called to him from the back door of the house. When he got to her, she placed a small bundle, wrapped in a napkin, into his hands.

"It's teacakes," she said, "baked just a little while ago. Take them along to your family."

The package was warm in his hands, and he could smell the yeasty sweetness through the cloth. "That was thoughtful, Miss Ivy. My babies will sho like these. They eyes are liable to pop right out of they heads."

The housekeeper gave him one of her smiles. He knew that she hadn't baked the cookies. He also knew that it would have never crossed the mind of the little woman who *had* baked them to send some of them home to his children. Minnie would as soon give cookies to a bunch of animals as she would to black folks. There was as much difference between those two women, he thought, as there was between this house and the sorry little hole that he would go home to tonight. He thanked Mrs. Ivy again, and left the yard.

Tucker walked down the sidewalk beside Broadway, the big trees of the great houses making a dense roof over him. He carried the napkin full of cookies in one hand, careful not to mash them. Their sweet smell blended in with the scent of the oleander and rose bushes along that part of the street.

Going from the Kempner house to the warehouse every day always seemed like a downhill progression to him. At least at the Kempners he was treated well, and with some respect, except by

Minnie, of course, but he had long since learned to just do whatever Minnie told him to do and to spend most of his time away from her. She was the cook, and his duties rarely took him into the kitchen. Minnie believed that she could tell anyone what to do at any time, but he had seen Mrs. Ivy set her right on that more than once.

The Kempners were Jews, and that had worried him some at the beginning. His mama had always told him that it was the Jews who had killed Jesus, and for that single reason none of them were to be trusted. He and Mae, his wife, had talked about it—Mae made all the decisions regarding religion—when he had first gotten the job, and Mae decided the Jews that killed Jesus had done it so long ago that it was unlikely that any of the Kempners' people had been involved in it. Another thing was that Tucker had always heard that Jews were mighty close to their money and not inclined to part with any of it. He even thought, for a while, that they were paying him way too little because they were Jews. But he learned, from yardmen and groomsmen at other houses, that everybody got paid too little, and it didn't matter if they were Jews or Baptists.

He and Mae were Baptists. They went to church every Sunday morning, and Mae had decided that they should pray for the Kempners, so that they could find Jesus. They hadn't shown any signs yet that they had, or even that they were looking for Him, but the preacher at Tucker and Mae's church said to just be patient, that God doesn't ever get in any hurry, and why should he, having all eternity to fiddle around with and all. So Mae went on praying for them.

Tucker clicked his tongue at a dog on the other side of a wrought iron fence. The dog barked and began to jump around like he wanted out of the yard, to play with Tucker, or maybe bite him. One of the new automobiles sputtered down Broadway, and the dog barked louder and jumped around more. The horses pulling wagons and buggies registered their opinions with snorts and prances. There were only two or three automobiles on the island, and Tucker hoped that Mr. Kempner wouldn't buy one, though he could certainly afford to. Tucker was pretty sure that he could never learn to operate such a thing, and he didn't even want to. He enjoyed the time that he spent grooming and driving the horse, and had passed many an hour just sitting in the buggy, waiting for Mr. Kempner or his mother to come out of a building or the temple, and, more often than not, the horse had been his only companion. Tucker liked those times, when he could sit and watch the happenings in the streets and along the sidewalks, and the horse, just by being there, and flicking his tail or wheezing every once in a while, was a comrade, to be talked to, and rubbed, and eased. He would have liked to call the horse by its name, but it didn't have one. Tucker didn't know if Jews didn't believe in naming horses, or if the Kempners just hadn't gotten around to it. Maybe they just hadn't thought of a good enough name for such a fine horse.

The automobile came to a sputtering stop at an intersection, then the motor died altogether, and the driver climbed out and did something at the front of it to revive it. The automobile passed, and the street returned to normal. Tucker hoped, again, that he would never have to drive one. Much having to do with the horse—its grooming and feeding and the fellowship it provided during the long waits in the buggy—was part of what made his job at the Kempners' a good one.

His job at the wharves was a different story.

He got the job, sweeping out one of the big warehouses by the docks every afternoon, when he heard that the man who had it before him had been fired. Tucker needed as much money as he could make, so he decided to go and ask about it. The foreman at the warehouse hired him, at an even lower wage than Tucker had suspected, and told him that if he ever failed to show up, or didn't pay attention to what he was doing, he would fire him just as quick. He fired the last fellow quick, and he would him too, if he had any reason to, he said. The foreman told him that he could replace him in just a very few minutes, that it didn't call for any particular ability to sweep a floor.

The men who worked there, moving bales of cotton into the shelter or out of it to be loaded onto ships, paid him little attention, other than to yell at him if he got in their way. By the time he got there every day, they had been at it for a long time and weren't in any mood to have to get out of the way of the sweeper.

Tucker was a big man, lean and muscular from the hard work he had done in his almost thirty years, so the men didn't antagonize him to the point that he might come at them, but their attitudes and comments were always tinged with the superiority that they assumed came with the color of their skin.

When he got there, after his long walk, he went past some of the men and got the wide broom from the corner. The men stayed off to themselves, talking in loud, sharp voices that echoed in the big building. One of them said, "The nigger's here," as if it was a way of telling the time.

Tucker swept. Some days he had more to sweep than others because of the amount of cotton in the building. Today it was pretty full, so he did most of his sweeping near the entrance, where he could hear the sounds of the wharves. Ships' bells clanged, waves sloshed against vessels and piers in a slow rhythm, seagulls squawked; the men of the wharves called out to each other in filthy curses of several languages.

Almost an hour later, Tucker looked at the sun through the big doors of the warehouse. It was considerably lower in the late afternoon sky than the last time he looked. The workers would be leaving soon, and that boy that the little foreign man had told him about would come, and he would have to have made his decision by then. He didn't want to make the decision at all, and now he would have to make it in the next few minutes.

He had thought about it since Saturday, when the little man made his offer. And he prayed about it, in church on Sunday with Mae and his babies, and a hundred times since then. He even decided, yesterday, to tell the little man he wanted nothing to do with it, to take his fifty dollars and to go find somebody else to help him.

Then he had gone home from his sweeping and sat down to the supper that Mae had ready for him. His three small children sat on the edge of a bed and watched him. The oldest was a boy, and the other two were girls. One of them held a homemade doll, made from an old towel stuffed with cotton that Tucker had kept from his sweeping, with buttons for eyes. He ate the supper and looked into the eyes of his babies. As he chewed slowly on the fried sidemeat—mostly fat —and a scoop of field peas, he looked back at the children and knew that their supper had been as small as his.

Mae was busy at some chore in the corner of the single room that served as the kitchen. As he chewed each bite slowly, knowing there wouldn't be any more food till breakfast—another strip from the same piece of sidemeat, with a glob of spoonbread fried in its drippings— he wondered what he would have to do to provide an existence where such a simple thing as a decent supper would be possible for his babies.

Later, he sat outside in the dark alley, on the upturned crate that he sat on every night. Mae was inside, snuggled beside the smallest of their children, and through the open window he heard her singing the slow verse of a song. Then she just hummed, as soft and natural as breathing, so Tucker knew that his babies were on the verge of sleep, lured there by their mother's sweet voice.

He smoked the cheapest of tobaccos—the spillage that the grocer had swept up off the floor—in an old briar pipe, the only heirloom that had been passed down to him from his father. He turned the pipe in his hands and thought of all the years his daddy had smoked it while he was owned by another man. Tucker had been his father's last child, born nearly fifteen years after the end of the war, but he remembered the stories the old man had told.

Tucker leaned on the crate and rested his back against the rough bricks of the alley's wall. He would have liked to have a bottle of whiskey to sip on. He had been partial to whiskey before he married Mae, but his lack of money and Mae's religious leanings had brought his whiskey drinking to an end. Still, a sip or two out under the stars would have been nice.

He looked around him and wondered if he was any better off than his Daddy had been, as a slave. Shabby, run-down buildings, three stories tall, framed the two sides and one end of the narrow alley, which opened into a street full of whorehouses and saloons. Sailors from all over the world stumbled and swore as they made their weaving way along the street, but they seldom ventured into the alley, except, on occasion, to relieve themselves of the cheap beer and watered down liquor they'd had in the bars. Prostitutes never brought their clients there, where black people lived; even the dingy rooms in which the whores trafficked their goods were more desirable than the alleys.

Tucker thought of the preacher at the church where he and Mae and the children went on Sunday mornings and how the preacher always went on about Jesus coming back and making things right. The nauseating laugh of a woman, probably a whore, came from the street, mixed in with the gaudy, tinkling music of a piano. The whores and the sailors in the bars were all full of good suppers, Tucker guessed, and whiskey. His babies, asleep now, beside Mae, had gone to bed with only a little bit of a supper in them that a sailor or a whore would have laughed at, and thrown on the floor.

The stars shone bright in the narrow space between the buildings, and Tucker had thought that if what the preacher said was right, then Jesus ought to come on back now, that the world was ripe to be made better.

What he wanted didn't seem like all that much, to Tucker: a decent place to raise his children in, not even a very big place, just a clean, safe one, where his babies could play outside, and not have to watch somebody piss on the side of their house. And something nice for Mae every once in a while, like a new dress, or a hat to wear to church. And some food on the table that would get somebody interested in eating it, and enough of it on the plate to get somebody full. And a comfortable chair by the back door, so he could sit and look at the stars at night. They'd be the same stars, he knew, but at least he wouldn't have to sit on a crate and look at them, and listen to whores and drunks down the alley.

Then Tucker thought of the bent little Englishman, and of the fifty dollars he had offered. By the time he went in to bed, much later, he still hadn't made up his mind.

Now he had to make his decision. That boy would be here in a little while. Tucker had gone back, twice today, and at least that many times on Tuesday and Wednesday, to look at the little bricked-in room at the rear of the warehouse, and at the heavy padlock in its hasp. This was what the little foreign man was talking about, he knew. What he wanted the boy to be able to get into.

He thought so much about what the little man had said to him that it almost made him sick and kept him from sleeping more than once since Saturday. Fifty dollars would put him pretty far ahead. But it wouldn't do much for him if he got caught and thrown in Mr. Ketchum's jail. He could imagine having fifty dollars in his pocket, but he could just as easily imagine sitting for no telling how long in a jail as hot as this warehouse, while Mae and his babies didn't have any money coming in at all.

He had the padlock in his pocket that the little man had given him, and had hidden the hacksaw that he had handed him up under a cotton bale. He looked at the sun again, and knew that there wasn't much time left.

Since Saturday, he had wanted nothing more than to talk to Mae about it, but he knew that she would just start praying and asking Jesus to forgive him for even thinking about stealing. He even prayed, himself, and asked for some kind of sign to tell him what to do. After all, Mae had been trusting Jesus for a long time to come up with a way to help them. Maybe this was it. He had listened more carefully, on Sunday, when the preacher hopped around and yelled out his sermon, thinking that Jesus might put the sign in there. But the preacher went on and on about a man who had been eaten by a big fish, and spat back up, and Tucker couldn't see anything in that story that had anything to do with any of this.

He leaned against his broom, and thought again of what Mae's opinion would be. It would be an easy decision for Mae. Then he thought of how he would either be here long enough to show that boy where that little room was, and to help him tote whatever was in it over to a ship across the docks, and to get his fifty dollars from the little foreign man. Or he could be home in just a little while, and not have to worry about Mr. Ketchum coming after him and throwing him in his jail. Or about Mae being ashamed of him.

Tucker nodded at his decision and walked to the back of the warehouse. He took the padlock out of his pocket, and put it under the cotton, with the hacksaw. He would meet the boy outside, and tell him what he decided, and then go on home.

He put his broom and pan away and reached down for the bundle from Mrs. Ivy that he had placed in the corner. The napkin was there, but the cookies were gone.

Several of the men were huddled off to one side, getting ready to go home. One of them, a little man named Davenport, who always reminded Tucker of a rat, was saying something in a low voice to his companions. He smiled and glanced at Tucker, then he laughed.

Tucker was sure he was the thief—the man even seemed to be sucking the remnants of the cookies from between his little rat-like teeth. But he was just as sure that a few teacakes were not enough of a prize to lose this job over. And lose it he certainly would, he knew, if he accused a white man, even a little weasel of one like this one. He stuffed the napkin in the pocket of his overalls and left the warehouse, hearing the laughter of Davenport and his buddies behind him.

When he turned to look at them, they stopped laughing and returned his stare, daring him, with their silent belligerence, to step over into their world, where everything was stacked against him. He held their stare for a moment, and turned around and walked back into the warehouse. He found the hacksaw and the lock. He would wait for the men to leave, then he would quickly saw the lock in the hasp on the little room, and wait for the boy to come.

He thought of his babies and of how just a few cookies would have made their lives a little better. He thought of Davenport, and of his confident smirk.

Then he thanked Jesus, for sending a strong enough sign, and not some little bit of one, that a man might miss.

The boy came just after the last of the workers had left. He came in quick, and came right up to him, at the front of the big warehouse. Tucker knew he must have been watching from somewhere, probably from behind some bales.

"Did you get the lock sawed off?" he asked.

Tucker said that he had, and the boy told him to show him where the room was.

They moved quickly between the stacks of bales, and came to the bricked room. The boy looked at the lock, and found the narrow line that the hacksaw had eaten through.

"Have you been in there?"

"No, suh." Tucker looked at the lock, too. "And I ain't all that sure that I want to."

The boy turned the bottom of the heavy padlock and lifted it out of its hasp. Tucker reached under the cotton and got the other lock and handed it to the boy, and he hung it on the hasp.

The boy pushed on the heavy door. The hinges squeaked loudly, so Tucker knew it didn't get opened very often. He expected it to be totally dark inside, but enough late afternoon light found its way through some air vents at the top to let him see the crates. There weren't more than twenty of them, if that many, and they weren't very big. Only two, that he could see from the door, might need both him and the boy to carry them. The boy studied the crates, too. None of them was very thick. The boy rocked one of them up on its corner, to see how heavy it was. Tucker figured that they could have them up by the front doors in four, maybe five, trips. Then they'd wait for it to get darker, and move them over to the ship.

He wondered what was in them, but wasn't about to ask the boy. The less he knew, the better, he figured.

They looked out the door into the warehouse, and listened. Nothing.

"Grab as many as you can carry," the boy said. "But don't drop any, or bang them against the door or anything. What's in there has got to be in good condition when we get it to the ship."

Tucker nodded his head, and leaned down to pull up a crate under each arm. He followed him out into the warehouse. Tucker tapped one box against a cotton bale at a narrow turn in the walkway.

"Damn it," the boy said. "I said to be careful."

Tucker mumbled that he would, and followed him to the front.

They stopped far enough back in the shadows to be able to look outside without being seen. Nobody was around.

"Come on," he whispered back to Tucker. "We got to hurry now."

Tucker kept up with him as he moved quickly across the open area beside the doors and laid the crates against the wall. Just as quickly, they were back inside.

"You done good," the boy said, as they hurried back through the maze of bales to the room. "Now we just got to keep doing that till we get them all." They were both breathing hard, now, and their shirts were soaked through with sweat. The boy took off his cap, and wiped the sweat from his forehead and hair with his hand before putting the cap back on and pulling it down low over his eyes. "There's two big ones that we'll have to get together," he said. "Let's go ahead and be done with them."

Two trips later, they had the biggest of the crates outside with the others, and they went back in to get some more. For the next little while, they went silently about the routine that they had established. They had already snapped the new padlock into place and were on their way out with the last of the crates when the spindly red-headed boy ran into them. Tucker was so surprised that he dropped the two he was carrying.

Before the first boy could say anything, the red-headed one had sputtered out enough information to tell them that somebody was coming. The first boy put the crates that he was carrying behind some bales and jerked Tucker and the red-headed one over beside them. The boy went back and collected the crates that Tucker had dropped, and by the time they saw the little man walking down the aisle that they had been using, they were all hidden.

The man walked past them, close enough for them to reach out and touch him, and then went on toward the back.

Tucker was breathing so loudly that he was sure they could hear him. He turned around and watched the man. He never even looked at the little room, but walked on past it and stopped further back and leaned down to pick something up. It was hard for Tucker to see in the darkness, but he guessed the man had come back to get something he had forgotten. He came back toward them, carrying a bottle.

They kept down low behind the bales and watched the man go by them. Tucker could still hear his own frantic breathing and hoped it wasn't loud enough for the man to hear it, too.

He was far enough away from them, now, for the boy to relax a little. He touched Tucker on his big shoulder, to let him know that it was all right, and Tucker jumped enough to push one of the crates forward. They watched it balance precariously for a short second, and then fall with a thud to the concrete.

The man turned around, and came back in their direction. The two boys looked at each other, and Tucker pushed them both back down.

He stood up, and stepped into the aisle.

The man stopped when he saw him, and squinted his eyes to see who it was.

"What the hell you doing here?" he said.

Tucker fought to get his breathing under control. "I'm just doin' my sweepin'." He tried to make his voice sound normal.

The man looked at him.

He smiled. "Then where's your broom?"

Tucker didn't move. He smiled, too. "I just got done and was headin' off home."

The man looked at the bits of cotton all over the floor. "It don't look to me like you're done," he said. He looked some more. "It looks to me like you ain't never started back in here."

Tucker looked at the floor, too. He had missed this section.

The man didn't say anything for a moment.

"You're up to somethin'," he finally said, and wagged a small finger at him. "You ain't done no sweepin' back here today." He smiled, again. "Now I wonder what the sweepin' nigger's doin' in here if he ain't sweepin'."

Tucker stood still and quiet.

"I'll just bet," the man said, "that foreman would be mighty happy to know that his sweepin' nigger was down here up to no good, in his warehouse, at night." He laughed. "I guess it's a good thing that I needed me a drink, and remembered I had me a bottle hid down here. Or you'd have got away with whatever you're up to."

"I ain't up to nothin'," Tucker said.

The man just kept on smiling. He pulled the cork out of the bottle he was holding and took a drink from it. "I think we'll just wait right here, me and you, till that guard shows up. And you can explain how you been doin' all this sweepin' without no broom, and with cotton all over the floor."

Tucker could feel his heart beating and knew that it was beating faster than it should be. Davenport squinted his ratlike eyes, and picked at his little teeth with his tongue, probably at bits of the teacakes that had been intended for his babies. Tucker took a step, to get past, but the man pushed him back against a bale. By the time he was back on his feet, the man had pulled a jack knife from his pocket, opened it, and was waving it in his direction..

"Now you better listen here, boy," he said, his rat's nose twitching. "I'm keepin' you here till that guard comes." He poked the knife toward Tucker. "That foreman will be glad to know that one of his workers took the time to catch a nigger tryin' to . . ."

The first boy was over the bale and to him before he had a chance to finish. He grabbed the man's arm, but it was the one with the bottle, not the knife. The bottle fell out of his grip, and exploded on the concrete floor.

The man pushed the boy away from him and turned on him with the knife. He sprang toward the boy and lunged the knife forward with such force that he could hardly feel it as it made its quick journey through muscle and bone. The boy's body went rigid for a second, then slumped down.

Everybody was quiet, and nobody moved. Mountains of cotton stood over them, rising up to the ceiling of the cavernous building. They could hear Tucker's loud breathing and smell the spilled whiskey on the floor.

The man let go of the knife and backed away, trying to figure out who it was. Then he saw that he hadn't stabbed who he thought he had. Whoever it was, he thought, as his mind raced to try to make some sense of what had just happened, he was ugly. All that red hair, and those big ears, and a mouth that seemed to cover the whole bottom half of his freckled face.

Tucker tried to back further into the bale of cotton, and made a weak, whining sound, like an animal might make in a trap. The first boy looked down at the red-headed one, then at the man. He had the knife out of the small body before the man had finished looking at the boy's face.

It was the last thing he would ever look at. The boy swung the knife's blade with a wide enough arch to dig deep into the man's throat. He staggered for a second or two and fell backward onto the floor. They could hear the wind from his lungs make its last, pathetic gasp to escape, and then he was still.

Much later, the brightest things that a bird, flying high overhead, might see in Galveston, even on a cloudless night like this one, were along the streets where the saloons and whorehouses sent out especially bright lights, as if they were generated by the vices being practiced inside. Two streets away, the wharves lay in darkness, the dark water of the bay moving only slightly, sloshing quietly against the hulls of ships, and against the wide, heavy pilings of the docks.

Tucker would have given his fifty dollars to anybody who could turn the clock back about five days. And gladly.

The *Maydelle*, her tall masts reaching up into the night, loomed over him. His muscles ached, and he leaned against a bundle of cargo on the wharves. He tried again to sort things out.

He had asked Jesus to send him some money. And now he had the money in his pocket.

Two dead people. A robbery. Nearly a whole week of headaches and rolling around when he ought to have been sleeping.

He didn't think he'd be asking Jesus for anything else anytime soon.

It was late, sometime after midnight, and Tucker couldn't remember ever being as bone-tired as he was right now. He hadn't slept much the night before. Tonight, when he had looked down at the two dead people on the floor of the warehouse, he knew that however exhausted he had been before, it wasn't anything compared to what he was about to be. He knew that that boy, who had been hanging onto the red-headed one till he died, wasn't going to be in any shape to help him. And, for once, Tucker had known what had to be done, without having to figure it out. He looked only briefly at the big doors at the front and hoped that the night watchman wouldn't get there till he was finished. Then he went to the stack of cotton sacks in a corner, told the boy to stand out of the way, and rolled the bodies up in several of the sacks. Then he got some water, and wiped up the blood and the whiskey and the broken glass from the concrete, and rubbed it dry with some more of the sacks.

He told the boy, who was quiet then, after all his crying and hollering, and almost as white as the dead boy, that he would have to show him where the ship was, and to carry some of the boxes, if he could. Tucker carried the bodies one at a time to the dock beside the ship, and laid them among some cargo stacked there. It would have been easier to drag them, but he was afraid that some blood might smear on the wharves, and he could go faster carrying them. He was glad that the dead boy and Davenport were not very big people.

The boy was able to carry two of the boxes while he stumbled, like a drunk man, over to the ship. Tucker had to go back and get the rest of them, himself. By the time he delivered all of them, he was sure that his muscles couldn't function anymore. He fell against the cargo the bodies were hidden behind and dropped his head between his knees.

He had dozed a little, he guessed, and when he came to he heard some of the commotion on the ship. A man was yelling, and Tucker could tell he was foreign. But it hadn't sounded like the little bent-up man who caused all of this. He looked over at where he had put the crates, but they were gone—somebody from the ship must have come down to get them while he had been sleeping. He pulled himself up and looked behind the cargo. The bodies, in their burlap shrouds, were gone too.

Tucker couldn't quit thinking about the red-headed boy and how he had jumped up so quick, out of nowhere, to get between Davenport and the other boy. So quick that it was almost like it was what he was supposed to do. Like it was what he was there to do.

Soreness was already settling into his muscles. He leaned back down against a box and moved his neck around slowly to stretch some life into it. He knew that he probably shouldn't be sitting out in the open, on the wharves, like this. If the police came now, all they had to do was load him up with whoever wanted those boxes stolen and haul him off to jail.

But he was too tired to move. If Mr. Ketchum came right then, he'd just have to catch him. He smiled and closed his eyes, realizing how tired he was, and he didn't have a thing to smile about.

When he woke up that time, the little bent-over foreign man was almost to him. Tucker was too weary to even try to get up. The man had already given him his fifty dollars—two twenties and two fives—and this time he just told him about Mr. Ketchum and how he had a good brain in his noggin, how he would figure a few things out pretty

101

quick. Then the little man found the darkest shadows at the edge of the wharves and disappeared into them.

Tucker thought he would rest a little more and then go on over and give the money to Mae. He was sure that Mr. Ketchum and his policemen would come for him tomorrow, or maybe even later tonight. He might have gotten away with it if two people hadn't ended up dead. But now Mr. Ketchum would have considerably more reason to ask a lot of questions than he would have without any dead bodies being involved.

He tried to think through it again, though his mind was as spent as his body, since it had done more thinking in the last five days than it had in as long as he could remember.

He hadn't killed either one of the people. But the man who killed the first boy was dead himself. And the boy who killed him was on that ship and not showing any signs of coming off of it. Tucker shook his head slowly, knowing that he would be blamed for one, or maybe both, of the deaths. Then Mr. Ketchum would throw him in his jail, and they might send him up to the state prison in Huntsville, where his cousin had been sent for just stealing some yard pigs, and not even killing anybody.

Tucker stopped shaking his head when the new possibility sank in. They might hang him. He knew that white folks didn't need much of a reason to hang people like him, and two dead white people would certainly qualify. He rubbed his thumb lightly on his neck.

He would just give Mae the money and take something to eat and then go out to the edge of town, where he could figure things out. He might even go down to the city hall tomorrow and turn himself in, now that Mae would have some money. But a night, and maybe a full day, of sitting in the dunes, sleeping when he wanted to, and watching the water roll up on the beach wouldn't hurt anything. He wanted to think everything through carefully this time, and not make any mistakes.

A sailor came to the railing on the ship's deck, and called down to him to unhitch the lines. Tucker pulled himself up, and went over to undo both of the heavy ropes. Two more sailors hauled them up.

He sat back down in the same place, and leaned his head back against the bundles. It was dark, and he had to strain his eyes to see the boy, standing on the ship's deck, with his cap pulled down low over his eyes. The boy had acted like a grown man, one who knew what he was about when they were doing their work. And he had come over that bale of cotton at Davenport like a mean dog, not even slowing down to think about it. But now he looked like he had while they walked over from the warehouse, when Tucker had to nudge him along. He had seen the boy's shoulders shaking a little in front of him, and knew that he was crying, and trying to not cry out loud. So he told him to just keep on going, and not to stop, or drop the boxes, and that everything would be all right.

The boy went up on the ship when they got there, and whoever had done all the yelling, the other foreigner, must have finally got the story out of him. Tucker didn't know—he was too busy hauling dead people and boxes, and he was worn out, too tired to do much more thinking or moving. He had been doing too much of both in the last few days. The little preacher yelled out, once, during one of his vigorous sermons, that sometimes storms start blowing in people's brains, when Jesus and the devil go to fighting in there. Tucker didn't know much about that, but he did feel, at the moment, like he had been knocked around pretty good by a storm.

The boy still watched him from the ship's deck; his hands resting on the rail. Tucker gave a slow wave in his direction, and the boy touched his finger to the brim of his cap, and nodded.

The ship floated away from the dock, and in a few minutes enough sail had been put up to catch the slow breeze and the schooner began moving quietly along the harbor, toward the Bolivar roads.

CHAPTER TWELVE

Shortly after three o'clock in the afternoon, the waters from the Gulf of Mexico met those from the bay, and Galveston island became part of the ocean floor.

Isaac Cline, still at the Weather Bureau office in the Levy Building, recited the message that he had carefully worded to his brother Joseph, who would telegraph it to Washington.

"This island is fast going under water," he said, and paused to think. "Great loss of life is imminent. The need for relief is urgent."

He took off his glasses, and wiped them with his handkerchief. "See if you can get it to the telegraph office," he said, "then come on home. There's nothing else that we can do here." The rain gauge had already blown off the roof, and the other instruments were teetering precariously when they had last gone up to read them.

"I'm going to be with Cora Mae and the girls." He looked at his brother. "Start for home as soon as you can."

One of the clerks, a bachelor with no family to go see to, had volunteered to stay here and enter conditions in the log. He would fare better here, Isaac knew, in a brick building, than people in frame houses. Cora Mae and his daughters were waiting for him in just such a house right now, separated from the beach by three blocks.

He prayed that three blocks would be enough.

Sister Elizabeth helped Zilphia and Samuel up on to the porch of the little store, where they staggered for a moment, and both fell back against the wall, exhausted. The muscles in Zilphia's legs and back felt as if they had been twisted tight, like wet towels being wrung out. She stretched her legs in front of her and rested her head against the clapboard siding.

"I take it," she managed to say, between deep breaths, "this store is closed."

Elizabeth smiled and reached for both of their hands. "Thank God you came," she said.

"Thank Reverend Mother, too," Zilphia said, loud enough to be heard over the wind. "She was about to come herself, I think. Or climb up on Mendulla, and paddle her over here like a boat."

The small building teetered on its blocks, the wooden sides and beams groaning like the masts of a ship.

"I had thought I'd just wait it out here," Elizabeth shouted, "but then it started all this bobbing around a few minutes ago. I was about to try to get the door open, and take my chances inside."

Zilphia pulled herself up. "It won't be long till there won't *be* any inside," she said. "It's about to be swept away, and we will, too, if we don't get off this porch."

Samuel eased himself down into the churning water and helped the two women down beside him. Zilphia showed Elizabeth how to bundle up the bottom of her habit, to keep it from pulling her under.

Elizabeth stood as still as the fast moving water would let her. She looked back at the building.

"We can't get back to the orphanage," she yelled, "it's too far."

"We have to," Zilphia shouted. "It's even further to the next buildings, and we wouldn't be any better off there than we will be at home." She looked at the gray, turbulent water that swirled all around her, swifter and deeper than it had been even a few minutes ago. "But we've got to go now!" She pulled on Elizabeth's hand. "Or we'll die here."

They moved as fast as they could, each of them stumbling several times, the other two helping that one up when they did. More debris was sweeping past them than it had on the first trip—they had to dodge the bigger pieces of driftwood. Elizabeth didn't get out of the way of two pieces, and the largest one nearly pushed her over.

Zilphia saw the problem. "You've got to keep your eyes open," she shouted back at her.

Elizabeth stumbled around until she regained her footing. "I was praying," she shouted back.

Zilphia grabbed her hand. "Then do it with your eyes open," she said, yanking her forward. "Or you'll be saying your prayers in person."

Samuel led the way, the foamy brown water splashing against his chest as he pushed through it. The wind howled past them, and the rain slammed into the gurgling water like pellets fired from rifles.

Zilphia held on to Elizabeth's hand and pulled her along. She could barely hear her mumbling behind her, and knew that it was one desperate Hail Mary being recited after another. Zilphia knew that she should be praying, too, and thought that when they got back to the orphanage, provided there was an orphanage left for them to get back to, she might make an attempt.

They didn't see the first rattlesnake until they were halfway home.

When Joseph Cline reached the Western Union office, he learned that the telegraph lines had been down for almost two hours. So he waded back to the Levy Building and climbed the stairs to his office. There was only one chance remaining, he knew, to get the last report out. He reached for the telephone on his desk, clicked the cradle a couple of times, and asked the operator for a long distance connection with the Weather Bureau office in Houston.

"You've got a few people ahead of you waitin' for lines," the operator's voiced crackled into the receiver.

Joseph mopped his forehead with a handkerchief. "How many?" he asked.

"About a hundred, would be my guess."

Joseph frantically explained the urgency of the situation, and only after having to recite it all again to the manager was given a connection. He read into the mouthpiece the report that Isaac had given him, word for word, and asked that it be sent, straightaway, to Washington.

Joseph was unaware of it, but the long distance wires were snapped by the wind only a few minutes after his call, severing the last remaining link between Galveston and the mainland.

Eighteen blocks away, Joseph's brother Isaac finally pulled his tired, soaked body up on to his own porch. He fell against the door and had to wait there for a moment to recover enough breath and energy to go on.

The storm was wailing all around him, sending debris skirting along the top of the water faster than a man could run on dry land. Isaac leaned close against the door and felt his breathing returning to a normal level.

People were dying now, he knew, as he had predicted. He saw one man, on the way home, nearly decapitated by a shutter that slammed into him. The body of a child was caught against a yard fence. Isaac waded over to it, but the girl was dead.

Galveston was coming apart in the fury of the tempest that boiled over it. Isaac had seen a produce wagon, on Sealy Street, slam into the front of a building. As it disintegrated, it freed, too late, the lifeless body of a man who had somehow been caught to it. The fragments of the wagon became lodged in the churning current and floated away. Then the man, his eyes still open wide, his face still showing the absurdity of his final predicament, followed them.

The porch tilted slightly, and he grabbed the door frame to keep from rolling through the several inches of water on the porch and into the churning lake that was his front yard. The house stood on blocks, to protect it from overflows. Many houses in Galveston had been built in the east and shipped in sections in the holds of ships returning to the island to be loaded with cotton. As he waded home, Isaac had seen several such houses already dislodged from their blocks and floating, like top-heavy, lumbering barges, until they crashed into whatever could stop them. He knew that soon most of the structures would be colliding into each other, like rows of giant dominoes being tipped over. But he had designed this house himself, and had gone with the carpenter to purchase the lumber, and watched as it had been built. It was sturdy, he knew. And if any house this near the gulf would come through the direct hit of a massive hurricane, this one would.

He got up, pushed against the door, and went into his front room. Water was already almost a foot deep and slamming pieces of furniture into each other.

He hurried up the steps, and found nearly fifty terrified people assembled in the upstairs rooms.

"Where's my family?" he shouted. Water sputtered out when he spoke.

A neighbor came forward. "They're in here, Isaac. Cora Mae will be mighty happy to . . . ."

He hurried through the crowded room to his bedroom, and over to his wife and three daughters, scooping all of them into his arms, and letting them cry into his soaked clothing.

The statue of Mary, on the high central tower of her cathedral, lurched slowly back and forth in the wind. Heavy slate shingles, which had been used as a precaution against fires, worked themselves loose, became airborne, and gathered enough speed in their long, slanting descent to slice people in half. Several of their victims already lay near the cathedral steps, and floated in the surging water that was Twenty-First Street.

Inside, over a hundred people who had sought refuge there huddled near the center of the nave, not knowing what to do, or where to go.

One man looked up at the high ceiling and tried to determine where the central tower stood. He knew that the tower, and the two smaller ones at the front of the church, might not survive the buffeting wind and if they didn't would crash through the roof.

He hurried among the crying, stunned people and urged them to get over next to the walls, as far away from the tall windows as they could. Those that were too shocked to move, he pushed. Soon, several others were helping him.

The man tried to lift an old woman who had knelt down to pray in the center of the church. She pushed him away.

"If that statue falls," he yelled at her, "you're right in its path."

She looked up at him and smiled. "She won't fall," she said softly, clutching a rosary in her hands. "And I've been in her path all of my life."

He looked at her for a long moment, then left her alone.

Thurmon tried to stay on what he hoped was the beach road, though he could barely feel it, as the wind kept pushing him further to his right than he wanted to go. And he certainly couldn't see it, since it was under so much of the gray, frothy water. It was raining so hard that he could barely see the surface of the water right before his eyes, much less any landmarks that might tell him he was going where he wanted to go.

He kept looking for the tops of the two tall orphanage buildings, but it was raining too hard for him to see anything. He hadn't been out here in ages, since he had gone fishing out at the west end of the island with Hap Bonner. And Hap Bonner had been dead for over ten years.

But Thurmon knew that the orphanage was still further out than he had managed to come. Maybe as much as a mile or more further. And he wasn't at all sure that he could go another mile. The dark Gulf of Mexico was already slapping waves up into his face, and he barely had enough of his arms up out of the water to steady himself.

He'd have to stay on the road, he told himself, as he fought for another few feet of progress. The road was the highest land out here, and when the gulf got deeper than he was tall, as it almost was already, then he would just have to try to swim, though he knew that surely would be the end of it. And he'd drown.

He felt of the bottle of brandy that Minnie had given him, secure in his pocket. It would be awfully easy now to just stop, and drink as much of the brandy as he could get down before the current pushed him under.

Only one thing could make him fight for a few more steps. One single image that was bright enough for him to see it through such a dismal day as this one. Her features were small, even her teeth were, and her slight presence seemed to say to not bother about her, that she'd just stay out of the way. Thin arms and legs were attached to her little body at fragile junctures, as if they were barely sufficient to hold all of her together. Her wrists looked brittle enough to be snapped, with little effort, like dry twigs. Her smile was beautiful, and her goodness radiated like light.

Sal.

Thurmon pushed himself forward, and looked again for the tops of the two houses that he was sure he wouldn't see for a while yet.

If he was ever to see them at all.

Quin looked at the two boys, who were inside now, standing in the twelve or so inches of water that he was standing in, too. He had seen the uselessness of leaving them outside, since they were determined to keep pounding on his door until he admitted them.

"Well," he said, "you got what you wanted. You're in." He surveyed the pile of his inventory, already being moved around in the increasingly swift current. "It ain't done you no good, however."

He felt in the deep pockets of his coat to make sure the wads of bills were still there. Then he waded toward the door.

"Where you goin'," the taller boy asked.

Quin pulled the heavy door open, creating a wave that moved slowly over and splashed into a stack of lady's handbags.

"That ain't none of your business, is it?" He fumbled with the buttons of his coat. "You beat the hell out of this here door long enough to get yourselves in." He tapped at the door with a crooked finger. "Well, you're in." He moved out to the sidewalk, and pushed against the brown, foamy water until he had gone a few feet.

He felt the tug at his coat, and turned around to see the two boys.

"Where we goin'?" the taller one asked.

Quin stood as still as he could. He very nearly laughed, then he pushed the boy away.

"*We* ain't goin' nowhere," he shouted, his misshapen body lunging to regain its balance. "Are you too goddamned simple to see that? *I'm* headin' for the middle of this cursed island, and findin' a dryer place to be."

He waded for another few feet, his small, bent body pushing through the flood. He didn't have to turn around to see that the boys were keeping up with them. He knew they were there.

"What the hell do I have to do?" he yelled, turning and facing them now. "Do I have to knock you in the head to make you see it?"

The boys stood close together, staring at him. Two more people who had been wading in the same direction stopped and stared, too. Then they went on.

"The middle of town is that way!" Quin shouted. "Go on if you want to." He pulled the collar of his old coat closer together, to try to keep some of the blowing rain out. "But you ain't goin' with me."

The boys didn't move, and continued to look at him. The somber expression on their faces hadn't changed since he had first seen them standing outside his door.

"We're goin' where you're goin'," the taller one said.

It took him only another moment to add what Quin knew was coming, what he knew was the boy's one driving tenet.

"We got nowhere else to go."

CHAPTER THIRTEEN

They managed to dodge the first two snakes that swept by them, and Samuel knocked the third one away with his arm.

"Did it bite you?" Zilphia screamed, spitting water out with the words, since the water was now up to her chin.

He shook his head, too exhausted to do any more talking than he had to.

In a few minutes, the fourth rattler, bigger than the others, slammed into Zilphia's shoulder, got caught in the bundled habit, and hung there for a long moment. She let go of the bunched up cloth, and the snake floated away.

Samuel pushed his way over to her.

"He didn't get me," she shouted. "Keep going."

"Maybe they all dead," he said. They moved forward. "Maybe they can't bite in the water," he added.

Zilphia pushed him forward. "Let's not test that theory," she shouted. She turned and looked for Elizabeth. The effort needed to go any further, or the last episode with the snakes, had been too much for her, and she slumped in the water.

They went back and secured her between them. Her head fell against Zilphia's shoulder.

"Leave me here," she said. "I can't . . . ."

Zilphia spat some water out and pushed her head away. "Damn you," she shouted. "*Damn you!*" She pulled Elizabeth forward with such force that it nearly knocked Samuel down. Zilphia tilted her head back and faced the stinging rain and wind. "And damn *you!*"

Samuel stopped wading and watched her, horrified. Elizabeth fell back against him.

"Don't help us!" Zilphia screamed, shaking her fist furiously at the wind. "But leave us be!" She pounded her fist into the water. "Leave us *be!*" She was crying, her tears mixing with the slicing rain. "Leave us be!" She nearly whispered it this time.

They went on, pulling Elizabeth along between them, until they could see the faint, gray outline of the first of the orphanage's buildings, and then the other one.

In a moment, three of the nuns waded out into the yard to help them, and the little group stumbled up on to the porch and through the flooded first floor and up the stairs.

Reverend Mother Camillus cradled Elizabeth in her arms, and closed her eyes. "God has found our lost sheep," she said, "and brought her back to the fold."

Zilphia looked around the big room. The children were huddled together in groups, most of them crying. The wind slammed against the side of the building, and rain blew through broken windows.

She shook her head slowly, and passed out.

Isaac Cline, still on the bed with his wife and daughters, heard someone shouting his name. A man rushed into the room.

"Joseph's here," he cried. "They're helping him up into the house."

"Is he hurt?" Isaac asked, as he hurried through the bedroom door.

"Just wore out, I think," the man said.

He met them at the head of the stairs. Joseph was gasping for breath as they lowered him into a chair. A deep gash on his chin was bleeding.

"Look in that cabinet," Isaac shouted to one of the men, "and get me something to tend to that cut." He gripped his brother's shoulders. "Are you hurt anywhere else?"

Joseph shook his head, and leaned forward. "Should have started sooner," he managed to get said before coughing up some of the water he had swallowed. "Didn't think I'd make it." He looked at his brother. "Didn't think you had made it, either." Then he leaned closer to him. "Most of the houses are breaking up, Isaac," he said, between breaths. "We might be next."

Isaac looked around the room at the people gathered there, then at the door that led to his bedroom, where his children and pregnant wife were. Then he looked back at Joseph.

"There's nothing we can do about it now," he said.

He was holding his spectacles but couldn't remember why. He slipped them into the pocket of his vest.

"Nothing to be done now," he said, perhaps to himself.

The lobby of the Tremont Hotel was so full of people that nobody could move. The stained glass windows in the rotunda, high overhead, were still in place, but several other windows had blown out. Large tables had been maneuvered through the crowd and were being held against the windows to keep the wind and rain out.

When the water rushed up over the high sidewalk, and flowed into the lobby, the hysterical mass of people started pushing up the stairs to the mezzanine.

The two businessmen from north Texas were pushed up with them.

"What now?" one of the men yelled, as he was jostled up the stairs.

The other man knew much about cattle, but nothing about hurricanes. "Just stay with the herd, I imagine," he said.

Quin and his two somber disciples made their slow journey along the flooded sidewalks. He hadn't found a place yet that offered what appeared to be a safe sanctuary. His body ached, the muscles in his legs registering their protest in sharp bursts of pain. The boys kept up with him, never talking, never complaining, never questioning the direction in which he was leading them.

They passed beneath a second story porch which was still intact. It was built into the recesses of a small alley and was out of the brunt of the wind. Several people were on the porch, singing what Quin recognized as a hymn. He looked at the people, then back at the boys.

"They got some room, looks like," he said, and pointed at the porch. "Crawl on up there and you'll be out of the water."

The boys did not move.

"They ain't no better place than that likely to come," he shouted.

The boys looked at the porch, then back at Quin.

"Ain't you goin' up there?" the taller boy asked.

Quin heard the singing, over the whistling wind and roaring water. One of the men on the porch was praying loudly. Quin shook his head. "I been there already," he said.

They continued to look at him.

He waved his crooked hand at the entire situation.

"Damn you," he said, as he kept on his way down the sidewalk.

They followed him, never once looking back at the porch, or its singing congregation.

Now that the Levy Building was rocking in an alarming manner, the lone clerk in the Weather Bureau was having second thoughts about volunteering to stay there. After a few more minutes of the rocking, he decided to try to get to the Tremont, where so many people seemed to be heading.

He didn't have any readings to record, anyway, since all the instruments had blown off the roof long ago. Only a few minutes had passed since he had entered the last wind speed registered before the gauge took flight. He carefully wrote the fatal words in the log.

During the last five minute period, before the instrument was destroyed, the velocity read eighty-four miles an hour. But for two of those minutes, it registered close to one hundred.

Zilphia awoke to Sal's smile.

"You're back," she said. Zilphia wasn't sure if she meant back from her travels, or back to consciousness.

"How are you doing, dear?" she asked, and touched Sal's cheek.

She shrugged. "I'm okay. But Mary and some of the others are pretty scared."

Zilphia sat up and listened to the wind continue to buffet the building. It was shaking now. Then she said the words that she didn't really believe.

"Maybe we're near the end of it. After all, it's been blowing for a long time. Even a storm has to end sometime."

Sal nodded.

"Go on back over to Mary and the children," Zilphia said. "I'll be over there in a minute."

She got up, and found Camillus.

"You did a fine thing," the old woman said, "and a brave one." She still clutched her rosary. Her weary eyes and small slumped body were testaments of her fatigue.

"I couldn't have done it without Samuel," Zilphia said.

Camillus nodded. "You couldn't have done it without God, child."

Zilphia stared at her.

"Surely you see that now."

She took her hand, and led her over to one of the few windows that was still intact. She pointed at the fury outside. Zilphia looked at the rolling waves in the yard.

"It's time," Camillus said, still clutching Zilphia's hand, "for all of us to make our peace with Him."

Zilphia smiled and nodded toward the window. "That doesn't look so peaceful."

Camillus shook her head. "But that's not Him, Zilphia. He *is* peace." She squeezed the hand. "Pray to Him."

Zilphia continued to look out the window. "I—I can't. Something caught her eye in the storm. Something small at first, and then it got bigger.

"Look," she said, and pulled Camillus over beside her. They both squinted their eyes to see it better.

"Someone's coming," Zilphia said.

They went down the stairs, and Zilphia stepped down into the water. She pulled herself along the wall on the porch, and waited for the solitary figure to reach the edge. Then she helped him up.

He was too big to pull up the stairs and too tired to help with the chore, so he lay on the steps, fighting a small battle for each breath.

Several of the nuns and children had appeared at the top of the stairs, and finally Sal worked her way through them to see.

She pushed everyone out of the way as she darted down the stairs. She hugged the man so tight that Zilphia was afraid she might squeeze out what breath was left in him.

They were both crying, and Sal finally sat up and cupped the sides of his face in both her small hands.

"I've been praying," she said, between her sobs, "and sitting real still, like you always say, and you were right." She lifted her eyes up and found Zilphia. She had to catch her breath before she could tell her.

"He always says . . . ," she began and started crying again and buried her face back against his neck. Everyone had to wait a moment to hear the end of it.

"That if you just sit still for long enough . . . ," she finally said. Then she looked at him again, and smiled. "That something good will happen."

He smiled back at her and cried and nodded his head that this was so.

In the very top of the big Kempner house, on Broadway, in the tiny room where the maid lived, Pearl could hear the storm raging outside and feel it pounding against the walls. She had given everybody soup and sandwiches until all the food was gone, and then she came up-stairs. She told Mrs. Ivy that she needed to get something.

Pearl didn't need anything from her room. What she needed was to be away for a few minutes, from Minnie's bickering, and Mrs. Ivy's constant hovering. She needed a quiet moment, to think.

She hadn't been crying, for she wasn't a cryer by nature. She had done enough crying earlier in the week, and was determined to not do any more. For she had seen enough of life in her fifteen years to know that sitting around crying was a waste of time that could be better spent taking some kind of action that might remedy the situation that made you want to cry in the first place. But she was sad. She hadn't formulated any philosophy about being sad.

The little room she was sitting in was the first bedroom she had ever had to herself. But the last few days it had seemed awfully lonely, especially in the late afternoons, with the night coming on, that would remind her of another night.

And then the stars. That would remind her of other stars.

CHAPTER FOURTEEN

PEARL

She always told anyone who asked—provided that she had determined that it was any of their business—that she had grown up at the St. Mary's Orphanage out on the beach road. The truth was that she had done very little of her growing up there. But it sounded good. And she figured that what people didn't know about where she actually grew up wasn't likely to hurt them.

She came to work at the Kempner's, as the maid, in the spring of her fifteenth year. One of the first things Mrs. Ivy asked her was when her birthday was. So Pearl made up a date.

She picked April Tenth, since it was only a few weeks off, and on that date Mrs. Ivy had Minnie make a frosted cake, which Minnie grumbled about, and Mrs. Kempner gave her a present wrapped in white paper, the first she had ever received: a set of combs.

She knew she was fifteen, because one of the whores, a cadaverous old woman who had somehow managed to lose most of her teeth, had told her, five years ago, that she was ten. The whore remembered that she had been born in 1885, but she couldn't remember even the season, much less the date, since she had spent much of that year liquored up, because the love of her life had sailed off to Tahiti and taken up with native girls.

When the position at the Kempner's came open, Mrs. Ivy, who was a good Catholic, had asked Father Kirwin at the cathedral if there were any girls out at the orphanage who were old enough to work. In not too many weeks, Pearl was hired, and had moved all of her possessions in one suitcase that would have still held considerably more things if she had had them.

Mrs. Ivy was awfully nice to her, and patient about teaching her the things she had to do. Mrs. Kempner was good to her, too, and her sons paid hardly any attention to her at all. Tucker always smiled, and asked how she was doing. Minnie's sour disposition was of the sort that Pearl was used to dealing with. She had to bite her tongue a few times to keep from telling the little Irish bitch to shove something or other up her wrinkled ass. But so far she had managed to keep her mouth shut.

At night, Pearl would lie in her bed in the little room at the top of the big house and watch the breeze play through the voile curtain. Sometimes she would hear Mrs. Ivy in her room down the hall, writing letters to her sisters, or humming a song that she was fond of. The big housekeeper went on up to her room every night, except on Saturdays, when she went to the German pavilion to listen to the band that played there, and to drink beer and eat sausages. She met her friend Mr. Kurtz there every week, and then he walked her home, and she climbed up the three flights of stairs, and soon Pearl would hear her snoring, louder than she did on other nights, no doubt due to the beer and sausages.

By the first of summer, Mrs. Ivy began to worry about her and noticed that, other than Sister Zilphia, and Sal, and herself, the girl had no friends at all, and never left the house, even on her half day off, except with Sal, sometimes, to go and wade in the surf.

So, one Saturday afternoon, after Mrs. Ivy had given Tucker and Minnie and her their week's wages, she suggested that she go with her to the German pavilion, to meet Mr. Kurtz, to eat a little bit, and drink some lemonade, and listen to the music.

Pearl didn't want to. But she put on the only dress she owned and let herself get dragged along.

And that was the start of it.

It was a glorious summer night, and darkness had taken a firm hold on the island by the time Mrs. Ivy and Pearl reached the *Garten Verein*, the Garden Club, at 27th Street and Avenue 0. The multi-colored electric lights draped throughout the thick trees in the park that surrounded the huge octagonal dance pavilion twinkled and sway-ed in the slight breeze, and a brass band was working its way through a polka. Waiters moved from table to table, with wide trays of cold sliced meats and cheese on their shoulders. Steins of beer, frothy and overflowing, seemed, to Pearl, to be everywhere, and baskets of coarse looking bread, as black as the night beyond the colored lights. Most everyone here, Mrs. Ivy told her, was German, since it was a German social club, and Pearl supposed that accounted for the red faces everywhere. Mrs. Ivy searched until she found the red face she was looking for, waved, and pulled Pearl over to be introduced.

It didn't take Pearl long to determine that Adolph Kurtz was a man of precious few words. When Mrs. Ivy approached the table, with her in tow, he lifted himself to his full five feet and a few inches, gave a slight bow, and muttered a chopped-off word that might have been hello. Mrs. Ivy sat down beside him, and he gave Pearl a short bit of a smile, then focused his red Teutonic features on the black bread and cheese that he was in the process of eating. Whenever he took a swallow from his stein of beer, he carefully wiped his mouth with the broad napkin he had stuffed into his collar.

Mrs. Ivy told him what a good girl Pearl was and how much help she was to her at the Kempner's. Then she began telling about the horrible day they had both had with Minnie. Mr. Kurtz listened to it all politely and ate his bread and cheese and drank his beer. He motioned for a waiter to bring Mrs. Ivy some beer, and some lemonade for Pearl. The same waiter brought several slices of liverwurst, and Mr. Kurtz and Mrs. Ivy ate it with the bread. Throughout all of this activity, Mrs. Ivy did the only talking that was done, and Pearl was beginning to wonder if Mr. Kurtz knew how to speak English, when he told the waiter to bring more liverwurst. His voice, she noticed, wasn't even heavily accented. She thought it must just be his nature to be quiet.

Mrs. Ivy slapped slices of meat on the thick chunks of bread, handed one to Mr. Kurtz, and took a generous bite, then a deep swallow of her beer. After a week in the house with Minnie, Pearl suspected, she must enjoy spending Saturday nights with a person who didn't have much to say.

The band was playing another polka, and several people were dancing in the pavilion. Pearl turned in her chair and watched some young people playing on the bowling green in the park. The big trees grew so closely together that their thick branches and leaves touched each other, making an uneven roof over much of the neatly trimmed grass and the walkways that wandered through it. The lights twinkled in the trees, and in the big open space next to the pavilion a wide expanse of sky was evident, pocked with real stars that were even prettier, Pearl thought, than their imitations in the trees.

Mrs. Ivy and Mr. Kurtz were busy with their food and drink, and Mrs. Ivy kept the one sided conversation going with occasional comments.

"I think I'll go walk around a little," Pearl said, "if that's all right."

Mrs. Ivy nodded her big head and gave her reply through a mouthful of liverwurst and bread. "You go right along, honey, and find yourself somebody to dance with." She shushed her away with her hand.

Pearl scooted her chair back, and got up. Mr. Kurtz removed the napkin from his collar, and stood up, too. He gave his little bow again. She sort of bowed back, figuring that if she said anything, he would feel obliged to say something too.

She walked along one of the brick walkways, taking it all in. The place was full of girls, dressed all in white, with bonnets and bows. Just the hats, Pearl guessed, had cost more than the dress she was wearing. The men wore summer suits and laughed politely when the girls said things. Several young people were gathered around one of the bowling greens. The men were putting on their coats at the end of a match. Pearl stopped in the shadow of one of the gigantic trees and watched.

"It never would have been any contest at all if it hadn't been for my wrist," the tallest of the young men was saying, as he flexed his hand up and down. The girls laughed. "Now, I'm serious," he said, in a voice that Pearl thought said he was not. "I've been working so hard at saving lives that I think I've picked up a touch of rheumatism."

There was more laughter, and another young man buttoned his coat. "No more work than you do, I wouldn't be surprised if that hand was suffering from lack of exercise."

The tall young man took empty glasses from two pretty girls in flawless white dresses. The girls joined the others and walked toward the pavilion.

Pearl stood in the shadows and watched him come toward her. His attention was on the four glasses he carried, and he didn't see her until he was beside her.

"Hello," he said, barely slowing down.

She smiled; he moved on. "I know who you are," she said. He stopped, and turned to look at her.

"You're one of the helpers at the infirmary." She stepped out into the light.

He shook his head. "Now I'm found out," he said.

"I saw you there when my friend Sal got stung by a jellyfish, you and one of those others." She pointed toward the group that was disappearing into the pavilion across the lawn.

"That's Scott," he said. "I'm James Tuttle." He held out the bottom of one of the glasses that he was holding with a thumb. Pearl wasn't sure what to do at first, then, when he jabbed it a couple of times in her direction, she shook it, like a hand. She smiled.

"I remember you now," James said. "You came in with that nun from the orphanage—who I was the first person to welcome to Galveston, by the way—and the little girl. She had an awful sting."

"She's better now," Pearl said.

James laughed. "Well, I hope so. That's been weeks ago. If I were to let somebody die from a jellyfish bite, I wouldn't be much of a doctor, don't you think?"

Pearl smiled again. It seemed easy to smile when listening to him. He couldn't be over twenty, she thought. "Sister Zilphia said you're not any doctor."

He gave an outraged look. "Did Sister Zilphia ever ask to see a diploma?" He shook his head, and nearly dropped a couple of the glasses. "Maybe we ought to ask to see *her* credentials; maybe she's not even a nun."

Without thinking about it, and without realizing that she was doing it, Pearl was laughing. She held her hands to her mouth.

James smiled back at her. "Well, anyway, I'm *going* to be a doctor. That's why I practice on children that get dragged in by nuns. If I were to mess up and let some rich and important person die, there's no telling how long that would set me back in my doctoring plans."

He looked at her and at her dress.

"Is your father a member here?" he asked her.

She shook her head. "I'm here with the housekeeper at the place where I work. Her friend is a member."

He nodded. "I'm a friend of a friend of a member myself." He looked around, and leaned closer to her. "I'm not even German," he whispered.

She smiled. "Me, neither." She could smell a faint trace of gin on his breath. Her mother used to drink gin, and she recognized it. She supposed that he was on his way to splash a little in the glasses to be filled with lemonade.

"Well," he said, "since we're both here under false pretenses, let's try to have a little fun before they toss us out with the stale beer." He tilted his head in the direction of the pavilion. It glowed like a gigantic lantern, framed by the soft greenery and twinkling lights of the trees. "When I've collected these drinks, I'm going over there with some other folks, and we intend to dance. Why don't you join us?"

Pearl shook her head. "I don't think so," she said.

"Now listen here . . . ," James said, and thought. "What's your name, by the way?"

"Pearl," she said. "Pearl Hart."

Well, listen here, Pearl Hart. There's a fine band in there, and lots of room to dance, and everybody's had so much beer that they wouldn't even care if they knew we're not even Germans. What do you say? Just one little dance."

She shook her head, again. "I don't want to."

James smiled. "Don't you know how to dance?"

She could feel herself blushing. "And what if I don't?" she almost blurted out, with more force than she had intended. "I never had any time to go dancing. I have to work for a living."

"Well," he said, "I, for one, don't do any work myself. I just spend all of my time down at the infirmary dancing with the patients."

She tried not to smile, but it was hard not to smile around him.

"Even the ones that are crippled," he went on, "I just get Scott to hold them up so I can dance with them, too." He stopped for a minute. The empty glasses he held reflected the various colors of the electric lights. "You know, in addition to being a great healer, I happen to be quite famous as a teacher of dance."

"Is that right?" Pearl said.

"Oh, yes m'am. Folks come from all over, and some just pay to watch. So, what do you say, Pearl Hart? How about a free lesson?"

She looked at the pavilion, bright and colorful across the lawn, and listened to the festive music and the laughter and chatter that came from it. "Not tonight," she finally said. "Mrs. Ivy will be ready to go soon, and I . . ."

Someone called James's name. One of the girls in the perfect white dresses came quickly down the path. "Where in the world have you been?" she called, before she got to them. "We've all been waiting, and Daddy is asking about you."

She stood before them now and looked at the empty glasses in James's hands. Pearl thought she must be about his age.

"I was just visiting for a minute," he said. "Mary, this is Miss Pearl Hart, and she's . . ."

"We're ready to dance," the girl said, then looked at Pearl for the first time. Pearl could feel her gaze, as it swept over her dress. "Could you hurry with those, please?" Not waiting for an answer, she turned, and swept away in the direction from which she had come, the pure whiteness of her long dress floating through the park like a cloud. Pearl and James looked at each other.

"I guess you better go on and get your lemonade," she said.

He looked at the glasses, then back at her. "I'm sorry about that," he said. "Mary's not usually like that. I kind of grew up knowing her. Her family and mine have been friends for a long time." He clinked the glasses. "Anyway, I apologize for her behavior."

"It don't matter," Pearl said.

James looked at her eyes. "Yes, it does. People shouldn't treat other people like that." He looked at her again. "I wish you would come. If for no other reason than to see that Mary's not a dragon all the time."

She looked at the ground and shook her head.

"Then how about next week. I'll be here next Saturday night too."

He maneuvered the glasses into the crook of one arm, and took her hand with his. "Come then, Pearl Hart. I won't let you go till you say you will." He squeezed her hand a little.

She looked into eyes that couldn't be more than five years older than her own. But this young man seemed to be bathed in a confidence and charm like she had never seen before.

"You'll drop all those glasses, if you're not careful," she said.

He didn't let go of her hand. "These glasses belong to the Germans; I'll bet they break more than these every time they start dancing to that Polka music."

They were both quiet for a moment.

"Maybe I'll come," she said. "That's a whole week off. I don't know what I'll be doing by then."

He let go of her hand, and turned away. He was already moving away from her when he shouted back the last words. "That means yes, Pearl Hart; I know it does." Because he was still looking at her, he almost collided with a couple on the walk. He apologized and kept on his way.

A week later, Pearl stood under the same tree. She hadn't made up her mind to come until just that afternoon, and had asked Mrs. Ivy if she would take her again. The housekeeper nearly knocked a tea kettle over in her excitement, and had brought the girl along with her, the scent of violets from her toilet water wafting along behind them.

Pearl sat at the table and watched Mrs. Ivy and Mr. Kurtz drink their beer and eat their sausage and bread for long enough to be polite, and then found her place under her tree. She watched the dancers in the pavilion and listened to the music and wondered if James was in there, dancing with one of the girls in the perfect white dresses.

She had thought about him from time to time during the week, as she went about her work at the Kempners. He wasn't on her mind all the time, or even close to it, but sometimes, as she was dusting the knickknacks on the tables in the parlor or making the beds upstairs or hanging out the wash in the back yard, she remembered something funny that he had said, and she smiled, and sometimes even laughed. She knew, from the expensive suit that he had been wearing, and the fancy folks he associated with, that he might have grown up in a house like the Kempners'. Besides, she knew, only people with money got to study to be doctors. The probability of the girl that he had been with last week being there again, to look down her nose at her cheap dress, had nearly kept her from coming. But the memory of James's laugh, and his funny remarks, had been the deciding factor. Besides, if the girl said too much to her, there wasn't anything to keep her from telling her to go to hell, and to take her white dress with her.

Pearl had told people to go to hell before, even when she lived at the orphanage, and had faced the wrath of the nuns for it. Especially Sister Mendulla, the one with the scar all over her scowling face, who looked for any reason to deal out wrath.

The branches of the big trees made long, weaving shadows on the lawn, like veins in the marble floor of the entryway at the Kempners. Pearl watched the lucky young people move across the lawn and knew that she would never be any more a part of their world than a servant in one of their houses. But just to watch it and touch it every once in a while on Saturday nights, when the band was playing and the lights were twinkling, was enough.

"Well, look here," he said, behind her, "if it isn't Miss Pearl Hart."

She must have jumped when he said it, because he laughed a little. "I didn't mean to sneak up on you," he said. "I imagine you thought I was one of the members, wanting to throw you out, because of you not being a German."

She smiled and straightened the bow on her dress. "No, I . . . ." She caught her breath. "I was just looking over there, and not expecting you."

"Well, why weren't you expecting me? I told you I'd be here, didn't I?"

She nodded.

"I generally pop up, when I'm supposed to, whether folks want me to or not."

"I'll try to remember that," she said.

She stood quiet for a moment, trying to think of something to say. When she was anywhere else, she didn't ever have a problem with it, but words didn't seem to come all that easily around this boy.

"Did you save any lives this week?" she finally asked.

"Not as many as usual, only about five. It was a slow week." He reached for her hand, and pulled her out of the shadows. "Now, look here," he said, "this dress is just as pretty as the one you had on last week."

She didn't tell him that it was the same dress. with a new bow at the middle. "It's not anything as nice as all of these girls have on."

He looked across the lawn at some of the girls. "Those things?" he said. "They're all exactly alike, like looking at a bunch of ducks on a pond. You can't tell one from the other."

It was quiet again, and they listened to the music.

He was still holding her hand. "Well, Pearl Hart, what do you say we go and have your dancing lesson?"

She looked at the pavilion full of people.

"Are your friends in there?" she asked.

He smiled. "They didn't come tonight, because they had to set dinner for President McKinley or the Prince of Wales or somebody. So just old Scott and I came down. He's over there somewhere filling his face with beer and sausage, I suspect."

She looked at him. He was as handsome tonight as he had been last week—she hadn't been mistaken about that. Her hand felt good in his.

"I don't want you to teach me in there," she said, pointing at the pavilion. "We can hear the music real good out here. Can't you teach me here, where everybody won't be looking at us?"

He bowed to her. "Whatever you say, Pearl Hart. But only on one condition. That when you get good at it, as you surely will, with me being your teacher, you'll dance with me in the pavilion."

"But that won't be tonight," she said quickly. "I can't get that good in one night."

"It may be, but if not, that's fine." He smiled, and squeezed her hand a little. "There's lots of nights."

They found an open space, away from the trees and their lights. James put his hand on her side, and lifted her other hand away from them. She was awkward at first, but began to get better by their second attempt. Soon, she fell in step with the music, and thought she had the knack of it.

James went to get them some drinks, and she rested on a bench. He sat down with her when he got back and handed her a glass. It didn't have any gin in it, just lemonade.

They sat for a moment. "How old are you?" she asked.

He crunched on some ice from his drink. "I'm either fifty-two or fifty-three. I've lost count." He watched her while she laughed. "How old are you? About forty?"

"I'm fifteen," she said, figuring it wouldn't do any good to lie about it.

"Fifteen," he repeated, and nodded, as if thinking about it. "That's a good age. I was fifteen, myself." He leaned over to her, and whispered. "I'm really nineteen. But I have all the folks at the infirmary thinking I'm older, so they'll let me do my doctoring."

The band started playing a pretty song. "That's a Strauss," James said. "He's a German, so I guess they try to throw him a little business. Do you like it?" She nodded that she did.

"Come on, then," he said, and led her back to their open place.

"This is a waltz," he said, "and has lots of turning. Are you ready?"

Every Saturday night, all through the summer, they met at the *Garten Verien* and danced. On the third week, he brought her flowers that he had picked from someone's bushes on the way there, and on the fourth week, under the electric lights that twinkled in the trees, he kissed her, gently and for longer than she had expected. On the eighth week, he asked her to go to dinner with him at Ritter's, and when she told him that her friend Sal always talked about Ritter's, because she liked to look into their windows, at the fancy tables and place settings, he suggested that they take her along.

That very week, they went. Sal sat quiet and small in the back seat of the rig that James had rented, and she and Pearl didn't have to do any talking, since James rattled on all the way across town.

Once there, Sal's eyes grew wider than they had been. She ran her finger around the smooth rim of the large plate in front of her enough times to know that there were no nicks there, and looked constantly around her, at the fresh cut flowers on the tables, at the white tablecloths, and at the waiters, in their white jackets, as they balanced the large trays of food above them. Even the disassembling of the starched, perfectly white napkin that had been standing on the surface of the plate commanded Sal's full attention. She took her time opening it, like peeling away the layers of skin on an onion, and Pearl knew that she was committing the folds to memory.

The menus their waiter brought were almost as big as newspapers.

"Why don't you order for me, James?" Pearl said. "You know what's good."

"Me, too," Sal said, and closed the menu.

James studied the choices. "Well, now, let's see," he said, "we could get us a mess of snails, if we wanted to . . . ." He looked over the top of the menu at the girls. "I don't much believe I want to, how about you two?"

Not waiting for an answer, he went on down the list of selections. "Here's something about rabbit. It says *if available*. So I guess if some rabbits hopped up to the kitchen door this morning, we can have some of that."

The girls laughed.

"I've eaten rabbit meat in stews," James said, "but I don't think this is a stew. It's got some French words after it, and I never heard about French folks eating many stews."

Pearl wasn't particularly interested in eating a rabbit. But if she was going to, she hoped it wasn't in a stew, since Minnie made stew at the Kempner's pretty often.

James looked up. "Now let's see, you're both Catholic, aren't you? So you have to eat a fish on Fridays. But this is a Monday. Do you have to eat any special kind of an animal on Mondays?"

They smiled, and shook their heads.

"I'm Episcopal, myself, and can eat anything I want to, any day of the week, though I draw the line at snails." He looked back at the menu. "Now, here we go. Here's roasted suckling pig, served up with potatoes and a cranberry and cinnamon apple sauce." He looked at them, again. "Neither one of you has any Jewish blood mixed in with your Catholic, do you?"

They shook their heads again.

"Well," he said, and closed the menu, "we can eat some of a pig, I guess, and not violate anybody's religion." He waved to their waiter and ordered the meal.

While they waited for their dinner, James talked about saving a couple of lives down at the infirmary that day, and Pearl laughed and said he ought to keep a record of all the lives he saved, since he might be in line for a medal or reward or something. Sal sat quietly across from them, and continued to look at everything.

The waiter brought their dinner, already served up on plates, which he traded out with the clean plates in front of them. Sal ran her finger around the rim of the new plate, and found no nicks on it either. Pearl studied the carefully arranged food. The slice of pork was covered with the cranberry and apple sauce, and several of the smallest potatoes she had ever seen, perfectly round and sprinkled with little bits of chopped green leaves, sat beside it.

The food was perfect, as Pearl knew it would be. The bread was soft, and the butter as sweet as sugar. The little potatoes were moist, their red skins so tender and delicate they could have been painted on them. The meat was juicy, and its outside was roasted to a crunchy, buttery texture. She tried to eat a little of the crust with each bite, and let it rest on her tongue long enough to savor it. Even the water in the crystal goblet tasted better than any she had ever had, though she didn't imagine there was much even the cooks at Ritter's could do to water to make it taste better than it already did.

She had some difficulty with her silverware once and catapulted one of the little round potatoes out into the center of the table. James stabbed it with his fork and said that if she didn't like his stories, she didn't have to resort to throwing food, but could just tell him. They all laughed, and James ate the potato.

When they were done, and the girls had laid their knives and forks in their plates as James had done, he signaled for the waiter, who came over and asked how they had enjoyed it.

James patted at his mouth with the edge of his napkin, folded it, and put it on the table.

"I don't know about these ladies," he said, "but I believe that was the best roasted suckling pig in cranberry sauce that I've had today."

Then he said to the waiter, "Now, look here, what's the chances of you having a big chocolate layer cake back there somewhere, with lots of thick, gooey icing all over it?"

The waiter said he had just noticed one on his way out.

"Well," James said, "I've been told that we have a great lover of chocolate with us here tonight, so I guess you'd better bring a big piece of it."

He asked Pearl if she'd like some, too, but she smiled at Sal, and said she was too full to eat it.

"I'm full, too," Sal said. "I don't need any."

James held up his hand. "No, mam. Anybody that loves something as much as Pearl says you love chocolate ought not be denied it." He nodded at the waiter, and he carried the plates away.

The wedge of cake, when it was placed in front of Sal, was huge, and moist, with tiny flakes of dark chocolate sprinkled on it. Sal touched it with her fork, and looked up. "There's an awful lot here," she said. "Why don't you two help me eat it?"

James shook his head. "I don't eat cake very often," he said. "I'm already sweet enough." He winked at Pearl.

"I want just a bite of it," Pearl said, and reached over with her fork. "Just to see if it's as good as it looks."

James picked up the small wrapped chocolate from beside his coffee cup. "See," he said, "everybody always tries to stuff sugar into me." He laid it beside Sal's plate. "You take that along for later."

She grinned at Pearl, thanked him for it, and put it in her purse.

The people at the other tables chattered away, and the waiters went back and forth with their trays, and James kept up his constant banter while he sipped at his coffee. But Pearl didn't see or hear much of it. Her entire attention was focused on Sal eating the cake. By the time she was aware of a new voice, and had looked up to see who it was, James was already on his feet, introducing them to the speaker.

She was a pretty girl, the one that had been at the *Garten Verien* on that first night. She was wearing the nicest dress Sal had ever seen. The girl gave a brief nod in Pearl's and Sal's direction, barely enough of one to acknowledge their existence, then turned her attention back to James.

"We haven't seen much of you lately," she said. "Daddy's been asking about you."

He said something about having been busy. Pearl noticed that he wasn't speaking as loud or as cheerfully as he had been.

The girl looked back at the girls, and at the half eaten cake in front of Sal. She asked if this was a birthday party.

James was still standing. He said that it wasn't.

"Do these little girls work for you at the infirmary?" the girl asked.

He frowned. "I'm an orderly, Mary. Nobody works for me. These are friends of mine. We came in for dinner."

She smiled and looked at Pearl for a moment.

"You're off to Beaumont soon, I think," the girl said, turning back to James.

"On Saturday, but just for a few days. Classes start soon."

She smiled. "Well, I'd better get back over there. Daddy's anxious to order." She looked back at Pearl. "You've got a little chocolate on your mouth, dear," she said. Pearl didn't move, or look at the girl. "I hope your dancing is coming along all right."

The girl took James's hand in hers. "You be sure to give my love to your family." She started to go, then turned back to him. "I assume you'll find some time to spend with Alice. After all, a man should do a little dancing with his fiancee from time to time."

She smiled at the girls, and walked away.

James stood for a moment, then sat down. Sal laid her fork beside the unfinished cake and looked at it. Then she looked at Pearl, who was staring at the folded napkin still in her lap. The minuscule smudge of chocolate was still on her lip.

They all sat quietly for a long moment. Sal looked at the large windows and at the people on the sidewalk, and Pearl knew that she wished she were out there, looking in.

Pearl wished she were out there, too. Out there where she belonged, on the other side of the bright lights that shone in the windows, away from the people who were eating at the tables, and talking of things that she could never have, or even understand.

The short ride from Ritter's to the building on Ship's Mechanic Street where Sal lived was a quiet one. The buggy's wheels clattered along, and the horse's hooves clopped on the pavement. The horse broke wind once, and Pearl almost wished he would do it again, just to add a little racket to the mute procession.

Pearl sat beside James, because she had sat there on the way to the restaurant, and Sal sat in the seat behind them, clutching her purse in her lap. She leaned forward only once, to show him the building, and let him help her down when they had come to a stop in front of it. She never quite looked at him when she said she had an awfully good time and enjoyed the dinner, and the cake, and thanked him for taking her with them. She looked at Pearl, who didn't look back at her, and told her good night, and that she'd be seeing her soon, she hoped. Pearl nodded, and smiled at her, and said she was glad she had gone with them.

They watched until Sal went up the stoop and into the building, then James clicked at the horse and jerked on the reins enough to get him going. When they were on Broadway, and heading back toward the Kempner house, he said that he was sorry that the evening had turned out badly, and that he wanted to explain something to her.

"Just take me home," she said, and kept her eyes on the street in front of them.

They rode between the big houses along the street, the buggy staying close to the esplanade in its center. As they came to a stop in front of the Kempner house, the horse broke wind again, louder this time, then plopped a mound of steaming manure on the pavement.

Pearl started to get out, and he grabbed her arm.

"At least let me tell you about it," he said. She tried to pull away, but he held tight, so she sat back against the seat's cushion.

"You haven't got anything to tell," she said. "You're gonna get married, that's all. There's nothing illegal about that. People do it all the time."

"But that's just the thing," he said, still holding on to her arm, "I'm *not* getting married."

She looked at him, then shook her head from side to side. "Then why did that girl . . ."

James waved the notion of the girl away with his other hand. "She's just . . . ." He hesitated, trying to locate the words that would best describe Mary. He found at least two, but common decency kept him from using those. ". . . just wrong, that's all. I've never asked anybody to marry me, and that's the truth."

Pearl looked back at her folded hands in her lap.

"There *is* a girl in Beaumont," he said. "Her name is Alice, and I've known her my whole life. Our families are friends, and everybody just always thought the two of us would . . . end up together." He watched Pearl's hands, as she fidgeted with her nervous fingers. "I thought so, too," he said, "for a long time." He looked, now, at her face, pretty and soft in the pale light of a street lamp. "But not now. I'd already decided to tell her that next week when I go there." He glanced down at his feet, and waited a moment, to make sure he said exactly what he wanted to say. "I had decided to tell her about the special girl I've been dancing with all these weeks."

He cupped his fingers under her chin and turned her face toward him. "That's the God's truth, Pearl Hart, and I swear it is. I've known all along that it wasn't right with Alice and me." He smiled. "It's not like I didn't give it enough time. I tried that one for my whole life, and I've only known you a couple of months."

Pearl shook her head, not knowing what to think. They sat quietly for a moment. The horse, through with his business, stood still. A dog barked down the street; another one answered him.

"What about that girl, Alice, and her family? And yours? Won't they all be mad?"

He thought, too. "Our folks will be disappointed," he said, after a minute. "And surprised, I guess, to find out their plan didn't pan out." Then he smiled, again. "To tell you the truth, Alice will probably be relieved. All this time she's had to follow me around, and write letters to me, and give me presents she didn't even pick out. Why, I imagine . . . ."

He stopped when he saw that Pearl was crying. Not sobbing quietly, but actually crying, the force of her weeping racking her so that she was rocking back and forth in the buggy seat. She had to catch her breath when she finally spoke.

"You think you've got it all figured out," she managed between heaves and sniffles. She pushed away the handkerchief James was trying to hand to her. "You figure you'll just tell that girl you changed your mind, and everything will be all right." She looked at him, now, tears running down her face. "Well, you better do some more thinking."

She almost choked now and had to wait for a moment before continuing. The words, when they came, were pushed in between the crying.

"Don't be stupid," she said. "Do you think your folks are going to throw a big party, so all their rich friends can meet the little house-maid that James brought home. Maybe that girl will be there, to laugh at my dress, and tell me I've got chocolate on my face."

"Now listen here," James said, "none of that matters any. If you and me . . . ." He reached for her hand; she pushed it away.

"But they're ain't any *you and me*," she shouted. "Can't you even see that? They're can't ever be any *you and me*, James. Not ever."

Before he knew it, she was standing beside the buggy, still crying, her lower lip shaking up and down, like the bobbin on a sewing machine.

"I wouldn't ever fit into those fancy places. I'd have to watch you all the time, just to know what fork to use, or how to pick up a glass, or . . ."

"All that stuff's not important," he said. "I don't even know all of it myself."

She stepped closer to the buggy and reached up to hold his hand in hers.

"Yes, you do, James." She lifted his hand and held it beside her face. "You've always known about it. Because that's who you are. And I'm who I am." She looked at him. He seemed about ready to do a little crying of his own.

"I know you weren't lying to me about Alice," she said. "And I know why that girl did what she did. But don't you see, James, they'll always be her, or somebody like her, to tell me to wipe my face, or to get a better dress, or to stand up straighter, or whatever. And, sooner or later, I'd get tired of it and tell them all to go . . . somewhere else, and then you'd start wondering what kind of a girl you'd ended up with."

He started to protest, but she put her finger to his lips to stop him. "Yes you would." She ran her finger beside his eye, and down his face. She made a low, shushing sound, as if she were encouraging a baby to settle down. "You would," she whispered. He dropped his head.

"And then we'd both be unhappy, I guess," she said, rubbing the back of his neck.

He kept his head down. "I don't see where other people ought to matter at all, or dresses, or forks, or anything. If we want to . . ."

She spoke loudly now, and the dogs started barking again. She had stopped crying for a moment. "You weren't the only one trying to keep a secret. I was, too." She saw his puzzled look, after he had a moment to think about it. "No," she said, and almost smiled, "it's not a boy. No decent boy would come within a mile if they knew about me."

James watched her. A new light had come into her eyes, as if some hidden well of energy had been tapped.

"You think I grew up at the St. Mary's orphanage, don't you? Because that's what I let you think." She slowly shook her head. "I was only there a couple of years, after my mother died." She stood up straighter to tell it. "I grew up on Postoffice street, in the back room of a place you'd never want to see." She stopped, to let that sink in. "I had to lay there at night, James, and listen to my mother . . . working, in the next room."

He stared at her, not moving, hardly breathing.

As she told the rest of it, the racking sobs slowly worked their way back, causing her to pause to breathe, and cry, every few words.

"My father was one of her customers. She never even knew which one. I grew up eating at the table with whores, and we didn't have but one fork each to choose from, and not any napkin to keep folded in our lap. All the napkins in that place were used for washing the sailors, to keep them from killing the whores with the diseases they brought there with them."

James was shaking his head now, and telling her to stop. But she couldn't have if she'd wanted to.

"I never had to work there, myself. I was too little, and the old woman that ran the place knew that the law would close her down. Policemen came there all the time, but as customers. So I never had to do what my mother did." Tears were running down her face now, and it was harder to get the words out. "But I got looked at enough, by every man that came through there, and they all hugged me, and ran their filthy hands into my dress."

She stepped away from the buggy. "So that's what you'd be getting, James," she said. "That's what you'd be taking home and dressing up in a white dress, and showing off to your family, and to that girl."

He was shaking his head, again, trying to make her stop.

"A little whorehouse brat," she choked out, "that's what you'd have to be so proud about." She was standing near the gate now, the new onslaught of crying racking her body. She pointed both hands back at herself. "I can't even read, James." She erupted into the gasping, frantic sobs that he had heard sick babies make in the infirmary. "I can't even write you a letter . . . ."

She turned, then, and ran through the gate, and around the side of the house to the kitchen door.

Inside, she leaned against the window, and watched James sit there in the buggy for a long while before he tapped the horse with the reins and headed in the direction of the place where he had rented the rig.

Pearl lay in her bed that night in her small room at the top of the Kempner house and closed her eyes and tried to think of something other than James. But all that would come into her mind was that second night at the *Garten Verien*, when she had first danced with him.

It had been a hot night, with not much of a breeze, and the sweat on their faces glistened. She looked, once, into his eyes, and saw him looking into hers. Then his cheek was beside hers. She fell into the rhythm of his dancing and it suddenly seemed effortless, as easy as walking down a street.

The Strauss waltz, prettier than anything she had ever heard, lifted up through the thick canopy of leaves in the big trees, and they moved in wide circles on the lawn. His face stayed next to hers, and his hand cupped her side.

Pearl had been dragged off to Mass every Sunday when she lived at the orphanage. She had never been impressed with the slow moving ritual, conducted by priests who appeared to be about as interested in it as she was, and with their backs to her for most of it. But she liked the rows upon rows of little candles in the corner of the cathedral, and the flickering light they gave to the dark place. She liked to squint her eyes during the Mass, and look at the candles, so that they became a multitude of bright pinpoints, winking at her in the dark.

Dancing with James, she had squinted her eyes like that, against the cool sweat of his face, as they swirled around in slow, full circles. And the stars in the giant summer sky looked, to Pearl, like all the candles of all the altars of every church in the world.

CHAPTER FIFTEEN

Galveston's people huddled in the upper stories of buildings and houses as the savage wind stabbed all around and above them and the raging water surged below. Many prayers were sent up, some frantically, some tranquilly. Some people hadn't prayed in so long that they had forgotten how, and stumbled over words that they hoped were right. Others had prayed for so long that every heartbeat and breath was a prayer. They didn't ask for anything now, but waited for whatever the night would bring.

Those people close enough to windows, usually broken ones, could see the cataclysm taking place outside. Bodies, of people and of horses, pounded against the sides of buildings—some were caught in the piles of wreckage. Entire buildings, or houses, would suddenly crumble, as if some all-important beam had snapped, and a flood-tide of bricks and lumber would boil out into the streets. The people in the top floors spilled out with the debris. Sometimes fifty or more men, women, and children would end up, within seconds, in the rushing water. Some were killed in the structure's collapse, some by flying wreckage. Some were so stunned by the fall that they drowned before they could right themselves, and some made it into the next building, hoping that it would prove sturdier than the last.

Some who were catapulted into the tempest searched for wives or husbands or children. Few found them, since the water was moving so swiftly. More than one parent, having watched their family die, gave themselves up to the fury around them and let themselves be swept to whatever fate awaited them.

Darkness began to fall on the island, which was no longer an island, but part of the sea. The people huddled in the tops of buildings and houses became aware of the fading light. They scrunched closer to their family or friends or, sometimes, complete strangers. Everyone was tired and hungry and afraid, and everyone wanted the assurance of other people next to them. Children cried, and many adults. Almost everyone prayed. Some sang.

The wind was blowing harder, and more structures were falling apart. The people huddled in the tops of buildings and houses had encountered this particular hell for hours, and now they must face it in darkness.

And hope that their building was a sound one.

One person not in the top of a building was Tucker, who was in the bottom of one, since that was where his home was, in the room that opened into the alley.

He had moved from the bed to the top of the table, and, when the brown water rose even to that height, to the top of the wide, tall chest of drawers that Mae had inherited from her mother. The water was almost to the top drawer now, just a few inches beneath him. There wasn't anyplace higher in the room to get, and, even if there had been, he wouldn't have been able to get there because he would have been crammed into the ceiling.

Other pieces of furniture bobbed up and down, like corks on fishing lines, and bumped against the walls. The dark, frothy water swirled around in the room, looking for someplace to go.

Tucker knew that soon he would have to wade through it, out into the alley, and then to the sidewalk, and do the same thing.

When James and Scott had finally returned from their futile journey to the Union Passenger Depot, early in the afternoon, having fought the storm across the city and back, James thought he had never been so tired. Then, after they had carried and guided the over one hundred patients from the doomed county hospital over to the St. Mary's Infirmary, he knew that he had endured levels of exhaustion that he hoped to never come close to again.

When the job was finally completed, there hadn't been beds available for them to collapse into, so they stretched out on the tops of two tables in an upstairs supply room. They didn't talk, but just lay there, happy, for the moment, to not be moving and carrying people and wading in water or climbing stairs.

Scott slept for a while and woke up to see an empty tabletop where James had been. He leaned up to a sitting position, and tried to stretch some life back into his spent muscles. He stumbled to the door and saw his friend standing with a nun and two patients down the hall. He recognized the two men—he had guided them both through the high water. For once, James wasn't doing the talking.

"We can't let you leave," the nun was saying, "and that's the end of it."

"That ain't the end of it," one of the men said. "Our families are out there, and we've got to get to them."

"You *can't* get to them," the nun said. "You just came in out of that water and wind, and you know that."

The other man, who had kept quiet till now, touched her arm.

"It's our families, Sister," he said, quietly. "Our people." He hesitated for a moment. "We know we might not make it, but . . . ." The others could tell that he wasn't used to doing much talking. He seemed to be weighing every word, before he used it. "Sometimes, you got to be with the people you care about, and need to look after." He looked at the other man, and lowered his eyes, as if he were embarrased to be saying such things out loud. "We got to try."

The nun still shook her head, but more slowly. "I can't stop you, I suppose, but I . . . ."

"I'll go with them," James said. All three of them turned toward him, as if they hadn't been aware that he was there.

Scott was standing beside him now. James looked at him.

"It's ten or more blocks over there," Scott said.

James nodded. "I guess I've eaten enough fish this summer," he said, "that I ought to be able to swim like one." He shook Scott's hand and went toward the stairs with the two men.

The nun started to go after them, but Scott grabbed her arm.

"But where does he think *he's* going?" she asked.

Scott watched as they went down the stairs. One of the two men, who had only recently had surgery on his foot, was limping.

"Where he feels like he has to, Sister," he said. He smiled. "But not to Beaumont, I'll bet."

The nun gazed at him and wondered if all of his heroics had affected his thinking.

Anyone trying to get to Beaumont tonight, she knew, might as well be trying to get to Egypt.

The people huddled in one of the big rooms on the second floor of the St. Mary's orphanage knew that, though it seemed impossible, the storm was even stronger now than it had been. The two long buildings sat by themselves, with no trees or houses to buffer the savage wind before it got to them. Only the lonely dunes had stood sentinel against the sea, and they had long since been washed completely away.

The building swayed this way and that, its wooden beams and timbers groaning as the storm hurled its fiercest wrath against it. Everything shook, and the planks of the floor jerked up and down in tiny, individual bursts of movement, like piano keys being played.

Thurmon had both arms around Sal, who had hers locked around Wee Mary. Sisters Zilphia and Elizabeth sat in the center of groups of children, many of them crying, some having cried themselves out. Five other nuns sat with more clusters. Sister Catherine, who loved to sing, attempted to get a song started, but hardly anybody had joined in. When she found that she was the only one singing, Catherine sang louder, rather than stopping, and the cadence of the pretty hymn rose above the crying of the children.

"You ought to sing with her, Pa," Sal said and leaned her head back against his chest. She was so afraid, her small teeth were clicking agaist each other. She tried to make them stop.

Thurmon hugged her closer and listened to the hymn. "I don't know that one, Sweet Potato. And it's far and away prettier than any of my songs." He combed her hair with his hand. "Why don't you sing it?"

She shook her head and tried to keep her fear out of her voice. "I can't sing."

Margaret, who was sitting beside them, nodded in agreement. "Naw," she said. "She can't. She tried to sing to us one day and near made some of the little kids cry."

Thurmon needed a drink. Badly. He knew that some of the shaking he was doing wasn't caused by the lively floorboards and the shifting building. He knew, too, that the small bottle of brandy that Minnie had given him was still in his pocket. Only once, during his long, difficult journey from town, had he stopped to drink some of it. There was plenty left.

The room lurched to one side, sending several children rolling along the floor. The crying became louder, and some of the children screamed. The nuns gathered them back close to them.

Thurmon hugged Sal and Mary closer and reached out his hand to hold on to Margaret and closed his eyes. His father would have known exactly what to do in such a situation, he knew, and would have taken charge of the terrified assembly and done it. But Thurmon didn't know what to do, other than hold tight to the most precious thing in his life, the only thing he had managed to do right. He'd leave the bottle of brandy alone for now, and try to keep his wits about him.

Mother Camillus stared anxiously out the side window at the other building, which she could barely see through the blowing rain. Several of the horrified children had tried to make their way to this building a while ago, and most of them had made it. She watched at least four of them as they fell and were swept quickly away in the surging flood. Zilphia had had to physically restrain her from going after them, telling her what she already knew, that there was no way she could get to them. That the water was moving so fast that the children were already dead, more than likely. And that if she went, she too would die, just as quickly, and what good would that do, Zilphia had wanted to know, when she would soon be needed here? Mendulla was still over there with the children that had stayed with her and the other two nuns. Camillus searched the dark outline of the structure, desperately trying to see any sign of life through its blown out windows. But she saw only darkness.

Then the entire building that she was watching rocked suddenly backward, and lifted itself up, higher into the dark night than she would have thought possible for it to go. After teetering there for a long moment, it crumbled in on itself.

The old woman watched in horror as it fell away, and then it was simply not there. She listened for the noise that it must be making, and for the shouts of its occupants. But all she heard was the storm.

Camillus managed to get to her feet and hold onto the wall that was pitching more terribly now. They only had one chance left, she knew, other than the prayers that she had been silently mouthing for hours.

"Now!" she screamed. "Do it *now!*"

The nuns knew what to do, for she had told them how to do it earlier. They reached for the lengths of clothesline that she had sent Samuel out to fetch that afternoon from the storage shed, long before it had blown away.

Frantically, each nun tied the children closest to her together with the line, looped its end around her waist, and secured it to her belt. Most of the children were in enough of a state of shock by now that it was easily done.

Thurmon fumbled at the line that he had been given and tied Sal and Mary and Margaret and two other children to it. He wrapped it around him twice and pulled the knot as tight as he could.

Sal looked at him.

"Don't be afraid," he managed to say.

She smiled and kissed him. "I'll try," she said, and held Mary close.

Time seemed to stop, then, as they all waited. Sal couldn't even hear the storm, though she was sure it was still raging, and making as much noise as it had been all day. Even more. She nestled tight to her father, so close that she thought for a second or two that she could hear his father's watch ticking in his shirt pocket. Then she knew that it was her own heart that she was hearing, or maybe her father's, or Wee Mary's. Maybe, she thought, as she closed her eyes, it was all of their hearts, everyone's in the room, pounding loud enough to be even louder than the storm.

The building sent out a pathetic, hopeless shriek, and they felt themselves being lifted.

Then the roof collapsed.

Chapter Sixteen

Quin had lived on Galveston long enough to know something of its topography, so he knew that the highest ground would be along Broadway, the grand, wide avenue that ran along the center of the island like a slightly raised backbone. He knew that his own back, not nearly as straight or as splendid as Broadway, couldn't take much more of the constant pushing along through water high enough to slap against his face, and fast enough to make his progress nearly futile. And he knew that the water wasn't getting any shallower, the closer he got to where the highest ground should be. So the whole island was under now, he realized. And, of course, he knew one more thing: that his albatross was still there, just behind him, close enough to not lose sight of him, but far enough back to be out of harm's way in case he finally decided to turn around and slap the hell out of the two of them.

He had been hit by several things during his journey. By bits of broken lumber and several slate tiles from roofs. A slopjar slammed into his shoulder hard enough to cause him to lose his footing, but he staggered and righted himself. A muffled groan behind him told him that it had hit at least one of the two boys on its way past. Two dead people floated by, and a dead cow, and several dead chickens caught up in a section of wire fencing.

Everybody else that Quin encountered was alive, and expending considerable effort to stay that way. Quin didn't bother to look at any of the people, since people were of no interest to him. But he knew that if he were to look, he would see that they were tired. Doubtless they were as exhausted as he was, after wading in this muck for so long, and having to fight to stay upright in the quick current and the stinging wind and rain.

Most of the buildings he passed had been so crammed full of people that the upstairs windows seemed to be overflowing. And Quin's abhorrence of crowds was strong enough to make the prospect of being wedged into a place so full of people that they were spilling out the windows even more disagreeable than standing out in a flood and a storm.

Finally he came to a building that was so old, and in poor enough condition, that folks had passed it by. Quin pulled himself through the open doorway and then pushed through the stale water on the first floor. This had been an upholstery shop until today. Ruined remnants of fabric floated in the black water. Cloth-covered buttons skirted slowly over the surface like corks being tugged along by hooked fish.

He found the stairs. The bottom steps had been washed away, but enough rotten wood remained for him to get a grip to pull himself up. He listened for any sounds from upstairs, but didn't hear anything. The building was shabby, the bricks uneven, with no evidence of the mortar that held them together. Like loose, brittle teeth in very old people. Quin didn't expect to find anybody up there, since everybody would have pushed themselves into the crowded upper stories of sounder places.

His muscles gave the very last of their strength and pulled his twisted little body up along what was left of the rotten ladder. Soon he fell against the floor of the second story and caught his breath. When he had breathed long enough to raise his head, he saw that the room was just as he wanted it.

Empty.

The room had no windows, which suited Quin, since most of the windows he had seen for the last couple of hours had been blown out. He could still hear the storm out there through the old, uneven bricks. And he could hear his own heart beating. The only other thing he could hear was the scraping and clattering on the steep stairs below.

Quin closed his eyes and had no doubts as to who was already dragging themselves up to him.

The lone worker in the Levy Building had tried to make it to the Tremont Hotel. But the water in the street was at least ten feet deep by then, and carried enough bodies on its swift surface to convince him to return to the office and ride things out there.

The barometer, the only instrument left working, had dropped to 28.48 inches. He wrote it in the log, not realizing, as he did it, that he was entering the lowest official barometer reading ever recorded by the United States Weather Bureau.

At the wharves, ships were tearing loose from their moorings. The British steamer *Kendal Castle* held fast for awhile, giving her captain hope that she could survive. Then the *Roma* crashed into her, followed closely by the small Norwegian *Guyller*. The remaining lines snapped, and the *Kendal Castle* was adrift. The roaring wind and water turned her sideways and propelled her into the channel.

The captain regained his feet. The windows of the wheelhouse were solid walls of cascading water, so the captain couldn't have seen where to steer his vessel even if steering were an option. The big ship bumped against smaller ones and kept its course.

The first mate pounded his fist against the low ceiling. "We're done for now!" he shouted.

"Well," the captain said, feeling his ship gain speed beneath him, "we're sure as hell going *somewhere!*"

"We'll get there when we get there, I guess," he said.

The two-story white frame house three blocks from what used to be the beach was still standing. But Isaac and Joseph Cline suspected that it was only a matter of minutes, perhaps seconds, before it would clatter into thousands of bits of debris, as its neighbors had already done. It was a stalwart house, as Isaac had intended it to be, but it was probably no match for the formidable tempest that it faced.

The second-story porches had already been ripped off and washed away. Joseph had gone out on the one facing town less than a half hour before and looked over at the next house. His neighbor was standing on his own upstairs porch, clutching the handrails, calmly watching the horror unfolding before him. When the water lifted his neighbor's house up, and rocked it free of its blocks, Joseph watched the man slowly turn and wave in his direction, as if he were on the deck of a ship embarking on a pleasure cruise. The house then moved forward, and Joseph watched as it picked up speed, before it exploded into the massive remains of another house two blocks away. Then he came back in a few minutes before the porch he had been on crumbled into the boiling sea that had been, until today, the front yard.

Isaac was still on the bed with his wife and youngest daughter. Joseph sat against the wall, keeping the two older girls pulled tight against him. The last time he had raised up to look outside, he had judged the depth of the water pouring past the sides of the house at fifteen to seventeen feet.

"It's going to fall apart any time now," Joseph shouted at the almost fifty terrified people assembled upstairs. "Remember to try to find something to hold on to." It was the best advice he could think to give, but, as he gave it, he knew that it would not help much, if any.

Tucker had never been much of a swimmer, but he was having to do more of it tonight than he ever had. Just getting from his roost to the front of the room had been a chore, especially since he had sat for so long all scrunched up on top of the chest of drawers, and his muscles had rebelled at first. Now he would have to swim under water in order to get through the door.

He floated for a moment, trying to judge where the door was, or at least where he thought it was. He couldn't remember ever having swum under water before and wasn't sure that he could hold his breath for long enough to get out into the alley. But one thing was certain: he was either going to have to get through it or drown in his own home. His head had already scraped the ceiling a couple of times.

He considered holding his breath for a little while, to see if he could do it. But then he decided that he either could or he couldn't— he'd find out soon enough.

He took in as much of the stale air as he could, clamped his mouth shut, and went under. He felt around for the door for a few seconds, didn't find it, and came up gasping. The door was open, he knew, because he had already watched the water push it out of its way. He ought to be thankful for that, he guessed, since he wasn't any too sure that he could open a door under water.

He collected another supply of air and went back under. He kept his eyes clamped shut, since the saltwater would burn them; he knew he couldn't see anything in this murk anyway. This time he found the opening and pulled himself through it. He shot so high up out of the rolling water in the alley, and coughed and gasped so loudly, that it startled the four women hanging on to the windows at the end of it.

One of them, who got over her surprise faster than the others, laughed, and told the other three, who had started to scream, to shut up.

She looked at the smallest of the three.

"Jesus Christ," she yelled. "You been praying for two damned hours for somebody to come help you, and then, when he does, you start caterwauling like a goddamned calf with his nuts chopped off."

The girl kept crying, along with the other two, and watched Tucker bounce up and down in the brown water until he worked his way over to a window sill to grab.

"I never would have thought it," the calmest, and by far the largest, of the four women said, not even loud enough for her three hysterical companions, or the bobbing black man, to hear.

"I guess even whores' prayers get answered sometimes."

Chapter Seventeen

QUIN

The brigantine that brought him to Galveston had not been a very fancy affair. Which suited him fine, since refined and elaborate things and situations tended to attract people to them. And he cared nothing about people.

He cared a great deal about money. And spent all of his time amassing it and then hoarding it away, as animals bury things for later, when they might need them.

But Quin never needed much of the money. The big room in which he lived—in a shabby building wedged between two others, just as shabby—hadn't cost much. He hadn't bought any articles of clothing in years, except in February of 1899, when a freak blizzard visited the island, and he reluctantly peeled several bills off his tightly rolled savings to purchase a heavy coat. He ate just enough to stay alive and sometimes would elect to remain hungry rather than go into a store and have to deal with the people there. He spent no money on whiskey, and neither chewed nor smoked tobacco. And whores were of no use to him whatsoever.

So he had most of the money that he had made from his various criminal dealings. The two voyages that transported him from halfway around the world had been more expensive than he had hoped for, but they were essential.

Very few things were essential, to Quin. He needed to control the group of thieves who worked for him, needed to know their every action, so they couldn't cheat him out of any more of his take than they already did. He needed quiet, and solitude, and darkness. He had to have them, and went to great lengths to stay hidden away from the world, his body hugging the deepest shadows and most remote corners of the island that he hadn't left, or even considered leaving, since he first arrived, in 1868, when he was not yet twenty.

And he needed opium. The drug itself and the ornate pipe he

smoked it in were his only extravagance, and he needed it.

He had bought the pipe from a whore on Postoffice Street. It was given to her by a Cuban sailor short of cash in payment for services rendered. This particular whore had had no need of an opium pipe, since her vices were of the sort poured from bottles, so she had sold it to Quin. As for Quin, he had had no need of the whore, other than to ask her where her son, who was one of his boys, had disappeared to. The boy had never returned, but the pipe that Quin purchased from his mother had been worth its cost. He had discovered opium years before, on the other side of the earth, but never had such a good pipe to smoke it with.

When he used the pipe, a velvet haze curled lazily through the putrid air of his room, the pale light from the single lamp filtering through it as it floated through particles of dust.

Quin liked to lean back against the rough wood of his chair and let the drug make its slow progress through his brain. The murky fog inside his head blended with the smoke of the pipe, and the dust in the air. It was all a cloud, thick and dark, and Quin would be part of it. And, every time, the cloud floated over something that he couldn't quite make out below.

After a while, there would be a small patch of light. He always reached toward it and tried to make the opening in the cloud wider by pulling at the edge of the tiny, wispy window. But he couldn't get a hold on it, and it always dissolved into curling strands of nothingness, oozing through his fingers. After much waving of his hand, the opening became big enough to see through. Then there were green fields, and clumps of trees down there, and sheep. The fields were spotted with fat, white sheep.

Some more of the cloud usually wandered into the small area, and Quin always brushed it away. Things were closer now. He always thought the cloud that he was in must have dipped lower. Two people were walking along a lane, bordered on either side by low walls made of stones. The wide expanse of pastures and trees rolled out around the people, a woman and a child, and short bushes grew up against the wall, sometimes so close that they had pushed some of its stones into the lane. Quin always knew, somehow, that there were hedgehogs in the bushes. He didn't know how he knew—he just knew that he had seen them there.

The boy was walking behind the woman, keeping a constant distance. The woman was reading aloud from a leather-bound book. She was obviously reading to the boy, who was paying as little attention to her as were the sheep on the other side of the wall.

When the cloud was close enough to them for Quin to hear the words, he knew that the book the woman was reading from was the Bible, and the passage was about sin and wickedness. ". . . but are like the chaff which the wind driveth away," she read, just lifting her eyes from the text enough so as not to stumble. "Therefore the ungodly shall not stand in judgement, nor sinners in the congregation of the righteous. For the Lord knoweth the way of the righteous; but the way of the ungodly shall perish."

The boy stayed quiet behind her, not listening to the words, but searching the rows of bushes for hedgehogs, and the sky for hawks. He didn't seem to see the cloud from which he was being watched.

Quin took another pull on the mouthpiece of the pipe then, and let the smoke fill in the window. He knew that the boy had been caught stealing in the village, and he knew that the scripture lesson he was receiving would not be the worst of his punishment. He would be thrashed soundly by his father when he got home, thrashed with the cane that his father took with him when he walked to the cottages of the people of his parish.

Quin always closed his eyes and could see the man clearly, approaching one cottage or another, tapping the tip of his cane along the ground, or on the stones laid before the doors. He was given tea in each home, and sometimes bread and jam, or meat pastries. He listened attentively to the lamentations of that house's inhabitants, their miseries and, not very often, their joys. The vicar drank his tea and offered words of hope and encouragement, and much scripture quoting went on. Quin smiled as the holy words and platitudes rolled off the vicar's tongue, as easily as water poured from a kettle. The vicar caressed the knob of his cane as he spoke and tapped its tip on the floor. Later, he would learn of his son's transgressions, and he would use the cane to strike the boy—who would be naked so that his clothes would not be damaged—about the backs of his legs and his buttocks.

Quin usually closed his eyes tighter as he watched the vicar, in a frenzy now, full of the wrath of his Old Testament God, as he made the cane an extension of his fury and moved its slashing force up the boy's body, across his back, and finally, when the vicar's ire was at its zenith, on his head.

He knew that later, before the hearth of the vicarage, a small flame dancing among the coals in the grate, the vicar and his wife would kneel and cry, each clutching their Bibles, each begging their God to wash the boy clean with the blood of Jesus, and deliver him from sin and wickedness.

Then Quin would inhale deeply and rub his crooked hand along the smooth surface of the pipe. And he would see, behind his closed eyes, another dark room, darker than this one, with the boy in its corner, still naked, not crying, not praying, stained with blood that had nothing to do with Jesus.

Quin liked the dark. On some late afternoons he walked out to the empty docks and waited for night. He liked to watch the eerie blanket of pale light that came for just a few moments before the darkness, draped over the docks and the ships, and the bay beyond them. This was that scarce few minutes of each day that people from his childhood called the gloaming. His mother had called it that, he remembered. He wondered if his father had. Probably not, Quin thought, if his father had ever taken the time to look at the last few moments of an afternoon. Unless the gloaming was mentioned in the Bible, in one of the hellfire and damnation parts that his father had spent his lifetime being concerned with, he wouldn't have thought it important enough to spend any of his time on.

He wondered if his mother had seen a difference between the late afternoons of China and those of England. He couldn't remember her ever voicing an opinion about it. But, of course, she had been more concerned with helping his father pull the ignorant Chinese heathen out of their Godless ways and washing them in the blood of Christ. Quin sometimes thought about that when he gazed at the fading red streaks behind the masts of the ships, and knew that, if his father had ever lifted his pious face and seen such a thing, he would have only beheld that blood there, as an affirmation of his life's work.

The passage to China had been a long one, and he had been sick for most of it. His parents saw the crew of the miserable ship as more souls needing to be saved, and spent their time on the voyage to that end, paying no more attention to their pale, vomiting son than the daily cramming of scriptures into him. He had finally memorized enough to satisfy them, at least enough to avoid some of the whippings with his father's ever-present cane.

He remembered the harbor they had entered, full of the odd little fishing boats that he would come to hate as much as he did the dwarf-like, slant-eyed people who sailed them. His father and mother had kneeled on the deck of the ship and begged God to give them the patience and resolve to do His work there: to save these useless creatures and bring them to Jesus. He thought that the crew of the ship, if any of them were given to prayer at all, had more than likely offered up thanks that they would finally be rid of the two meddlesome missionaries and their sick little boy.

He had grown stronger in that pathetic place, but not bigger. It was as if he had become infected with whatever growth-stunting curse that plagued the Chinese. And he had found it easier to steal there than he had in England, because the Chinese didn't seem used to having things stolen, and because the town and countryside weren't full of busybodies that enjoyed nothing more than reporting his thievery to his father.

By the time he was fifteen, he had developed and perfected a network of stealing that would serve him well thereafter. He had picked up just enough of the twangy language to recruit a few younger boys to do the actual filching, then he had paid them a small percentage of what he knew the sailors on ships in port would spend for the bounty. If he had been a praying man, himself, he would have given thanks that his zealous parents had found enough sinners to save in the first town in China that they set foot in and never found it necessary to venture inland. For the seaport had been a treasure trove for his new enterprise. He honed his craft there and hid away enough money, in the currencies of several nations, to put that miserable place, and the two worthless abominations that were his parents, behind him.

He had waited for that day, lived for it. He was seventeen, and his small body had already been twisted into the warped and awkward thing that it would always be. As he grew older, the applications of his father's cane and the slobbering delivery of his sermons as he administered them had grown more vicious. His mother had prayed loudly and spat out Old Testament indictments while he gritted his teeth and suffered it all.

Finally, the day of his delivery arrived. He booked passage on a departing ship and sewed his money into the lining of his clothes. The few articles that belonged to him he threw into a small bag, except for the Bible that had been a gift from his parents. He wouldn't be needing that, he knew. The boys in his employment would just have to figure it out that he was gone. So he had only two people to bid farewell.

He found them at their prayers before breakfast. He walked slowly to the table and tilted his mother out of her chair as easily as if he were tipping a bushel of apples out of a basket. He kicked her hard enough to keep her from getting up for a little while and then collected his father's cane from the corner. The vicar was up from the table by then, his face locked in a mixture of alarm, anger, and piety that Quin would carry with him for the rest of his life, as surely as if the look were a watch, or a trinket. One wide sweep of the cane sent him sprawling to the floor. He heard the skull crack in the quiet room. Then he beat the man so badly that he doubted he lived through it, but he hadn't stayed to see. His mother managed to summon enough breath to bellow out at him, as he walked calmly out the door, a final curse. That he was lost forever, now, and would surely never find salvation. He wasted none of his own breath to tell her that he just had.

Later that morning, as he watched the little seaside town grow smaller behind the stern of the ship and then disappear completely over the horizon, he hoped that the vicar had not gotten up from his beating, but found himself standing before the cruel, vindictive God that he had served so well.

The ship had brought him to New Orleans, where he stayed for a little over a year, and then another one brought him to Galveston. And here he had stayed, and prospered, and limped along in the darkness of shadows for over thirty years. As one group of boys grew up and sailed away, or died the early deaths that were common to them, he had recruited new ones, who knew so little about the bent little man that they didn't know if Quin was his first name or his last.

Chapter Eighteen

James had worked his way along the high sidewalks with the two men until they went off in the directions of their homes. He knew that one of them hadn't made it—he watched as he was rammed with what was left of a buggy, traveling at considerably faster speed than it ever had when hitched to a horse. The man tumbled over and over with the thing and then disappeared.

Pulling himself along from one post to another, James made it to a cross street and managed to get across the highest part of the island by finding enough wreckage to hold on to. He even used dead bodies for leverage when he had to.

The current was a constant problem, but the big pieces of broken lumber that had been until a little while ago parts of houses and buildings, presented an even greater danger. He had seen enough people swept under by them to know that he had to dodge everything. The one thing that he didn't dodge, a huge section of a wagon that had stayed intact, proved to be his savior. It bolted past him, just grazing his side, and by the time he was over the astonishment of the collision, he found that he was caught on it.

He struggled to free himself. By the time he did, he saw that it had delivered him to within a half a block of his destination.

Sal closed her eyes, and gave herself up to her death.

The clothesline pulled against her side and tore into her flesh. She felt her father's arms around her, and then she didn't feel them. She felt her own arms around Mary and then she was gone, too.

Sal pulled on the clothesline, wanting either her father or Mary to materialize. Then the biggest of the heavy things that were falling came down all around her.

She was under water. Then she wasn't.

The heavy things—parts of the roof, she guessed—were still falling. She opened her eyes and looked for her father and Mary. All she could see were the mammoth sections of timbers and shingles

151

from the roof that were flying everywhere like confused birds. Wind and rain filled up the place now, as if they were angry for having been denied it.

She saw Sister Catherine. She wasn't singing now, but rolled over and over, the children that were tied to her with the clothesline rolling with her. One of the biggest parts of the roof spilled into the place where they were.

She saw Reverend Mother Camillus die, also, as she reached through the fury around her for any children that she could find. The old woman gathered a boy into her arms, and another one of the heavy things swallowed them up.

Things were still falling. Sal didn't know how there could be anything left to fall, then she noticed that the walls themselves were coming down. She saw another group of children for a second or two before the wall fell on them.

One of the children was attempting to stand up, but the others that she was tied to had been caught under some of the big things, and she couldn't move.

Sal couldn't feel any tugging on the line tied to her. All she could feel was the need to go to sleep. It was ridiculous, she realized, to go to sleep right then. But she had never been so sleepy.

As she closed her eyes, she made the most amazing discovery of all. None of the horror going on around her was making any noise. The crashing down of the building should be loud, she knew, and the roaring of the storm. The children should be crying and shouting. Even as they died, they should be screaming. But they weren't. Everything was so absolutely quiet that she could hear her own heart beating.

When she blinked her eyes open, she knew that she had been under water. She floated on the top of it, and the water moved her along. The clothesline jerked at her. She could see that she was beside what was left of the building now. Big pieces of it bumped against her and floated all around her. It was raining hard, and the rain stung her face. It must be a very loud rain, she suspected, but she couldn't hear it.

Something pulled against the clothesline, twice, and she went underwater again. She had to cough several times when she came up this time, and she wondered if this was how she would die, by drowning. All of the roof had fallen, and the walls, too, she guessed, so now drowning was what was left.

She tried to look around at everything, but she kept dunking under the water, and the line kept pulling her around. It was raining so hard that she couldn't see much anyway. And she couldn't hear anything except her heart.

The foamy brown water rushed past her, and over her. It looked like chocolate, she thought. Enough of it flowed over her to push her under deeper than she had been.

So this is how she would die, she knew. In swirling, quiet chocolate.

Three miles away, a section of trestle, held together by rails, was ripped from its moorings and tumbled over once before gathering wreckage in front of its two hundred foot length and pushing it forward. It traveled almost three blocks before it slammed into the first obstacle it encountered.

Isaac Cline's house shuddered at the impact and rose from its foundation. It floated for a moment, then tumbled over.

Joseph, still clutching his two young nieces, was propelled backward through one of the windows that was still intact. All three of them crashed through the glass and the storm shutters and rolled around on what, until a moment before, had been the side of the house. Joseph reached for the girls and pulled them back close to him.

Everything rocked violently as the house sought to adjust itself and re-settle. When it had, Joseph raised up and looked around him. He and the girls were the only ones he could see who had made it out.

Quin was so exhausted from the slow journey across the city and from the nearly impossible effort it had taken to pull himself up what had remained of the rotten staircase that he had fallen into a crumpled heap in a corner of the empty room and gone to sleep. When he woke up, the first thing he saw in the faint light that crept in from a hole in the roof was what he would have expected to see, if he had had time to think about it.

Both boys sat, side by side, staring at him.

The storm was raging with more strength and vigor than it had been before Quin found the building. And the muted light that came in the damaged roof was of the sort that he knew best, the eerie light that comes at night. Rainwater poured in the hole in the roof also, so he wasn't any drier than he had been when he had fallen asleep.

"I thought you was dead," the taller boy said.

The old building rocked in the high wind, and Quin repositioned himself to keep from rolling along the plank floor.

"Just sit there and wait," he said. "You'll likely get to see it yet."

*   *   *

153

On Broadway, James let himself be washed into the entryway of the Kempner house. He hit the bottom of the wide stairs hard enough to stun him for a moment, then he grabbed the banister and held tight.

His head was throbbing from the wallop the stairs had given it, so he stayed where he was until he felt that he could go on. He was damned well not going to die here, he decided, at the foot of the stairs that would take him where he wanted to go, after fighting his way through hell to get there.

When the throbbing had subsided a little, he pulled himself up one step after another, using the banister as his anchor. At the top, he turned and saw a set of closed double doors. He made his way over to them and pounded as hard as he could, knowing that if anyone was behind the doors they couldn't hear him over the raging tumult.

Summoning the last of his energy, he got to his feet, backed up a few steps, and lunged his side against the doors with sufficient force to send them flying open.

He staggered for a moment at the threshold and looked at the surprised assembly in front of him. Most of them were sitting on the floor. One man, who had been standing, got to him before he fell and lowered him gently down.

When he looked up again, he saw her, walking slowly toward him. She wore her maid's uniform, and a strand of her brown hair had fallen over her eyes. They were pretty eyes, still as pretty as they had been when he had first seen them, reflecting the twinkling lights in the *Garten Verien*. She knelt down beside him and cradled his head in her arm.

She breathed his name.

"I pop up sometimes," he said, finding just enough breath to deliver the few words, "when folks don't expect me to."

She smiled.

"How many lives did you save today?" she asked.

He leaned his head against her shoulder, closed his eyes, and, for the first time since he had been a small child, he cried.

The four women watched Tucker as he held on to a window sill in the flooded alley. One of them was still alternating between crying and screaming. The biggest one, who was also the calmest, reached over and slapped her hard on the side of her face.

"I done told you to shut up, Lucy," she yelled. "I don't want to have to tell you again."

The girl touched her face and whimpered.

"That's better," the biggest one said, and laughed. "We wouldn't want our friend here to think we got a goddamned idiot on our hands."

They all held on to whatever kept them in place. The deep water swirled around in the alley, splashing against the brick walls at the sides and the back. The women looked at Tucker.

When she had determined that the man wasn't going to say anything, the biggest woman nodded in his direction.

"That building you've glued yourself to," she shouted, "if you ain't noticed yet, is rockin' around more than our place of business does on a Saturday night."

Tucker felt it now as it shifted.

"Now, like I been tellin' these gals," the woman said, "I ain't no expert, except at certain things, but I do believe we'd best find a better place to be." She looked up at the top of the three story structure, as it swayed in the wind.

Tucker looked up, too. "I don't know if they is any better place to be," he shouted back at her.

He knew the building would probably collapse eventually. He knew, too, that the roaring river at the end of the alley would be an awfully bad place to have to go to. He'd have to take these women with him now. And he didn't even want to think about what kind of fits that littlest one would throw if they tried to get through that deep, fast water and all that wind.

The stinging rain pelted against his face, and the building he was holding on to shook enough to almost make him lose his grip. Then he made up his mind.

"Maybe we ought to try to move on," he yelled. "Before this place falls down, and catches us under it."

The woman laughed. "Well, honey," she shouted, rainwater sputtering out with the words, "I spent most of my life up under things. But I never had no intention of dyin' there."

CHAPTER NINETEEN

The hellish water spat Thurmon out and sent him surging forward. His head was spinning even faster than the water was and his lungs had spent the last of their air. Before he could figure out where he was, or where he was going, he had to get more of it.

He gasped and coughed, lunging upward to swallow as much air as he could get. Some water came in with it, and he had to cough it up. The clothesline tied around his waist wasn't helping his breathing any—it jerked him along, squeezing out the little supply of breath that he had managed to collect.

His face slammed against the water a couple of times and then into something substantially harder.

He woke up to more water racing past him. But he wasn't going with it anymore. He shook his head and blinked his eyes. The clothesline tugged at his middle, and then he heard a voice.

He couldn't find her at first, but had to work his way along whatever it was that he was holding on to. Then, there she was, just her head above the water line.

"I was afraid you weren't going to wake up," Sal yelled.

He held onto her for a long moment, then rose up a little to see around him. Mary's small head bobbed beside Sal's, and a few others, on the other side of her. He couldn't see how many there were.

"What are we hanging on to?" he shouted.

"A piece of the roof, I think," Sal said, spitting out the words when her mouth rose clear of the water. "You got knocked out, and I got your arms over that board, so you wouldn't go back under."

He leaned against the wreckage, and breathed in more air. "Is everybody still tied to the line?" he asked.

She nodded.

He knew that they needed to stop talking. The yelling they were having to do, to be heard, was too exhausting. And they needed every bit of strength they had left.

He raised up again and looked at the surface of the large section of debris he was fixed to. He leaned down on it to test its buoyancy, then turned back to Sal.

"We've got to get up on top of this," he shouted, and tapped the wreckage. "Something will crash into us if we stay down here."

She nodded that she understood.

He lifted her up first, then handed Mary up to her. He untied the line from his waist, so he could reach the others. He pushed a girl up, and then a small boy.

The last child wasn't moving. Thurmon pulled him over to him, and his head bobbed under the murky water. When it came back up, he saw that a deep gash ran from his eye to his throat. Both eyes were open. He felt for a heartbeat, but the pale face and vacant eyes had already told him there wouldn't be one.

Thurmon untied the line from the boy and cupped the side of his face in his hand and kept it there until the current pulled him away.

He lifted himself up.

"Lay flat, on your bellies," he shouted when he was on board. "There's enough holes for you to hold to. Use both hands, and hang on tight."

He found the end of the clothesline and tied it back around his waist. Then he made sure it was still secure around each child. A thick board protruded from the roof. He pulled hard against it, to convince himself of its sturdiness, and wound the other end of the line that had been attached to the dead boy around it several times. He tied it off with three tight knots.

The makeshift sanctuary pitched up and down, but was stable for the moment. Thurmon knew that the howling wind and bolting water would probably break it loose—there wouldn't be anything to do then but hold fast and ride it.

He hugged tight to the thick board with one arm and laid the other one, heavily, on Sal's shoulders.

Isaac Cline felt his house rolling slowly over. He held Esther, his six-year-old daughter, tighter, and they were thrown from the bed. The last thing he saw, before a huge dresser slammed into him, was his wife reaching out for him. Now he and the girl were pinned against a mantle. He struggled to work them free, but was unsuccessful. His home did it for him.

The house pitched forward, and then sideways, sending the heavy piece of furniture across the floor and onto a group of people wallowing in the corner.

Isaac was free now, but was underwater. He groped around for his daughter, found her, and made for the surface. When they reached it, his daughter's screams joined others in the room. He held her tight against his chest and looked for his wife. When he didn't see her, he began stabbing his hand under the surface.

The water level rose as quickly as if a dam had broken, and Isaac was sure they would be crushed against a wall. When he glanced up, he saw that there were no more walls, only rain and wind. He and the girl reeled around several times, and were knocked back under by something.

They would die now, he was sure. He clutched his daughter as hard as he could, and kissed her forehead. The dark water spun them around for a long moment.

Then they were floating. He felt his feet scoot along something solid, and pulled them out of the water, and onto it. Holding his daughter with one hand, he looped his arm over what had been one of his bedroom windows. A piece of the drapery that his wife had made was still in place on a rod.

He tugged the girl up beside him and collapsed against the window, his face buried in the fragment of floral print curtain that Cora Mae had worked so hard on.

The second story room that the three vagabonds had found commenced its death rattle. The structure around it groaned and shrieked, and the walls and floor and ceiling of the room itself joined its anguish, as it took on a new and contorted shape. One end of the room rose, as if being pushed from beneath, the boards of the floor separating themselves from each other and snapping apart.

Quin rolled along the slanting floor and came to rest against a wall. A hole materialized in the bricks of the outer wall, and the front of the building fell away.

Both of the boys, who had been near that wall, fell with it. It was as if Quin had blinked and they were no longer there.

He tried to stay pressed against the wall, but the room lunged again and hurtled him out into the rainy night. His last conscious thought was not a new one to him.

He was flying, he thought, for the few seconds that he was allowed to think. He was whole and robust. And he was flying high above a world where twisted creatures must limp along in shadows, and where boys get beaten with canes.

The largest of the three women pushed the smallest one along in

158

front of her, kicking her when she slowed down. The girl was still screaming, and the woman kicked her harder to shut her up.

Tucker was in front of the group, pulling himself along from one window to the next. When he got to the alley and saw the angry river that was racing down the street, he had second thoughts about the wisdom of the plan and turned to tell the biggest woman so. But her face was locked into a determined frown, and he knew that she'd probably start kicking him, too, if he gave her any reason to.

He anchored himself to the window frame, and waited until the four were closer. He pointed to the street, where wrecked buggies and wagons and parts of buildings rolled through the swift water.

"That's awful deep," he shouted. "The sidewalk's a good four feet up off the street."

The biggest woman, who had obviously elected herself to do the thinking and talking for the other three, gazed at him.

"It's way over our heads," he said, in case she didn't grasp the difficulty of the situation. "One of them wagons would hit us in the head, I reckon, even if we could get across it."

The woman still looked dumbfounded.

"Well, goddamn!" she finally yelled, causing Tucker to lose his perch for a second. "How long did it take you to figger all that out?"

Tucker reattached himself to the window frame.

"I ain't seen no damned sign that said we have to *cross* the son of a bitch! All we got to do is work our way down beside it, till we get to a better building to get up in."

The other women looked at the turbulent water and the heavy pieces of debris rolling in it.

"Jesus!" the smallest one said. "Jesus! We'll get killed if we go out in that." She started crying again, which suited Tucker better than her screaming.

It didn't suit the biggest woman, though. So she slapped her.

"You and Jesus and can stay here, then," she yelled. "And when this building falls on you, maybe you'll roll out from under Jesus and come find us."

Tucker studied the street again, and the river charging down it. The water didn't appear to be moving any slower at the sides than it was in the middle.

"Maybe there ain't no better buildin' down there," he said. "Maybe there ain't no buildins left."

"And maybe," the biggest woman said, as she pushed him toward the alley's opening, "there's a goddamn sailboat tied up down there, and you can take us out for a ride, and we can fish a little."

"We won't know, will we," she said, as she shoved the other

women forward, "till we get there."

Atop her cathedral, the statue of Mary still swayed in the furious gale. Inside, one of the largest of the stained glass windows exploded in the wind, and countless fragments of glass and molding sprayed out into the nave with the blowing rain.

The massive two-ton bell pulled against the iron bands that held it in place. The bands groaned in high-piched agony and broke, popping like rifle fire, and the bell crashed through the roof and fell to the floor.

One of the front towers of the cathedral lurched forward, then seemed to balance in a moment of indecision, before plummeting into the submerged street.

In the rectory next door Father Kirwin and the bishop, along with several other priests and the household staff, were upstairs, away from the flooded first floor.

Through a broken window Kirwin watched the destruction taking place before him. He saw many bodies, and knew that there must be even more inside the church. The windows of the cathedral, and in all the buildings and houses that he could see, had been blown out, their casings and edges standing jagged and torn.

He turned away from the window and saw that Bishop Gallagher was standing beside him.

The old man laid his hand on Kirwin's arm and looked at him for a moment. When he finally spoke, his voice was soft, but, oddly enough, Kirwin could hear it perfectly above the roaring wind.

"Prepare these priests for death," the bishop said.

The bodies that weren't caught under the orphanage when it collapsed were lodged against its wreckage. Thurmon had seen several as they were whisked past on the surface of the churning water.

The muscles in his arms were aching, but he held tight to the thick board and to Sal. If he had another arm, he thought, besides the two that were in use, he would take out the bottle of brandy that Minnie had given him, if it wasn't already broken, and have himself a much needed drink.

Sal lay on the roof, one hand gripping the hole it had found, and the other on Mary, who was huddled next to her. She felt her father's arm on her back, pinning her down.

She had been praying for the last few minutes, now that she was on something that was still enough for her to do it. She asked God to help everybody she could think of. She prayed for her mother, and for Joe, and asked for them to be somewhere that was safe.

She knew that some of the nuns, and many of the children, were already dead—she had watched some of them die.

As she lay flat against the shingles of the roof and kept her eyes fixed to her father, Sal wondered if the nuns and the children were already in heaven. She wondered how long it took to get to heaven, once somebody died. Not long, she figured. Heaven was pretty far away, she thought, but surely dead people didn't have to make a long journey to get there. She hoped it was a quick trip, and that all those children and the nuns were already there, safe and dry and looking at God.

Mother Camillus was with the children, she knew, and Sister Catherine, and whatever other nuns had died, so the children wouldn't be scared. Sister Mendulla was probably dead, too, since the building she had been in had fallen down first. She thought that even Mendulla would be happy, and nice, in heaven. Sister Zilphia might already be there, also. Maybe she was looking down at her right now and asking God to help them. If she ended up dying tonight, Sal thought, she could read to the children, if they had books in heaven.

She looked at her father and asked God if he would let him die, too, if she did.

So they wouldn't have to miss each other.

Chapter Twenty

Father Kirwin

He had never even seen the sea until he was an adult.

He was born in Ohio, just as the Right Reverend Nicholas Gallagher, the bishop of the diocese of Galveston, had been. Circleville, the town where Father Kirwin was born and raised, seemed about as far removed from the ocean as any place he could imagine, and when he was back there, on his regular trips home to visit his mother, he missed the close proximity of it and the salty air. When he was in Ohio, he felt that part of him was still in Galveston, among the dunes, and wharves, and the clock-like predictability of the tides. Father Kirwin put much of his strong faith in the unexplainable mystery of the will of God. And he was ever thankful that a small part of that will seemed to include his being there.

Even on a hot morning, like Thursday morning had been, on his way out to the orphanage in the buggy.

Several of the children ran down the beach road to meet him and skipped along beside the rig as it came to a stop by the picket fence and its gate outside the orphanage. He climbed down, and ruffled the hair of some of them, and pinched their ears to make them giggle. One little girl—Margaret, he remembered—tugged on his sleeve and asked if he was going to say the Mass on Sunday.

"And what if I don't?" he asked. "Won't you listen if another of the priests does it?"

She shrugged. "I'll listen," she told him, "but I won't like it."

He laughed. "Well, you need to listen and *like* it, whoever does the preaching. Reverend Mother told me you've been sick. Are you well now?"

She nodded. "I *had* to get well. They wouldn't let me come outside till I did."

She followed him up on the porch, where more of the children had gathered to greet him. "That's as good a reason to get well as I ever heard," he said. Then he began pinching and patting the other youngsters.

Reverend Mother Camillus received him in her small study, as she always did. They talked about several of the children, and he agreed to speak to a couple of them regarding lapses in good behavior. One of the boys had been adopted, and he wanted to know all of the particulars about that, and about a new child who would be coming soon to live there.

When all of their business seemed to have been completed, Camillus turned in her chair and looked at the open journal on her desk, expecting her guest to dash out the door in his usual quick stride to find the other sisters to visit with. But he hadn't moved.

"And what of Sister Zilphia?" he asked. "How's she doing?"

"Sister Zilphia?" she said, surprised. "She's doing fine. Her medical training has been quite useful, and she gets on well with the children."

The priest nodded, and smiled. "I'm sure she's a great help to you and the sisters." He leaned forward a bit in what he always thought was the hardest chair he had ever sat in. "But I'm asking about *her*, not her duties. How is *she* doing?"

Camillus closed the book and laid her pencil on top of it. She waited a moment before she spoke. He knew she was choosing each word carefully before she used it.

"Sister Zilphia is"—she shook her head slightly—"questioning her path, I think. Perhaps her faith, also." She looked at him. "It hasn't affected her work here," she quickly added.

"Has she confided in you, or sought you out, so that you can help her through this . . . *questioning?*"

The old nun took off her glasses and rubbed her eyes with her fingertips. "We've visited just the one time, in here, other than small talk at meals, or discussions about the children."

He looked out the tall window beside her desk. Several children were milling around in the yard. Two sat on the steps of the porch, where the sea breeze washed over them. He had brought a photographer out only a few weeks earlier to take a picture of all the children, arranged in rows on those steps, the nuns standing stern and stiff behind them.

"Was it a good visit?" he asked. "Did she ask for your advice, or guidance?"

Camillus clasped her fingers together in front of her, not in an attitude of piety, Kirwin thought, but out of long custom. "It confirmed what I already knew, that she is unsure of herself, and her calling. God brought her here for His good purpose, and when it is time she will know it."

Father Kirwin readjusted himself in the chair. The walls of the narrow room seemed always closer together every time he saw them. He wondered how she could bear to spend so much of her life in the cramped box.

"And if she should ask for help in seeing God's will, I know that you'll listen, and guide her. She may need that."

The old nun pushed herself away from her desk and stood up. "She needs God," she very nearly snapped at him. "His will is sufficient. Anything that I, or you, could say to her would be of not much importance." She straightened her habit, and looked at the door, an obvious sign that it was time for him to find it. She offered the last word on the matter: "She needs to pray."

"Yes," he said, as he rose to leave. "We all need that."

He found a few of the nuns to say hello to and sought out the two children that Camillus had asked him to speak with. He suffered through the usual few moments with Sister Mendulla, as she cataloged the infractions of several of the orphans for him. Her eyes, set in the dark birthmark that covered much of her face, sparkled as she told on the children. Mendulla's eyes always appeared, to Kirwin, to be as hard as the stones that he was often tempted to remind her not to cast.

Outside he saw Sister Zilphia hanging clothing on the line to dry in the sun and breeze. A child he had not seen before was with her.

"It's wash day, is it?" he shouted, as he walked over to her.

"Good afternoon, Father," Zilphia said around two wooden clothes pins clinched between her lips. "No, that's on Tuesdays, when the yard is filled up with drawers and dresses." She swept one arm in a wide semicircle to include all of the numerous lines strung between poles. "We've just been getting some of their beach things dry." She looked at her helper, who stood quietly by, out of the way.

"Oh, Father," she quickly said, "this is Sal Casey, who is a big help to me here." She pointed in her direction. "Sal, this is Father Kirwin, from the cathedral."

He held out his hand and Sal shook it.

"And how long have you been here, Sal?" he asked, thinking it odd that Camillus hadn't mentioned a new girl.

"She doesn't live here, Father," Zilphia said. "Sal lives in town, and is good enough to come out and see me. The children love it when she comes—she reads to them."

He said that it was an awfully nice thing to do, to come all the way out from town to help at the orphanage. Then he asked if he could have just a moment of Sister Zilphia's time. When Sal said goodbye to him, before she went off to leave them alone, he rested the palm of his hand on her head for just a second, as she crossed herself.

"Do you come to the cathedral, Sal?" He couldn't remember ever having seen her. She told him she went to St. Patrick's, with her mother, and walked toward one of the buildings. Two small girls met her halfway and took her hands. Together the three went up the steps and inside.

Father Kirwin watched them. "She's a sweet one," he said. "How did you find her?"

"She's the friend of the girl who used to live here, who works as a maid at the Kempners. Sal's mother is the cook there. Her father's a drunkard, by all accounts, and her mother is . . . difficult." She reattached the corner of a bathing costume to the line. "Now that it's summer, she was just sitting at home all day, with nothing to do, so I pushed her to spend some of her time here. It's good for her, and for the children, too."

"I agree," he said. "And it's good for you, too, I imagine."

She looked at him. "Well," she said, "I enjoy having her about. She's cheerful, and likes to talk about the books that she reads."

"That's good," Father Kirwin said and reached into the basket on the ground and handed her another suit to be dried. "And she obviously needed you, and this place."

Zilphia slowly pinned the suit to the line.

"You know," he said, pulling the top of the suit tighter and repinning it, "it's just possible that God led that child to you, in the same way that He led you to Galveston."

She looked down at the basket of wet clothes.

She rested a hand on the line. He covered it with his own. "There's nothing wrong, you realize, with seeking help. You don't always have to give it."

She looked at him now. "I don't know how much help I could give, Father. Or what I need. And I don't know about being led places." He saw a cold glint of determination in her pretty eyes. "I wonder if we don't just find our own way, and make the best of it wherever we end up."

The wind brought them the sound of the waves on the beach, on the other side of the dunes. The fresh, salty air felt good to Kirwin.

"Perhaps," he said. "I don't know either. But I believe. And one of the things I believe is that the power that made us also loves us, and wants to help us. If we'll let Him."

She took her hand away and reached into the basket for the next suit.

"Well," he said, and turned to go, "I'm glad the girl comes out here. I'd be happy for the company if she needs a ride back to town."

"I'll bring her later," she said. "I have to come in to the Infirmary for some things."

He nodded and took a few steps toward his buggy. "Sister," he called and turned around. She looked up to face him.

"Just one question. When I brought you here, you looked at these buildings and said something about coming to your . . . *sentence*, I think you called it."

She thought of that day, months ago.

"Do you still see it as that?"

She looked at the buildings and at several of the children on the porches.

"No, Father," she said. "I see it as a blessing." She smiled. "Which you already knew, or you wouldn't have asked."

A large yellow dog ran up to him as he walked past the porch. Margaret, sitting on the steps, watched him lean down and pet it.

"How's Chester?" he asked, rubbing the dog's neck.

"He got bit again," Margaret told him. "Sister Zilphia had to doctor him."

Father Kirwin stood up. "I'm afraid one of those snakes will be the end of old Chester one of these days," he said.

"Naw," Margaret said. "He just keeps on living."

CHAPTER TWENTY-ONE

$\mathbf{T}$he house was beginning to break up, and Joseph Cline knew that it would soon be tumbling, in pieces, toward the center of town. The section of outside wall that he and his nieces were on seemed to be holding together pretty well, so he decided that they would take their chances on it.

The girls were pressed against his sides, and were crying. He had continued to scan the short distance that the storm allowed him to see for survivors, but so far he hadn't seen anyone.

Their part of the wall shifted, and began to break free from the structure.

"Just hold on tight to me," he shouted to the girls, "and we'll be fine." He got the best grip that he could and felt the newly born raft float free.

The platform spun around slowly, as if determining which way it would go, then moved forward. It picked up speed, and Joseph saw two figures holding onto the side of the house.

He shouted at them and leaned over far enough to grab the largest one's hand. The raft almost tilted over as he pulled them on board. It righted itself, and sailed forward.

When he had regained his balance and glanced to make sure that his nieces were still with him, he looked at the two new passengers.

The Cline brothers stared into each other's eyes.

"Cora Mae is gone," Isaac said, as he rubbed his youngest daughter's back. He shook his head slowly.

Joseph nodded and watched his brother's arm move mechanically over the child's back. He couldn't see Isaac's eyes very clearly, but he knew that if he *could* see them they would be empty of the vigor and the gleam that he was used to seeing there.

"But *you're* not," he said. "Or your children."

Then he looked at the ruined buildings and houses they were passing. They'd hit something eventually, he knew.

He grabbed his brother's arm.

"We're all still here, Isaac." he said. Then he touched his face, for what was surely the first time in their lives.

"And you've got to help me, now." He nodded quickly, as if agreeing with himself. "You've got to help me."

They held onto the girls, and the vessel propelled them into the darkness.

Sal felt her father's arms lose a bit of their grip on her, and she knew that he had dozed off. They were tied to the section of roof with the clothesline, so she didn't see any harm in letting him sleep for a few minutes. She still clutched Wee Mary tightly to her, with Margaret and the other boy beside her. All of them were quiet, either sleeping, or in shock, or too frightened to make a sound.

Sal leaned against her father and closed her eyes and thought again of all the people she had just seen a little while ago and talked to and read stories to, who were now dead.

She wondered if her mother was dead, in town. And Joe. And Pearl. She was pretty sure that Sister Zilphia was dead, or they would have seen her by now. Or maybe she got swept off in the water. She raised her head up just enough to see the flood that still raged over what was left of the buildings, and to hear the howling wind, still as loud as a train. She didn't suspect that Sister Zilphia could live through any of that.

She closed her eyes again and leaned close against her father's chest. She could feel the small bottle in his pocket, and his father's watch. She wondered if it would even work any more, after being in so much water. It had never been in much water before, she suspected. And neither had she, before today.

In the Kempner house, on Broadway, everyone sat on the floor of the upstairs parlor. Ike Kempner had told them, several times, that they were in one of the sturdiest houses on the island, and they prayed that he was right.

They prayed, too, for people who weren't in it.

Mrs. Ivy prayed for Mr. Kurtz, and Mae prayed for Tucker. What Pearl had been praying for had been delivered, and leaned against her now, sound asleep. But she had prayers left, concerning two long buildings out on the beach road.

Minnie Casey fingered the beads of her rosary and wondered where her family was. She knew where Sal was, and where Thurmon was, too, or at least where he was trying to get to. But she had no idea where Joe was. She didn't know if they were safe, or dry, or hungry, or—she worked more frantically at the beads—if they were even alive. She prayed that they were at least that.

Thurmon had been on her mind, how he had bolted out the door and through the gate. She smiled at that, her slight hint of a smile that still sometimes came. But she couldn't keep her mind on him going through the gate. When she tried to, she kept seeing him in that little eatery where she had worked just after she had come to Galveston. All that banter, and nonsense, and how he would sing.

Minnie thought of that as she recited her rosary. And she skipped over all the other years, the darker, harder ones, and then would end up at that gate, outside this very house. But when she thought of it, it wasn't right at all. For Thurmon wasn't going out the gate.

He was coming in.

Tucker stayed as far in front of the biggest woman as he could. He heard her back there, yelling out words he was used to hearing from dockworkers and sailors. The woman didn't hesitate to use the words, and they rolled out as easily as all the other words she was using. Tucker was getting used to hearing the big woman use the words but didn't think he could get used to the way she kicked or slapped anybody within her reach when it crossed her mind to do it. So he kept a healthy distance between them.

They had emerged from the alley without losing anybody. Tucker reached around the side of the building, with just his face above the lurching water, and edged himself from brick to brick. He knew there was a sidewalk down there somewhere, but it was deeper than he would be able to touch. So he did what he had done in the alley: found enough things to hold on to.

So far there had been enough window frames and chinks in the brick walls. Only once did he have to press himself even flatter than he already had, and scoot along slowly, with nothing to anchor himself to.

The wind and water pushed against their backs and tried to peel them off the face of the building. Frothy brown waves splashed against their heads, passing debris churned into them, and stinging rain pelted down on them. The smallest woman had started crying a couple of times, for no other reason than she felt it was time to. The bigger one slapped or kicked her when she did, so she contented herself with chanting a constant, desperate prayer.

The first two buildings they pulled themselves along were in as bad, or worse, shape than the one they had left. The windows had been blown out and washed away, and while what was left offered convenient places to hold on to, the shaking interiors didn't promise much in the way of a safe haven.

Tucker turned and looked at the biggest woman.

She stopped, and leaned her ample face against the rough bricks. "Don't you start talking to me about they ain't being no buildings for us to go up in," she yelled. She spat some water out. "They's bound to be one directly."

He had been about to suggest that they rest for a moment or two, and just hold on to the wall. But the big woman was already moving again.

Tucker looked up the street to see how many things were floating down it. Some big things were—one whole porch, with the handrails and the roof still attached, careened from one building to another. He didn't like the look of the thing bouncing toward them, but he liked the look of what was propelling it even less.

"Oh, my lord," he shouted and pushed against the water to get back to the others. "Get a holt of somethin'," he shouted.

"What the hell . . . ," the big woman started, then she looked back and saw it too.

The smallest one didn't have to look back. Tucker's reaction to whatever it was, and the fact that the woman had stopped yelling in mid sentence were enough to convince her that it was something bad. She didn't have enough time to get off all of one good scream before it was on them.

Chapter Twenty-Two

Most of the two big buildings were gone now, washed away in the wind and flood. Oddly shaped pieces remained, rocking and tilting, but continued to hold their grip in the swirling, gurgling water. Thurmon and Sal and three children held onto the section of roof that was lodged to enough wreckage beneath the surface to keep them from being propelled off to wherever most of the rest of the building had long since gone.

Thurmon's back was hurting, the muscles there and in his shoulders and legs throbbing with a dull ache. He still held tight to the thick board and to Sal. He didn't know how long they had been there, but the platform began to groan and sway, and he could feel the mass of rubble that was beneath them start to readjust itself as the current pushed against it.

The wind was not blowing as fiercely now, but it was still strong enough to do them in if they gave it the chance to. He looked up and saw that the clouds had broken in places. He even saw the moon peep through once, briefly. It was still raining, though not as hard.

He eased his grip on the board enough to lean down to Sal. She raised up enough to meet him.

"Not much longer," he shouted. "You've got to keep holding on tight. Can you do that?"

She nodded that she could.

"We've just got to sit still, don't we, Papa?" she shouted.

He smiled. "That's right. We'll just sit still."

Margaret, on the other side of Mary, lifted her head up. "I can't be any stiller," she yelled. "What I need to do is move around a little." The boy beside her nodded in agreement.

"We'll get to move around soon, I think," Thurmon shouted. "Just keep hanging on, and we'll . . . ."

He stopped, and listened. "Do you hear that?"

They all listened now.

"Somebody's hollerin'," Margaret yelled.

They all heard it now, a single voice over the lessened roaring of

171

the storm. Thurmon looked in the direction it was coming from, but couldn't see anything.

The voice came again, blowing over them with the wind.

"Somebody over there needs help," he shouted, and looked at the pitching waves between their platform and the next clump of debris.

"They're over there, I think," he said.

Sal pulled Mary tighter against her side and reached up to grab her father's arm.

"You can't go, Papa," she yelled. "You're too tired. And that water's too fast and deep."

He touched her hand and then her face.

"Somebody needs help, Sweet Potato," he said. "It's not too far, I think."

She started crying, and held on to his arm.

He looked back at the pile of wreckage.

"Can you hear me?" he shouted, as loud as he could. He listened, but there was no response. He called out again.

This time, the voice called back.

"We're here."

Thurmon leaned as close to the edge of the section of roof as he could.

"Are you hurt?" he shouted into the blowing rain.

The only sound now was the wind.

"Are you hurt?" he repeated.

"One of us . . . ," the voice came back. "One of us is."

He looked around, and considered his options. The current was still moving fast between the two piles of wreckage. He cupped his hand around his mouth, and yelled back toward the voice.

"I can't . . . ," he started to shout, but he had leaned too far forward and lost his hold. He hurried to get it back and looked behind him to see that the children were all still in their places.

"I don't think I can get to you because of the wind," he shouted. "But it's letting up. Hold on tight to whatever you're on."

He listened, but the voice didn't come back.

"Can you do that?" he yelled.

He listened again and heard a new sound.

He looked at the dark outline of the debris the voice had been coming from and saw a darker shape behind it. It was huge, and he knew that the roaring sound he had just heard was coming from whatever it was.

"Hold on tighter now," she shouted at the children, "as tight as you can. There's a big wave coming."

By the time he had finished, it was there, rolling over them. The clump of debris that the voice had been coming from was there, too, crashing into their own.

The wave knocked him loose from the thick board that he had been holding on to and drove him under the surface. He turned himself upright and reached for anything that he could find.

When he opened his eyes, the wave had pushed past them. He saw the edge of the section of roof and reached up for it. Something held him down. People were scurrying around on the roof, then he saw Sal reaching her hand down to him. He grabbed it, but the thing still held him tight.

Then he felt something slam into him. It wasn't lumber, but was soft. He let go of Sal's grip and groped at the soft thing. He felt an arm, then a waist. He got his arm around whoever it was and pushed them up. Sal reached down again, this time grabbing not her father's arm, but someone else's. She pulled and with Thurmon's pushing managed to pull the body up and over the side of the roof.

She looked at the face, and held tight to the arm.

"I thought you were in heaven," Sal said.

Sister Zilphia blinked her eyes and coughed up some brown water. She looked at the same wind and rain that she had looked at for hours, and heard the same wind as it whistled past. She touched Sal's face.

"I don't think I am," she said. "Yet."

The scraggly piece of Isaac Cline's house that he and his brother and his daughters were riding on slammed against several obstacles, but bounced off them and kept moving.

Isaac had recognized the tall tidal surge as it lifted them up and over a particularly large collection of rubble that would have probably been the end of them and prolonged their journey.

They all clung to each other and to their vessel as it spun around in the wake of the big wave. A sudden gust whipped across them. When the fury had subsided enough to let them see, the Cline brothers looked helplessly at each other and pulled the girls closer to them.

The dark outlines of the city's buildings, what was left of them, and the big piles of wreckage were getting smaller in front of them. Neither of them said it, but both understood the grave dilemma that had presented itself.

They were being swept out to sea.

Quin wasn't flying now. He tried to gain his focus but couldn't quite. He knew that he was lying on hard things—bricks, no doubt—

and that his body was even more bent and crippled than it had ever been before.

The slow gasping he was doing, and the general sensation of something inside being awfully wrong told him that he was badly hurt. Something even deeper told him something else.

He was dying.

Strangely, the oddest sensation came not from any of the damaged places, or the more important ones, but from his hand. Someone was holding it. He squinted his eyes enough to see the shorter of the two boys. He wore a cut or two on his narrow face, but he seemed to have fared well enough.

Quin tried to ease himself up a bit, but couldn't. He looked around. The water still raged along the street, but he was up above it, apparently on a pile of rubble. The boy must have hauled him up on it.

He didn't see the other one. He made a sound that might have been a question, but the shorter boy, who he remembered didn't do any of the talking, just stared at him and held his hand. Quin settled himself against the bricks and felt the boy's hand on his. He tried to remember the last time someone had held his hand, if anyone ever had. It must have been, he thought, oh, long ago, and awfully far away. He supposed that all mothers, even bad ones, sometimes did get around to holding their children's hands.

He coughed up something vile and breathing came more painfully now. He gripped the little hand harder, and the boy patted the hand with his other one.

But it wasn't the boy, he thought, as the night became darker, and he slipped irrevocably into it.

It wasn't a boy's hand at all.

The huge wave dislodged the little group hanging on the side of the building.

When Tucker came up, after doing more spinning around and kicking than he had ever done, he couldn't even see a building, much less try to hang on to one. He couldn't see much of anything else, either, except water, and the big things, like wagons, that were being pushed along in it with him.

One of the big things, he knew, was the woman who had been doing all the cussing. He tried to look around for her, since he wasn't any more anxious to be run over by her than he was a wagon. At least a wagon wouldn't start kicking and hitting him, like the big woman was likely to.

On the few occasions that his head bobbed up over the surface, he could see that he was moving fast. That worried him only long enough for him to reason that he was probably moving faster than the wagons and the whole porch that he had seen before he saw the big wave.

Tucker didn't think that he could live through getting hit by a fast moving porch. Of course it wasn't something that he had ever had to worry about, that he could remember.

There wasn't anything that he could do except let the water take him wherever it was taking him. He knew that it was heading for the wharves, and then, he guessed, the harbor.

He couldn't hear any cussing, or any screaming or praying either, so he knew that at least two of the women must be off somewhere else in the flood. Or they were dead.

Chapter Twenty-Three

SAL

In the Spring, Sal had gone to the Kempner house one early morning to get a dollar from her mother so she could go to Boone's grocery store to buy stew meat and an onion for that night's supper. Mrs. Ivy introduced her to the new maid and decided that she would send the girl along with her, if that was all right, to get a few things that Minnie had said she needed in the kitchen.

And so Pearl Hart came into her life.

Her mother didn't like the idea, and when the housekeeper swept quickly out of the kitchen—with Pearl in her wake, to get some money—Minnie told Sal to not be chumming up to this girl, because she was an orphan and had no proper bringing up and that she didn't trust her as far as she could throw Mrs. Ivy.

The two girls walked through the gate of the wrought iron fence that separated the Kempner yard from Broadway. Since Sal was the one who knew where they were going, she made a shy point toward town and took a nervous step in that direction. Pearl fell in behind her. They walked along the sidewalk beside the wide street, already busy on a Saturday morning. The scent of oleander, plentiful there, drifted along with them. The salty odor of the gulf, only ten blocks away, was there, too, but neither girl detected it, since they both had been born on the island and accepted it as the way all air smelled.

Sal walked beside the older girl, who was taller and prettier than she was. Sal was small-boned and short, like her mother, and she sometimes wished that she had inherited some of her father's height. She had seen a photograph of him, taken years ago, in the 1880's, when he was tall and muscular, not stooped and sluggish and tired like he was now. She could have used some of those good looks, too, she thought, since she was wishing. What she had ended up with was her mother's scrawny structure and pale, bland features. She had worked hard at not bearing her disposition.

Now this girl walking to the store with her, she thought, had gotten
lucky in the looks department. Her skin was smooth and the color of
a bowl of cream in a faint shadow. Sal hadn't touched her hands, but
she knew that they would be soft and delicate, not like her own small
hands, which looked like the bony bodies of starved little birds.
Pearl's hair was brown, and as soft and clean looking as her hands.
Sal knew that Pearl's beauty was not of the kind that had to be
worked at—it was simply there, like a pretty sky, or a handsome tree,
to be looked at and enjoyed if you wanted to, but no worse off if you
didn't. Her maid's uniform fit her perfectly and showed off her
shapely body, with neither too many bulges nor too few. She glanced
quickly at her, to confirm her perfection.

"How far is it to this store?" Pearl asked, in a neither friendly nor
unfriendly voice, just wanting to know.

Sal pointed and realized immediately that it was a stupid gesture,
since the store would obviously be in the direction that they were going
in. She was almost afraid to talk, since even her voice would be
inferior to Pearl's.

"Not far," she scratched, losing her volume on the second word.
She cleared her throat, and this brought on a coughing spell.

Pearl slapped her on her back, dug in the pocket of her uniform,
and produced a lemon drop. "Suck on this," she said, slapping her
again. "Mrs. Ivy keeps them in her pocket, and gave me some."

Sal sucked on the candy and nodded her head. The coughing
stopped, but she decided not to talk just yet. "Thank you" was longer
than "not far," and there was no telling what type of seizure she would
fall into if she attempted it.

Pearl said that she hated to start coughing and handed Sal some
more of the lemon drops. She said to take them for later, that Mrs.
Ivy had tons of them and was always giving them away. Sal wondered if Mrs. Ivy ever gave them to her mother. Probably not, she
figured. It wouldn't make much sense to give a person with her
mother's temperament anything sour.

They stopped a few times so that Sal could look into the windows
of stores, to see how the merchandise was arranged, and restaurants,
to see the fancy ways the tables were set, or, if the tables were
occupied, to study the meals laid out on them. She told Pearl that they
were serving breakfast now and showed her the little glasses for the
fruit juice, and the cups and saucers for the coffee. A couple was
eating, but they were too far away for her to see what they were
having. Sal said that she bet they were eating omelets, full of ham and
peppers and onions, and that there was marmalade for their rolls.

Finally, they came to the store. Dust floated through the light from the tall, dirty windows, and more dirt was in evidence on the wooden floor.

Sal went back to the meat counter, where the huge butcher, Boone, in a dirty apron and with a half smoked cigar wedged into the side of his mouth, was slicing thick strips of bacon from a slab on a wooden block. Sal had been there before, and knew enough about the man's gruff nature to know that any attempt at small talk or pleasantry would be wasted, so she simply announced that she wanted a pound of stew meat. Lean, please.

The fat butcher weighed it up, never taking the cigar from his mouth. He had not shaved that morning, nor the one before that, from the looks of it, and Sal could see little particles of meat in the stubble on his face and ample chin, from rubbing his big hands there, she guessed. He first noticed Pearl, who was looking at some items on the shelves, when he handed the wrapped package over the counter. After a moment, Pearl walked over and handed Mrs. Ivy's list to Boone. He gave her a long appraisal, taking his time with it, removing his stogie from the corner of his mouth and rolling his huge tongue over where it had been. Then he looked at the list.

Everything was out on the shelves, he said, except for the salt— he'd help her to get that directly. He smiled at her, and sent his big tongue on another swipe across the stubble of his chin. Sal wondered if he would spit the little pieces of meat out if he came across one of them, or if he would just eat them, since they were there.

"Go on, girlie," he said. "It's all out there where you can find it." He said that his old lady was home sick with the female troubles, or she'd fill it for her. Then he took another long look at Pearl over the top of his counter.

"You're old enough to know about female troubles, ain't you, Honey?"

Pearl looked back at the man for almost as long as he had looked at her, and Sal thought that she was about to tell him something, but she didn't, but came over to where she was standing and said, in a low voice, that she needed her help.

"I want you to tell me what's on here," Pearl said, jabbing at the list with her finger. She looked at the floor for a moment. "I never had any school." She made sure to whisper, so Boone wouldn't hear. "One of the sisters at the orphanage tried to teach me, but I don't think we did most of the words on this list."

Sal read it, and smiled. "It's Mrs. Ivy's handwriting, I think. I can't hardly make it out either."

In a moment, they had found all the things, except the salt. They told Boone they needed it, and he rolled a tall ladder along its track near the ceiling, and told Pearl to climb up to fetch it.

She looked at Sal for a moment, then at the butcher, who smiled. "They's too much of me to get up this ladder," he said, "and the old lady ain't here, like I told you. Now, if you want the salt, you got to go up for it."

Pearl put a hand on the ladder and moved it enough to see that it was stable. She handed her groceries to Sal and stepped on to the bottom rung.

"I'll hold it for you," Boone said, clasping one fat hand around the side of the ladder. Then he pointed to the salt on the top shelf.

Pearl slowly made her way up and took one of the packages of salt. Holding it in one hand, she used the other to steady herself before coming back down.

"Don't you fall now," Boone said. Then he placed his big hands on the back of her thighs, just under her behind. The three people in the store stood still for a moment, frozen in an odd tableau, illuminated by the dirty light from the tall windows. Then the butcher moved his thumbs in small, slow circles to get a better feel, and said he sure wouldn't want her to hurt herself.

In one quick motion, fast enough to make Sal drop some of the groceries she was holding, Pearl was off the ladder and in the fat man's face, weighing the bag of salt in one hand, heaving it slowly up and down, as if to judge its value as a weapon. She spat out the words faster than Sal would have thought she could have even thought of them.

"I'm not the one will be getting hurt, if you try something like that again."

Boone tried his best to look amazed, and innocent. He sputtered out enough words to say that she had misunderstood, that no disrespect was intended. He even smiled.

Pearl didn't smile. When she had had enough time to collect her thoughts, she started slowly, and then the word's came faster, and louder.

"Just you try to remember, you filthy bastard," she said, taking the groceries from Sal, who, wide-eyed, was still clutching her dollar in her fist, "that I work for Mrs. Kempne   And there is other grocery stores in Galveston, in case you didn't know it, you blubbering son of a bitch, and if you can't keep those slimy hams off of me, or that pig's mouth from spitting out shit, then Mrs. Kempner will have to find her one and tell all her friends in the big houses on Broadway to do the same."

The butcher stood still, truly amazed this time, Sal suspected, at the fact that Pearl, who had used so few words at first, had suddenly found so many, and that they were exactly the words that she needed to cut him to the quick.

Pearl didn't intend to wait for a reply. She grabbed Sal by her thin arm and moved her through the door. Sal barely managed to leave the dollar on the counter. They were two blocks down the street before anything was said. Sal hadn't even glanced in Pearl's direction, and, when she finally spoke, it was so low that Pearl had to stop to hear her.

"I said I have to go home," Sal repeated. She pointed behind her. "It's the other way."

Pearl saw her wide eyes and touched her arm.

"It's all right now," she told her. "Just don't you say nothing to your Mama about it, you hear?" Sal nodded. "She'll just tell Mrs. Ivy, and she might think that I done something to make him act like that." She patted Sal's arm again. "You go on home now."

When she had taken a few steps, Sal stopped and turned. Pearl was still standing there, holding her groceries.

"How did you know what to do to that man," Sal asked, "to make him stop bothering you?"

Pearl looked at her. "He ain't the first man like that I've had to put up with." Then she walked in the direction of the Kempner house.

On her way home, with the pound of stew meat and the yellow onion, Sal determined that this girl, who could do a thing like she had just seen her do, would be her friend. She didn't care what her mother thought about it or what she would say, and she didn't even consider what Pearl's opinion might be on the matter.

And then there was a particular Saturday morning in the summer. Saturday was Pearl's half-day off, and she dragged Sal out to the beach.

Even Pearl's feet were perfect, Sal thought, as she watched them move along the sand. Not very large feet, they were rounded and soft looking, not pinched and sickly white like feet that are forever in shoes, though Sal knew that they were in shoes most of the time. They were feet like Sal had seen in paintings of saints and angels. Sal and Pearl had become close friends in the last two months, but she had never seen Pearl's feet before today, nor thought about how they might look. But if she had, she would have predicted that they would look exactly as they did.

The two girls walked along the crowded beach. With every step, Sal saw one of her own feet, narrow and bony like her hands—she thought they must be sending out their whiteness like a signal. She had considered wearing her shoes right down to the water, but knew that she would have to take them off when she got there anyway.

The girls hadn't rented one of the two-wheeled bathhouses that concessionaires rolled out into the water, so that occupants could, after changing into their bathing suits, simply step down into the surf and, later, change back into their street clothes, then hoist up a little flag to signal for the concessionaire, who would bring his horse down and pull the thing up to the road, sparing bathers all that sand on their feet or in their shoes. Pearl had enough money to rent one, from her wages at the Kempner's, but she figured it was money she could save by just changing her clothes in the public bathhouse.

The beach was crowded. Several buggies were parked, their horses sniffing at the sand for something to eat. Mostly children were in the water, some of them running a race against the waves, charging and making quick retreats as the sea breathed in and out. A group of boys about the same age as Pearl stood in the surf splashing water on each other. One of the boys, bigger than the others, seemed to be the ringleader. He had already noticed Pearl and said something to the others that caused them to shake their heads in agreement.

Some of the ladies on the beach wore long, full white dresses, and had on hats with wide brims tied under their chins with ribbons. Two or three men wore suits and stood with their hands in their pockets, appearing to have nothing to do, which, of course, they didn't, since they were on a beach in suits. A few ladies carried parasols, and wide, black umbrellas were in abundance, to protect sensitive skin from the sun. Some people wore bathing costumes, all stripes and loose sleeves. Only very small children and very young boys exposed their chests. For a man to have done so would have been in extremely bad taste, and for a woman to would have been illegal, and punishable in the courts. The only parts of the body that could be seen here that could not be seen in any other part of the city, at any other function, were bare feet.

Sal looked at hers again, and saw the sad, anemic things making their way along the sand. Then she looked at Pearl's, as natural and flawless as the feet of a native on a south sea island.

The girls reached the edge of the surf, and Pearl stepped into it. She leaned down and scooped up enough foamy water to splash her face and shoulders. Then she turned around and motioned for Sal to come in.

Sal stood on the shore and wished she had her shoes on. In fact, she wished she had them on in the front room of her home over on Ship's Mechanic street. She had been born on this island, and had lived here for all of her eleven years, but she had only been into the gulf a few times, with her father, who had grown up swimming in it, and with her brother Joe, who used to do such things. All her life her mother had warned her of the dangers of the sea. Several of her family had been sailors in Ireland and had met watery fates, and she often told Sal about the mysterious force that would come out of nowhere and grab one's ankles and pull its victim to their death. Sal looked at the gulf lapping at her feet and wondered if one of its sinister functions might be to drag members of Minnie Casey's family off to its depths.

"Come on, Sal," Pearl called, impatient to go out farther. She had been born here, too, and spent many hours in the water, especially when she had lived at the orphanage, which was right on the beach, several miles to the west of this one, and never crowded. "It's warm," she said.

It's warm up here, too, Sal thought, but she took a tentative step toward Pearl. Pearl took her hand and led her out a little deeper. Sal stopped for a minute and then let Pearl lead her out a little farther. She felt the first faint touch of the undertow and knew immediately that it was the hidden suction that her mother had so often described. She took a few steps back.

Pearl shook her head, and laughed. "There's nothing that will get you," she said and pointed to the many people, mostly children, who were playing and splashing in the waves. "If there was, it would have already got somebody."

Sal stayed where she was. It would be hard for her to explain it; she wasn't afraid of anything *in* the water, but of the water itself, of its deep mystery and dark potential. She had seen the gulf every day of her life but had never grown to trust it. She had always known that there was something about it, some secret and hidden part of it, that could come up on the land and do great evil. Her brain thought all these things now, but all her mouth could say was, "I don't want to."

Pearl looked exasperated. If they had gone to the trouble to come down here on her half-day off and change into bathing suits, only to turn around and go back home, she would be pretty steamed. "What are you afraid of?" she asked, her hands on her hips. Getting no response, she continued. "Are you scared of fish?" Pearl was often bumped by the tiny mullet that fed near the shore when she swam. "The fish won't bite you—they're afraid of you."

"I'm not afraid of fish."

Pearl shook her head again. "What is it, then?" She searched her mind for possibilities. "There's no snakes in here, and I already promised you I'd hold on to you, so you won't fall down. And even if you did, you would just get right back up. It ain't deep." She bounced up on her toes to show her.

Sal pointed to the horizon. Several ships sat on it. "It's deep out *there*," she said.

Pearl looked at where she was pointing. She squinted her eyes. "I wasn't intending," she said, after a moment, "for us to swim all the way over to Europe."

Sal decided not to tell her that they would hit Florida before they got to Europe. Pearl had never been to school, so she couldn't know that.

"I can't swim anywhere," Sal said, her eyes still on the straight line where the sea met the sky. "I can't swim."

"I know that," Pearl said. "That's why I'm going to hold on to you. Besides, we won't get in over our heads, or anywhere close to it."

Sal finally let herself be led into waist-deep water. She held tight to Pearl, who said that there was nothing to worry about.

"What if there's a storm?" Sal asked.

Pearl gazed at the perfect late-morning sky. Gulls floated around on the slight breeze, their squawking blending in with the shouts of children.

"Well," she said, "I ain't no expert, but I'd personally be pretty surprised if we had a storm in the next few minutes."

They splashed around for a while, and Sal finally felt confident enough to let go of Pearl's hand and take a few wobbly steps on her own. Pearl dove into one of the small waves and came up shaking the saltwater off. She was standing in water that came up to her thighs, and her bathing costume clung to her like a wet towel. The light fabric did little to conceal her features, which were shapely and full, and there, now, for anyone to see.

The group of boys who had been waiting and watching saw them quickly enough, and made their way over get a better view.

Pearl took Sal's hand again and moved her toward the shore.

The biggest boy was to them now and stood between them and the beach. The others gathered around. The boy pulled his thin shirt away from his skin, and let it cling back to him, to better outline his chest and stomach. He shifted his weight from one foot to the other, and Sal knew that he was scanning whatever brain he had for the right words to impress his disciples.

"This water must be colder than I thought it was," he said, and pointed to the top of Pearl's suit. The other boys laughed.

Sal looked, too, and saw that Pearl's full breasts were perfectly displayed, her nipples erect, and straining at the fabric, like two perfect pebbles on upturned bowls.

Pearl turned and faced the boy. Rather than covering her breasts with her hands, as Sal thought she would do, she seemed to push them out even farther toward the boy. She took a long look at him, and let her eyes wander slowly down to a bulge in his own suit. She pointed at it. The boy looked down, and realized that she had made more of an impression on him than he realized. He let his hands fall to cover the evidence.

"I guess it *is* awful cold," Pearl said, shaking her head. "If it shrunk that down to that little bit of nothing."

The boy called her a bitch and waded away. The others laughed and followed him.

The girls stood for a moment in the shallow water and Sal watched Pearl as she attempted to stretch and arrange the folds of her bathing costume to better conceal her body. Pearl's body, Sal knew, was one that would always be on display, with curves and bulges that refused to be hidden. It was a body that would always demand to be looked at, while *her* body, flat and pale, would always blend into the surroundings, and hide itself there.

They went to the beach together several times after that, until the day that Sal was stung by a jellyfish and Pearl hauled her up to the beach road, where Sister Zilphia was sitting in the buggy reading a novel while she waited for them. She took them to the St. Mary's Infirmary, where the doctors and nurses were too busy to fool with such a minor injury and the girls first saw James Tuttle, who helped Sister Zilphia tend to it.

On the first day she met Pearl, after the incident with Boone, Sal had wanted to tell someone about it. She thought about it all that day, and by suppertime she was fairly bursting to tell how this girl had made the fat butcher back away from her. Of how she had put him in his place as quick as a hiccup—as her father might say it—with not all that many words. Of course, Sal wouldn't have actually said the exact words. But she remembered them.

The trouble was that she didn't have anybody to tell it to. Pearl had told her not to tell her mother, and she wouldn't have had the chance to anyway. She told Minnie that she had lost the change from her dollar. She couldn't tell her that Pearl had yanked her out of the place before she could ask for the change without telling what had happened. So Minnie went on for some time about that, about how, in her day, a good Irish girl would never be so careless as to lose any of the money that her Ma had worked so hard to earn.

She couldn't tell Joe, who had complained that the carrots in the stew were too undercooked and said they might as well be eating rocks. Minnie bristled at that and said that this wasn't no cafe she was running, where people could complain about the food. Then Joe pushed his bowl of stew away and said God help her if she was to try to sell such as that in any cafe.

Then Minnie had launched into one of her tirades, and Joe took his cap from the peg by the door and looked for a shirt to put on. Minnie said that no decent Irish lad would come to table with no shirt on, even if he was eating by himself, and surely not with his mother and his sister there. Joe yawned and stretched his arms. The taut muscles of his stomach and chest were well defined under his smooth skin. His father thought that he would become a barrel-chested man, and, with those eyes and eyebrows, he'd end up being the misery of many a woman, more than likely. Minnie always said Joe looked like her father. though her father, a coal miner who died when she was small, had been an ugly little man who in no way resembled this boy.

Then Joe left and Sal wanted to tell her father. But Thurmon had finished his supper by then and ruffled her hair with his hand, and, without a word to his wife, who was by then clanging the dishes in the sink, he was off to the first saloon he came to to sing one of his songs, and to receive his payment in a glass.

Late that night, Minnie's yelling woke Sal up and she stumbled into the front room to watch the scene that was played out all too often.

Thurmon slumped against the tattered sofa, and Minnie was calling him everything that came to mind and reciting the usual litany of the crosses that she had to bear. She ended, as she always did, by saying how happy she was for one thing at least—that her blessed family was no longer alive to see how America had treated her. Even then she wasn't done, which didn't surprise Sal, and she asked Thurmon, who couldn't hear her, what possible good he was to any living soul, she'd like to know. It wasn't, she said, as if God *needed* him to drink up all the liquor in the town, which was the only thing that he was at all good at. And him with a sainted father who was still a hero to Galveston.

And then Minnie made her clicking sound with her teeth and tongue and stomped off to bed. After a moment, Sal sat down beside him on the sofa and leaned her head against his big shoulder.

He smiled when he realized it was her, and took her small hand in his large one.

She wanted to tell him about Pearl, but he wouldn't hear her, she knew. Or understand. She wanted to tell him that people can stand up to the world and make themselves be heard. That people can gather up enough of whatever it takes to make whoever or whatever is tormenting them leave them alone.

She leaned closer to him, and closed her eyes and thought again of that morning, in a dusty grocery store.

She wanted to tell him that she had finally seen it done.

CHAPTER TWENTY-FOUR

Thurmon floated.

His body floated, at least the top part of it, the part not caught in the bends and twists of the submerged wreckage, floated beside the edge of the section of roof. And his mind floated, between awareness of where he was and of the new predicament he was in, and the dark, quiet refuge promised by sleep, or unconsciousness, or whatever it was that called him away to the womb-like, gently rocking place.

When he woke up this time, Sal was still there, leaning down to him, her hands holding his.

He was hurting too badly to do much talking, but he needed to tell her to lie back down and hold on, before she got blown off into the water. He didn't know how much of it he got said.

"The wind's let up some," Sal said, not having to shout as much now. "We can even see the moon sometimes."

He tried to tilt his head enough to see it, but something deep in his back, at the base of something that had to do with the tilting of his head, didn't allow it.

Sal rested her face on the side of the rough shingles, close to his. "Sister Zilphia says that the water will go down soon, Pa." She squeezed his hands. "Then we can get you loose."

He smiled at her. "Did she . . . find that girl?"

Sal shook her head. "But she's still looking. She said she was already hurt pretty bad, and maybe she didn't get to hold on tight enough when their stuff washed over to ours."

He pulled himself up a little, and spit out some water. "How are the children?" he asked.

A hint of a smile appeared at her lips. "Margaret's bored, and ready for the water to go down. And Mary's already asked if big storms bring lots of shells with them."

He looked at Sister Zilphia, on the other side of the platform, still scanning the waves for the lost child.

Sal looked too.

"Her arm's broke, I think," she said. "It's just kind of . . . hanging there. And she's real sad, about the girl—Virginia—and about . . . everybody."

She rubbed the back of his hands, then kissed him.

"You sit still, Papa. Sit still and wait."

He did. At the moment, he had no means, nor inclination, to do otherwise.

Isaac and Joseph didn't know how far out into the gulf their raft had taken them. They kept the children in front of them, and their own backs to the wind. In that position, they wouldn't have been able to see where they were going in the brightest of conditions, much less in the pitch black hell they were bolting through.

For a while they spun helplessly around, sometimes fast enough to dislodge them. But they kept their holds, and then the vessel bobbed for a few minutes before lurching forward. Soon the tiny dots that must have been the flickerings of oil lamps, blinking in the darkness like dim, desperate eyes, appeared in the black outlines of buildings that stretched along what was once the shoreline.

They were going home.

Tucker recognized the porch—it still had its roof and most of its railing—before he crashed into it. The last thing he thought about before he reached it was to wonder how the porch got up ahead of him. It had been behind him when he first saw it. Maybe the big wave had pushed it up over him while he was turning over all those times down under the water. He didn't have any time to think any more about it, since he was there now.

He hit something hard enough to sink pretty far into it. He wondered if he would just go on all the way through whatever it was and then hit something else. When he had seen that he would hit the porch, he had assumed that he would hit boards, since it was made out of boards.

But whatever he was pulling himself out of wasn't any board, he knew. It was more like a mattress, or a sack of cotton.

He pushed himself up and looked into the set of eyes less than three inches from his own.

"Well, shit!," the biggest of the women said. "I thought you never was gonna get here."

Sister Zilphia strained her eyes to search the choppy surface of the waves for the girl who had been with her. The wind had subsided somewhat, and they were able to rise up to a sitting position, or, if they were careful, to even stand up, using their outstretched arms to balance themselves, like high-wire walkers. Zilphia had to be particularly careful, since one arm hung useless at her side.

The waters from the gulf weren't flowing quite as fast as they had been, either. But they weren't slow enough yet for Zilphia to leave the section of the orphanage's roof and go looking for the girl.

Her mind kept returning to St. Louis, even as she called out for the girl, and to that huge hospital where she had been a nurse. Even while her eyes searched in the wind and rain for the small body that she really didn't expect to find, her mind was back there, in the tall-ceilinged wards and the big surgery. Warm, bright rooms, with frosty windows, and the slate-gray winter outside. And James was there, of course. Her own James, not Pearl's.

He was just as tall, and his mustache was trimmed just as neatly, and his black hair was just as unkempt as it always had been. His handsome eyes seemed to have a query in them. They seemed to be asking her what on earth she was doing here, in this storm, with so much death, when she could have been there. With him.

She laughed at the question. Because they both knew the answer.

She hadn't even liked him at first, with his slapping things around in the surgery, and his constant opinions about everything. Later, when they talked of it, he found that awfully funny, because he had originally been put off by her pushy, opinionated manner.

They worked together every day during that particularly cold winter and talked of many things. She talked of the power of faith— he dismissed it as foolish and impractical. They were agreed about women's suffrage. He held out that some women would never vote correctly, and she maintained that most men didn't, if they bothered to vote at all. They came to know each other's routine in surgery so well that they never asked for one instrument or another, or offered, or spoke at all.

He knew she went to Mass every day, but he had never spoken of it. He never even asked her how she became a nun, and she would have gladly told him. It was simple enough—she had been raised by nuns in an orphanage, and when she was too old to be an orphan, she became the only other thing she had known anything about.

She prayed for him and asked God to show Himself to him.

After the first month or so, they took long walks in the park near the hospital. Winter had taken its firmest grip on the city by then, and everything was snow and ice. Ponds and birdbaths were frozen over, and long, spindly icicles hung from the black skeletons of trees.

Because of the snow, the sky was darker than the ground. They wore their biggest coats, with mufflers at their necks. Their words, about the things they had read in the newspapers, and about new and interesting medical techniques and advances, had materialized in the cold air between them and hung there for a few seconds before they disappeared. They each wore thick gloves, so they figured it wouldn't really matter if his hand found hers on their walks, since it wasn't really their hands that were touching, but the gloves.

And he was married, or course. But not living with his wife, who knew and cared only enough about the world to know that she didn't care for St. Louis, especially with all the Negroes who had settled there, and that she had better go back to Scranton, to visit her folks. It had been a long visit. Almost a year. And neither of them expected her to come back, but they never talked of her, or of a romance of any kind.

When it was almost Spring, they kissed each other in the supply room near the surgery. It was a long kiss, and her first one, and they had held tight to each other for a good while.

It turned out to have been their only kiss. The wife returned from Scranton and wouldn't listen to any talk of divorce and treated her long absence as nothing out of the ordinary. All of the right people travel, she said. Her father, chief of staff at a big hospital, expected James to come there. That had been the plan. And the wife and her father seemed determined to follow the plan.

He told her that he would leave his wife and abandon the plan, that she would quit being a nun and that all would be well.

She had stared at him a long time, and hadn't told him that leaving her order wasn't as simple as walking out of a job at a bakery. She prayed about it, and decided to talk it over with her Provincial, to ask for a little guidance, and to discuss her options. The Provincial, a somber lady who hadn't been particularly young when the Civil War was fought, was of the opinion that no options existed. Before it was done—and it was done quickly—a priest was called in and James was on his way to Scranton and Zilphia was on her way to Galveston, and her faith in the church was gone.

And her faith in God?

She looked at the wreckage of the two buildings that the gulf waters were rushing over. She could see several dead children from where she was, their bodies hung up on the debris, held there by the clotheslines that Samuel had cut.

Reverend Mother Camillus's little study was under there some-where, Zilphia thought, and all of her books about faith. And the old nun was under there, too, she supposed. What had all that praying done for her?

She shook her head. She didn't know the answer to that. But she knew this—she knew that the look on James' face, as the people in charge of their lives shipped them off in opposite directions, would always haunt her. That look of stubborn persistence, mixed in with a bit of amazement at the fact that they were surrendering, and a touch of the betrayal that he must have felt, would be her constant companion. Reminding her that plans can be broken, and that free will can actually be followed.

That, at least, Zilphia had faith in.

Margaret and Mary and the boy were all asleep. Thurmon was too, or was unconscious. Sal held his hands so his face wouldn't slip under the water. Zilphia sat down beside her and rubbed the back of her neck.

"Why don't you let me hang on to him for a little while?" she said. "So you can stretch your arms out some."

"They're all right," Sal said. The wind had died to such an extent that they didn't have to yell at each other now. "You need to keep looking for Virginia."

Zilphia shook her head. "She's gone, I think." She looked out over the dark waves again. "I would have heard her by now. She was almost gone before that wave knocked us loose."

Sal shifted her position and rested one hand behind her father's neck. She could feel his breathing.

"If Virginia is dead," Sal said, "is she already in heaven?"

Zilphia leaned forward, frowning at the pain in her arm.

"I think so," she said. "I hope so."

Sal rested her head against her lap and Zilphia found a strand of her hair to twirl around in her fingers.

"Are they all dead, do you think?" Sal asked.

Zilphia waited for a moment, looking for a softer answer than the one that she knew Sal had long since figured out for herself.

"I think they may be," she said. "Some of them might have found something to hold to. But most of them died when the roof fell, I imagine. We were lucky enough to be near the side. We fell out somehow."

They sat quietly. Sal listened.

"The wind's letting up," she said. "And it's not raining as hard. Do you think we could try to get Papa loose now?"

Zilphia shook her head. "The water's still moving too fast," she said. "It'll go down quickly, I'll bet, when it starts. We need to see what we're doing, so we won't hurt him any more than he already is."

Sal nodded. The three children slept behind them, and her father slept on the side of the platform. Zilphia stroked her hair, and Sal knew that she was falling asleep, too.

"Heaven must be getting awfully full," she mumbled, as she drifted into the soft cradle of sleep.

Zilphia felt Sal's rhythmic breathing against her leg. She nodded her head slowly.

"It did a land office business tonight," she said.

Now that the Clines' raft was returning to town, the brothers had to worry about where and how it would deliver them. The current was not nearly as strong now, but it was still swift enough to bash them into the side of a brick building, provided there was a building left standing after the hellish night.

They were passing piles of debris now, so Isaac and Joseph knew they were back over the island. They both looked ahead of them to try to locate the assortment of wreckage, or the structure, that would be their destination.

As it happened, they didn't see it at all, since it wasn't in front of them, but below. The straggling pieces of broken boards under their raft caught on something solid enough to bring them to a jerking halt. When the raft stopped, the five Clines didn't, but were thrown forward into the dark, wet fury of what was left of the storm.

On Broadway, the people in the Kempner house stood at the many tall upstairs windows and looked out at the clear patches in the clouds and at what they hoped was receding water in the yard and the street. Most of the glass had been blown out of the windows, but the people stood there anyway.

Ike Kempner had already left, with a few of the other men, to check on other households on the street. Mrs. Ivy had made her way up to her room in the very top of the house, to "arrange" herself, after sitting on the floor for so long, and to splash on some of her violet toilet water. Ike Kempner's mother was busy seeing to her guests, and to her children.

Minnie had put her rosary beads away and looked out the window for any sign of clearing, for any evidence that things would get back to normal. She looked at the gate, at least she looked at the hole in the tall, ornate fence where the gate had been, since it had been torn loose and washed away sometime since the last time she looked at it. Minnie wondered if she had any family left to come back through that gate sometime today. She looked around her at all the people who had kept the long, dark vigil with her, and wondered what old Ivy intended for her to cook for all these people for their breakfast.

Pearl and James stood at one of the windows too. They didn't talk, and didn't need to. James lightly cupped one hand on Pearl's back, as he had so often when they had danced.

He wondered if the pavilion of the *Garten Verien* still sat in its pretty park. He wondered if the thousands of tiny lights still stretched through the trees.

If there were still trees there.

Tucker knew that he had run right into the big woman, with enough force to bury his face deep into her middle. It must have hurt her, he thought, and he couldn't figure out why she wasn't already kicking and slapping him.

But she was leaning back against the wall, her fat legs pro-truding in front of her. She was even smiling.

"I never figgered on ending up on no goddamned porch," she said. "And it's a goodun, too. I might just keep it, and nail in on the front of my business."

The porch had lodged against a building on top of one of the tall sidewalks, high enough up out of the water so that its floor was not submerged. It seemed to have found a good place to land, Tucker thought, and didn't seem to be about to go anywhere. Maybe the big woman, sprawled over most of it, was holding it down.

Tucker looked at the water rolling by in the street. "It ain't going as fast, now," he said. "And the wind ain't blowin' as hard."

The big woman didn't say anything, but sat on the floor of the porch and inspected her arms and legs for cuts and bruises.

"I wonder where them other three is." Tucker said.

The woman pulled at her dress, a fluffy pink affair, almost exactly the same color of her skin, that didn't cover up as much of her large body as Tucker wished it did. She lifted the fabric away from her huge breasts, and let it splatter back against them. After a moment, she lifted one big leg slightly and emitted the loudest, longest fart that he had ever heard.

He tried not to look surprised. She smiled and looked relieved.

"One of them is over yonder in that winder," she said, and pointed a fat finger across the street.

Tucker looked till he found her there, hanging on with both arms wrapped around the center post of what had been a wide window.

"She'll just have to hold on," the big woman said. "Till it's over."

Tucker leaned back against the rail, glad that the wind had slowed down enough for him to relax a minute.

"It'll be over 'fore long, I reckon," he said.

"It might be over for Lucy and Betty right now," the big woman said. "I ain't seen 'um. Nor heard 'um. And with all the hollerin' that Lucy was doin', I guess I could hear her over a goddamned steam engine. I ought not have any trouble hearin' her over the last little bit of a storm."

He looked at several bodies lodged against piles of wreckage and in the recesses of buildings. From where he sat he counted nine that he knew were bodies. Another three might have been, but they might as easily have been towsacks, or dogs, or pieces of furniture. It was still dark, and his eyes were tired of looking for things anyway.

"I hope they all right," he said, thinking about the loud, little woman and the other one. "It don't hardly seem right, folks going through a night like this one, and then dyin' at the end of it, when the wind and the flood be about to quit."

The big woman looked at him.

"What's your name?" she asked.

"Tucker," he said, and spat into the water.

"Well, Tucker" she said, "them girls is whores, you see. So they ain't had much experience with things bein' right." She scratched her wide neck. "But I'll tell you this. If they *are* dead, they ain't any more or less dead than all them other ones you been lookin' at."

"When it comes to bein' dead, Tucker," she said, "bein' right or wrong don't amount to much more than a puddle of piss."

CHAPTER TWENTY-FIVE

Thurmon felt the shifting before the others did. His shoulders hurt, and his head. He knew that he ought to be hurting in his legs, but he couldn't feel anything there, or in his hips or waist. So the shifting of the mass of debris that held him wasn't really a feeling, but a tugging. Not a drastic one, or his head would be under the water now, but a slight one, almost a teasing.

Sal was asleep, her head resting in Sister Zilphia's lap. The nun's hand rested behind Thurmon's neck.

The wind was from the south now, and considerably diminished. The rain had settled into a softer, steady shower, no worse than any of the thunderstorms that had swept over the island since Zilphia had first come there.

"I wonder if it's midnight yet?" she said.

She looked at the sky, clearer of clouds now than it had been. She could see some stars, and the moon. Thurmon didn't respond, so she answered her own question.

"Maybe so. It seems like it should be midnight about a week from now, doesn't it?"

He grimaced and nodded.

She looked at Sal and the other three sleeping children, and then back to him.

"Are you hurt badly, do you think?"

He lifted his head. "The places that I can feel are all right. Just sore." He blinked his eyes. "I can't feel anything under my belly. But I must be mashed up some down there. There's some blood been coming up to the top."

"I've seen it," she said. She leaned down closer to him. "The water should start going down soon, I imagine. Now that the wind and rain are slower."

He nodded.

"The thing is," he said. "This roof is . . ." He didn't get to finish, since the section of roof did what he was about to describe. Something at its bottom shifted and the whole thing rocked heavily, throwing

Zilphia off of it altogether, and sending the four children sliding toward the edge.

Sal woke up before she entered the water and managed to grab Wee Mary before they both went under. When they surfaced, Zilphia was already back on the platform, and reaching down to help them up. Margaret and the boy were hanging onto the side.

Zilphia was glad that the current was slow enough now to let them move themselves around. If this had happened even a half an hour before, all of them would surely have been swept away.

"Is anybody hurt?" she yelled, as she pulled Sal and Mary on board.

Nobody answered. She crawled over and lifted up Margaret and the boy with her good arm.

Margaret blinked rapidly and sputtered for a moment, once she was sitting on the edge. Zilphia slapped her back a few times.

"Did you swallow too much water?" she asked.

"Naw," the girl answered. "But I wasn't figgering on swallering none." She coughed once more. "That's what set me off, I guess. Getting throwed in the water while I was asleep."

Sal screamed, and Zilphia turned and crawled to where she was. Thurmon had been repositioned when the section of the house shifted. His head and shoulders had been above the water level before, now only his face was, and barely that. Each wave sloshed over him. He had already judged the short span of time between them so he could steal quick breaths.

Sal tried to pull his head up, but that brought such a pained expression to his face that she stopped. She hadn't been able to lift his head very far, anyway—whatever held him had a secure grip.

"We got to get him loose," she yelled, as Zilphia gazed at the new situation.

Sal lowered herself over the side, and was underwater before she could stop her. In a few seconds, she was under with her, both of them pulling at the twisted wreckage.

The three young children sat close together on the roof and watched as they came up for air time after time before they pulled themselves back under.

Zilphia saw the hopelessness of the task before Sal did. But she kept at it, pulling and pushing until her lungs were nearly bursting, before going back up for more air.

Finally, they both leaned on the edge, exhausted, their faces resting on the rough shingles. The whole thing settled another fraction of an inch into the sandy ground at its bottom.

Sal leaned over and cupped her small hand under the back of her father's head. The water was almost to his mouth now, and he had to arch painfully upward to breathe, or speak.

"Sit still, Papa," Sal said, and kissed his forehead. "It'll go down anytime now."

He winked at her.

Zilphia looked at the sky, which wasn't any clearer than it had been the last time she looked at it, and at the water, which hadn't begun to fall yet.

"We just have to wait, now," she said, and touched Sal's arm. They both knew that no amount of tugging and pulling would dislodge what gripped what was left of Thurmon's legs. When the water receded, they could at least try to make him comfortable, until someone came who could get the debris off of him.

She rubbed Sal's arm. "There's nothing else we can do for now."

The roof moved again, tilting Thurmon nearly an inch deeper. Sal tried to hold his head up. His mouth was underwater now, and the painful look in his eyes was replaced with panic.

Sal looked at his eyes, and turned to look at Zilphia.

"You can pray!" she shouted.

Zilphia saw his eyes, too, and the water that was sloshing around his nose and mouth.

"You've got to *pray!*" Sal screamed.

The raft that had served the Clines so well, and taken them so far, was gone now, and all five of them wallowed in the deep water.

Isaac and Joseph knew that conditions had improved greatly. The wind wasn't as high, and the current was slower. But they also knew that five people, three of them children, being swept and blown around in water full of debris wasn't a good idea even in the best of conditions. And conditions on Galveston still fell far short of being ideal.

Isaac twisted and turned and looked for his girls, but all he could see was more water, and darkness. He floated for a moment, and had started to look around in all directions when he heard his name being called.

Before he could respond, or even turn in the direction of the voice, someone grabbed his hand and pulled him up out of the current and into a window.

He shook his head and was suddenly being hugged by all three of his daughters. He looked around.

Whatever house this was, it had stayed in one piece. They were sitting in an upstairs room, and a framed picture still hung over the mantle.

Joseph leaned against the wall, his features and his clothing looking like they had been through what they had been through.

"It's almost like we were back where we started," he said.

Isaac hugged his girls closer to him, and thought of Cora Mae.

"Almost," he said.

He looked at his brother.

"That's twice, tonight," he said, "that you gathered these chicks up and had them waiting, while I hung on to the side of a house, or floated in the water."

He was holding his youngest daugher; he leaned his face against hers.

"I guess I'll have to give you a raise," he said.

CHAPTER TWENTY-SIX

Once the wind had stopped its roaring, Tucker heard the screams coming from somewhere behind the relocated porch. He crawled over to the edge and tried to see what was going on back there, but he couldn't.

He turned to the big woman.

"You hear all that?" he asked.

She nodded that she did.

"You reckon we ought to go see if they need some help?" he asked.

The big woman, still resting comfortably against the back of the porch, dug something out of her ear with a short, fat finger. She inspected it and flicked it away.

"I don't see no anchor shoved up your ass," she said, "so I guess you can go see about anything you want to. Now me, I intend to see about stayin' right here, till that street's as dry as a drunk's throat."

Tucker sat still for a moment, and listened to the screaming.

"I reckon I'll go see about it," he said.

He looked across the street, at the woman who still clung to the center post of the window frame.

"I guess you can watch after her," he said, to the big woman.

She slowly turned her huge head, and found the woman in the window.

"I guess I can," she said, "at least as good as you can, from across a goddamned mean river like that one." She scratched her leg. "You couldn't skin her offa there with a claw hammer, anyhow."

Tucker edged his way around the side of the porch and stepped down into water till he found the sidewalk. The current wasn't moving nearly as fast as it had been, but it was still moving fast enough for him to know that he had to be careful.

He didn't have to go far.

The outside wall of the building that the screaming was coming from was gone, leaving only a vast, open first floor. Terrified people hung on to the several support poles. Some of them were making considerable noise.

Tucker suspected he knew who was doing the loudest of the screaming. He pulled himself through the dirty, dark water and finally found her, yelling out one of her prayers.

She was holding so tight to the pole that Tucker didn't see how there was any blood left in her arms and hands.

She recognized him, screamed a little more, and then shut up.

"Betty's dead," she said, with as little emotion as she might use to tell him that his pocket was unbuttoned. He guessed that all of her emotion was required in the screaming. "I seen her bash up against a building. Her head cracked open, and she floated off."

Tucker nodded at the report.

"Them other two is all right," he said. "That . . . big one is up on a porch just around that corner. We can go on back over there, I guess, if you want to."

She had hung on to the pole as long as she intended to. She let Tucker help pry her arms from around it.

"Now, hang on to me," she said. They headed back over to the sidewalk.

Tucker looked down once, and saw several bodies caught against the back wall. Two were children, and one was a baby, naked, no more than a year old, he figured. He thought of his own children then and hoped they weren't pushed up against the dark side of a building, floating around in dirty water.

When they got to the sidewalk, and the faster current pushed against them, the woman started screaming again. Tucker wished the big woman had come with him, so she could slap her. But she hadn't, and he figured he'd better not do it, since all the water would go down after while, when the storm had moved on, and then the little woman would probably start screaming about that. And then Mr. Ketchum, if he lived through this night, would have another thing to come after him about. Mr. Ketchum surely wouldn't approve of a black man slapping a white woman, Tucker thought, even if the woman was a whore.

So she kept screaming and he kept pushing her in front of them, and they came to the back of the porch.

He worked his way around its side first, and was ready to tell the big woman that he had found the little one when he saw that she wouldn't be slapping her, or anybody else.

The piano, a large upright, had hit her square in the center of her large body. She must have been leaning with her head forward, Tucker thought, because it was enough of a mess for him to be able to tell that it was the first thing hit. Her big pink arms floated helplessly on either side of the piano, her hands, like small hams, moving up and down in the waves, like she was making the first, slow effort to fly. Her face, what was left of it, looked surprised.

The small woman worked her way around the side of the building, and saw the piano and its victim. She stopped screaming as quickly as she had started.

"I think that's the piano from our own place," she said.

Tucker looked across the street, to see that the woman was still holding onto the window pole. Then he looked back at the big woman.

"It's a shame," he said.

The little woman nodded.

"She had took a liking to this here porch," he said. "Said she might even put it on the front of y'all's place."

The little woman shook her head, and looked at the piano, to see if it was the one she remembered.

"Probably there ain't no place to put a porch on by now," she said. "It was just about gone when we got out of it."

Tucker leaned down beside the end of the piano that the big woman wasn't attached to and closed his eyes.

He had wished a lot of things in the last week and especially, in the last few hours. But, right now he just wished it would be morning.

All over the city, those of Galveston's people who had made it through the night wished for the same thing.

It was still raining, and the wind was still blowing. But they had seen rain and wind like this many times. This was rain and wind that folks could get out and around in, if they had to.

But the flooding was still a problem. Those of Galveston's people who had seen overflows before knew that the water would go back into the gulf and the bay more quickly than it had come out. They had never seen so much of it come over the island before, but there was no reason to expect, they figured, for it go down any slower.

They just wished it would go ahead and do it.

Some of the people who had watched members of their family die, or their friends, or who had heard or seen or felt whatever had been their home crashing down behind them as they fled, weren't so sure that they were ready for the flood to subside, or for the sun to come up, as it surely would, in not much more than an hour.

Because they weren't all that sure that they were ready to see what the morning's light would show them.

North of the island, the center of the storm moved over pastures and farms, ripping the late summer crops from the reddish dirt, tearing whole branches of fat, ripening pecans from trees, and stirring up the water in stock ponds and creeks.

But it was doomed now, and dying, singing out the furious finale of its death rattle. With no warm ocean under it to fuel it, it was starving.

But still it howled, and pushed itself forward, northwest, toward the center of the continent that would finally kill it.

Near Alto, in the steep, pine covered hills of East Texas, a farmer and his family sat in the largest room of their small house and listened to the wind, and watched the rain slap against their windows. The storm had awakened everybody a couple of hours earlier than usual, so they had crawled out of their beds to watch it. The sky over the tiny farm exploded with lightning and thunder, and the oldest of their children, a girl, said that she thought that she had seen the steeple of the Shiloh church in the bright light.

The farmer nodded. His wife, who had as many plates of break-fast to get on the table this morning as she did on any other, went on with her work at the stove, and said that she doubted it, since they couldn't see the Shiloh church from anywhere on the place on the clearest of days. And it probably didn't get any closer in a storm.

Sal had prayed for as long and as hard as she could, but her father still wasn't loose, and the water still hadn't fallen. Sister Zilphia was praying too, she guessed, as they took turns keeping their hands cradled under Thurmon's head.

She was so exhausted that she barely heard him when he called her.

"Sweet Potato," he managed to say as he stretched his neck up enough to get his mouth out of the water. She held both of his hands in hers, and squeezed them tighter, to let him know that she could hear him.

"Sweet Potato," he said again, and coughed up some water that he had swallowed. "It's moving again, down there. I can feel it."

She shook her head. He smiled at her, and lifted one of her hands up to kiss it. Almost all of his energy was gone now, and his words came out in little more than a whisper.

"It'll be over soon," he said.

She clenched her small lips into the slightest of smiles and nodded. He shook his head slowly.

"This part will," he said. He held her hand next to his face. "We did our best, didn't we?"

She was crying now. "When the water goes down, Papa," she said, "when . . ."

He put his hand to her mouth. Zilphia was behind her, now, her hand on her shoulders.

"Sal," he whispered, barely able to get the word past his pain, and the water. "It's no good. I'm all crushed up under here. Awful bad, I guess." He paused to catch his breath.

"Even if the water . . . ."

But Sal was crying so loud now, racked with gasping sobs, that he stopped trying to talk.

Zilphia held her and leaned down to him.

"I prayed," she shouted, whether at him or somebody else, Thurmon couldn't tell. "I prayed and prayed and prayed!" Tears streamed down her face with the rain.

Now he put his finger to her lips, and she was quiet.

"I know that," he whispered. He winked at her. "And it worked."

She stared at him and continued to cry.

"Reach in my shirt pocket," he managed to say.

She felt the bottle, miraculously unbroken, and lifted it out. She held it in front of him.

He smiled, and shook his head.

"Not that," he whispered. "Not this time."

She reached in again and found his father's watch. She put it in the palm of his hand. He clamped his fingers around it.

"Sweet Potato," he sighed.

Sal was back in front of him now, still crying. He handed her the watch, and cupped his big hand over hers.

She leaned down against his face, and cried harder, so hard that it was impossible to speak for a moment. When she did, the words were not much more than frantic gasps.

"No, Papa," she cried, "no, please. When the water goes down, we can . . ."

He reached up, painfully, and put his hand over her mouth.

"We can do something better right now," he whispered.

Her horrified eyes were still shaking back and forth.

"We can just sit still . . . ," he said, and the bottom of the debris shifted. He had to strain to raise up enough, now, to get a few more of the words out.

". . . and wait for . . . ."

And then he was gone.

The three small children sat as still as statues on the section of ruined roof. Zilphia and Sal watched in silent horror as the face disappeared into the brown water.

Sal leaned forward and reached for her father's face, but the wreckage had shifted harder this time and dragged him deeper. Both of them were over the side as quickly as they could get there, but the debris had pulled him so far under it that they couldn't even find him, much less help him.

Zilphia pulled Sal back, before the shifting clutter could catch them too. She pushed her back up on to the platform, then pulled herself up with her good arm.

Zilphia fell backward, and collapsed into a fit of crying.

Sal held the watch in both hands against her face. The little energy left in her sent out a last shrill cry, and then she fell back against Zilphia.

The rain pelted down, softer now than before. The first trace of a clear sky full of stars appeared through the tattered clouds. The three children crawled over to the edge of the section of roof, and watched the dark, rolling water where the man had been.

CHAPTER TWENTY-SEVEN

JOE

On Wednesday night, the captain's cabin of the *Maydelle* had swayed softly, and Barkley, the captain, concentrated on the quartering of an apple. When he finished, he lifted the wedge of fruit to his lips with the blade of his knife. His pleasure with the sweetness of the apple was apparent, and caused Joe, who was standing before the Captain's worktable, to remember how hungry he was. He hadn't eaten since early that morning, and that hadn't been anything to brag about: two dry biscuits left over from his family's supper of the night before.

He had swung by their dingy rooms early, making sure that he had waited long enough for his mother to be at work. He knew that his father would either be at his job at the Cotton Exchange or off on one of his binges, probably the latter. His sister, Sal, had been sound asleep when he took the biscuits, the only food he could find.

The remaining slices of Barkley's apple, fat and glistening in the light of the oil lamp, looked awfully inviting to Joe. Then the captain reached into an open drawer of the table and lifted out a parcel wrapped in oilcloth. He delicately raised the corners of the cloth, and there was a half round of cheese, bright yellow under its red wax skin.

Barkley cut a generous portion and then took a bite of it with the apple. Joe watched the process and would have been grateful for a chair—his knees had begun to tremble. From the hunger, he told himself, not anything else.

When Barkley finally leaned back in his chair, and spoke, it was through a mouthful of apple and cheese. Some of the juice found a zig-zag trail down his rough chin and throat. A thick British accent, not quite harsh enough to be Cockney, but well short of refined, came through the chewing.

"So this here is the boy you been telling me about."

Quin nodded that it was. Barkley looked long and hard at Joe, before feeding himself another wedge of apple with the knife and taking another bite from the cheese.

"Tell me, lad," he said, when he had chewed enough of the food to get the words out, "would you be willing to prove your worth in a tight situation, in exchange for passage out of here?" He continued to chew, then stopped and waited for an answer. He leaned forward in his chair. "Quin here tells me you're mighty interested in getting off this island."

They stared at each other.

"Well, what's it to be? I got to hear it from you, not from him."

The small man behind Joe had pushed him roughly forward. Joe, clutching his cloth cap in both hands, nodded that he was willing. Barkley leaned back again, and resumed his chewing.

"Quin tells me that you're Irish." His face cracked into the slight suggestion of a smile.

"Knowing, as I do," he said, watching the boy for any response, "that all Irish are liars and thieves and not to be trusted or depended on, tell me why I should take you on."

Joe returned the captain's stare, denying him any evidence of emotion.

"I guess it's for thieving and lying," he finally said, his first words to the man, "that you're wanting me."

Barkley stopped his chewing again, and Quin very nearly stopped breathing. None of the three spoke or moved. The only sound in the cabin was the squeak of the lamp hanging from the ceiling keeping its balance as the ship swayed.

Then Barkley's rough face broke into his broadest smile yet.

"I guess that's right." He looked at Quin. "Let's take this brave Irish lad on for our little adventure." Then he tossed the remaining wedge of apple to Joe. "He looks smart enough to know better than to do us wrong, and to keep his trap shut if things fall apart."

He reached behind him, opened a cabinet, took out a bottle of brandy, and a single cup. He poured out half a cupful and lifted it in the air.

"To the Queen, gentlemen." He sucked at a piece of apple lodged between his teeth, retrieved it, and spat it on the wooden floor. "A sad, pathetic old package of bones and fat, and on her deathbed, by all accounts, but still," he sighed, "the Queen."

He drank the toast alone, leaving Joe and Quin with nothing to do but watch him do it. Joe ate the slice of apple.

Barkley wiped the sweat from his forehead with a rag, then tossed it on the cluttered table in front of him. Both portholes in the cabin stood open, but no breeze had found them.

"It's too goddamned hot in here to even think," he said, standing up quickly and pushing his chair away from him. "Let's go out where we can breathe."

They followed him up the narrow ladder and were soon on the deck. The sailor who had led them down into the ship was not there, and Joe knew that the rest of the crew were over in the whorehouses and saloons, catching up on their vices after the long voyage from England.

It was a hot, still night, with not enough of a breeze to bother any of the rigging on the ships tied to the docks. Barkley took a small cigar from his pocket, bit the tip off and spat it into the water, and struck a match against the railing. He touched the tiny flame to the end of the cigar, watched the match burning in the windless night until it nearly reached his fingertips, then flicked it over the side.

Joe stood quietly, knowing that all he was expected to do was listen. Quin was even more skittish out on the deck than he had been down in the cabin. He stood back away from them, in the shadows of the wheelhouse. There were many things in Galveston that Joe knew he wouldn't miss when he was away from here, on this very ship, and the smelly, nervous little man for whom he had stolen for the last year was near the top of his list.

"It's got to be tomorrow night," Barkley said, the cigar lodged in the corner of his mouth. He spat into the murky water.

"We sail as soon as it's on board, and I don't want to tarry around here. I don't intend to wait on neither you or the stuff you're bringing." He looked at Joe, who nodded.

Barkley leaned on the rail, and stared off into the night. "If you don't get here in what I figger is the right amount of time, then you don't get your money." He turned to find Quin, in the shadows, and nodded in his direction. "Cause he don't get his."

Then he looked back at Joe. "And you don't get your passage." He lifted the cigar out over the rail, tapped an ash into the water, and looked back out at the dark bay. "If you do your job right, and I get what I'm wanting, and not any of it banged up or damaged, then I'll take you to New Orleans, or even up to Boston, if you want to go that far. Though you might have to spend a day or two in New Orleans, anyway, while we wait out a storm I've heard is bearing on Florida. But then you're on your own. You'll have enough of my money in your pocket to get you started, but you and me will be done with each other. Understood?"

Joe nodded, again, but Barkley didn't even watch him do it.

In a moment, when he had finished staring at whatever had held his interest, Barkley turned and walked across the wooden deck to the opposite side of the ship. He pointed in the general direction of the wharves.

"You'll be going into that warehouse, the big one, just before dark, after the workers have left and before the night watchman gets there." He jabbed a finger toward his fellow countryman, still standing, bent and restive, in the darkest place he could find. "Quin has been watching, Quin has, and he tells me the watchman ain't any too good about gettin' to his work on time. So that leaves us a little while, when you can get in there and find what you'll be looking for."

Joe walked over to him and found the huge building, its outline barely visible in the darkness.

"I ain't never seen nothin' around there but cotton bales," he said.

Barkley laughed. "That's what everbody is quick to tell me," he said. He pointed the cigar at Joe, its glowing tip bright red in the night. "But I know a little something about it that everbody else don't."

He hiked one leg up, rested his boot against the rail, then leaned forward and turned the small cigar in his hand.

"The old man who owns that warehouse, and all that cotton, is planning on building himself a house. A mansion, bigger than all the other ones over there on that fancy street. I know that, because I been hauling the best woodwork and bricks over here for him for the last two years."

Joe looked at the dark blob of a building again, and hoped the Englishman wasn't expecting him to tote out boards and bricks.

"Now that old man," Barkley said, "is no different from any of the other rich men in this town. He wants that house to be the biggest and fanciest that he can put up, since that's what people like him figger other folks judge him by." He looked off into the distance, over the low tops of some of the city's buildings. If it were daylight, he would have been able to see the steep roofs of some of the big houses on Broadway. "Now a man," he said, "can only do so much to make his house bigger and grander than another man's. There's only so many archways and towers you can put on one house." He leaned down, again, over the rail. "But what goes *in* the house, now that's a different thing. When a man wants to make a showing there, they ain't hardly no limits to what he can do. That's what I'm after."

He was quiet for a few moments.

Joe decided to go ahead and ask the question outright, since he was tired of having to guess about it, and since Barkley obviously wasn't any too anxious to tell it.

"So, what am I supposed to steal?"

Barkley smiled, and looked at him.

"Pictures."

He said it so low that Joe thought he must have heard it wrong. "Pictures?"

"Just some pictures," Barkley said. "The heaviest thing about them is the frames, and a strong, young Irish lad like you should be able to have them out of there and on board the *Maydelle* in no time, without even breaking a sweat."

Barkley laughed, again, louder than the last time. "Now you're wondering, I'll wager, why I would go to all this trouble and expense to get some pictures." He didn't wait for a confirmation. "But these here ain't just any pictures, boy. They're paintings, with the names of some of the most famous artists in Europe on the bottom of them. Any museum would be proud to have them, and pay well to get them. But I can't sell them to no museum, since they would know where they came from. But I know people who will buy them, provided they ain't damaged any." He turned to look at Joe. "So you'll have to be careful."

Joe thought about it. "Why would he keep them in a warehouse? He owns one of the biggest buildings in Galveston, and a bank, too. Why don't he keep them there?"

Barkley smiled at that. "Now I ain't asked him personally," he said, and laughed. "So I don't know. Maybe he don't want anybody to know he's got them. Maybe he intends to save them for that big mansion he's going to build and then have a big party and say 'Look here what I've got', and start rattling off the names of all those dead artists like they was a grocery list."

He leaned back down over the rail, removed the cigar, looked at it, and dropped it between the ship and the dock. "I just know they're in there, stored in crates till he gets his house built. Some of the fellows who brought them to him told me that much." He peered at the pitch-dark cotton warehouse, and thought of the fortune resting in it. He had done his research and knew that, while none of the works were masterpieces, there were enough lesser known canvases by some of the masters to make up an impressive collection. He, too, had wondered why the old man would store them there, rather than in a more secure place. Probably, he had finally reasoned, because the agents and their dealings had been of a somewhat shady nature, and the cargo should be kept in a place where no attention would be called to it. What better place than in a sprawling warehouse full of the one commodity that was so plentiful that only an idiot would think to steal it?

Joe looked at the building, again. "It's a big place, and full of cotton. How am I supposed to find some pictures in it, in the time I'll have?"

"I doubt," Barkley said, "that somebody as smart as that old man is going to store anything that valuable up under a bunch of cotton bales. Don't you?"

Joe just looked at him and waited for his answer.

"So," Barkley went on, "there's a room—made of brick—with a heavy lock or two on the door."

Joe thought for a moment. "I might be able to find a room, I guess, if there's enough light. But how am I supposed to have time to cut any lock, or two or three, before that guard gets there?"

Barkley turned to Quin, who still hadn't said anything. The little man ambled forward, and held onto the rail.

"They's a nigger what sweeps the place out ever day, right before dark," Quin said. "He knows where the room is and can saw the lock while he's supposed to be sweeping, and leave it lookin' like it ain't never been touched. He can even help you tote the things out. Some of 'em might be too big for you to handle."

Joe frowned. "I got to trust a nigger to help me?"

Quin came closer to him. "I talked to him already, and I could tell that he wants the money he'll get for this as bad as you want to ride this here ship out the Boliver roads."

"But has he said he'll do it?" Barkley asked, a note of irritation in his voice.

Quin nodded. "He ain't said it. But he'll do it. That money's been workin' on him since Saturday. I doubt that he's thought about anything else." Then he sighed, as if he had already used more words than he had intended.

The next morning morning, Joe ate the breakfast that Sal cooked for him—biscuits with butter—but he was still hungry. He wished he had himself a plate of sausage and bacon and eggs with a couple of flapjacks hanging over the edge. Now that would be a breakfast to take some time with, not like the scraps thrown at him at home. He figured that if he could just start out all his days with a big breakfast like that, then he would go far. It was one of the promises he had made to himself, to be able to eat a plate of good food whenever he wanted to.

The wharves this morning were already bustling with the constant loading and unloading of ships, but it didn't take him long to find Danny, his one true companion, sleeping among some bales of cotton, curled under a fold of tarpaulin. Awake, Danny spent much of his time maintaining a malevolent frown which he projected to betray his age—he was only twelve—and his slender boy's body. Asleep, the scowl was gone, and he looked even younger than he was, curled up against the damp morning. Joe pushed on him till he woke up—he didn't want him looking like that. He liked the frown better.

"I ought to let you be," Joe said, grabbing the tarpaulin and throwing it to the ground, "and let some dockhand hook you up with this cotton and haul you into a ship and tote you off to England or somewheres."

Danny still lay on his bed, letting the morning light work slowly into his eyes. He scratched and yawned. He had been dreaming about whores and didn't much appreciate being called back from them so suddenly, even by his only friend.

"I'd go," he said, smacking the sleep from his mouth. "If they got women in England." He yawned. "It don't matter much to me where I am, long as they got women."

Joe slapped at him with his cap, and sat down on the bale. Danny leaned up to sit beside him. "There's plenty of women here," Joe said, "and I ain't noticed you botherin' them any."

Danny rubbed the last of the night from his eyes, felt around until he found his own cap and put it on, then locked the muscles of his face into the stern, no foolishness attitude that he had so perfected. He spat in the direction of the buildings across the street from the wharves.

"There ain't nothing here but dock whores and la-de-dah old fancy women." He spat again, and shouldn't have—the last of it ran down his chin. He quickly wiped it away. "I wouldn't give you a nickel for all of 'em."

"You ain't got any nickel," Joe told him.

Danny surveyed the area around them and didn't speak until he was satisfied that they were alone. When he did speak, it was in a low, conspiratorial voice. "I got more than that by a mile, and you can bet on it. I been savin' up, and when me and you light out of here, I plan to have enough put by to pay my way, and to have some fun with."

Joe smiled and slapped at him with the cap again. "If you mean to just spend all your time and money on all these women that you're hoping for, I might reconsider taking you with me."

A look of concern came over Danny, and for a few seconds his frown was replaced by the soft features of a little boy. But the moment passed as quickly as it had come. "You'll take me," he said, leaning back against the cotton, "because that's always been our plan."

Joe found the *Maydelle* in her berth and stared at her. Suddenly he didn't want to talk about plans anymore. Besides, his hunger was calling to him again.

"Come on," he said, pulling Danny off his perch, "let's go see if there's any bread left."

They left the wharves, crossed the road, and walked along one of the streets of the city. The handsome Moody Building, four stories tall, rose up beside them, and they stopped at its corner to look up and down Avenue B. People moved along the streets and sidewalks and into and out of the big doors of the stores.

Danny yawned and scratched his groin. He had forgotten to piss, what with Joe being right there to talk to him when he woke up. And a good, steamy piss was pretty high on his agenda at the moment. He told Joe he needed to.

"There ain't no alleys along here," Joe said. "Hold it in till we get over to Postoffice—they's plenty of places there."

They walked along for another moment. A woman was coming down the sidewalk toward them, still almost a block away. She wasn't paying them any attention, and was focused on where she was going.

Danny leaned close to Joe. "Do you reckon she'd see me if I just went against this building?" His voice held the urgency that he was suddenly feeling. Joe didn't answer. Danny leaned close again. "Would *you* care if I did?"

Joe sighed and shook his head. "I don't give a damn what you do. But if she starts yelling for a cop, it's your business, not mine." Danny didn't respond. "Hell," Joe went on, "if you can't wait for two more blocks, you ought to be in a damned diaper."

Danny held it in, the words burning almost as much as his bladder. In a moment, the woman passed them and, in what seemed like an eternity longer, they came to Postoffice street. He ran into the first alley they came to and relieved himself.

As he was finishing, he heard a slight movement, from deeper in the alley. There, in the dark shadows of the tall buildings, sat a small child, a black girl, holding what looked like a homemade doll. The child sat on an upturned crate, and watched Danny as he concluded his business. He wished she would look away, because he needed to shake out the last bit, and he didn't particularly want to do that in front of a girl, even a black one. But she continued to watch, so he finished, and was through buttoning his pants before he saw the woman, no doubt the girl's mother, standing in the doorway to what must be their home.

The woman called the girl to her and told her to go inside. When she spoke, her voice was not angry—Danny thought it was almost friendly. But she wasn't smiling.

"Why you got to do that in front of a chile?"

Danny just stared at her, and, in a moment, the woman went inside and closed the door.

He had to run to catch up with Joe, who hadn't waited on him.

"Did you know that niggers live in the alleys?" he asked, when he got to him.

Joe laughed and slapped at him again. "Where did you think they lived, in them castles on Broadway?" He laughed some more. "Why? Did you piss on one?"

"I just never knowed that there was places to live in off of those alleys. I guess I never looked back far enough back in one."

Joe laughed again. "Well, that's good. When you're pissing, you'd better keep your eyes on your business, and not be looking around at the scenery."

They stopped far enough from the bakery so that they could see what was going on there, but so that they wouldn't be noticed. Joe and Danny had done this before, and they knew that they had to wait for exactly the right moment, when the baker was in the back room where the ovens were, and the front room was empty. Then, while Danny watched for anyone coming down the street, Joe would run in and take whatever was there, or whatever he could carry, in the way of fresh, hot bread.

At the moment, the baker was in the front room. They could see him through the window, placing rolls in a basket for delivery to one of the fancy restaurants. The boys had only been caught once, when the baker came in too quickly, and found Joe with his arms full of bread. Joe had suffered two slaps on the side of his head that time and a lecture. The baker recognized him and went on and on about how he wouldn't call the police out of respect for Joe's grandfather, God rest his soul, and how if he didn't mend his ways, he would turn out like Joe's father, though he had never known even him to stoop to stealing, and what a disgrace it was to the memory of a great hero like his grandfather. When it was over, Joe resolved to never get caught again, not because of any sense of remorse, but as a practical matter. The man knew him. There could be trouble.

When the baker had his goods arranged to his liking, he went back to see to his ovens. Joe looked up and down the street, which was practically empty. Now was the time.

He motioned for Danny to keep watch, and he darted across the street and into the shop, taking care not to make any more noise with the door than necessary. He didn't have time to pick and choose, so he grabbed the first basket he came to and left as quickly as he had come. He didn't slow down when he got to Danny, and the younger boy fell in with him. People on the street watched them as they ran, but nobody tried to stop them, either not wanting to get involved, or not inclined to work up that much of a sweat on such a warm morning. They ran to the nearest cross street, turned down it, and ran for almost two blocks before falling to the curb, lunging forward for each breath, like hungry horses after apples.

After a minute, Joe pulled Danny up and they went on toward the docks. He didn't think that the baker would come that far to recover a basket of rolls, but it was still a chance. And if there was one thing that Joe had learned working for Quin during the last year, it was to not take unnecessary chances.

They didn't talk on the way, except once, when Danny reached into the basket and showed Joe how one of the rolls looked like the rear end of a naked woman. Joe told him to shut up, and added that Danny wouldn't recognize a naked woman if one jumped on him, which one wasn't likely to do.

When he had found a comfortable bale of cotton to sit on at the wharves, and when he had eaten all of the yeasty, warm rolls that he could get down, Joe took out a small sack of tobacco that he had lifted in a store the day before. He expertly rolled it into a paper, crimped the ends, and rested it on the very edge of his clinched lips. He found a match, struck it with a quick snap of his fingernails, and lit the cigarette. He leaned back on the cotton and blew out a long, steady line of blue smoke.

"I wish that son of a bitch would make pots of coffee," he said, pulling his cap down lower over his eyes and spitting out bits of tobacco. "I could sure stand a cup of coffee."

Danny was still eating the bread. When given the opportunity, he always ate until he couldn't manage even one more bite, since he never knew when he would eat again. "We couldn't run off with no pot of coffee," he said, through a full mouth. "It would burn us, and we'd drop it."

Joe shook his head and took another pull on his smoke. Sometimes he wondered why he had ever hooked up with such a dimwit. He closed his eyes and enjoyed the cigarette. He had only recently taken up smoking, and he liked it. He decided that he would steal his next packet of tobacco from the same place—it was good quality.

Danny was through eating now, having reached the point where he nearly gagged. He folded his legs under him and perched upright. He pointed to the cigarette. "Why don't you roll me one of them?"

Joe didn't open his eyes, but just pulled his cap down lower over them. "Because you'd start to hack and spit like you done the last time, and wake up half the damn town."

Danny sat still, and considered eating another roll. But he knew that if he did, he would probably throw up. He looked at Joe, stretched out and enjoying the morning and the cigarette, and figured Joe's opinion of him wouldn't go up any if he threw up. Finally, he offered his opinion. "Well, how am I ever going to learn to do it if I don't never get to practice?"

Joe took the last long draw on the cigarette and flipped it on the dock. The smoke came out with his words. "Why don't you just *talk* about doing it, without ever really doing it. Like you do about screwing whores."

"I ain't never said I screwed a whore," Danny said. He gave up on getting a cigarette and leaned back on the bale. He didn't know how the conversation had come around to whores, when it had just been about cigarettes. He was pretty sure that the only way he would ever have sex would be with a whore, and have to pay for it. He was ugly, he guessed. He had red hair and his ears were certainly bigger than they needed to be, and his mouth sort of splayed out all over the bottom of his face. And he had more freckles than there appeared to be stars in the sky. He had never known who his father was, and he barely remembered what his mother looked like, but he guessed he had inherited the worst physical traits of both.

He had once thought about asking Joe if he was ugly. But he had known that he would just hit him with his cap and tell him to quit asking stupid questions that don't mean anything. Women and girls never gave Danny a second look, nor even a first. But he had noticed that they sure looked at Joe. In the last year, he had gotten taller and bigger, with muscles in his arms and his chest, and Danny had heard one girl say what pretty eyes he had, though he didn't know how she could see them, since he kept his cap pulled down low over them all the time. He guessed that Joe wouldn't have any problem getting a woman to give it to him free.

"And if I *was* to screw one," Danny said, "I damned sure wouldn't tell you about it, on account of you would just carry on about it all the time. Like you do now, when I *ain't* even screwed one." Joe didn't move, nor open his eyes.

"I took a billfold off a drunk fella last night and carried it over to give to Quin," he said. "But he wasn't at his place." He waited for Joe's response. He had a long wait, but finally it came.

"Quin was with me, down here at the docks."

"Doin' what?" Danny didn't like the idea of Joe going off and doing things without him, or, at least, without telling him about it. Joe was quiet again.

"It was about the job tonight, for Captain Barkley," Danny said.

"Wasn't it?" He leaned up, toward Joe. "If I'm in on that, then I ought to be in on plannin' it. I ought to know what's goin' on."

Joe lifted the narrow visor of his cap and looked at him. "Nobody said you was in on it. It's you done all the talk about bein' in on it."

Danny ran a dirty hand along the edge of the bale of cotton. "But I thought . . . ," he started. "I figured . . . ," he started again.

He looked down at the dock. Gulls circled overhead, calling out to each other, sailing through the damp, gray morning.

A church bell tolled in the distance, and the bay quietly sloshed against the wharves and the ships. "I just figured me and you would, you know, be in on it. You and me always . . . ."

Danny stopped talking and it was quiet for what seemed like a long time. Finally, Joe sat up and looked at him.

"You got to let me do the setting up, Danny. I've told you that before." Danny nodded that he understood, but Joe could tell that he was close to tears. "After the job's done, and were're ready to sail, I'll talk to Captain Barkley about takin' you, I promise." Danny continued to sit quietly, afraid to talk; he thought that if he tried to talk, he might start crying, and crying in front of Joe would be worse than throwing up. Joe went on. "You hear me? I promise you."

Danny nodded, and pretended to watch a seagull that was swooping not very far above them.

Late that afternoon they crept along the same wharves, Danny as close and quiet behind Joe as a shadow. This was what they had been thinking about, and talking about, and even dreaming about for such a long time that it seemed almost impossible that the moment had arrived. But there was the warehouse and there was the reddish sunset sky that said it was time, and there was the *Maydelle*, not far away, pulling at her ropes, waiting for them.

Joe tugged Danny down beside him behind some bales of cotton and looked around. Several of the workers were still milling around in front of the large doors of the warehouse. The boys had arrived a little earlier than Quin had told them to get there, but Joe wanted to get a good look around and not walk too quickly into anything that would foul up the plan. The plan was everything to him, and now he could quit thinking about it, and worrying about it, and just do it, and get it over with, and go off into the night on a handsome ship, and be done with Galveston forever.

He had been trying to decide whether to leave the ship at New Orleans or Boston. Barkley had said he would take him as far as Boston, if he wanted to go there. All he knew about Boston was that it was cold there in the winter, and it snowed. He had read a story about a boy who lived in Boston back before he had given up on school, and he remembered that the boy in the story had had to put up with a lot of snow. The only snow that Joe had ever had to put with was during a short-lived bizzard a couple of winters ago. But he had had to endure more than his share of hot, sweaty days, so he had just about decided to go on up to Boston, and take his chances with the snow. New Orleans was too close. People came to Galveston from New Orleans all the time, so he figured that just as many people must go there from here. And Joe didn't want to ever see anybody from Galveston again. It was a hell of a trip from Galveston to Boston, and he didn't imagine it got made very often.

He looked at Danny, who was peeking over the top of a bale like a kitten in a basket. He hadn't asked him which place he would prefer, New Orleans or Boston, since he knew that Danny would happily follow him off the ship if it delivered them to the North Pole.

The men by the warehouse were moving on now. In a minute or two the section of the wharves in front of the big building would be deserted and Joe would go in and find that black man who would lead him to the room.

Joe had not said good-bye to his family. But he had looked at each one of them, after supper.

He would miss Sal, he guessed. He had worried a little about how she would get along, but had finally decided that there wasn't anything he could do about it, and hoped that she had enough grit in her little self to survive their useless parents and find her own way to get out. He thought about his grandfather's pocket watch, which, by rights, ought to be his someday. He had even considered stealing the watch, but didn't want to give his father any reason to come after him. He almost laughed when he imagined Thurmon following him to Boston. He might go there if all the whiskey in Galveston had been hauled off to Boston, but he was unlikely to go there in search of a misplaced son and a stolen watch.

Joe had left a sealed envelope with the bartender in one of the saloons that his father frequented. It was addressed to his father and contained a single slip of paper on which a few simple sentences said that he had gone off to find work in another town and that he shouldn't be come after and he might write to them sometime. He had printed his first name at the bottom.

And that was that, he thought, as he watched Danny watch the wharves. It was almost dark now, and he knew it was time.

"I'm going on in," he said. Danny nodded.

"You watch close for that guard. If he starts coming, get in there as quick as you can and tell me."

Danny nodded, again. And Joe was gone.

Danny stayed crouched behind the cotton, trying to watch in all directions in equal measure. After about half an hour, he had turned his head so many times that it was starting to get sore.

He had gone to his special hiding place, that nobody knew about, not even Joe, this afternoon and taken out all the money that he had been saving. He had counted it out again, even though he knew, to the penny, how much was there. Almost seventy dollars. It had taken the whole year that he had been thieving for Quin, to save it. He hadn't spent much on himself—a coat last winter, and a new pair of shoes once. Hardly any of it had gone for food, since food could be as easily stolen as bought. So most of the coins that Quin had dropped into his palm in that year as his percentage of the take were there, and making up the lion's share of it was the money that he hadn't handed over to Quin when he had lifted a wallet, or a purse, or dipped into a cash box when a store clerk hadn't been paying attention.

Seventy dollars, he thought, as he kept his eyes peeled for anybody that might wander up. That would get Joe and him off to a good start wherever they were going. That and the money that Quin would give to Joe for tonight's job. Even if they had to pay something to Captain Barkley to get him to take him along with Joe, they'd still be set up awfully good.

He had seen Joe and the black man come up to the front of the warehouse with the wooden boxes four times. They were back in there, now. He still couldn't understand why anybody would pay any money to steal a bunch of pictures, and he didn't care. He was just happy that somebody wanted them bad enough to provide Joe and him a chance to finally put their plan into action. He didn't even care where they were going, as long as Joe would be there, and they would have a lot of money in their pockets. Joe had said that they may not even take up stealing when they got there, but get real jobs, and a place to live in.

The man was almost to the wharves before Danny saw him. He was a little man, and wasn't walking very fast. But he was walking toward the warehouse.

Danny kept down low as he hurried around behind the cotton bales, and only had to run across a narrow bit of an open place to get to the big doors. When he was inside, he ran toward the back, not knowing any other direction to go in.

It was later now, and the man that the black man had called

Davenport lay dead near the shattered bottle of whiskey that he had been holding.

Joe turned to Danny and fell down to him. He worked his arm under his head, and cradled it there. Danny's features weren't locked into the scowl that he had perfected, to make himself look older. He looked now, Joe thought, like he did when he sometimes found him asleep on the wharves. He looked like a little boy. A scared one. He was trying to breathe, and his face was even whiter than it usually was. Blood continued to come out of the gash where Davenport had thrust the knife. Danny's shirt was soaked with it.

"Just lay still," Joe said.

Danny tried harder to breathe, and choked a little. He looked at Joe and tried to smile. "I can't . . . ,' he started, attempting to think of what it was that he couldn't do, and tell his friend about it at the same time.

"Shhh," Joe said. "Don't talk." He leaned closer to him and kept his head cradled in his arm. "Lay still."

They stayed like that for a long moment, while Danny fought harder to breathe. When he realized that he wasn't going to be able to, he managed to slip his hand into his pocket and pull out the wad of bills. He nudged them toward Joe.

Joe looked at the bills, then back at Danny's face, whiter now than Joe had ever seen a face. He shook him with the arm that was under his head.

"No," he whispered. Then he said it louder. "Don't you die," he shouted. "Goddamn it," he yelled. He was crying now, and nearly choking on the words. *Don't you die!*" He was shouting and crying in Danny's white face, and slinging his tears on him as he shook.

"You got to do what I tell you! *You hear me, goddamn it!* You always do what I tell you! You can't . . . ." He was shaking so hard now that he couldn't hold the head still. "You can't . . . ."

The body was limp in his arms, and Joe was still shaking so hard that he wondered if he would ever be able to stop.

CHAPTER TWENTY-EIGHT

Morning came. And a brilliant blue sky, and a calm sea. The wind still blew, but gently, as it would on most September mornings. The people in the tops of those houses and buildings that were still standing came out slowly into the cluttered streets, and beheld, in the bright light of morning, devastation even more horrible than they had been conjuring all night.

Bodies were everywhere, some even caught in the branches of trees that had managed to stay rooted to the ground. Mountains of ruined lumber and bricks rose where structures had been. Many buildings were only half there now, their ragged walls jutting up like shards of broken pottery. Parts of roofs were all over the place, since roofs had taken flight early on in the storm. The floors of the buildings were covered with a foot or more of slime, as thick and dark as axle grease, left behind when the water retreated, before daylight, to the gulf and the bay.

It was probably the slime that produced the foul smell, since the thousands of bodies had not had time to cause it. But the stunned people of Galveston, as they wandered like zombies into the streets, didn't attribute the odor to the slime. It was the smell of death, they knew.

There were more leveled houses than standing ones. Whole blocks, especially near the beach, had been swept clean, with little evidence left to show that there had ever been houses there at all.

People in the houses that had remained standing took in those who were now homeless, and did what they did every day, with whatever food and fuel they found. They cooked breakfast.

At the city hall, Ketchum had moved what was left of his police department into one of the least damaged rooms. He went out into his mutilated city when the sun came up and moved as slowly and wide-eyed from one horror to the next as everyone else. On his way home, he saw a buggy, still upright, with a dead horse hitched to it. The driver, also dead, sat on the seat, reins gripped in his clinched fist.

He found his house still standing and his family serving breakfast to most of the neighborhood. He ate some of it himself, and went on with his inspection.

On Broadway he saw that most of the big houses were, for the most part, intact. Some of the ornate porches were gone, and the wide yards were filled with uprooted trees and other debris, but the doors, if they still had doors, were thrown open wide, and the injured and hungry survivors of the dark night were being helped through them.

He stopped at the Kempner house to tell Ike about a meeting the mayor had called for ten o'clock at the Tremont Hotel. Some of the island's influential citizens needed to get together, the mayor felt, and make some decisions. A delegation needed to be dispatched up to Houston, once a seaworthy vessel was located, to make the first arrangements for relief supplies.

President McKinley should be notified, and the Governor. Martial law might need to go into effect, and consequences for looting and stealing jewelry from the dead needed to be laid out. There was much to talk about.

Ike listened to all of it and asked him if there still *was* a Tremont Hotel. Ketchum told him he had just seen it.

He looked around the busy kitchen, the high water marks clearly evident on the walls near the middle of the tall windows. Several of the Kempner boys were just finishing shoveling some of the mud and slime from the floor. A big housekeeper, who looked none the worse for wear, was busy helping a small woman cook breakfast. A red faced man sat at the table, beside a young black woman and her three small children.

Ike identified some of the people for Ketchum, told him he didn't know who the hell most of them were, and offered him some coffee. A young maid was helping to serve breakfast to everybody. She kept glancing over at a young man who was tending to injured people, and touched his shoulder every time she walked by.

As he was leaving, Ketchum listened to the little cook as she complained about how much certain people were eating, and how she hadn't noticed that Jesus had showed up yet, to turn what little food they had into more of it.

Nobody in the big room full of people was paying any attention to her, he noticed. Least of all the big housekeeper, who was standing right beside her.

Father Kirwin surveyed the ruins of his cathedral. Men were

already carrying bodies outside, and entire families huddled against the walls that remained, as if they weren't quite confident enough, yet, to move away from the safety they had provided.

The rectory had made it through the night, and the people inside it. The cathedral had sustained heavy damage—all of the windows were gone, and one of the towers, and most of the roof. But the central tower, that had rocked and swayed all night, was still there. And the statue of Mary still sat on its zenith, her soft eyes directed at the ruined city laid out before her.

There would be no service this morning, even though it was Sunday.

There would be no services anywhere in Galveston, since most of the churches had been destroyed. But there would be an abundance of prayers sent up, full of gratitude. And grief.

And questions.

At the Tremont Hotel, the two businessmen from North Texas stood at the edge of the mezzanine and looked down at the slime that covered the floor of the lobby.

They had heard that a meeting would be held there at ten.

"I don't guess we need to go to it," one of them said.

The other one pulled the last soggy cigar from his coat pocket and bit the end of it off.

"Personally," he said, as he clamped the cigar in the side of his mouth, "I don't intend to go to any more meetings south of Dallas."

At the St. Mary's Infirmary, Scott had finally fallen asleep, sometime before daylight, in a closet. What he saw when he came out of it, and walked out into the bright Sunday morning, made him want to go back in and shut the door.

The doctors, most of whom hadn't slept at all, worked on one injured person after another, and Scott made ready to see to some of the cuts and scrapes that didn't require a physician.

One of the nuns pulled him over to the side.

"I know you're tired," she said. "And I hate to ask you to do one more thing, after all you've done."

He waited. He would do it, of course. Anything short of wading twenty blocks through flood water, and back again, and hauling a building full of sick people through a river and up the steepest stairs he had ever seen was obviously within his power.

"We're all tired, Sister," he said, and smiled. "What is it you need done?"

She asked him to walk out the beach road, if there still was a beach road, or find a horse to ride, if he could, and see if they needed help out at the orphanage.

He ate breakfast first and headed out. He'd stop at the Kempner place on the way, he thought, to make sure that James had made it there. Then he'd make the long walk out to check on the nuns and the children.

The captain of the *Kendal Castle* leaned on the rail outside the wheel house and gazed at what his best chart identified as Texas City, on the northern shore of Galveston Bay.

His first mate stood beside him.

"What do we do now?" he asked.

The captain studied his mammoth steamship, tilted only slightly to starboard. He shrugged his shoulders.

"Damned if I know," he finally said, and looked over the side, at what he estimated to be less than three feet of water.

Isaac Cline left his three daughters sleeping in the upstairs room and walked down the stairs of the deserted house with his brother Joseph.

Outside, they looked around, and then at each other, not knowing whether to laugh or cry. The raft that had raced them through hell and back had deposited them within two blocks of where their own house had stood.

CHAPTER TWENTY-NINE

Three hundred miles away, across a large, calm section of the Gulf of Mexico, a boy, not a very big one, sat hugging his knees in some low sand dunes and surveyed his surroundings.

The large pile of broken planks and timbers being pounded by the surf was what was left of a ship. It lay on its side, like the carcass of a big, stupid creature who had wandered too close to the shore.

Several of the sailors were still breaking open the wooden crates that they had dragged in. But they weren't working as diligently at the task, since they had already broken enough of the crates to know that all the contents had been ruined. Great, heavy bales of cotton, swollen with seawater, sat in the rolling surf and on the beach like enormous bloated cattle.

When the boy had last seen the captain of the ship, he was standing off by himself, spitting out the filthiest words at his disposal. He didn't see him now.

The boy had heard one of the sailors say something about it not being too far to New Orleans. Some people had already come down to the beach in wagons to look at the wreck. So he figured he might get a ride back with them, for as far as they were going towards New Orleans. Then he would walk the rest of the way, if he had to. At least it was a pretty day for it.

A huge river ran through New Orleans, he remembered from his brief venture at schooling, with boats on that river that could take him north. He didn't know enough about the rivers in the United States to know if you could get from New Orleans to Boston on one, but he figured he had enough money in his pocket to get there either on a river boat or on a sailing ship. After his experiences of the last couple of days, he would just as soon take his chances on the river boat and leave the seagoing vessels to other folks. But he would do what he had to do.

Boston had been his plan for a while now, so he had decided to let it still be. It was far enough away, he figured.

He felt, again, of the money in his pocket. Part of it was Danny's, he remembered. But it was his now. He had determined to not let himself think anymore about Danny, at least for a while. Not until he got to wherever he was going. To Boston, he figured. He had told Danny they were going to Boston.

He looked at the wrecked ship again, and at the activity on the beach. Then he stood up and brushed the sand from his pants.

North, he thought. There wasn't anyplace to go now but north. He was ready.

Something was wrong. he had to think a moment to decide what it was. He felt over his eyes, and made his discovery.

He had lost his cap.

The two women didn't hug each other when they were reunited. They just nodded, and looked at Tucker.

"I guess you saved us," the littlest one said, her voice raspy from all the screaming she had done.

Tucker was too tired to talk, or even to think.

"I reckon we all saved each other," he said.

Then the two women wandered off down the street.

The big one was still lodged behind the piano, on the porch that she had thought so highly of.

Tucker barely had enough strength left to put one foot in front of the other one, but he headed off up the street that had caused him so much difficulty.

The building that the biggest woman had been so sure would fall down was still standing. His own room, off the alley, was puddled with water, and the furniture was all ruined, as he knew it would be. By the time he had walked five blocks, he was too exhausted to go on. He was to Broadway, now, and leaned down against an iron fence. He needed to go to sleep, he knew. But he ought to wait till he got to where he was going.

The trouble was, he didn't *know* where he was going.

It would be a blessing, right then, to have a place to go to. But Tucker was hesitant to ask for any blessings, since the last one he had asked for had been delivered, and cost a couple of lives, and probably his family.

Just a little sleep would be a blessing right then.

When he opened his eyes, the man was standing in front of him. Tucker knew who he was, even before he looked at the badge pinned to his sweat-soaked shirt.

"You look to be pretty wore out," Ketchum said.

Tucker nodded.

"You mind if I join you for a minute?" Ketchum asked. "I'm pretty wore out myself." He lowered himself down beside him.

"Your name Tucker?"

He nodded, too tired to use any more words than he had to.

Ketchum kicked at the sidewalk with one foot, and leaned his head back against the iron rails of the fence. He pointed up the street.

"Your wife and children are over there at the Kempner house. I just saw them, all in good shape and eating their breakfast."

Tucker lowered his head, then nodded again.

"You go on over there, when you get your wind back. They'll be mighty happy to see you, I imagine."

They sat quietly for a few minutes.

Tucker still looked at the ground. "I reckon you been lookin' for me," he said.

Across the street, two men were trying to dislodge a body from a tree. Tucker and Ketchum watched until they had it down to the ground.

"Well," Ketchum said, still looking at the men going about their grim business, "I've had one or two other things on my mind the last couple of days."

Someone called him. He waved a hand in his direction and got slowly to his feet.

He took a couple of steps, then turned back.

"You sweep out that big ol' cotton warehouse, down by the docks, don't you, Tucker?"

Tucker watched the men across the street load the body into a wagon.

"Yes suh," he sighed.

Ketchum took off his hat and wiped some sweat from his forehead with his handkerchief.

"The damnest thing," he said, as he put his hat back on. "That whole place got blown away in that storm. The old man that owns it is going to be mighty sad to hear that all his cotton got washed off far enough from Galveston that he'll never see it again."

He turned and moved slowly toward the man who had called him.

"Yes suh," Tucker said, not even sure if he could hear him. Then he closed his eyes.

CHAPTER THIRTY

Three miles away, on the lonely part of beach where the two big buildings had stood, Margaret looked out at the calm sea.

"I guess Chester's dead," she said.

Sal only nodded. She had already seen one dead nun, Sister Elizabeth, with seven dead children tied to her. The rest, she guessed, were up under the rubble, or washed off somewhere away from there. So she was pretty certain that the dog was dead, too.

The brown waves had finally broken the debris up enough to release Sal's father and had taken him with them when they returned to the gulf.

The water went down quickly, when it had finally decided to do it, like someone had opened a gigantic drain somewhere. Then the moon appeared, and the stars, and the very last of a wide summer sky outdid itself, as if nature was apologizing for the past few hours.

Sister Zilphia was off by herself, with her head down. She had made sure that none of them was injured once the water had receded, and then she moved away from them, busy at whatever kept her head gently rocking up and down.

The boy was over where the dunes used to be, looking for things in the sand. Wee Mary was just sitting, having already announced that she was hungry. Margaret went to see what the boy was up to and left them sitting beside some of the wreckage.

Mary, who hadn't done too much crying during the long ordeal, suddenly started crying for no particular reason. She continued to cry, and Sal came over and sat beside her, then pointed down the beach road.

"Keep looking off down there," she said, "and I'll bet you'll see somebody come to help us."

That didn't stop the crying, so Sal gathered her up next to her, and rocked her back and forth.

"Just sit still," she said.

The sky was as blue as any that Sal had ever seen. And the gulls had come back from wherever they had gone to be safe during the night. They sang out to each other, and made wide circles over the gulf, like they did every morning. She pulled Mary closer, and she stopped crying and looked down the road.

"If you sit still for long enough," Sal started, and closed her fingers over the watch she was still holding. She pressed the side of her face against the child's and sighed.

"Something good will happen," she said.

They watched the road for a long time, until a small dot appeared at the end of it. The dot slowly became a man, a tall, young one. They kept their eyes fixed on him as he got bigger.

EPILOGUE

He was coming home. Though he had never been here before. He looked through the slow sweeps of the windshield wiper at the low, flat mass of land at the end of the causeway. The murky water of the bay was being pushed by an early autumn breeze, and the caps of the waves weren't white, as he was used to seeing on lakes, but a dull and uninspired gray, foamy at their tops, as if churned up from a particularly dirty laundry. He slid past an eighteen-wheeler that threw up dingy splatters on the windows.

The island stretched out before him.

He hadn't had much to do with islands, other than the numerous small ones that spotted the lakes of upstate New York, near the farm where he had grown up. He had been to Manhattan and Coney Island, but they hardly fell into the same category as the one making its appearance under the bridge. In less than a minute, Interstate 45, which he had taken down from Houston, became a residential street. He strained to see the street sign when he stopped at the first red light. Broadway.

The light changed and he drove on. Huge plants—oleanders, he imagined, from the reading he had done about the place—were everywhere, along both sides of the street, and filling up the wide esplanade that ran down its center.

It was early January, and a cold snap was causing the dismal weather. He had predicted it, had watched its ragged edge creep across the monitor on his desk, the powerful radar sounding out, in various colors, every squall and break in the system's advance. It started to rain harder and he turned the wiper up a level.

At the next red light, a large cemetery was on his right, beyond an ancient iron fence. Its old-fashioned and too big tombstones were dark silhouettes in the slow, gray rain.

In not too many minutes, he turned on twenty-third street and drove through several blocks of a rundown neighborhood. He leaned forward on the steering wheel and looked at the sad milieu, supposing that Galveston must not have any more zoning laws than Houston, which he knew had none. Shanties, in various stages of disrepair, were interspersed with Mom and Pop grocery and liquor stores. Iron bars were on the windows and doors to protect the places at night from the customers they probably served during the day.

Larger houses were here, too, relics of times long gone, their elegance still straining to emerge, through broken cornices and fragments of chipped, delicate woodwork. He thought they must be hacked up now into as many narrow, mean apartments as possible. The big green plants were less abundant here, but occasionally one appeared, having pushed up through cracks in the pavement.

He seemed to be going up a hill, an unlikely thing on such a flat place. Then he remembered. The seawall. Several miles of the city nearest the beach had had to be built up to accommodate it. He couldn't remember where all the dirt necessary for such a task had come from—surely he had read it somewhere.

He watched the street signs, turned right on Avenue Q, then counted three blocks before stopping beside the curb. He studied the small yards and old houses until he found the lot where the house must have once stood. He leaned back in his seat and looked at the broken, uneven sidewalk. It could have been here, he thought. It looked old enough to be the same sidewalk that his ancestors, two brothers with names plucked right out of the Old Testament, must have walked on countless times.

They had been weathermen a century ago, and he had heard about them first when he was no more than a boy, on that farm in upstate New York. He learned the story from old people in his family who told it with awe, and reverence. The story that haunted him when he sat for countless hours above a high meadow, and watched clouds roll across the countryside. He identified each cloud in a book, and knew, even then, that this fascination with weather would be his life. That the lure of the secrets of wind and rain and the seasons had made its slow journey from those two brothers, across decades, and finally found him, sitting on his hilltop.

And he knew the brothers—uncles, preceded by two "greats"— who had watched their last clouds amble along sections of sky long before he had been born. His veneration of Isaac and Joseph Cline must, he sometimes thought, be not unlike that felt by many musicians for those stoic men who played the final hymn on the slanting decks of the *Titanic*. Men who gazed into the teeth of Hell itself, and went calmly on with the tasks they had been allotted.

He looked again at the tract and for any type of marker. There was nothing to indicate that anything, or anyone, of importance had ever been here. The house that sat here now was much smaller, he knew, than the brothers' house had been. This one could use a fresh coat of paint, and a multitude of new boards to replace rotten ones. The front door was closed against the cold, wet weather; an ice chest stood upturned on the dilapidated porch. Plastic toys lay in the yard.

He drove to the end of the small block, turned left, and, after a few more blocks, the street dead-ended into a much wider one, on the other side of which the world fell off into nothingness. The bleak neighborhood gave way to taller, bigger buildings, and then to the Gulf of Mexico, broad and majestic, even in the slow, dismal rain. Its dingy gray became darker as it stretched out toward the horizon, making it difficult to find the line that divided the sea and the sky.

He parked the car on the beach side of the wide street. Hotels and motels and shops and restaurants lined the other side, and a few shops were built out over the beach on piers. The steep steps of the shops were covered with brightly colored gadgets of all kinds, giant conch shells and twirling kites and wind catchers, and wooden pelicans of the sort that neither a wildlife artist nor a Walt Disney animator would have had anything to do with. It looked to him like it had all been belched out of the shops on to the steps. He leaned over to try to see the beach, but it was obstructed by the high seawall.

The gaudy kites, splashed with an unfortunate mix of bright colors, twisted helplessly in the stiff, damp gulf breeze. He got out of the car and walked to the edge of the sidewalk. The beach below him was nearly deserted, except for a very few determined and hearty souls who wouldn't be denied a final pilgrimage before even colder days arrived. Waves washed up on the gray beach in a constant rhythm, rolling over each other before finally playing out into nothingness on the dark sand.

He stood at the edge of the high seawall, the salty mix of breeze and rain stinging his face, and let his gaze follow the wall's graceful curve along the shoreline off into the distance. If only it had been here then, he thought, before catching himself, and smiling. For "if only" came quickly to mind when he thought of Galveston, and of her darkest night. If only the seawall had been here. If only there had been radar. If only. If only.

He looked again at the slow, uneventful activity on the beach. He had dreamed of coming here since his childhood, and now here he was. And the island seemed as disinterested as the few people wandering along the sand.

After college, he had survived two stints as the weatherman at television stations in small, uninteresting cities. He was finally accepted into the Weather Bureau, where his two ancestors had served in its infancy. Then the big break came, a turn as a staff meteorologist with NASA, just outside Houston. One of the deciding factors had been its close proximity to Galveston.

Now he was driving along Seawall Boulevard, between the gray, rolling surf and the numerous eateries and souvenir shops. He drove with the confidence of someone who had lived long in a place, though it was his first time on this street, in this city. He had committed the general shape and features of the island to memory the first time he had seen a map of it, when he was a boy, in one of the books he had read about the storm. And he learned its dimensions and elevations even earlier, from the book written by Isaac Cline himself. It was called *Storms, Floods and Sunshine*, and he had found it on his grandfather's shelf when he was ten. It was the start of it, his clarion call.

He turned on second street and drove past apartment buildings and residential neighborhoods, palm trees and oleander everywhere, until he joined the line waiting for the Bolivar ferry. In a few moments, the big boat maneuvered its way into the slip, and, when the vehicles had driven off, he followed the car in front on to it. It was full of teenaged boys and music loud enough to reverberate through the car's frame. One of the boys was drinking beer from an oversized can.

He pulled up to where the attendant indicated for him to park. Several people were getting out of their cars and hurrying in the cold rain to the center structure of the boat. They clutched their coats and jackets close to them, and squinted against the wind. He knew there was an observation deck up there.

The teenagers had piled out of their car, and were shouting and whooping on the upper deck. One of them was still singing the song that had been blaring out of the car. Another one threw Fritos at squawking seagulls hovering in the heavy, slate colored air.

He watched them from his car, in their ragged clothes and with various ear and nose rings and tattoos, and wondered what the earlier travelers on these waters would have made of them. The new arrivals from Europe, the cotton merchants, the pirates from the Caribbean.

When the ferry churned away from the slip, he got out and stepped around a couple of puddles on the asphalt deck and stood at the rail. The rain was only a drizzle now. He huddled inside his coat and turned the collar up.

In the open channel, he watched the Coast Guard station slide by, then the empty, desolate tip of the island. He remembered that a quarantine station had been out there somewhere, once, when Galveston received enough immigrants to distinguish her as a smaller version of Ellis Island.

The ferry's horn bellowed out its deep, rumbling moan, and the bow of the wide, heavy boat collided with the cold waves, sending spray high into the salty air, then falling like thick raindrops, splattering on the front row of cars. The wind gusted over the choppy water at such a brisk speed that even the gulls were having trouble with it. Several large cargo ships sat at anchor out past the end of the island, and a big cabin cruiser full of particularly determined fishermen bounced through the rolling waves. With each lunge it fell quickly back to the water, thudding like a fat man doing a belly flop in a pool.

He knew that he was in the Bolivar roads now, clear of the island. He gripped the rail and listened to the whistling of the gust and the slow chugging of the engines. Gulls sang out to each other, and the teenagers continued to wail and stomp on the upper deck.

It would seem odd, he knew, to other people, to leave an island so soon after driving on to it. But he wanted to see the roads, and this short voyage offered the best vantage point. He gazed out at the turbulent, churning surface of the water, where the world had come to Galveston since it had first found reasons to. It was the doorway.

In not too many minutes, the ferry made its wide, slow turn toward the Bolivar peninsula, and he saw the lone lighthouse of a long stretch of the gulf coast.

Everyone had returned to their cars, and the boys were sending the throbbing music out again. Everyone had to drive off the boat, and turn around to get on again if they intended to go back to Galveston.

He drove as close to the lighthouse as he could get and turned around in the narrow highway. The boys, in the car in front of him, continued on toward other adventures.

He didn't get out of the car on the return trip, but sank back into the soft cushions and watched the roads, and the Houston ship channel, and then the flat dark expanse of Pelican Island move slowly by outside his window. He wondered, again, what his two ancestors would have thought of the city now, of its tourist-centered, Atlantic City type ambiance. And how amazed they would be at the advances in their science. Radar could now declare with chilling accuracy the smallest of weather occurrences. Anyone with enough intelligence to turn on a television or a computer could have, in seconds, hundreds of times more climatic information than Isaac and Joseph Cline could have ever hoped to receive over the telegraph, or on the single telephone in their weather bureau office on Market Street.

Now, a monster the size of the 1900 storm couldn't sneak up on anyone. Alarms would be sounded days in advance. Evacuations would be ordered. He closed his eyes and the statistics hit home again. The greatest natural disaster in the history of the United States, a record it still held, a hundred years later. A thriving, bustling city, and the entire island it occupied, submerged. Over six thousand deaths. And that was the most conservative estimate.

The bodies had been hauled out to sea, only to return with the next tide. Then they had burned them, in huge bonfires that must have glowed in witnesses' memories for the rest of their lives.

If only . . . he let himself think. If only.

Back on the island, he turned left off the ferry road and drove through the hospital complex, then the street curved its way beside some docks and finally emerged into what he knew was the Strand district. Many of the old brick buildings lining the elevated sidewalks had obviously undergone refurbishing. Iron grillwork adorned some of them, and tall, old fashioned doors and windows were closed against the cold morning.

He knew that the whole neighborhood, once the busy center of the city, had gradually dissolved into a slum before the city and several rich citizens undertook to bring about its renaissance. Now it was trendy, full of shops and galleries, and on summer nights people filled the same streets that, not too many years before, would have been considered too risky to visit even in the daylight.

He recognized the Moody Building on its corner. He had seen pictures of it in books, both as a three-story structure, as it was now, and with a forth floor, before it was sliced off neatly in the storm. He knew that in its offices clerks had once entered numbers into massive ledgers that represented the buying and selling of much of the cotton crop of the South. It now housed what appeared to be a large Army surplus store.

Turning left, he made his way back toward the gulf, reading the street signs along the way: Mechanic, Market, Postoffice, and Church. There was the statue of Mary, on the tallest tower of her cathedral. And there was the Catholic high school, which had been known for most of its existence as Kirwin High. Then the street names became letters of the alphabet, and he turned, to the right this time, on Seawall Boulevard and drove the almost two miles to the place that he most wanted to see. The place he had to come to.

The place that had haunted him since he first heard its story.
He slowed to a stop and double checked to make sure he was at the right place. Sixty-ninth street and Seawall.

A big Walmart store was there, beyond its vast, almost empty parking lot. An apartment complex took up the other corner, facing the beach. He searched for any identifying marker, or monument, but found nothing to call attention to the place, as if the island had forgotten something it should have remembered.

He parked beside the seawall and got out of the car. The rain had stopped, and the stiff breeze from the gulf stung his face. He didn't know where the two long buildings had stood, a century before, but he knew that they had been here, close to where he was standing now. The cold wind whistled along the lonely place, and the waves tumbled unto the empty beach. A few persistent seagulls squawked and performed their graceful acrobatics above the dingy water.

He closed his eyes. And listened.

The wind sang its ghostly song, and he could almost hear them. The sounds of children.

He was still there in the late afternoon.

He had sat for so long on the sharp edge of the seawall that he had to stand and stretch life back into his legs. It was almost evening, and the cold wind, even colder now, still wandered across the vast place. The cars on the wide street didn't slow down here, unless the light at the intersection turned red. Even the huge Walmart, beyond its wide parking lot, seemed to be doing a slow business. The sand at the base of the seawall swirled and relocated itself in the wind, and the several constant gulls that had been his lone companions all afternoon dipped and swayed over the churning, eternal sea.

It was time to eat, he knew. He had left the place, in mid-afternoon, for long enough to walk over to the Walmart, and its McDonald's, and brought his lunch back and eaten it on his perch. Most of the fries had gone to the gulls.

He was hungry again, but knew that he wouldn't go into one of the island's seafood places and sit down and eat a meal. Maybe he'd pick up another burger and take it back to his new apartment near NASA. It was less than an hour away. He'd eat it there, among the unpacked boxes.

He didn't want to sit in a restaurant right now and listen to the conversations from other tables, banter as meaningless as the clacking of silverware or the tinkling of ice in glasses. Not tonight. Not after this day.

He had known, since he was ten years old, that he would make this journey. That he would come to this island, and to this specific spot. He had even known, for all of those years, that it wouldn't be a particularly impressive place. Unmarked. Forgotten.

He looked again, for perhaps the hundredth time today, at the long, graceful sweep of the seawall as it followed the curve of Galveston in the last of the day's light. Maybe, he thought, this was the best memorial anyway, the most fitting tribute the city could have come up with. And the only one needed. The occupants of the two long buildings had paid for it, along with the thousands of others who hadn't made it through that darkest of nights. The seawall itself said it better than any memorial or statue. Not next time, it said. Never again.

He looked around him at the quickly changing afternoon. It was his favorite time. That few minutes of magic between daylight and darkness, when the day gives itself up, and gives itself over to its ending. Some parts of the world called it the gloaming, he knew. He remembered what Longfellow called it, when shadows became goblins as darkness falls. There could be no better term for it here, on this particular stretch of beach.

The children's hour.

Soon the first stars would be out. And it would be a clear night, with the stars shining down on the silver, rolling gulf. But he would save that for another time. He had done what he had come to do today. He had kept his lonely vigil.

His new job would begin on Monday, in a nice office at NASA. He'd have, at his instant disposal, equipment and technology that his ancestors, Isaac and Joseph Cline, would never have thought possible. His calculations and predictions would determine when space shuttles would be launched and brought home, and weather satellites that he would help design would one day wander among the stars that would soon shine over Galveston. The same stars that he had watched from his hilltop, above the high meadow, in his boyhood.

He stretched again and walked toward his car. He opened the door, and turned to look one last time at the lonely beach, as the darkness found it.

Maybe he would do a little unpacking tonight, from the boxes of clothing, and books, and pots and pans. One small item, carefully folded in a towel, would be the first to be located and unwrapped. He would hang it above his desk, in his new office, so that he could see it often. It had hung in his bedroom when he was a child, then on the wall of his dormitory in college, and then in his offices in the two television stations where he had been the weatherman.

The frame was nothing fancy, for he had selected it when he was a little boy. Polished wood, a few chips evident at the edges. The mat was plain, and almost the same color of the photograph. It was a small and slightly crumpled picture, carefully sliced out of a book about the storm.

It was black and white, of course, and the subjects sat stiffly in rows, on the steps of one of the long buildings. The girls wore long dresses, all the same, light color, each buttoned up to the small, pinched necks. The boys wore shirts the same color as the girls' dresses, and dark britches.

Everyone had on their best pair of shoes. The stoic nuns stood at the back, on the porch, unsmiling, like a tribunal sitting in judgment of a most hideous crime. One of the nuns, even more somber than the others, had a dark blotch across much of her face, because of a scratch on the negative, he always thought.

The children weren't smiling, either, since this was probably the first time that any of them had been photographed, and they might have been nervous. Maybe someone had told them not to smile.

When he looked at it, as he did several times every day, he could see, in the hundred faces, the potential for smiling. He often caught himself hoping that, right after the photographer had gotten his shot, the children had smiled a great deal, and been allowed to run upstairs and put on their everyday clothes, and take off their shoes, and go out to play at the water's edge.

He didn't know if that had happened. But he knew what had happened not too many weeks after they had sat on the steps of the orphanage and stared at the photographer and his strange contraption. For a date was printed in the corner of the picture. August, 1900.

And he knew this. That wherever he went, for the rest of his life, the picture would go with him. The hundred years that separated them would be as narrow as the glass in its frame, the nearly forty thousand nights that had fallen on Galveston—as this one was doing now—would be as nothing at all. He knew that, whatever he did, as he calculated, and predicted, and warned areas of potential dangers, they would watch over him, as they sat straight and in rows on the steps of one of the long buildings, all of them leaning forward slightly, as if to see him better through the full century.

To make sure he did it right.

Acknowledgments and Comments

It was on the annual family vacations to Galveston when I was a child that I first heard stories of a long ago storm. Even then, as a gangly pre-adolescent, all elbows and knees and a crewcut, I first became haunted, and *The Windows of Heaven* began to grow. I've spent some of my best days visiting the island, and her fine Rosenberg Library was most helpful in my research. So Galveston herself, the grand old lady of the Texas Gulf coast, deserves much gratitude.

A wonderful assortment of books, dog-eared and well marked by the end, were my guides. John Edward Weems' *A Weekend in September,* the best chronicle of the hour-to-hour events, was my constant companion. *Death From the Sea,* by Herbert Molloy Mason, Jr., proved an essential source, especially regarding the formation and route of the hurricane. Gary Cartwright's *Galveston: A History of the Island* and David G. McComb's *Galveston: A History* gave great insight into the topography and architecture and government of the city. A pair of books intended for children, *Dannie: A Tale of the Galveston Hurricane of 1900* by Madeline Darrough Horn and *The Great Storm* by Sybil Hancock, produced wonderful images of the island at the turn of the century. Irving Stone's *They Also Ran: The Story of the Men Who Were Defeated for the Presidency* took me into the life of William Jennings Bryan, and *Storms, Floods, and Sunshine,* Isaac Cline's memoirs, were, of course, most useful.

For specific matters pertaining to Roman Catholicism (which I should have known without asking) I turned to my colleagues at St. Thomas High School in Houston: Fathers Belish, Hannah, Schwenzer, and Vela, good Basilians all and, happily for me, good friends. I had the privilege and good fortune to come to St. Thomas, to teach writing and English, at the start of its centennial year, the school having opened its doors to its first students within days of the Galveston storm.

The archives of the Villa de Matel produced a wealth of information about the good works of the Sisters of Charity of the Incarnate Word on Galveston and specifically regarding the sisters who died at the orphanage. Father Belish and Sister Monica were most helpful in this particular research.

I'm in the debt of birder and naturalist Jim Renfro, who enlightened me on the behavior of birds and snakes during turbulence and floods. The late Salvatore "Sam" Pistone, whose barber shop sat beside St. Mary's Cathedral Basilica and who served as its unofficial guide, gave me a tour of that church that was unequaled by any I've received in Notre Dame or Chartes or Canterbury.

Dr. Paul Ruffin, at *Texas Review* Press, was well established as a good friend prior to our association on this project, and then he passed the test, in flying colors, of a good editor. Special thanks, too, to Sam Houston State University, my alma mater and the home of the *Texas Review* Press, for underwriting much of the cost. We are in our third generation of Bearkats in the Rozelle family, and are quite proud of it. Dr. Donald Coers was also most helpful in bringing the University on board. I am almost as grateful to him for that as I am for his opening my eyes, a long time ago, to the sheer wonder of great writing, when I was his student in the first undergraduate literature course I ever took.

Kellye Sanford, who designed the cover and did the layout, was wonderful to work with, and the book benefited greatly from her artistic vision. Teresa Stevenson read the proofs of one of the final drafts. And many thanks to Jacques de Spoelberch, my agent, for his guidance, his hard work and his confidence.

Finally, I'm thankful to and for my wife Karen and our girls, who put up with me through the initial idea, the research, the six drafts, and the revisions. This is our second book together, and their support and love made these books possibilities at the beginning and realities at the end.

A couple of notes touching on fact and fiction. Many of the characters in the story actually lived, among them the Cline brothers, Father Kirwin, Bishop Gallagher, Ed Ketchum, the Kempners, and many of the nuns and children at the St. Mary's Orphans' Asylum. Most of the other characters are of my own invention. Sister Camillus was, in fact, the superior at the orphanage in 1900, but she was actually a much younger person than the lady I envisioned for the story line. Sisters Zilphia and Mendulla, who never existed in real life, should have had names of saints, of course. But, since I imagined the women themselves, I took full advantage of artistic license and conjured up their patrons as well. Zachery Scott was in fact a young orderly at the St. Mary's Infirmary and he did carry many patients to safety, without the assistance of his friend James, who is fictional. Zachery Scott was a highly respected and much loved physician for many years, and was the father of the movie star of the same name. Finally, although Ritter's was an eatery in Galveston, it probably fell short of the splendor of the restaurant described in the story.

Other historical facts do, I hope, pass the scrutiny of purists, and, if they don't, it is due to either an unintentional oversight on my part or the need for some readjustment of times or events to better fit the scope of the novel.

A photograph was actually taken of the children and the nuns on the steps of the orphanage not too many months before all but three of the children died in the storm. A framed copy of it hangs on the wall of my study, over my desk. They watched over me through the entire project.

Ron Rozelle

Ron Rozelle is the author of *Into That Good Night* (Farrar, Straus & Giroux, 1998), which was a finalist for the P.E.N. American West Creative Nonfiction Prize and the Texas Institute of Letters Car P. Collins Award. It was selected as one of the best works of nonfiction in the nation (1998) by the *San Antonio Express News.* The author taught high school English for over twenty years before starting the creative writing program at the Basilian Fathers' St. Thomas High School in Houston. He is currently teaching creative writing in the Brazosport School District. He teaches and speaks at numerous writing conferences and was the memoir teacher at the Newman University Milton Center Workshop, held in July of 1999 at Mississippi College. He is the recipient of *Image* magazine's Artistic Merit Award, and lives in Lake Jackson, Texas, with his wife Karen and their daughters.